# THOMASES' COSTUMERY

Printed in Australia

Cover and internal design by New Found Books Australia Pty Ltd
Images in this book are copyright approved for New Found Books Australia Pty Ltd
Illustrations within this book are copyright approved for New Found Books Australia Pty Ltd

First printing: SEPTEMBER 2024

New Found Books Australia Pty Ltd
www.newfoundbooks.au

Paperback ISBN 978 1 9231 7237 1
eBook ISBN 978 1 9231 7249 4
Hardback ISBN 978 1 9231 7261 6

Distributed by New Found Books Australia Distribution and Lightning Source Global

 A catalogue record for this work is available from the National Library of Australia

More great New Found Books Australia titles can be found at: www.newfoundbooks.au/our-titles/

*We acknowledge the traditional owners of the land
and pay respects to the Elders, past, present and future.*

# THOMASES' COSTUMERY

## WJ Richardson

*To my wife Christina for her love and support,*
*and my CFS family for having my back as I have theirs.*

A huge thank you to Marg Ludwig for her encouragement and proof reading of the early drafts of this novel, it would not have come to fruition without your invaluable input. Thank you to Loni, Tracy, and Rumball for being just who you are and helping to make the characters in this story come to life. Finally thank you to the team at New Found Books Australia Publishing for taking a punt on aspiring Aussie authors whose voices would be lost to the world without their help.

# CHAPTER ONE

## WARRNAMBOOL, AUSTRALIA,
## JULY 16TH 2117 CE, 23:57 HOURS

IT WAS CLOSE TO midnight and the rain was bouncing off the road like hail. Detective Constable David Thomas watched a cat scurrying up the alley he and his partner had been observing for most of their shift. He lowered his night vision glasses, then gently nudged Jen, who had her head back and mouth open, snoring.

Jenifer Rostig had been David's partner since he first made detective a year ago. David knew he lucked out the first day he had been assigned as Jen's partner; she was a good cop, one of the best, who had built a reputation over 20 years for playing by the rules, while not taking shit from anybody. He couldn't have hoped for a better partner and mentor.

David studied Jen's sleeping form. She was still a very attractive woman, not that the current picture was screen saver material. Jen was medium height, dark haired, with the odd grey strand that had somehow missed the monthly hair dye session, but she was in good shape. She worked hard at it and it showed.

Jen was single, because that's the way she wanted it and had one of those smiles that made you feel good when she chose to use it. David really liked her as a friend. He would do just about anything for Jen, take a bullet for her, like they used to say in the days when cops carried lethal weapons. It didn't seem as committed to say he would take a stunner blast for her.

David tapped his partner's shoulder.

'It's knock off time Jen.'

Jen abruptly stopped snoring.

'What?'

'Knock off time, sleepy head.'

Jen shook her head, then rapidly blinked her eyes to force them open. She leant forward, peering into the alley.

'I wasn't sleeping, I was just resting my eyes. Anything happening?'

David used the night vision setting on his glasses to peer through the car window again.

'No.' He turned in his seat.

Jen who was looking at the dark spot on her shirt with displeasure. It was a tomato sauce stain from the takeaway they had purchased at her favourite retro themed restaurant.

'Bugger,' she said, putting a finger on the dark spot.

'Do you want to call it in? I'll start heading us toward home.'

Jen spoke the key words, 'Call comms, 34 Bravo to Central dispatch.'

A holographic projection of a uniformed officer appeared on the windscreen and said, 'Central Dispatch receiving unit 34 Bravo, send, over.'

Jen recognised the dispatch officer as a friend but kept the communications traffic formal as per the book.

'34 Bravo is terminating surveillance. Nothing showing, returning to station, over.'

'Central dispatch received. 34 Bravo clear of scene, returning to station, over.'

'Thank you dispatch, 34 Bravo out.' The hologram disappeared.

'Ok young David,' she yawned, 'whisk this slightly older, but still way too hot for you, lady homeward. I hear my bed calling.'

David was taking one last look at the alley and realised something was different.

'Have a look to the left of the dump bin. Does the rear door on that warehouse look open to you?'

Jen picked up her surveillance glasses, even in the near perfect vision, provided by the latest technology, it was difficult to tell in this amount of rain. She tapped the side of the glasses, changing the view to an enhanced thermal setting. Instantly, it changed to shades of grey and white.

'Sneaky bugger,' Jen muttered.

The thermal image showed a narrow band of light against shades of pale grey and black, indicating the relative temperature of the background and objects that were in, or had just passed, through the field of view.

'I think our mysterious burglar is wearing a stealth suit, but it's a bit short in the legs.'

David tapped his own glasses; he could see a fading white line that looked like the path of two ankles rising and falling as they glided along the rear of the building. The line disappeared inside what was, an obviously, closed rear entry door. He and Jen were now very much awake.

Detectives Rostig and Thomas had been on the case of a mysterious burglar for two months. There had been a string of seemingly random illegal entries into buildings across the city. Alarm systems, motion sensors and laser trip alarms had all been negotiated without activating and video surveillance systems had failed to provide images of the intruder.

The occupants of the affected buildings reported that somebody had made entry, taken nothing, but things were not as they had been, prior to the break in. A photo on the desk was slightly angled too far to the right, the seat on the desk chair had been raised to an uncomfortable position, their coffee cup had been moved to the left side of the bench, rather than to the right, where it always sat. This could be dismissed as just the workings of an overactive imagination, except for the fact that the visitor, while taking nothing, left behind a gift to mark their visit.

Propped in a prominent position would be left a real paper and print book. The covers varied in colour and design, some were well thumbed and careworn, others appeared as if they had just rolled off a printing press. Inside the front cover, printed in slightly apologetic script was the declaration that this book had been supplied by the *Gideon's*, or the *Gideon Bible Society,* or *Gideon International.* David could think of few objects more disturbing to be confronted within.

Crime was not greatly different in the 22nd century than it had been since the establishment of the rule of law. Crimes of passion, stupidity and violence, fuelled by egos or, often as not, illicit substance abuse, were still the bread and butter of the world's law enforcement agencies. The thirst for power and dominance over others still raised its head in criminal behaviour, but the norms of society now mostly kept this in check.

Sadly, the desire to possess that which belonged to somebody else, still emerged on occasion; the perpetrator believing they deserved it more than others, so the object of their desire should therefore belong to them. This included material goods and often the affection or control over others. Luckily, society had now evolved to the point that what most people valued above all else were personal experiences. You couldn't steal them, they had to be lived.

Life was a fairer and less stressful existence than what had gone before; nobody had to go hungry or die from lack of medical care, or the funds to afford it. No person had to fight for existence because of their nationality, sexual orientation, nationality or ethnicity, colour, spiritual beliefs, language or social standing. And yet, society still had unrest, the six percenters, the proportion of the population whose brains were wired in such a way they just could not fit into society without some form of conflict, still existed. You could screen an embryo's DNA for genetic abnormalities, but it was still not possible to detect if an unborn child would become a sociopath, psychopath, egomaniac, narcissist or just a plain dick.

David wondered which of these may have slipped through the rear door of the warehouse.

'Call it in Jen, while I will take a look.'

David made his way to the rear entrance of the building in a set of small hops and sideways leaps across the growing puddles. He studied the door for a bio scanner, which read an individual's DNA code to confirm their identity, before any secure door would open. Criminals loved these security systems; they were simplicity itself to circumvent. All you needed to do was lop off a finger and you could carry anybody's DNA to wherever you wanted to open a door.

The police called them *Meat Cleaver* security systems and could not recommend them based upon the nickname alone. To David's surprise, the door had a keyhole lock with a D shaped handle to pull the door. David gripped the handle and the door moved as he gently applied pressure. He locked eyes with his partner and indicated with a nod that the door was unlocked. Jen left the warmth of their police vehicle and made the same skip and jump approach as David to the building's rear entrance.

'It doesn't look like I am getting to bed early,' said Jen as the rain flattened her hair and soaked her shirt with its red sauce spot. 'I would hate to think we are getting soaked because somebody forgot to lock the door and the neighbourhood cat has left a nice heat signature for us to follow.'

'Only one way to find out,' said David, checking his police issue stunner side arm, placing it back into its holster, then sliding through the open door. 'By the way, I like what you have done with your hair,' he grinned.

Jen gave David a scornful look, checked her side arm then followed her partner.

As had always been the way, undesirables and the six percenters could arm themselves with guns, knives, lumps of steel and wood with which to do horrible things to other humans. With the exception of specialised armed response teams, law enforcement officers no longer carried lethal weapons. They were equipped with defensive armaments designed to disable an opponent with a neuro shock blast.

These stun weapons were designed to incapacitate for a few minutes, or a few hours, depending on the setting used. They could still be fatal if fired too close to the skull or if the target was in poor health. The use of non-lethal force to subdue those who could do harm to others was a cornerstone of modern policing, however this high-tech humanitarian approach could and did have very bad consequences on occasions for both the offender, and the law enforcement officer.

David was hit by a feeling of familiarity the moment he stepped through the door. It wasn't just the bricks and mortar; it was the smell of cloth and the filtered light at the end of the corridor they found themselves in. David didn't know why, but he knew this place; he had been here before. He indicated for Jen to follow his lead, backing up a couple of metres behind, using a standard building search pattern, David looking forward, Jen checking their rear as they moved. Wet footprints led down the corridor toward the source of light. David and Jen drew their weapons.

'Not a cat,' whispered Jen, flicking wet hair from her eyes.

'A big two-legged one if it is,' replied David, moving forward and leaving his own wet footprints.

Jen stopped, raised her wrist to her mouth and spoke quietly into what looked like a watch.

'Central dispatch, 34 Bravo requesting back up to our last location. Can confirm intruder inside of premises. We have entered the building from the rear alley and are investigating. Request backup to come silent and cover front entrance. We suspect the intruder is wearing a stealth suit. Assume they may be armed, over.'

There was a muffled response. Jen held her wrist against her ear to dampen the sound.

'Affirmative, Bravo 34 out.'

She indicated for David to continue his slow search down the corridor, rechecked her stunner then followed her partner.

David held his stunner two-handed, aimed a couple of metres ahead of his progress, pointing down. His index finger rested along the length of the weapon's ceramic body, just above the trigger guard, where it could move to fire in an instant. A weapon aimed at the ground was easier to raise to a firing position than it was to bring it down from above. If need be, the weapon cold be discharged early, hitting legs, knocking targets off their feet as one moved to cover the centre body mass. Standard practice.

David checked each room along the corridor, moving from one side to the other as he and Jen made their way toward the light at the end of the passageway. He found boxes on shelves in one room containing laundry detergent, fabric softener and cloth dye; in another, bolts of cloth of varying colours and textures; in another, footwear and hats of a wide range of descriptions. Familiarity again. Something was nagging at the back of his head.

David slid up to a door with a glass observation window. Along one wall was a line of industrial steam presses used to iron laundry and standing next to each was a matt white ironing robot. David now knew where he was with absolute certainty. This was bad.

Jen looked at her partner. David seemed frozen as he stared through the observation window.

'David,' hissed Jen. 'What?' she mouthed silently.

David said nothing, then indicated for her to continue down the corridor while he entered the room.

Jen shook her head, 'We stay together.'

David shook his head.

'There is a room behind the laundry, I need to secure it before we go on. You can still cover my rear while getting a look at what's up ahead.'

Jen reluctantly nodded her approval. She waited for David to disappear through the door before moving off. She set her glasses to heat signature mode. It might help even if they were chasing somebody wearing a stealth suit.

David crossed the laundry without pausing to look left or right until he reached a door at the rear of the room. Squatting on one knee next to the exit, David moved his finger inside the weapon's trigger guard, tapped his glasses to bring up the thermal mode, took a deep breath, then thrust his body through the doorway.

Jen had reached the end of the corridor where a double door with one-way observation windows secured the exit. She peered through the glass. The room in front of her contained a large open space surrounded by three stories of smaller rooms accessible via a wooden staircase. The walls were decorated with wood panelling and crystal chandeliers hung from the ceiling. Even in the pale glow of the emergency exit signs, the room reeked of opulence.

A red torch flared. It appeared to be floating unsupported at waist height as it moved along the row of doors at ground level, Jen assumed, due to the operator wearing an illegal stealth suit. Genuine military grade stealth suits were impervious to detection by movement sensors and had a chameleon mode which allowed them to change colour to reflect a selected background. In daylight, they stood out as soon as the wearer moved. As good as the technology was, it could not fool the human brain. In the dark, they were almost impossible to detect.

Jen turned the thermal imaging off; it was of no value against this level of technology. When the torch was still, the shape holding it blended into the background, disappeared. Luckily, the torch kept moving, searching for something. With her naked eye, Jen could just make out the outline of a human. Given its shape and the way it moved, the body appeared to be male. It disappeared through a door. Jen turned, looking for David but there was no sign of him.

'Damn it!' she whispered to herself.

A bang followed by what sounded like, steel scraping across concrete reverberated through the empty space. Jen jumped at the noise. She stared towards the door where the body had disappeared. A moment later, came the sound of shattering glass.

'What the...!'

More banging and crashing; the guy was trashing the place. This couldn't be the Bible depositor, they had never left a mess or caused damage. Jen risked a call over her communicator.

'David, where are you?' No reply. Jen tried again, 'Officer Thomas, please respond.' Nothing. 'David, get your butt up here mate, we have an issue with our cat.' Still no reply.

Jen could now see the red glow associated with flames emanating from the door.

'Shit!' Jen moved, talking rapidly into her wrist.

'Central dispatch from Bravo 34. Over.'

'Dispatch receiving. Send.'

'Additional backup required urgently. Intruder has started a fire in the premises, please respond the fire brigade. Can confirm suspect is wearing a stealth suit and should be considered dangerous. Am moving to apprehend the suspect who is currently on the ground floor of the premises. Bravo 34 out.'

Jen sprinted across the room, pulling up against the wall alongside the door. Taking a deep breath, she called in her most authoritarian voice, 'POLICE!'

Jen waited three seconds for her call to register.

'All exits from this building are now secured, there is no possibility of escape.' As if to emphasise the point, the sounds of multiple sirens could now be heard in the distance. 'Stop what you are doing, come out with both hands above your head. Once you get outside the room, lie face down on the floor. Spread your arms and legs, make like a starfish on a beach. If you fail to follow my instructions, I will shoot you.' Jen let this sink in for a three second count.

'If you don't come out, you will die in that room. It's no skin off my nose either way mate, but I think I would rather face a magistrate than burn to death.' Jen waited another three seconds. 'That fancy suit of yours won't protect you for long.' Nothing. No noise, no reply, no anything. *Where the hell was David?*

'All right. I am coming out,' replied a male voice. 'Just don't shoot me, I am not armed.'

Jen moved away from the door to give herself space. Smoke was starting to billow from the doorway, the brown cloud of soot and entrained toxic gases were rushing towards the ceiling.

'Quickly,' Jen urged. A tall body, arms held high emerged to spreadeagle on the floor four paces outside the room.

Jen holstered her stunner, put one knee in the back of the figure, then reached for a wrist to attach a handcuff. As she did, Jen felt a presence behind her.

'About bloody time, Dave. Shut that door, we can probably confine the fire for a while at least.' The figure didn't move. Jen turned her head.

'David, did you hear what I said? I don't know what's up with you, mate. Didn't you hear my radio calls?'

As she moved, Jen felt a solid thump against the small of her back, as if somebody had kicked her. She was startled by the knock, then an instant later, agonising pain shot through her body. Red liquid gushed from beneath her sodden shirt; it spilled down her side, slowly spreading on the floor beneath her knee. Jen reached with her hand to the floor, trying to steady herself, the red spread beneath her fingers.

'Shit!'

There was a second strike, something solid rather than sharp. It struck the side of her head, then bounced off. An object flashed in front of her face. It was a fist, closed around the handle of a sturdy knife. The blade was ugly and tarnished, not something designed for kitchen use. Jen lost her balance; it had only been maintained by pure bloody-minded determination not to go down on her face. Jen knew, if she collapsed to the floor, every part of her body would be exposed, she would not be able to defend herself. With two halting slides, she slumped across the torso of her now ex-captive.

'Two of you bastards,' she swore through the pain.

Hands gripped her by the belt, dragging her sideways. She tried to resist, to get up, her efforts received a boot in the ribs taking away her remaining breath. The room began to go fuzzy, then faded to black as she watched two sets of legs walking away.

David returned to the corridor, immediately tapped his wrist band to reactivate his radio and body camera. By shutting down the device, he had ignored and circumvented operational procedure.

David smelt and saw smoke wafting down the length of the corridor at ceiling level, a red glow illuminated the end of the passage where he had expected to see Jen. The light was coming from what he remembered to be the big entrance hall. To add to his concern, David could hear multiple sirens in the distance.

'Jen, what's happening?' he whispered into his wrist. No reply. David ran towards the glow. 'Jen? Talk to me Jen, where are you?' No reply.

David reached the end of the corridor, dropped low and peered into the hall. Weapon out, extended, finger inside the trigger guard. Scanning the room from right to left, he could see a shape lying in front of a glowing doorway. Smoke was pouring through the opening in a pulsing torrent towards the ceiling. Touching his glasses to zoom in, David recognised the shape lying in a pool of dark liquid. His heart raced as he charged across the space, speaking loud and rapidly into his left wrist.

'Bravo 34 to dispatch, officer down at my location. Urgent medical assistance required and armed response backup.'

Kneeling alongside his partner, David was struck by the amount of blood on the floor. The liquid was coagulating into a steaming red jelly from the heat emanating from the room only metres away. Grasping Jen's arms, David dragged her toward the front entrance of the building.

'Jen, can you hear me?'

Jen's eyes flickered, then popped open as they reached the rosewood and brass entrance doors.

'Give me a minute to catch my breath. I can walk by myself if you let go of me,' she grimaced. Pain flickered across her face; she coughed, leaving a dribble of blood on her chin.

Smoke continued to fill the room, super-heated fire gasses above their heads radiating heat downwards and oxygen levels were falling. David felt his chest tighten as his lungs struggled to cope and the water on his clothing began to turn to steam. As he reached for the door handle, the building's sprinkler system burst into life sending a deluge of water tumbling from hidden pipework.

Now that the risk from the fire was being taken care of, David searched for Jen's wound to staunch the blood flow. Turning his partner onto her stomach, he located the wound low on her right side. Dark red liquid was seeping out rather than gushing. That was a good sign, at least, it wasn't a spurting arterial bleed. The flow was being diluted by the sprinkler downpour, spreading a pink puddle down her hips and onto the floor. David tore Jen's shirt around the wound, then removed his sodden shirt, scrunched the fabric to form a wad, placed over the gash and applied pressure.

Jen opened her eyes, and spoke in a raspy voice, 'Did you just rip my new shirt?'

'The colour didn't suit you and I doubt you would have gotten the sauce stain out anyway.'

'Bugger that,' coughed Jen, blood dribbled on to her chin, 'you owe me a shirt.'

David struggled to reply. What could he say? Blood continued to soak through the cloth he was pressing against Jen's wound. He was about to remove his t-shirt to add to the wound dressing, when the doors behind him swung open. Two firefighters in breathing apparatus, pulling a fire hose, made entry into the room. They dropped beside David; one began to unfurl a drag mat used to move casualties, the second was speaking into a radio, calling in a sitrep. No sooner had they knelt, when a second pair of firefighters entered with a second hose line. The teams exchanged a quick word. The first pair moved off to the seat of the fire, taking their hose with them.

'We have this,' came a female voice through the fire fighter's face mask.

David looked at Jen.

'Are you ok to go without me?'

The firefighters had manoeuvred Jen onto the drag mat. It looked like a canvas sleeping bag with one side mostly cut off, leaving an enclosure for feet to rest in. Wide straps with push in clips, held the occupant in place. Jen was face down so that one firefighter could keep pressure on the wound while the second lifted the head end of the mat and dragged her toward safety.

Jen could see David kneeling at her side; she fought to stay focused.

'There are two of them,' *cough, wheeze.* 'One male, educated Aussie accent. The other didn't speak, but stuck the knife in, no hesitation.' Jen raised her head as well as she could, the grimace on her face showed David how much pain she was in.

'Take no chances with the bastards, Dave.'

Jen coughed open-mouthed, her body arched. She let out an agonising half-choked, growling noise as her face twisted in pain. Her eyes rolled, flickered and she slumped limp. David could see Jen's chest rising and falling. She had succumbed to shock, loss of blood and stress, he could do nothing for her now. A quick exit to medical help was her best hope of survival.

The internal deluge from the sprinkler system slowed, then stopped. The fire suppression isolation valve had been closed by the firefighters. David held Jen's hand as the firefighters dragged her through the exit doors; he could see two fire appliances and an ambulance on the road outside. The glaring white light from the fire appliances' lighting towers cast dark shadows down the street. Further sirens could be heard approaching from a distance.

David knew police backup had yet to arrive. If they had, there was no way the firies would have been allowed into a building containing armed and violent criminals. The true situation on scene had probably yet to fully register and trigger the required response. It would come, it would come quickly. An officer was down, all hell would be let loose. A tactical armed response team would arrive within an hour from Melbourne.

In the meantime, local law enforcement would begin by sealing off the surrounding streets, but that would already be too late. Even if fleeing on foot, wearing stealth suits in the rain would make them almost impossible to detect in the dark. If they had transport, they should have breached any containment perimeter before it was established.

David picked up his and Jen's weapons from the parquet floor, put one stunner in his holster, then checked the other, setting it to maximum stun. He held the weapon out in front, his finger resting on the trigger, not standard practice. David feared the intruders had no intention of leaving the building by conventional means, it wouldn't matter what perimeter was thrown up to lock down the neighbourhood. If he was right, it would make no difference whatsoever.

David flattened his body against the wall to peer sideways through the laundry door glass. He would enter the room low and fast. It was expected, assumed, that an adult would come through the door at head height and not on their hands and knees. Doing the unexpected could make the difference between being the hunter, or the hunted.

David dropped to one knee, weapon through the entrance, head, shoulders, eyes left to right, up toward the ceiling and pause. No obvious threat. Up, weapon extended, rapidly across the room, his senses tingling as they worked to analyse the inputs surrounding him, the weapon tracking with his eyes. Down on his haunches, side- on to the door, listening. He could hear a hum, the sound of electronic static remembered from his childhood, from before he and his sister were banished from visiting the room behind the laundry.

David was going to go in quick, weapon up, pointed toward where they would be. They couldn't afford to wait and neither could he. They had hurt Jen, that was not acceptable, it never could be.

When David realised where he was, the memories of secret conversations and late-night meetings between his uncles and her in their family home, had come rushing back. David had not thought about her, or it, for years. Not until tonight. Then there it was, standing there like it had when he saw it as a child, smaller than he remembered, looking innocent and basic. It was stunning to think it had taken this long for somebody to find it and want to use it. This thought brought back the gut knotting fear he felt when he realised what Jen and he were walking into.

David calmed his breathing. He remembered it was not instantaneous, inputs had to be made, machinery had to warm up. If they knew what they wanted, knew when and where, it would be faster, just not instant. The sound of sirens had stopped, there was no more time, he had to act now.

David swung left to face where it stood 30 metres away in the dark. A glow illuminated its interface, reflecting off the glass of its elongated box shape. Two figures were behind the glass, holding hands: one a tall woman, dark haired, trim figure, holding the strap of a backpack, stuffed to the point of bursting, resting on the floor of the machine.

The other was male, older than the woman by probably 10 years; his blonde hair was immaculate, despite having been contained within a balaclava only minutes before. He looked at David and smiled; it was a handsome face.

'You're too late, I am afraid. If I were you, I would go home and make the most of your life as it is. Things are going to change; they will never be the same again.'

David recognised the voice and the smile from somewhere in his past. Then it came back to him like a kick in the guts. He started to run.

'I know you,' he yelled. 'I'll find you and bring you back.'

David fired his weapon. The energy blast whooshed across the gap as he pulled the trigger in rapid succession. The glass deflected it, the box had been engineered by David's father to endure far higher forces than could possibly be generated by the sidearm. He knew it was futile to keep firing, as did the face grinning back at him.

The face stopped smiling; mutual recognition dawned; the grin re-emerged.

'The people you bump into at the oddest of times. It's David Thomas all grown up. You remember I told you about him, Dwight's son.' The smiling face turned to address the rapidly approaching David. 'Please say goodbye to your mother for me, while you still can.'

With this, a bright green glow emerged within the box, pulsed three times and David was alone.

'SHIT!' he yelled at the top of his voice whirling in frustration and anger. 'Shit, shit, shit,' he spat, glaring around the room for an answer to his expletives.

He was in the dark, well almost dark. The glow from the machine's computer interface continued to spread a pool of greenish light. David stared at it, a memory, a memory of long ago, Uncle Emil pushing buttons on a keyboard to make the machinery work. David walked toward the glow.

'I've got you,' he breathed. 'I am going to hunt you down and bring you back.'

# CHAPTER TWO

**ADRIAN WAS AT THIS** moment feeling emotions ranging somewhere between excitement and dread. While David had promised adventure on their little getaway and the chance to pick up some artefacts with which to impress the members of his local genealogical and fancy-dress association, he had never mentioned the possibility of being crucified on a hill, overlooking a village populated with goats and donkeys, some 2000 years before he was born.

*Take that Julie Diesel,* Adrian thought, imagining topping her story about a priest ancestor, which for some reason had enthralled the association members. Normally, at the monthly get-together, it was a case of members trying to outdo each other with tales of a forebear whose achievement had brought them either fame or fortune, but instead Ms Diesel had gone for simplicity and a decided lack of anything noteworthy in her ancestor's life. Perhaps it was the way she told the story. Adrian had to admit it was a refreshing change from the usual presentation. It did have a certain humble quality, which quite put Simon Zuckerberg off his talk about an ancestor who did something important with computers.

Adrian found the study of history enthralling, but he was the first to admit that he tended to get things mixed up. Never mind, he could always refer to the Great Wikipedia Data Base, the font of knowledge containing the worlds collected wisdom, to check his facts. As he reasoned, why keep such things in your head when you can just look it up?

While Adrian had enjoyed the most amazing fun, things did look a bit grim. Here he was, erroneously detained by the local authorities after accidentally becoming involved in some local dispute which he was reasonably certain could be explained as a dreadful mistake, and if they let him go, he would promise not to mention the incident on his social media blog.

Studying the men with whom he was being detained, Adrian noted they seemed to be a bit down. Most were staring at the ground; one was even muttering something he assumed to be a prayer. Their expressions reminded him of his Uncle Dwight, the day the Australia was soundly thrashed by the Dutch in a world cricket cup test match final. Given it was by an innings and 562 runs, on the third day, before tea, they were looking very depressed.

Adrian decided to, as the ancients used to say, *carpe diem,* which people erroneously interpreted as, *seize the day,* but more literally meant, *act now,* or, *there is no time like the present.* Again Wikipedia. He turned to the chap alongside of himself and took charge of the moment.

'Excuse me,' started Adrian, conjuring up his most winning smile, 'I know we haven't been introduced, but my name is Adrian, Adrian Thomas.' He extended his hand as part of the introduction. 'I know I really shouldn't be asking, but I was wondering if you might be willing to help me explain my situation to the chap in charge?' Adrian paused, noting that he had the attention of all his new companions, 'That I wasn't actually involved in your demonstration, whatever it was about. A good cause I have no doubt, having brought so many of you out on such a fine sunny morning.' Adrian raised his arms, then addressed the sky to emphasise the glory of the day. 'Lord knows, I have signed enough petitions to stop real estate developers knocking down historical buildings just to put up multi-storey carparks. Let's face it, most people are too apathetic to get involved, which just means kudos to you gentlemen for taking an interest in local events.' Adrian patted his nearest companion on the shoulder in a sign of solidarity, then carried on, 'You know, I donated credits toward saving the endangered Amazonian Tapir once, a decidedly ugly looking beast to be honest. From what I was told, it has an important role to play in the regeneration of rain forest trees, something to do with eating fruit then excreting the seed after it has been through the beast's digestive tract,' Adrian paused to let his point sink in. 'As such, I am sympathetic to your right to protest, whatever your cause, which I assume is very close to your hearts.'

'Are you mad?' exclaimed a beardless youth who was the youngest of the group.

'No, I don't think so.'

A huge, bearded individual with one black and swollen eye, his face screwed up in anger, pushed past the youth to stand in front of Adrian. If the look on his face wasn't confronting enough, the man reeked of rotting fish, combined with a breath-taking body odour.

'What was that you said, stranger?'

Adrian found it difficult to maintain eye contact, and not just because of the smell emanating from the gentleman.

'I merely stated to your friend, that perhaps he, or in fact possibly yourself as the group representative, may be able to help me explain that I am being held by mistake. As you are aware, I had no involvement in your group's protest, other than being in the vicinity at an inappropriate moment.'

'Is that so?' hissed the man. 'You and your friend have got us all killed, you do realise that? You might as well have snuck into our homes and slit our throats while we slept.' The angry face shook his head in disgust. 'What the hell were you thinking, jumping off the roof on top of us? Didn't it register that it was probably a stupid thing to do, even if the Romans weren't there on the street in front of us?'

'I can only apologise on behalf of myself and my cousin David,' replied Adrian, 'it was purely unintentional. If we had been aware of your planned activity, we would have come earlier in the day to avoid, as it were, dropping in unannounced. There are few more irritating things than uninvited guests, it upsets the catering arrangements, if nothing else.' Adrian saw the look of disdain on his new acquaintances' faces.

'Sorry, I am embarrassed by my ignorance, but did we disrupt something really important?'

'Do you think we were lying in wait to attack Roman soldiers, armed only with sticks and rocks, if it wasn't important?'

'Ah, I see your point.'

'You see my point! You may have not noticed stranger, but those Roman dogs who you want to appeal to for freedom have invaded our country, defiled our temples, taken our women, stolen our beasts and seized our grain as taxes for the privilege of their presence as an occupying force. Does that sound as if it could be an important reason to fight back?'

'Sorry, I hadn't realised,' answered Adrian sympathetically. 'Here I was, thinking that you were probably involved with a local environmental action group, or something similar. I hadn't realised it was a political protest.' Adrian rolled his eyes as if it all suddenly made sense. 'Now I understand, you chaps are part of a left-wing alternative lifestyle political movement.' Adrian leant forward to whisper conspiratorially, 'I assume that's why you have an aversion to chemical deodorants.'

The eyes of the group's leader flared in astonishment, then his hands wrapped around Adrian's throat.

'Do you understand this?' screamed the leader of the group, tightening his grip until the veins on the back of his hands swelled under the strain.

Adrian, his eyes wide and fearful, grabbed the man's arms in an attempt to break his grip. This just seemed to increase his assailant's anger.

'If you hadn't leapt on top of us, just as we were about to spring our ambush, we wouldn't be in this bloody mess.'

The remaining prisoners wrestled the angry man bodily away from Adrian. He stood two paces away, held by the arms, leaning menacingly towards Adrian.

'You have killed us. You have killed all of these good men, you fool. If we survive, I swear I will end you myself.'

Adrian moved as far away from this assailant as his surrounding Roman captors would allow.

'I apologise,' he gasped between gulps of air. 'I don't know what else a chap can say. I am sorry, it was an accident.'

'An accident?' hissed the angry man.

'What are you trying to do, Peter? Get the Romans angry and make it worse for us?' pleaded the beardless youth.

'What do you mean, make it worse? If you haven't noticed, John, it is already as bad as it can get. We have been summarily tried and sentenced to death and it's not quite lunch time, I strongly suspect the afternoon is already ruined.'

'It could have been worse,' replied John.

'What do you mean, it could have been worse?'

The youth looked at each man in the bedraggled group.

'Crucifixion is not the worst way to die. I know it's going to be awful, especially when the crows come for our eyes, but they could have chosen a nastier way to finish us off.' John's forehead furrowed in worry. 'They won't use nails, will they? I have heard that is really unpleasant.'

Peter stared at John in disgust. Adrian could see a vein in the side of the man's neck bulging, it was obvious the man was about to explode. Adrian tried to move further away, but it was too late. Peter flung himself at John dragging the entire group into a writhing heap in the dirt and dust.

Octavian Drusis Flagelon was an important man. His official title, as the head of administration for the Sixth Legion Ferrata of Emperor Tiberius's Imperial Roman Army, was that of *Praefectus Castrorum*. This literally translated to camp prefect. The title carried with it, not only an administrative burden, but also the responsibility of being the third highest ranked officer within the 5000 strong military unit.

Today had been particularly productive for Octavian. He had fulfilled a promise to his business partner and managed to eliminate the risk posed by 13 members of the so-called Jewish Resistance to the stability of Roman rule, thanks to his informant in Nazareth. The man had been reluctant to cooperate. That changed when Octavian had made a few pointed remarks about the business dealings they had over the supply of horses to the legion. Business practicalities had overruled any real or feigned community loyalty.

The information paid for, had allowed for the capture of the bait, then the reeling in of the whole school. The irony of this was not lost on Octavian. It had been money well spent, the funds coming from his business capital, rather than the legion's purse. It was a business expense after all.

The resistance group had proven as predictable as Octavian had hoped. The rebels had rounded themselves up, announced their presence and would soon meet their fate with minimum effort on his behalf. Shortly, the troublemakers would be crucified on the hill that dominated Nazareth as an example of the power and reach of Rome. Octavian should have had the men nailed to the crosses, but nails were expensive, and the crime didn't warrant that level of pain.

Octavian took no pleasure in the death of these men; it could lead to further unrest and women and children were often the innocent victims of irrational acts of violence. Octavian found this abhorrent. His decision to remove the group was tactical, designed to act as a deterrent to those not yet fully committed to the cause. As the *Praefectus Castrorum* he was required to stamp out dissent; it was fortuitous that, on this occasion, the Empire's needs aligned with his and the request of his business partner.

Octavian was even going to make a small financial return as a result of what had been hinted at, but not directly asked for. It was as if avoiding the actual words, the requester was not tainted by the act. It would happen. Eventually. The request had been for the prize to be captured and removed; Octavian was technically meeting his half of the bargain.

Octavian surveyed the township and its surrounds; Nazareth was unremarkably ugly. Squat, flat roofed sandstone buildings were laid out in a lattice of narrow streets and alleys surrounded by family vegetable plots in a sea of sand and rock. There was a central square filled with stalls selling bread, vegetables, hand crafts and home spun clothing. A carpenter shop, wheel wright, flour mill, bakery and a blacksmith's forge made up the town's industrial base. The temple, that met the religious needs of the population, sat on a high point away from the centre of commerce. The roof of the temple, the tallest structure in Nazareth, had been requisitioned by the Roman garrison as an observation post.

Patches of green hugged the Tzapori River that skirted the village. At the base of the hill, nestled a grove of orange trees and newly planted olives being grown for the future use of the occupying Romans. A few goats and sheep were watched over by boys armed with slings to ward off wild dogs, and female forms could be seen beating cloth against rocks in the river to remove the dirt and dung that seemed to cling to everybody.

Octavian reminded himself that in two years, he could return home as a full citizen with all the privileges that service in the military bestowed in Roman society. He could put up with all of this for another two years, now that he had a plan for the future, a plan for his family.

Octavian's reflection was broken by an outburst of raised voices. He gestured, pointed to the next senior officer present to approach.

'Centurio Maximus, what is going on?'

A broad shouldered Centurio, with a puckered scar running from the tip of his chin across the length of his left shoulder, approached.

'It would appear our Jewish friends are taking it in turns to throttle each other.'

'I can see that, Max,' replied Octavian, using the shortened version of his trusted friend's name. Such familiarity between ranks was frowned upon, but these two men had served together in many battles and had more than a professional relationship, which could be shared when out of earshot of others.

'Unfortunately, Max, protocol dictates that we must be seen to be in charge. How would it look if our Jewish friends died before we had the opportunity to demonstrate the consequences of their rebellious activity?'

Maximus shrugged.

'The silly buggers were never a serious threat. A quick death for stupidity is probably more deserving than what's in store.'

'Agreed, but you know the rules as well as I do.' Octavian looked towards the brawling prisoners. 'Let's just get this done with as little fuss as we can. Make the point, but don't spend time rubbing it in the locals faces. We are trying to encourage following the rules, not incite further dissent.'

'By your leave, Praefectus,' replied Maximus. The centurio touched his fist into his chest, then strode purposely down the hill. As he marched, orders were issued to *sort this sorry mess out*. The writhing mass was broken apart, then formed into an upright bedraggled line.

'Right, you lot of scruffy molesters of goats and small children, this ends now.' Maximus stood tall as he addressed the assembled gathering. 'I have a job to do, the same as you gentlemen. Part of mine is to put the idea out of the heads of your friends and neighbours, that acts of stupidity like happened today, have a happy ending. They don't. Not for you, not for my young soldiers.' Maximus paused, then sighed deeply. 'I have nothing personally against any of you, I can see that you are brave men. I understand that you were only doing what you believed to be right. I salute your bravery, but you lost, and we won. If I were you, I would hold my head high and face the end as brave men, not as an embarrassing rabble.' Maximus let this thought settle. 'I have no desire to inflict more pain than is necessary, I promise to come after dark and push a spear into your hearts to end your suffering, that's as much as I can do for you unfortunately.'

Maximus surveyed the prisoners' faces. A youth without a beard smiled, it was as if the promise of a quick death was a relief to the boy. One man glowered in anger. That was to be expected, but most appeared dazed, suffering the anticipated terror of their fate. Then much to Maximus's surprise, one thrust his hand into the air and took a pace forward.

'Excuse me,' interjected Adrian, 'there seems to have been a dreadful mistake.'

Maximus was taken aback. Usually, the condemned became either morose and submissive, or angry and aggressive. This was the first time a prisoner had prattled on a rambling explanation about accidentally falling on top of everybody at an inconvenient moment, then went on about being a tourist embroiled in local politics purely by chance and was just finishing the part about it being their little secret, that he wouldn't mention it if they didn't, when Maximus came out of his daze.

'Are you crazy?'

Adrian frowned. 'You know you're the second person that's asked me that.'

Maximus drew a dagger, his *pugio,* and jammed it up under Adrian's chin.

'Who the hell are you, Jew? You don't smell like a goat; you have no beard, and your clothes are as clean as if they were just woven. You speak with the accent of a Roman nobleman, but only nonsense comes out of your mouth.' Maximus searched Adrian's eyes for a hint of deception, it was like looking into the face of an innocent child. 'Which means you don't fit. This makes me anxious; I don't like feeling anxious, it makes me do rash things, sometimes, bad things.'

Up until this point, Adrian had been enjoying the adventure. Now, not so much.

'Firstly, my name is Adrian Thomas, and I don't actually speak Latin, though I am speaking it now, while thinking in English, which I know is rather confusing. Technology, it's an amazing thing,' said Adrian with a lopsided half grin. 'Secondly, I think beards are horrible scratchy things, so I shave every day and thirdly, the clothes are new, as you noticed, thank you very much. I am an atheist, not Jewish, but I can't swear to my ancestry on that score, and I pride myself on personal hygiene. I find it a bit embarrassing, sweat and all of that.'

Maximus, pushing the pugio a little harder against Adrian's skin.

'Tell me why you are here again?'

'It was my cousin David's suggestion actually; you know a last-minute weekend getaway to take in a bit of the local culture, try some of the food, check out the arts and craft stalls in the local farmer's market.' Adrian could see the soldier's eyes narrowing in suspicion. 'I thought we could have a couple of drinks at the pub over lunch and do the usual touristy type things. It seemed like a perfect opportunity to get one up on boring old Julie Diesel and her great and pious ancestor stories, for once.'

'What in the name of Apollo are you rambling on about?' hissed Maximus, gripping the front of Adrian's robes and lifting him off his feet to stare into his eyes. It was at this point that Adrian squealed in fright, causing Maximus to release his grip in disgust.

'Right, you lot, where is this David this fool is talking about and what in the name of the gods, is a Julie Diesel?'

From behind, came a polite cough as one of the legionnaires interjected.

'There was a Jew that wounded three of our men. This Jew called him David.'

'Where is he then? I don't see a body and none of these men seem capable of wounding a real soldier in a fight.'

'The Praefectus Castrorum ordered him sent to Tyre with the next export of slaves, Centurio Maximus.'

Maximus nodded; it made sense. If this David was young and strong enough to put up a reasonable fight, there was profit to be made by selling him on the slave market and Octavian had a quota to fill.

'Which one of you lot searched this David?'

'Sir?'

'Don't play games, lad.' Maximus held out his hand, the soldier handed over

21

a bracelet which had at its centre a glowing green object the size and shape of three Roman sestertius coins stacked on top of each other. Maximus took the bracelet then raised an eyebrow as he studied the dial. He had seen glow worms in grottoes give off a similar light. This however was something new to him. The object had raised squares on its front. Touching one, the green glow brightened as the illuminated shapes it displayed rapidly changed until he released his finger. Maximus was no fool; it made sense that this object must be linked to the nearest other strange thing that he didn't understand and that would be the man standing in front of him.

'What's this?'

Adrian reached to take the object from the centurio. As he did, his sleeve fell back to reveal an identical bracelet. Maximus grabbed Adrian's arm, twisting it to get a better look.

'If you can let go of my arm, I can show you what it is.'

Maximus shifted his gaze from the bracelet to Adrian.

'All right, show me. But if you try anything, you will live in agony long enough to dream about being crucified.'

Adrian took the bracelet with slightly trembling fingers, touched his and the one belonging to David, together and was instantly surrounded by a bright, green aura. Maximus lunged with his dagger. It was all too late. Adrian and the surrounding air rapidly pulsated three times and he was gone.

# CHAPTER THREE

WILLIAM THOMAS, KNOWN TO everybody, except his mother, as Will, was a typical 14-year-old schoolboy. He was an average student, attending an overcrowded state-run secondary school in a country town where everybody knew everybody else's business. He was also typical in that he was struggling to come to terms with the normal problems associated with being 14. This included puberty, an overprotective mother and his younger brother Brian, with whom he shared a bedroom.

On this particular evening, Will had his bedroom all to himself. Brian was spending the weekend with one of his friends. Will was lying in bed thinking about the opposite sex, well one girl in particular, Jenny Patzel, from school who seemed less hostile towards him than his other female classmates. He just wished he was better looking, not prone to pimples and frankly, less frightened of being rejected if he did ask Jenny to go to the school social with him. His thoughts of 14-year-old girls were having an uncontrollable effect on his body, which teenage boys found embarrassing when it occurred at the least appropriate moments. Will's thoughts were interrupted by a polite knock on his door.

'William, are you awake?'

In a panic, Will pulled the covers of his bed up higher and dropped one of Brian's Phantom comics strategically on the bed to cover his lap.

'Can I come in?'

'Yes Mum,' replied Will, trying to cover his embarrassment by pretending to read.

Will's mother, Mary, sat on the edge of the bed and kissed Will's forehead adding to his discomfort.

'I have to go next door and watch Mrs Sullivan's baby for about an hour. Wendy has to go to the late-night chemist to pick up some medicine for the poor little soul. Your father is still out playing cards, so I'm going to have to leave you by yourself for a while. If you need me, I'll just be next door. I have written down the Sullivan's number and left it next to the phone just in case something happens.'

'Mum, I wish you wouldn't do that,' said Will, exasperated.

'Do what?'

'Treat me like a baby.'

'William, no matter how big or how grown up you become, I am always going to be your mum and you will always be my little boy. It's one of those things that you are just going to have to live with. Besides, Ita Buttrose wrote an article in the *Women's Weekly* about how children can drift away from their parents during their teenage years if you don't put in the extra effort as they grow and change, I am just following her advice.'

'If Ita told you to jump in the lake, would you do it?'

'Don't be so silly William,' said Mary rising off the bed, 'Ita would never suggest such a thing. I'll see you in about an hour.'

'Goodbye, Mum,' waved Will to his disappearing parent's back as he went back to pretending to read. As he did, something happened, something which was to change his life forever.

It started as a barely discernible breeze; the movement of air grew until strong enough to rustle the pages of Will's comic. Will looked up at his bedroom window. It was shut. He looked at his bedroom door. It was closed. The wind stopped. Will shrugged his shoulders and returned to his reading.

There was an almighty crash, an explosion of light and noise and wind, all contained within the four walls of the bedroom. Will's laminated wooden wardrobe disintegrated into pieces spewing dust, clothes, shoes, coat hangers and comic books through the air.

Will screamed, his bed flew through the air, landing on its side against the far bedroom wall.

'Oh my God,' whispered Will as the eruption settled and he tried to extract himself from the tangle of blankets, clothes and comic books that threatened to suffocate him.

'David, where are you?' came a voice from across the room.

To say Will was surprised would be a major understatement.

'David, is that you?' came the unidentified voice again from the dark.

Will wriggled his head clear of the carnage. Standing in his bedroom was a figure dressed in what appeared to be biblical robes, clutching what looked like a digital watch, while surrounded by an eerie green glow swirling in ever decreasing circles. Will's family were no more religious than any other he knew, right now, however, all the Sunday school sessions he had been subjected to were coming home with a vengeance.

'Oh my God,' whispered Will, seeing an avenging angel come to punish a sinner who only seconds ago had been entertaining impure thoughts about a slightly plump 14-year-old girl who sat in front of him during roll call at school.

Will did the only sensible thing he could and crawled back under the blankets.

'Hello, is there anyone there?'

'Go away. My mother told me never to talk to strangers.'

There was silence for a moment, then, 'You know, my mother used to say pretty much the same sort of thing when I was a young chap. I used to think it was fairly sound sort of advice, until I discovered that my mother met my father selling cosmetics door to door. If my mother had taken her own advice, she would never have spoken to my father who was a stranger when they first met. They never would have married and I would not have been born. I have, therefore, come to the conclusion that it would be far more sensible if mothers would tell their children to be selective about which strangers that they talk to, rather than imposing a total ban on communications.'

Before Will could decide whether he should reply, the voice carried on, 'I mean if you never spoke to strangers, how would you ever meet anybody, or for that matter ever be able to purchase anything from a shop unless you knew the individual behind the counter? It would impede an individual's social development no end. Just imagine how your life would suffer if you had to wait for a mutual acquaintance to introduce you to anyone who caught your eye. Before you knew it, the world's dating agencies would be over-crowded with frustrated potential customers who couldn't become a member because they didn't know the admin clerk and so couldn't tell them that they wanted to sign up.'

Will cautiously withdrew the coverings from his head. The room was now lit by starlight as the ceiling globe and its lampshade had become victims of wardrobe shrapnel. The initial fluorescent green glow surrounding Will's visitor had gone leaving the room in darkness and shadow.

'Who are you?' whispered Will.

'My name is Adrian Thomas, I'm, whooooaa...' Kathump. Adrian had successfully failed to negotiate the obstacles in Will's bedroom and collided with the floor.

Will found the torch which normally resided under his bed and shone the beam until he located a crumpled heap slowly rising to its feet.

'Are you alright?'

'I think so, apart from a few bruises, I'm physically alright. Mentally, I'm not quite so sure about.'

Adrian felt his way across the debris to sit on the edge of Will's bed.

'I have had one of those days when everything which can go wrong, does go wrong.'

Will found his table lamp which miraculously had survived undamaged, when he pushed the on switch the room was flooded with light.

'Bloody hell!'

'I say,' gasped Adrian, surveying the carnage.

'Mum's going to kill me,' cried Will, staring at the shattered furniture and scattered clothing.

'I say,' repeated Adrian, 'I'm dreadfully sorry about the mess.'

Will stared at Adrian open mouthed.

'You've demolished my bedroom!'

'I don't know what to ... say,' apologised Adrian, running out of words as he focused on the table lamp. 'You have electricity!' he whispered in surprise.

'I used to have a wardrobe and a bed as well.'

'I mean you have ... electricity!'

'No thanks to you, I do,' said Will, standing up and surveying the room in disbelief.

'But you have electricity,' repeated Adrian as if surprised.

'What were you expecting? Kerosene lamps?'

'No, I had thought maybe olive oil lamps, but not electricity!'

'What am I going to tell Mum?' whimpered Will, sinking on to his upturned bed.

Adrian surveyed the room taking in what remained of the furniture, the clothing and the comic books.

'What is the date?'

'What?'

'What is the date, please?' asked Adrian with a sense of urgency that struck Will with such force that he momentarily forgot about the surrounding mess.

'It's the fifth, I think.'

'The fifth?'

'Of August,' continued Will spurred on by Adrian's pleading look.

'What year?' asked Adrian in a rough whisper.

'1975. What year do you think it is?'

'1975!'

'Yes 1975,' said Will quietly, as he watched Adrian's face sag. He looked so depressed that Will felt ashamed for having raised his voice.

'Is there anything I can do?' asked Will holding out his hand. 'My name's Will, by the way, Will Thomas, though technically it's William, but only my mum calls me that.'

Adrian took the proffered hand.

'I am terribly sorry about your room. Adrian Thomas is my name, which coincidentally is the same as yours. Thomas, I mean, not William.' Adrian shook his head, 'I don't understand. David said all I had to do was to touch the recall devices together if one of us was lost and the machine would find the other. There were some technical thingies that limited the range, something to do with electromagnetic interference and atmospheric stability, I really wasn't listening to be honest. I do recall that David said, that as long as the time circuits were correctly aligned, it could find either of us over a range of around 10 kilometres.'

Adrian's speech trailed off. He looked at the digital watch look-alike clasped in his hand. The device did indeed indicate August 1975, not the year 15.

'Of course, the soldier!' His head snapped up, eyes fixing an unblinking stare on the face of his new young acquaintance.

'What?' asked Will, feeling uncomfortable. 'What are you staring at? You're not one of those strange men my mum is always going on about?'

'Good heavens, no,' replied Adrian, 'it's just not often that a chap gets to meet one of his ancestors in the flesh.'

Now it was Will's turn to stare.

'I see,' said Will, clearly not seeing at all. 'I think I hear my mother calling.'

Will stood, wanting to put as much distance as possible between himself and this strange man.

'Wait Will, please,' pleaded Adrian. 'I know I sound insane, and in the last few hours there was an occasion when I thought that maybe I had made the odd irrational decision, but I assure you, that I'm not. Insane that is.' Adrian looked imploringly at Will, trying to give an impression of honesty and integrity.

'What do you mean, one of your ancestors?'

'Ah,' said Adrian, 'the important thing is that I assure you I mean you no harm, that would be totally counterproductive if what I think has happened has.'

'What?'

'Sorry. I am not making myself very clear and probably not making you feel overly comfortable. I realise that my appearance must have come as a shock, however if you can spare a few minutes of your time, I can explain everything and then we will get along famously. I know this is a lot to ask, but could you please, please find it in your heart, as a fellow member of the Thomas family, to allow me to prove to you that fate has brought us together for a reason.'

'I really think I should find my mum; you should talk to her.'

'Please Will, just a few minutes, that's all I ask.'

Will looked at the man sitting on his upturned bed. He didn't look dangerous, in fact he looked more lost than anything. Will folded, he couldn't help himself.

'Ok, but if Mum comes home, you have to talk to her.'

David had demonstrated the memory recall system to Adrian and explained how it worked. The problem was, Adrian had only been half listening. From memory, all he needed to do was to put one lead from the device on the story teller's forehead and the second, on the chap's head who he was telling the story to. The machine would interpret his thoughts and transmit it to the other person. It would seem as if they had lived through the experiences themselves. The only drawback with the system was it was reliant upon the honesty of the memory donor for its program content.

When first invented, the memory storage and retrieval system had been intended for use by law enforcement agencies to establish a suspect's innocence or guilt by directly tapping into a person's memories, but it had a fatal flaw, which saw its use discontinued by the police. The device was, however, a commercial success when offered for sale for recreational purposes.

The electrode on Will's forehead began to pulsate with flashes of light. Adrian rushed on with an explanation.

'What you are about to experience, is one of my childhood memories from far in your future. The basic facts will be correct, how I choose to recall them will colour how the story unfolds. Not only that, but how you want to interpret them may also change the way you experience the memory.'

Will looked blankly at Adrian.

'What?'

'Don't worry it will all make sense in a moment. As I was saying, people in my time do not need to work. Artificially intelligent machines, scientific and technological type thingamajigs have taken away the need for human labouring. People do still work; it's a matter of choice, not need. So, you may ask William Thomas from 1975, what does humankind do if they don't have to labour to support themselves? They seek out higher, more meaningful activities to fill their days. Intellectual pursuits, to broaden their minds. You know: tennis, space exploration, that sort of thing. But the biggest, well actually the two biggest pastimes of mankind in my present and your future, are fancy dress parties and genealogy.'

# CHAPTER FOUR

'**WELCOME TO THOMASES COSTUMERY,**' smiled Emil Thomas as he greeted Miss Cynthia Horrigan, the daughter of one of the wealthiest and most influential families in Australia. It was an impressive establishment, solid wood panelling, crystal chandeliers and an imposing rosewood staircase leading to the upper-level fitting rooms. 'We literally have thousands of costumes to meet any client's particular taste for their next costumed soiree.'

'I have been told, Mr. Thomas.'

'Emil please. I insist that all of our valued clientele call me Emil.'

'All right, Emil,' she replied, returning the smile. 'As I was about to say, Emil, you were recommended by my friend, Margriet Van Der Horst. I know I left it to the last minute, but I need a costume for my university genealogy association's fancy dress ball this weekend.'

'That is very kind of Margie. So, tell me, what was it exactly that you had in mind? Something elegant? Perhaps, something adventurous?'

'No, what I am interested in is something...how shall I phrase this?... authentic. What I want is an authentic historical costume.'

'Margriet has perhaps mentioned a service that we offer to very discerning clientele.'

'I believe it is called a Fabric Reconstruction Cabinet?'

'Actually, it's a Fabric Dissemination and Historically Oriented Reconstruction Cabinet, but I've never been one to quibble over titles. You do understand how exclusive the service is?'

'Yes, I do,' replied Cynthia, handing over her gold credit disc. 'I need a costume which will make an impression for reasons that are too ridiculous to mention but may well affect my future career prospects. I am hoping you can help me.'

'I am sure we can,' replied Emil, passing the credit disk over a scanner. 'Do you have a host garment with you?'

Cynthia held aloft a suit carrier.

'Yes, I do.'

'Good. Then if you would like to accompany me, I will escort you to our private costume selection area,' said Emil relieving Cynthia of her luggage.

'This is very kind of you Emil.'

'Believe me Cynthia, the pleasure is very much all mine.'

Emil escorted Cynthia across the grand hall, stopping occasionally to speak to a customer, or answer an inquiry from one of the uniformed costumiers. As they walked, Emil remained witty, and courteous while explaining the numerous customer service and fitting rooms. He opened one of the storage cabinets, to allow Cynthia to feel the quality and see the detail of the rental garments as they made their way to a corridor leading away from the main store to a door marked "Laundry".

'When my great-grandfather started the business, everything was done manually, from making costumes, to their laundering and the restocking of the display cabinets. Since those days, our family has built the business to what you see today, embracing the latest in technology, while retaining a personal interaction customer experience. We were the first to introduce electronic cataloguing, the first to introduce interest free, short-term financing and now, we are the only costumery on the planet to possess an Historically Oriented Fabric Dissemination and Reconstitution Cabinet.'

Emil led Cynthia through a door at the rear of the laundry to a subtly lit room. Two of the store's costumiers were busily attending to two gentlemen. One was flicking through the pages of an illustrated history book, the second was passing a three-piece suit, a wide brimmed hat and a pair of leather shoes to his attendant.

'Good morning, all.'

'Good morning, Emil,' came the chorused reply.

'And how are you, Mr Fowles?' asked Emil, addressing a plump, fortyish gentleman in business attire.

'I am very well, thank you, Emil. That 18th Century Patagonian peasant's dress you recommended went down an absolute treat with Geraldine on her birthday.'

'I am pleased,' replied Emil with a brief smile. 'And what are we looking for today?'

'I'm not really sure. Geraldine and I have been invited for cocktails at the French Embassy for the Bastille Day celebration in Canberra. I had thought that perhaps I could find something appropriate in your reference library.'

'In that case, I would recommend Auguste Racinet's excellent illustrated book, *The Complete Costume History*. We have a copy on our shelves.'

Emil went to lead Mr Fowles toward the stores library then realised he was about to neglect his other client.

'Cynthia, please forgive me, I was getting quite carried away.'

'No, that's alright Emil, go ahead, I'll wait.'

'Are you sure?'

'It's fine, I can wait.'

'That's very kind of you, Cynthia.' Emil gestured towards Mr Fowles' attendant. 'Could you please supply Ms Horrigan with some refreshments, Tonya, while she is being so patient?'

'With pleasure, Mr Thomas,' nodded Tonya, who was dressed in the subtle grey and mauve livery of a costumier at Thomases Costumery. Her platinum blond hair was pulled back and tied with a matching bow.

'Then I'll leave you in Tonya's care while I track down Auguste Racinet's excellent book for Mr Fowles.'

'Go right ahead, I'll be fine.'

Emil turned, leading Mr Fowles towards the library.

'Bastille Day, you said. What an interesting period. The guillotine, political intrigue, invention of the pearl stitch, we are going to have some fun.'

'And what may I get you, Ms Horrigan?' inquired Tonya.

'A Pimms, with a slice of lemon would be nice, thank you.'

'One Pimms with lemon,' repeated Tonya as she noted the order in a gilt-edged book. 'If you would excuse me for a few moments, I will make up your order.' Tonya closed her book then indicated toward her fellow costumier with a slight, but friendly smile. 'Mr Damian will look after your needs while I am away. If you have any questions, please don't hesitate to ask him.'

'You won't be long, will you?' asked Cynthia, looking at her antique watch with a start. 'I have an appointment before six.'

'I should only be a few moments. Perhaps Mr Damian will be kind enough to show you the *Cabinet*, as we like to call it, in operation while I am gone?'

Mr Damian, who was standing behind Cynthia, shook his head at the suggestion, then changed to a radiant smile as Cynthia turned.

'That will be a pleasure, Ms Horrigan. I don't suppose you have met Mr Cooper?' Damian indicated toward Cynthia's fellow customer.

'No, I don't believe that we have.'

'Then let me introduce you,' hurried Damian, while watching the exiting Tonya's back. 'Mr Cooper, this is Ms Horrigan.'

'Oh, how do you-'

'Ms Horrigan, this is Mr Cooper.'

'Hello.'

'I'll let you two get acquainted for a moment while I catch up with Ms Tonya before she leaves.' With this, Damian turned and almost ran to catch his fellow costumier. 'Tonya, hold up for a moment.'

'Yes, Damian?'

'Where are you going?'

'I'm going to get Ms Horrigan's drink.'

'Come on, you know I want to knock off early. If you go wandering off, I'm going to get stuck here baby-sitting your customer.'

'She's not my customer,' hissed Tonya, 'She is Emil's. Besides, I'm sick of covering for you.'

'What do you mean?'

'You snuck out early Monday and twice last week. I'm the one who got left looking after your customers and it's not going to happen today.'

'Come on, have a heart, I've covered for you before.'

'No, Damian,' hissed Tonya.

'Please, Tonya,' pleaded Damian, giving Tonya his most pathetic and apologetic look.

'I said, no, and I mean, no. If you can't organise your social life outside of working hours that's your problem, not mine.'

'Are you jealous because I'm going out with your friend?' asked Damain feigning surprise.

'Cheryl is not my friend, not anymore.'

'I don't see what that has got to do with me?'

'Do you know what she did?' said Tonya balling her fists in anger.

'No. Should I?'

'I bet you and Cheryl think it's a huge joke,' said Tonya on the edge of angry tears.

'I really have no idea what you are talking about,' replied Damian pretending confusion.

'I thought she was my friend, how stupid of me.'

Damian found it entertaining watching Tonya's reaction but maintained his look of confused innocence.

'I'm sorry, but I don't see what any of this has got to do with me wanting to get away early.'

'Do you know what it's like to pour out your heart to someone, only to find they use that knowledge to humiliate you?'

'No, why would I?'

'Of course not, all you think about is your own self-gratification, I bet you have never met a mirror you didn't like.'

'What?'

'Did you ever think to ask me how I felt?'

'What?'

'All she had to do was wiggle her arse in your direction and you followed her like a puppy being offered a treat.'

'Look Tonya, all Cheryl did was ask me out for dinner,' replied Damian indignantly. 'You and I are not married to each other; I don't see a ring on any of my fingers. Yes, we slept with each other a couple of times, I enjoyed it; I know you did too, but it was nothing more than sex. Besides, you were the one that introduced me to Cheryl.'

'I just knew that you were going to throw that in my face,' retorted Tonya angrily.

'You're shouting,' whispered Damian looking toward Cynthia and Mr Cooper, 'they will hear you if you're not careful.'

'I don't care who hears me. Just don't blame me when it all ends in tears.'

'You are you jealous?' smirked Damian.

'How dare you!'

'You're shouting again,' smiled Damian, catching a glimpse of himself in the mirror in place for customers to admire their costume choices. Damian turned left, then right to admire the reflection.

'Go to hell, Damian.'

'What have I done?'

'You know, I was almost willing to help you out, but you can just go and-'

'Look Tonya, I don't know what has gone on between you and Cheryl and I don't care. All I know is that as soon as I've finished with Cooper, I'm out of here.'

'No, you can wait until I get back.'

'No, I'm gone,' said Damian turned his back on Tonya.

'If you leave before I get back, I'll, I'll—'

'You'll what? Never speak to me again because I dated Cheryl?'

'I don't give a fuck what you do, or who you go out with.'

'Good, then we don't have a problem and you'll be able to cover for me.'

'Cheryl would never have even considered going out with you, if I hadn't-'

'If you hadn't what?'

'Just fix up Cooper's stupid cowboy outfit and look after Ms Horrigan until I get back. For once, do the job that Emil is paying you to do.'

'No, I won't.' Damian turned toward his customers with a huge smile on his face.

'Is everything alright?' asked Cynthia.

'Yes, Ms Horrigan,' replied Damian with a reassuring smile.

'Could we possibly speed this up, I really do have another appointment?'

'Of course. Normally, all new customers who wish to prevail themselves of Thomases Costumery's exclusive service are given a tour of our facilities by Mr Thomas himself, followed by a demonstration of the *Cabinet*.'

'Emil has already given me the tour,' replied Cynthia pleasantly.

'Then if you like I will run through the operation of the Fabric Dissemination and Historically Oriented Reconstitution Cabinet as we create Mr Cooper's costume.'

'Thank you, Damian,' replied Cynthia checking his name badge.

'It is my pleasure. Now, Mr Cooper, have you selected a costume?'

'Shucks yep, pardner,' replied Mr Cooper, slipping into an imagined character based upon historical Hollywood westerns to match his chosen costume.

In real life, Mr Cooper was an unattached, middle-aged accountant whose successful, but dull, life had been completely turned around by his discovery of Thomases Costumery.

'Let me guess,' winked Damian over the accountant's head, 'you wouldn't have selected a costume from the American Wild West period by any chance?'

'Dang, how do you do it, pardner? You know, Miss Horrigan, I come in here every week and this young whipper snapper picks what sort of duds I want every dang time.'

'Really, Mr Cooper?' smiled Cynthia, enjoying the over-the-top performance from the man who only moments ago had been the epitome of a shy, self-effacing, city executive.

'Yes Ma'am, it's almost as if he can read my mind.'

'I assure you it is not anything paranormal, simply a matter of record,' Damian addressed Cynthia to explain the procedure. 'When a customer chooses to use our Fabric Dissemination and Historically Oriented Reconstitution Cabinet, they may know exactly what they desire, or they may only have a preference for a particular period of time or location. Mr Cooper is a fan of early North American culture, from around the era of 1820 to 1880. Isn't that so, Mr Cooper?'

'Dag nab it. I told you he was good, Ms Horrigan.'

'Amazing,' replied Cynthia glancing at her watch.

'Mr Cooper, like many regular customers, prefers to use our reference library to select the costume he desires.' Damian tapped the keyboard of the *Cabinet's* control interface. 'What have we chosen today, Mr Cooper?'

Mr Cooper lifted a leather-bound volume onto the pedestal that held the *Cabinet's* controls.

'This is the one that stuck in my craw.'

Cynthia noted the page contained an old newspaper article.

'The Battle of Little Big Horn. An excellent choice,' replied Damian. 'As Mr Cooper has made his selection, all that remains is for the relevant data to be fed into the *Cabinet's* control station here.' Damian flicked a switch, activating lighting which illuminated what looked like a shower cabinet surrounded by a mass of fibre optic cables and electronic hardware. 'Then we place the garment, which is to be reconstituted, inside the *Cabinet* over there.'

'How does it actually work?'

'Let me demonstrate,' started Damian, sneaking a look at his own time piece. 'Firstly, we enter the menu,' Damian tapped a keyboard, the video screen displayed a list of options which could be selected.

'This is a replica of an early personal computer?'

'Yes, Mr Thomas had it installed to add a feeling of history.'

'It does have a kind of rustic charm,' said Cynthia leaning in to get a better look.

'I'm sure that Mr Thomas would be pleased to hear you say so,' smiled Damian. 'Now having called up the menu, it is simply a matter of entering the required information as the computer requests it. It is also possible to short cut the process by requesting a specific historical event.'

'Like Mr Cooper's Battle of Little Big Horn?'

'Correct,' replied Damian. 'The computer will then automatically home in on the specific event.'

Cynthia nodded following the explanation.

Damian hurried on. He had yet to sleep with Cheryl and following his discussion with Tonya, was looking forward to it, for no other reason than he could.

'So, if I select, *Historical Event*,' Damian touched the screen, 'then type the event,' Damian two finger typed Battle Little Big Horn, then tapped *Enter*. The screen flashed and displayed a list of names.

'Lakota Sioux, Cheyenne, Arapaho, Seventh Cavalry, Crow Scout,' read Cynthia studying the list displayed on the screen. Cynthia knew this was a roll call of participant groups in the iconic and disastrous 19th century battle.

'That be the costume types available,' interrupted Mr Cooper, chewing an imaginary chaw of tobacco.

'Mr Cooper is correct, Ms Horrigan, I assume Mr Cooper, also knows exactly which costume he desires.'

'Seventh Cavalry,' stated Mr Cooper standing to attention.

'Seventh Cavalry, it is,' repeated Damian touching the screen before relieving Mr Cooper of a coat hanger loaded with clothing, which he placed inside the glass *Cabinet* and closed the door. 'Tap the key marked, *Enter*, like such, and the magic begins.'

'You just watch this dang contraption, Miss Horrigan,' enthused Mr Cooper, grasping his belt as if adjusting for the weight of an imaginary six shooter.

'What you are about to witness is quite extraordinary,' said Damian Treffer in a well-practiced feigned sincerity. It was corporate policy to provide a reminder of just how exclusive access to this device was. 'Though still only a prototype, the results are most fascinating.'

Cynthia watched the display unit scroll data across its screen.

'The first thing to occur will be a search of the computer's data base for the chosen time period for a specific location and, in this case, a specific event. Once the criteria selected is loaded, it is sorted and validated,' explained Damian.

'It sorts the wheat from the chaff,' interrupted Mr Cooper, wishing he had a spittoon for his imaginary chaw.

'It does in fact, as Mr Cooper metaphorically put it, sort the wheat, from the chaff. The information is then used by the *Cabinet* as a template to change the molecular alignment of the fabric in the host garment.'

'The dang thing rips your old clothes to bits, then turns them into the duds you want.'

'Thank you, Mr Cooper, I'm sure Ms Horrigan appreciates your simplified explanation of the Fabric Dissemination and Historically Oriented Reconstitution Cabinet,' smiled Damian.

'It's purely my pleasure, Ma'am,' grinned Mr Cooper, wishing he had a hat to tip.

'So, what you're saying is that the computer looks at all the information it has stored in its memory bank on a selected subject, collates all of the relevant data into a new sub directory then uses that information via the *Cabinet*, to rearrange the molecular structure of the material placed inside to replicate a selected costume.'

'Yes, that is a fair description of the basic process,' nodded Damian.

'Using what, a particle accelerator coupled to a fusion drive? Are you using superconducting electromagnets to focus the molecular separation?'

Damian was surprised by the questions; it was not often he misjudged the clientele who were vain enough to part with the amount of currency required to utilise the *Cabinet.* There was obviously more to Cynthia Horrigan than just money and youth. He smiled at the thought of potentially adding Ms Cynthia to his list of conquests, it could be far more entertaining than anything he was likely to experience with the tedious Cheryl. Then he thought the drudgery of Cheryl was still worth the effort, just to see the look on Tonya's face. It was the simple pleasures that were often the best.

'I believe that may be the case.'

'Then how is the accelerator guided? Is it a directed beam breaking each molecular bond one at a time, or is this some sort of mass decoupling? I don't know how you could control the energy output if that was the case. The heat generated would be substantial.' Cynthia paused to think on the problem. 'What are you using as an interface with the accelerator guidance system? Surely, it's not run through those fibre optical cables? If it is, how is it being cooled? The electromagnets would need to be chilled to at least minus 271.3° Celsius to ensure there was no resistance to the passage of electrical current?'

'I believe that is classified,' replied Damian using the standard corporate position for these sorts of questions. He had no idea how the machine operated. Dwight built the machine and he wasn't about to give its secrets to anybody. Damian had suspicions that even Emil didn't really know.

The video display ceased scrolling. *Ready To Proceed* glowed in green on the screen. 'Now the *Cabinet* is ready,' said Damian, stating the obvious and pushing the *Do* key. 'It can take a few moments for the actual process to begin.'

'The dang thing has to think about it, I suppose.'

'Quite probably,' quipped Cynthia, glancing at her watch.

Finally, the *Cabinet* glowed bright green, the clothing inside appeared to pulse three or four times, folded in upon itself, then disappeared.

'As you can see Mr Cooper's suit appears to have vanished.'

'Where?' asked Cynthia in surprise.

'The current theory is that the molecular structure of the host garment has been converted to a vapor, though that has not been able to be confirmed.'

'You mean you have no idea at all?'

'No, not really.'

'But if it's gone, surely the particle accelerator has simply blasted it into oblivion?'

'If that was the case, I wouldn't be able to do this,' said Damian typing, *Return* then tapping the *Enter* key.

'This is the bit that plum tickles me half to death,' smiled Mr Cooper.

The *Cabinet* shook violently, followed by a miniature sonic boom. What appeared to be a weather-beaten Seventh Cavalry trooper's uniform materialised amidst a slowly decreasing circling green glow.

'How?' gasped Cynthia, stunned by what she had witnessed.

'Indeed, Ms Horrigan. That is pretty much the reaction that I had the first time I saw the *Cabinet* in operation,' replied Damian.

'But?'

Damian looked at his watch while he retrieved the costume.

Cheryl may not be in the same class as Cynthia Horrigan, but she was immediately available. A bird in the hand, or something similar.

'We had best collect that replica Springfield rifle you picked out from our prop department, Mr Cooper, then you can be on your way home. I assume you are fair fit to bursting to enjoy your new costume.'

'Yes. Yes, I am,' replied Mr Cooper reverting to his accountant persona in the excitement at the sight of his purchase.

'But how?' Cynthia asked herself.

'That concludes the demonstration of the *Cabinet*, Ms Horrigan,' said Damian disrupting Cynthia's thoughts as he escorted a now hatted and belted Mr Cooper toward the exit. 'If you would like to take a seat, Tonya should be with you at any moment.'

'A pleasure meeting y'all, Ma'am,' called Mr Cooper, tipping his cavalry trooper's hat. 'Adios, until next time.'

Cynthia raised a hand, as if to wave.

'Bye,' she whispered then caught sight of her watch.

Time. Hell, she was going to be late! Cynthia scoured the length of the room; there was no trace of Emil or anybody else for that matter. She strode to the entrance of the room. There wasn't any sign of the wayward Tonya, so she drifted back to the *Cabinet's* control station where she flung her suit carrier across the keyboard in frustration. The machine beeped in reply.

'Whoops!'

The monitor began rolling information down its screen. It was the same list of costumes that had confronted Mr Cooper.

'Touch information icon, then subject selected if more data is required,' mouthed Cynthia reading the text on the screen. 'Okay, I'll bite.' Cynthia brushed the screen with her finger.

*Beep.*

Cynthia read the list, selected a costume then touched the screen.

*Beep.* The screen displayed the front, back and side view of a rough, textured, beaded and tasselled smock-type dress. It looked very rustic, earthy, and more importantly, *authentic*. Again, Cynthia looked the length of the room. Nobody. She looked at her watch.

'Come on, I've got to be out of here.'

*Beep.* A prompt message had been added. *If you wish to proceed, press the enter key.* Cynthia looked at her watch again.

'Hell.' She looked again, still nobody. 'Bugger it.' Cynthia tapped the *ENTER* key. 'I haven't got all day.'

*Ready to proceed*, flashed on the screen.

What did Damian press? There, top row, right side. Push. Cynthia stood back and waited; then looked down, her suit bag was still at her feet.

'Bugger.'

Cynthia swept up the clothing and hurried to the *Cabinet*, pulled the handle and the door swung open. She leant in to hang her outfit on the internal hook. It fell off.

'Bugger.'

She stepped inside the machine, picked up her suit to put it back on the hook.

'Cynthia, are you alright?'

'Oh. What?' Cynthia looked up to see Emil hurrying toward her.

'Miss Horrigan!' called a startled Tonya, approaching and carrying a frosted glass.

'I'm just—' started Cynthia. Then, the unthinkable happened. The *Cabinet* swelled with green light. It pulsed, once, twice, three times. Cynthia appeared to fold in the middle, along with the surrounding air, then she was gone.

# CHAPTER FIVE

'WOW!'

'Welcome back, Will, I hope you enjoyed my story.'

'It can't end just there, not with Cynthia just disappearing like that. What happened to her and what about Emil, Damian and Tonya?' asked Will.

'Sorry, I forgot to mention that the memory retrieval system has a built-in cut out timer. It's there so that you have to come back to reality, just in case the house has caught fire while living on somebody else's memories.'

'You are joking, aren't you?'

Adrian shrugged.

'It has been known to happen.'

He leant over and pressed the button on the recall device again.

'You are almost up to the point where my presence here can be explained. To make it easier, my father is Gerald Thomas, that is Emil's older brother. David is the son of Dwight, Emil's younger brother, and you, William Thomas, are one of those from whom we Thomases are descended.'

# CHAPTER SIX

## WARRNAMBOOL, FRIDAY 16TH APRIL 2102 CE, 1735 HOURS

TONYA SCREAMED, THE PIMMS and lemon crashed to the floor.

'Oh, shit,' gasped Emil staring at the *Cabinet*.

'Mr Thomas!' Tonya couldn't take her eyes off the glass box. 'What are we going to do?'

'We are going to remain calm,' replied Emil, trying very hard not to expel the contents of his stomach. Turning away from the *Cabinet,* Emil looked directly at Tonya. 'Where is Damian?'

'I don't know, Mr Thomas,' sobbed Tonya, tears streaming down her face.

'Get a grip, Tonya, getting emotional is not going to help.'

Tonya looked at Emil; her lip quivered.

'The last time I saw Damian he was going to leave early. He wanted me to cover for him. I said no but he just wouldn't listen.'

Emil shook his head.

'What are you saying? Has Damian left the costumery?'

'I'm sorry, Mr Thomas, he said he was going. I don't know if he has left yet.' Tonya wiped her face on her sleeve. 'What are we going to do? Miss Horrigan can't be, just gone?'

'We are not going to panic,' stated Emil, taking Tonya firmly by the shoulders and looking directly into her eyes, 'are we Tonya?'

'No, Mr Thomas,' replied Tonya, sniffing back a tear.

'What I need you to do is, get onto security and have them intercept Damian if he is still on site. Can you do that?'

'I ... yes, Mr Thomas.'

'Good. While you are talking with security, I'll try and work out what's happened.'

'It will be alright, won't it, Mr Thomas?'

'No, it won't. But we will do what has to be done to do the right thing.'

Within minutes, Damian was being briefed by Tonya as they made their way to the *Cabinet* room.

'One minute she was there and then she wasn't,' said Tonya searching for a way to explain the horror of what she had witnessed.

'She was inside the *Cabinet*?'

'It was horrible. Mr Thomas and I were calling to her, and then...'

'The green glow, pulses? Everything?'

Tonya nodded. 'And then nothing.'

'But how?'

'I think that is obvious,' stated Emil, gesturing for his assistants to join him. 'Miss Horrigan has somehow run the program for operation of the *Cabinet*. Look at the screen, the machine is still running.' Emil pushed the down arrow to reveal the previous commands. 'Historical event, Battle of Little Big Horn, costume selection, it's all here.'

'But how?' asked Tonya.

'The only way would be if someone left the machine running,' said Emil.

'I left her in Damian's care while I went to fill her drink order.'

'You're not dumping this on me,' arced up Damian. 'Mr Thomas left her in your charge, not mine.'

'Yes, but I gave you specific instructions to look after her until I got back.'

'No way, she was your responsibility; I was looking after *cowboy* Cooper.'

'And you just couldn't wait to get him out the door so you could go on your dinner date.'

'What are you implying?' bristled Damian.

'I am stating the fact that I left her in your care and when I came back, you were gone and Miss Horrigan was inside the *Cabinet*.'

'I don't know what you are trying to say, Tonya. The facts are that Mr Thomas left her in your care and now she has disappeared. You say, via the *Cabinet*. That, I can't prove one way or the other, but I have Cooper as a witness to vouch for her well-being while she was with me.'

'Are you denying that you left her alone with the *Cabinet*?' bristled Tonya.

'No, I am saying that she was your responsibility, Cooper was mine. I saw my customer safely off the premises. But yours, well...?'

'You arsehole, Damian Treffer. I was wrong, you and Cheryl do belong together.'

'Enough,' interceded Emil. 'Blaming each other will get us nowhere. We are all in this together. Firstly, Miss Horrigan was my responsibility. I shouldn't have just left her to go off with Mr Fowles.'

Tonya opened her mouth to protest. Emil raised his hand to halt her interjection. He continued in a calm, and measured tone.

'Secondly, you shouldn't have left her in Damian's care for any longer than was absolutely necessary.'

'Yes, Mr Thomas,' whispered Tonya.

'And you can wipe that silly smirk off your face, Damian. I may have left Miss Horrigan in Tonya's care, but you left her unattended with the *Cabinet* still running.'

'But—'

'But nothing, we are all responsible.'

'What are we going to do, Mr Thomas?' asked Tonya, regaining her composure.

'That, I don't know.'

'You have looked inside the *Cabinet*?' asked Damian in a hushed tone.

'Yes, there is not a trace of her.'

'Then she really has gone?' asked Tonya.

'I'm afraid so,' said Emil.

Damian opened the *Cabinet* door.

'It's like she was never here.'

'Or ever existed,' whispered Tonya in horror.

Damian slowly closed the *Cabinet*.

'That is an interesting thought, as if she was never here.'

'Oh, grow up Damian,' snapped Tonya, 'you don't honestly believe that Mr Thomas and I would ever consider trying to cover this up?'

'No, I suppose not.'

'No, we wouldn't,' said Emil in disgust.

*Beep.*

Damian turned to face the computer monitor.

'Can you imagine what would have happened if you had tried the return command?'

'What?'

'Can you imagine the mess if you had tried to bring her back?'

'Bring her back, of course!' Emil elbowed Damian away from the monitor. 'Tonya, fetch the first aid kit.'

'Yes Mr Thomas. Get out of the way, Damian.'

'What are you doing?!' gasped Damian, realising exactly what Emil was attempting. 'If you do this, we are going to get a lovely authentic costume and a pile of offal that used to be Cynthia Horrigan!'

'How do you figure that, Damian?' grunted Emil as he typed *RETURN* then poised his finger above the *Enter* key.

'You may be able to blast clothing apart with a particle accelerator and then put them back together, but you can't do that with a person.'

'What particle accelerator?'

'The one that operates the bloody *Cabinet* of course.'

'Do you believe everything you are told?' grimaced Emil as he nodded at the returning Tanya to stand by the *Cabinet*.

'I hope she's alright, Mr Thomas,' said Tonya snapping open the latches on the first aid kit.

'So do I.'

'You can't do it for god's sake!' hissed Damian grabbed Emil's wrists to prevent him from pushing the *Enter* key.

'Listen to me,' said Emil shaking off Damian's grip. 'The *Cabinet* does possess a particle accelerator, but it's not connected.'

'What?'

'When Dwight built the *Cabinet,* the particle accelerator was at the heart of the machine. The *Cabinet* did what we wanted it to do, most of the time, but now and then the accelerator would turn the costumes into a pile of charcoal. Then six months ago, Dwight disconnected the accelerator for maintenance but forgot to tell Gerald. Gerald had an order from one of our American customers he wanted to fill, as you know, he has been very keen to expand in that particular market, so he used the machine out of hours. The funny part was the *Cabinet* worked perfectly. There was no overheating, no disintegration, in fact, absolute trouble- free operation. And the costumes, well, you have seen them, it's as if they are originals, not replicas.'

'What are you saying?'

'What I am saying, is that this machine takes sets of clothing, makes them somehow disappear, then replaces them with what appears to be genuine historical articles and we have absolutely no idea how it is happening.'

'But what about the story we spin the customers?'

'That's business, Damian. As long as we keep the illusion that a particle accelerator is at the centre of its operation, no one else is likely to copy our success, at least not in the short term.'

Damian looked at the glass box.

'What has this got to do with our Miss Horrigan?'

'The particle accelerator is not connected, so Cynthia Horrigan cannot have been blasted to pieces by it.'

Damian shook his head as if to clear it.

'So, she hasn't been turned into an ionised vapour?'

'No, she hasn't.'

'Then where is she?'

'If I knew that, we wouldn't be having this conversation,' said Emil.

'What are you going to do?'

'Try and bring her back, if it's possible.'

'You can't be serious?'

'I believe it's about the only option open to us.'

Damian stood there staring. Finally, he gave a shrug and headed toward Tonya and the *Cabinet*.

'Ok, but heaven help us if you're wrong.'

'Don't you mean, heaven help us if I'm right?'

'Oh, shit,' said Damian as the realisation of it all came crashing in.

Emil pressed *Enter*, the *Cabinet* shook, *boomed* and a very much alive person materialised inside the glass box. It was a woman with long braided plaits of brown hair that hung past thin shoulders, nestling a blue and white banded calico dress, gathered at the waist by a beaded belt, holding a thick bladed knife in a beaded sheath. On her feet, she wore deer skin moccasins and, from the right wrist hung a leather thong through which were threaded fish that had been pierced just behind the head.

'It's Miss Horrigan,' gasped Tonya.

There, in front of Emil stood, most definitely, Cynthia Horrigan, though not the 23-year-old blonde he had met little over an hour ago. Maybe it was the change in hair colour or the dark burned tan that had replaced her fair complexion. No, not even that explained it. Gurgling noises were coming from the haversack nestled against Cynthia's back. Yes, that was it. Miss Horrigan was most definitely not accompanied by an infant when they last met.

'Ok, Damian, Tonya,' whispered Emil, 'stay calm and follow my lead.' Emil slipped on his smile, then gestured toward the *Cabinet's* door. 'Damian, assist Miss Horrigan, she must be tired after her misadventure.'

Damian had no desire to go near the *Cabinet*. He also had no desire to spend time in a correctional facility, so he went to Miss Horrigan's assistance.

'Miss Horrigan, I must compliment you on your costume, it is outstanding. Don't you think so, Mr Thomas?'

'It is. If I may say so, Cynthia, absolutely authentic of the American West in the mid to late 1800s. It is a costume that could win first prize at any genealogical association event.'

Cynthia had been standing, head bowed, knees slightly bent under the weight on her back. Her head flicked up, the knife from her belt was in her hand, pointing directly at Damian's face.

'Get out of my way.' Damian cannoned backwards.

'Do you remember me, Cynthia?' called Emil putting his body in front of Tonya to shield her. 'Do you know where you are?'

'Where I am?'

'Do you remember Damian? He was showing you the Fabric Dissemination and Historically Oriented Reconstitution Cabinet. Do you remember Tonya? She was getting your drink order. If I remember a Pimms and—'

'Pimms and lemon,' interjected Cynthia, 'how could I forget?'

Cynthia closed the gap between herself and Emil, bringing her knife to rest under his jaw while one hand gripped the front of his jacket, a thin trickle of red flowed down the blade's shaft.

'Believe me, Emil. No, I couldn't.'

Emil froze, 'I'm sorry, I don't quite—'

'Understand? Neither did I. When I realised I had been abandoned in the past, I began to hate you. Not the everyday annoyance you feel from being ignored while the shop assistant is taking a personal phone call. No, I am talking about being at your boyfriend's most obnoxious buddy's wedding, watching your boyfriend being partnered in the bridal party with his ex-girlfriend, hate.'

'Oh, Miss Horrigan,' whispered Tonya with tears in her eyes.

'I hated you for dumping me in the midst of a genocidal war.'

'And now?' asked Emil, trying not to struggle against the blade.

'I no longer hate you, Emil. But I will kill you, unless you do exactly what I want.'

'What is it that you want?' asked Emil, locking eyes with the woman holding a knife at his throat.

'What I need, is for you to send me back.'

'Send you back where?'

'To my husband and my family. To my home.'

'You got married!?' exclaimed Tonya.

'Yes, I married a good man named George Taylor. I am carrying our son, Michael, on my back,' replied Cynthia, keeping her eyes fixed on Emil.

Before Cynthia could even think, Tonya was at her side.

'Can I see him, please? I don't know why; I just know that I have to.'

Cynthia risked a glance at Tonya and saw only empathy in her eyes.

'It might be a good idea if you take him while Emil and I talk.'

Tonya reached into the bundle that lay wriggling upon Cynthia's back. 'Aren't you a handsome little man? What did you say he his name was?'

'Michael, after his grandfather, and Wapasha, after his Lakota uncle, the son of my Lakota mother. Wapasha died the day my family rescued me,' stated Cynthia quietly.

Tonya stroked the little boy gently, something in Cynthia's voice had brought a feeling of sadness to the room.

'I promise to keep him safe.'

'This is crazy,' burst out Damian.

Cynthia looked over Emil's shoulder to where Damian was cowering behind the control console. 'Perhaps I should kill Mr Damian instead.'

'WHAT? No!' squealed Damian, tripping over his feet as he retreated.

'I would prefer it if nobody actually had to get killed,' said Emil calmly.

'You know, I haven't seen that drink I ordered,' said Cynthia, 'it might calm my temper if I wasn't so thirsty.'

'Damian, do you think that you could—' Before Emil could finish the sentence, Damian was on his feet and going.

'Pimms and lemon coming right up, Mr Thomas.'

'I think we need to talk,' said Emil as he watched Damian run from the room

Cynthia lowered her blade.

'Can you feed Michael, please?'

'Yes, of course I can,' replied Tonya looking at Michael in wonder.

'You don't want to stay?' asked Emil using a tissue to staunch the trickle of blood on his throat.

'No.'

Emil turned to Tonya; all trace of his famous smile having evaporated.

'Please take Michael to the cafeteria to feed him and see what our Mr Damian is up to. Take your time, Cynthia and I will need time to talk.'

Tonya hesitated; Emil raised the barest hint of a smile.

Go on, we'll be just fine,' nodded Cynthia.

'Ok, if you need anything at all, call me.'

'A toothbrush,' said Cynthia, 'I will trade you my fish for a toothbrush. Hell, I would trade my knife for one if I had to. And toothpaste. I can't remember the last time I brushed my teeth with a real toothbrush.'

'I have a spare in my locker,' replied Tonya, 'and toothpaste. I will get it now.'

'I would prefer if you fed my son first.'

'Of course, I will do that first, Miss Horrigan.'

'Call me Cynthia. It's funny the things you miss, like hearing your name spoken in an Australian accent.'

'I will, Cynthia.'

'Thank you,' called Emil to his departing assistant's back. 'I think you had better tell me what happened. Don't leave anything out, not a single detail. Then if I can, if you still want to, I will do everything in my power to send you home.'

# CHAPTER SEVEN

'THAT WAS SO COOL, Damian was really packing it when Cynthia pulled that knife.'

'Packing it?' asked Adrian.

'He was scared, you know, really frightened.'

'Would you mind if I make a few notes?' asked Adrian removing a notebook from his robes. 'Your language, especially the use of slang, is fascinating.'

'Pardon?'

'Your speech, Will. We may be speaking English, but the passage of time has some what changed its usage.'

'Huh?'

'Well, for example. If I said to you that this room,' Adrian waved his arms gesturing, 'was absolutely dope and that you were, lit, what would you say?'

'I'd probably say that you seem to be a dope as well. You know, not the full two bob.'

'Why, thank you,' grinned Adrian.

Will grinned back, realising that he liked Adrian.

'The brain movie you showed me was great, but I still don't understand what you are doing here?'

'I'm just getting to that. After the incident with Cynthia there was one hell of a kerfuffle. My father, Gerald, was horrified. Not that there was anything strange in that. Father is one of those people perpetually horrified by most things in life,' chortled Adrian. 'He was all for destroying the *Cabinet*, while my Uncle Dwight was enthralled with the idea of time travel and what it could mean for the advancement of science. Uncle Emil, well, that was an entirely different story,' reflected Adrian. 'Uncle Emil demanded that control of the *Cabinet* be handed to him until a safe way was found to send Ms Horrigan back to where she had come from. After that, Uncle Dwight and Father could do what they wanted with the machine. We were all sworn to secrecy. I remember Damian Treffer came to our home the next day. There was an awful row and I never saw him again.'

'So, what happened?' asked Will.

'Well, Uncle Emil and Uncle Dwight locked themselves away with the *Cabinet* every night for weeks conducting experiments. They used the store cat as a guinea pig, putting it in the *Cabinet*, sending it back and forth through the machine. Each time it took a trip, it would come back a little older, with a different collar, having obviously had kittens after one trip, once incredibly fat, and finally dead from old age. While this was happening, Cynthia, that's Miss Horrigan, closed her apartment and moved in with Uncle Emil. That really did horrify Father,' grinned Adrian. 'I remember David, he was seven at the time, being a great fan of her stories, especially the ones about bears and wolves.' Adrian stopped, lost in his own thoughts.

Will prompted him to continue. 'What happened to Cynthia?'

'Well, my bedroom adjoined the office in our home. I could often hear what was being talked about through the wall. I remember Uncle Emil explaining that the cat proved it was possible to send a living creature through the *Cabinet* and have it return safely. Father started going on about how it proved nothing, and that a cat was not a person. Miss Horrigan said a few words I couldn't understand, then Uncle Emil starting up again. I guessed at the time that Miss Horrigan might have shown Father her big knife. Uncle Dwight said the experiments proved that the passage of time was different at the other end of the journey than was being experienced by those left behind. I can remember Uncle Dwight drawing up charts and graphs and Father scowling about the whole thing.'

Adrian leaned closer.

'I actually think, if I may borrow that wonderful description from your lexicon of language, that he was packing it. I did get that right, didn't I?'

Will nodded. He could imagine his mum having a meltdown if a woman claiming to be a time traveller from the future showed up at their house asking for help. Mum was not a Doctor Who fan so he doubted she would get it.

'Anyway,' carried on Adrian, 'Uncle Dwight concluded that it was safe, as far as could be determined, to send somebody into the past via the *Cabinet*. Going to the future couldn't be done, because the *Cabinet* had no point of reference to send an object forward to from its current existence. That makes sense if you think about it. A chap can't go to someplace if you don't know where it is, or how to get there.'

Will asked a question.

'So, you can't go into the future to see if you get a super-hot girlfriend, or become a mega football star?'

'Correct,' beamed Adrian, 'then there is the issue of time travel being a precarious activity. You could end up being your own grandfather or thwarting the invention of cricket. Uncle Dwight was adamant that, however the

*Cabinet* was used, it was absolutely critical that,' Adrian put one hand over his heart and raised the other as if saying an oath, '*we must take all necessary precautions to avoid the Grandfather Paradox*. When Uncle Dwight said this, he put his hands in the air, then wiggled two fingers up and down on each hand. Apparently, it was a gesture from ancient times used to signify deep importance.'

Will nodded, then explained, while making air quotes.

'This means, "*Quote*". It's used by some people who think they are important. Dad says it's really code to say,' Will made the air quote hand gesture. '*I am a wanker.*'

'Really?' asked Adrian, delighted at having learnt something to add to his notebook. 'Are *wankers* a sort of sorority like the Masons or Rotary?'

'No!' replied Will in surprise.

He was not sure how to answer the question, though his father did refer to the Masons as a bunch of strange *wankers*.

'A lot of people are called *wankers* because of how they behave, but in the true meaning it's sort of a-' Will furrowed his brow realising he had steered the conversation in a direction he definitely didn't want to go.

'To be honest, it's sort of a, well a sort of hobby some people have,' he said, feeling his face redden. 'People who do it, the hobby, like to keep it secret because it's embarrassing to admit you might-. Will stumbled on how to explain, while feeling increasingly embarrassed, 'there are really two different types of *wankers*. Those that do it in private, as a hobby, and there is probably nothing wrong with it, because you won't actually go blind, no matter how many times you do it. Nobody admits to it, but I am pretty sure most of my friends probably have, you know, had a go at the hobby,' he said, avoiding eye contact.

'Then there are those people that are called *wankers*, but might not actually do actual, *wanking*. Or they might but behave like a *wanker* in front of everybody. Dad calls them, *real wankers*. When they really upset him, *bloody wankers*. If he really hates them, because of what they do or say, he calls them *absolute wankers*. Dad says most politicians are *absolute wankers*. Dad told me that whatever I do in life, I had to be sure that no matter how successful I might be, I must never, ever, behave like a *wanker*. Dad says this is a sure way for people to lose respect for you and a sure way to prove you had become an *absolute wanker.*'

'I am not sure I am following the complexity of the difference between an innocent hobby, *wanker* and a *real wanker*. Or, from what you just explained, the high pinnacle of social abhorrence, being an *absolute wanker*, it seems rather complicated.' Adrian referred to his notes. 'Being a hobby *wanker*,' Adrian looked to Will for confirmation, 'is acceptable as long as you conduct the activities associated with the hobby in secret. Lots of people enjoy, or perhaps that's too strong a word? Maybe, participate?' Adrian looked to Will for confirmation. Will half nodded in embarrassed agreement, his eyes wide open but focussing on his feet.

Adrian made a revised entry, then carried on with his thoughts.

'I also understand that it won't cause you to go blind, no matter how often you participate in the hobby.' Adrian furrowed his brow. 'Is it a dangerous hobby? Do you need to wear safety glasses when you participate?'

Will shook his head, his face burning in embarrassment.

'In comparison, a *real wanker* might or might not be a hobbyist *wanker*, but conducts their *wanker* activities where it can be upsetting to other members of society. Do I have that right?' asked Adrian, delighted at having grasped such a complex concept.

Will nodded, wishing he was dead.

Adrian had a light bulb moment.

'Will, I hope you can excuse my curiosity, but do you mind if I ask, and I know you indicated that it is very much a private hobby, but are you...?'

'NO! No!' exclaimed Will, eyes wide in horror. 'I am sorry Adrian, but to ask a bloke that, or even suggest it. It's not even something that you could talk to your parents about, even if you were going blind.'

'I am sorry, Will, I didn't realise that it was a taboo to ask a chap if he was a,' Adrian mouthed the word silently, '*wanker.*'

Will rotated the recall device in his hand.

'Adrian, why did you give me this to hold?'

'I don't want you to hold it Will, I want you to lick it.'

'Why?'

'I should continue to explain, it had been proved you could travel back in time and return, but not go forward in time.'

'Yes, I got that.'

'The big issue was, is, will be, that while the *Cabinet* could send objects through time and space, there was no way of controlling the time lapse in the past from the machine itself.'

'So, you need something like this to travel back to the *Cabinet* when you want to?' questioned Will holding up the recall device.

'Well done, Will,' said Adrian, raising his sleeve to reveal an identical device. 'This is a Wrist Mounted Time Travel Device. Uncle Dwight likes to be descriptive when he names inventions. I just find it difficult to remember. As you guessed, it allows the wearer to operate the *Cabinet* remotely when you need to return home.'

'How can it do that?'

'I have absolutely no idea,' smiled Adrian.

'You seriously don't know how it works?'

'I don't think Father knows either, which was one of the many things that upset him. Father also believed the temptation to use travel in time for personal gain was too high. He went on and on about the risk of creating a grandfather paradox until my uncles agreed to separate access to the *Cabinet* and the W.M.T.T.Ds so that no one person could use both without the agreement of the others. As Father had no desire to use the *Cabinet* for anything other than generating currency for the business, it was agreed he should be the one to keep the *Cabinet* under lock and key.'

'Dad sometimes says he would die for a copy of tomorrow's paper so he could pick the winning lotto numbers and tell his boss where to stick his job.'

'What's a lotto?'

'It's a sort of gambling game. You can win a lot of money by guessing the first six numbers from 30 numbered balls that a machine spins around then spits out one at a time. It's on the telly every Saturday night.'

'Do lots of people gamble on the balls?'

'Almost everybody. Mum says that it would make our family if we won, even second division would be enough to pay off the car and maybe get a new washing machine. Mum says she likes to dream big no matter what the odds.'

'What an interesting thought.'

'So, the W.M.T.T.D thing allows you to go back to the *Cabinet* when you want to?'

'It does more than that. Once you travel back in time, you can use the W.M.T.T.D in steps to make your way back to base if you will. You can't go any further back in time, but you can hop your way home.'

'That's how you found me?'

'Yes, and unsurprisingly, no. For the *Cabinet* to transport you, it locks on to your DNA. You do know what DNA is?'

'Yes, DNA is the double helix strand of atoms and molecules that contain the genetic code to make all living things.'

'Well done you, Will. It sounds like you are a far better student than

I ever was. As you know, things made from inorganic materials do not contain DNA, so cannot be retrieved by the *Cabinet* unless they have a DNA marker, for example a skin cell, or a hair from your head.'

'Or spit from somebody licking it?' suggested Will.

'Exactly old chap.'

'So how come you found me?'

'That's the fascinating thing. It was supposed to lock onto my cousin David's DNA and take me to him, not to you. David and I became separated and he lost his W.M.T.T.D when we landed on top of a few local chaps that were in dispute with the local authorities in Nazareth. I believe it was something to do with the inequitable sharing of produce and the misuse of goats. Unfortunately, when we arrived, we did so with a bit of a bang.'

Adrian indicated the mess in Will's bedroom to illustrate the point.

'Sorry again,' he grimaced. 'The local law mistook us as part of the group. I tried to explain the misunderstanding to the officer in charge, but he wasn't that sympathetic, I am afraid, and it didn't help that David resisted arrest rather vigorously, knocking down at least three Roman legionnaires before they knocked him unconscious and dragged him away.'

'You got into a fight with Roman soldiers!'

'It was more of a scuffle really. Did I mention that David is a police officer?'

'Your cousin is a cop!'

'Yes, David became a police officer rather than join the family business.'

'That's just so cool.'

'You say *"cool"* a lot Will, does it have a particular cultural meaning in your time?'

'It means it's spectacularly good.'

'Does it really?' said Adrian scribbling in his book.

'I still don't get how you ended up in my bedroom.'

'What I think happened is that when the local official, the one who was less than understanding and, quite frankly, rather confrontational, was examining David's W.M.T.T.D.' Adrian looked at the device on his wrist.

'Will, I am sick of spelling out the letters for this thing. What was Uncle Dwight thinking? Shall we just call it something else? What's the name of your favourite sports team?'

'Saint Kilda, the Saints. They have only one premiership, which they won by a point after the final siren off a dodgy free kick against Collingwood. Dad reckons it was the best day of his life when the Saints won that game, even better than the first time he kissed Mum. Mum gives him a dirty look when he tells that story. I think she doesn't like being second to a point kicked off a dodgy free kick.'

'Ok then,' nodded Adrian, 'I hereby name the Wrist Mounted Time Travel Device, the *Sainter* for all future conversational purposes.'

'Agreed,' nodded Will, holding up the device in salute.

'As I was saying,' continued Adrian, 'my guess is that while the soldier was examining the *Sainter*, he changed the time setting. When Uncle Dwight designed the recall device, he included a homing function designed to take you to the person closest matching the DNA imprint on the device as a safety feature, which obviously works, given that we are here together. David did say that it can only work properly if the time coordinates are aligned, which means that both people are in the same time period and within a roughly 10-kilometre radius.'

'But it found me,' said Will, 'because I am the person in 1975 who has the nearest DNA to David, because I am his closest relative?'

'As I said, Will, you are an ancestor from whom the future Thomas family are descended.'

'You know what this means?'

'No, but I am eager to find out.'

'It means that I am going to have a girlfriend, maybe a wife, and we will have a child. You know, that's a scary thought.'

'Or,' countered Adrian, 'you may never have a girlfriend, or children and one of your current brothers, or sisters, or any future children your parents may have, will be the parent of the child from who the future Thomas family will descend.'

'Does that mean I might be a pathetic loser till I grow old and die?'

Adrian putting his arm around Will's shoulder. 'With luck you might die young and never have to worry about being old and alone.'

'I hadn't thought of that!' said Will in shock.

'It's facts like this which make the study of genealogy so fascinating, Will. In my time, people have everything they could want or need, and more leisure time than they know what to do with, so they need something solid to wrap their existence around. If their life is plain, predictable and boring, then the past holds a wealth of fascination. For me, to discover you living the life of a peasant in 1975 is fascinating, and quite frankly, more than a little life affirming. Take that Julie Diesel, I say, take that.'

'I don't think we are peasants,' countered Will. 'Dad says we can hold our heads up and be proud that we work for a living. He says we owe nothing, to nobody and that's important.'

'I like the sound of your dad. Say, what does he do, Will? I assume he has an occupation, some form of labour that he performs for currency?'

'Dad's a diesel mechanic. I'm not sure he likes it that much, but Dad says it pays the bills.'

'A tradesman, how wonderful!' exclaimed Adrian scribbling in his notebook.

'Dad's work is pretty dirty and smelly. Mum goes absolutely ape shit, sorry, droppings, when he forgets to take his work boots off. Mum says she has enough to do without trying to get greasy footprints out of the carpet.'

'What a life you have Will, manual labour, debilitating disease and war around every corner. Never knowing where your next meal is coming from. I must say that I envy your short, but eventful existence.'

'I hadn't thought about my life like that.'

'I wouldn't worry, I am sure you will do fine,' said Adrian, patting Will on the shoulder. 'Do you have any questions for me?'

'How come you and David were time travelling?'

'To tell you the truth, it came as a bit of a shock when David came to my apartment to put the proposition to me. I hadn't seen him in years.'

'So, why did you go back in time?'

'It was something David and I had talked about when we were growing up. I am a big fan of classical music and dreamed of visiting New York City during the punk music era,' Adrian sighed. 'David and I talked about finding out what sort of cake Marie Antoinette actually liked. I wouldn't mind betting that Marie was a double chocolate mud cake girl. I doubt she got that derriere from drinking low fat dairy products and hitting the gym three days a week.'

'Did she have a fat bum?' asked Will. 'Mum is always worrying about her's getting bigger. Dad says if a woman asks about it, don't answer, no matter what. You're better off being yelled at for ignoring the question than telling the truth.'

'Your dad is a wise man.'

'I reckon he is,' agreed Will.

Adrian continued, 'David and I knew about the *Cabinet* and what had happened to Miss Horrigan. Father drummed it into our family that if the story of the *Cabinet* got out it would not only ruin the family business but could also be extremely dangerous.'

'So, what happened?'

'There was a meeting after the issue with Ms Horrigan was resolved. Uncle Dwight wanted to use the *Cabinet* for the benefit of the business and for scientific exploration, while Father wanted it destroyed one moment, then argued about its commercial importance the next. I thought he was rather confused; but mostly he was worried that the *Cabinet* would be misused and somebody would be seriously hurt.

'Uncle Emil proposed a compromise, making the point that the *Cabinet* was not only a major breakthrough for science, but it was the company's major customer draw card and not in their interest to destroy it. It was also obvious that safeguards were needed if they were to continue to use the machine.

'Uncle Dwight had invented the *Sainter*; he could make more if they were destroyed, so there was no point in trying to restrict his access to them.

'Father was the legal owner of the premises where the *Cabinet* resided for tax purposes but didn't have access to the *Sainters*. He also had no desire to travel through the machine but believed the *Cabinet* to be an integral part of the financial viability of the company.

'Uncle Emil pointed out that he didn't have control of either the *Cabinet*, or the *Sainters*, and, since they had successfully helped Ms Horrigan, he felt it safe to relinquish sole control of the machine. Uncle Emil proposed that Father should retain control over the store where the *Cabinet* resided, thus managing access to the machine. Uncle Dwight would continue to manage the business technical requirements and retain control of the *Sainter* and the intellectual property associated with it. He wouldn't have access to the *Cabinet* without the approval of Father and Uncle Emil. Uncle Emil would continue to be the face of the business, as well as managing personnel matters. He would hold the codes and a DNA signature which would be added as security to allow operation of the *Cabinet*. By doing this, the company could continue to produce, as Father wanted, *"top of the range, authentic costumes at a premium price, for a small set of exclusive clientele,"* but only with the consent and presence of Uncle Emil. Uncle Emil and Uncle Dwight couldn't use the *Cabinet* without the presence of each other and access to the *Cabinet* provided by Father.'

'Were they happy with this?'

'No, but they agreed to the compromise. The business empire expanded, Uncle Emil and Uncle Dwight moved away with their families to run the other costumery stores and the original store became a storage and cleaning facility. If you did not know the building's history, it could easily be mistaken for a simple warehouse. I saw David less and less, until we drifted apart. David coming to visit was a complete surprise but definitely not unwelcome. We were best friends as children.'

'Are you saying that David came to visit you, after years of not seeing each other, and talked you into going for a trip in the *Cabinet*? Didn't you think it was strange for him to just show up and talk you into travelling back in time?'

'Well, if you think about it,' mused Adrian, 'it probably was. The thought never occurred to question why. We had lunch, gossiped about the family and went to the pub for a couple of very nice drinks. One thing led to another, before we knew it, David produced two *Sainters* and I was unlocking the old costumery building.'

'I thought you couldn't use the *Cabinet* without Emil?' asked Will. 'Doesn't the *Cabinet* need a secret code and your Uncle Emil's DNA to get it to work?'

'Yes, that's right,' agreed Adrian, 'but Uncle Emil showed up completely unexpected. I have always liked Uncle Emil; he was more than happy to help.'

Will's eyes widened in disbelief. 'You didn't think it was a bit strange?'

'Sorry?'

'Just think about it. Your Uncle Emil shows up the same day you get a visit from David, who you hadn't seen in years, and he's happy to help you go on a trip using the machine that nobody in your family wants anybody to know about, much less use, just for a bit of fun.'

Adrian's eyes opened wide with surprised understanding. 'Do you think?'

'I know if one of my cousins turned up and suggested we go for a ride in Dad's Monaro, I am pretty sure if my Uncle Bruce showed up at the same time and handed over the keys, I would be more than a bit worried.'

'I never thought,' said Adrian in surprise.

'What do you think is going on?'

'I don't know. Uncle Emil and David wouldn't have just tricked me for no reason. I assume, they did trick me, didn't they?'

'No point asking me. About an hour ago, I didn't even know you existed.'

Adrian nodded. 'I think I may have been a little bit gullible.'

'Dad says we can all be a bit dumb when it comes to family. Dad says you will do anything for your family, because they are your family, and so you must. He reckons that's why Mum keeps asking my Uncle Bruce and Aunt Beryl for Christmas even though, when they do come, it makes Mum angry and grumpy. It's not because she wants them to come, but because she has to. If she doesn't, it would make her feel guilty. I don't get it either way.'

Adrian furrowed his brow.

'I think I may have been a bit of a, what would you call it, Will?'

'A bit of a dill,' Will suggested. 'Don't worry, Dad says if you haven't stuffed up, you haven't lived. Dad says you can tell the quality of a bloke by what he does when he is in the wrong, as much as you can when he is in the right.'

Adrian reached for his notebook and began to write.

'When this adventure is over, I think we should consider publishing some of your father's wisdom. But right now, what's important is not that a chap has been tricked by his favourite cousin and uncle, but that David is lost and nobody but myself, and of course you, know about it.'

'What are you going to do?'

'The same thing I was going to do before we met: rescue David of course. But now, I am convinced it can only be successfully done with the help of those whom one can have absolute faith and trust in.'

'You mean with the help of family?'

'Exactly.'

'I'm only 14,' said Will guessing what Adrian was implying. 'I might look strong, but I am bloody hopeless at football and probably not that brave if it came down to a real fight. I have only ever been in one. I got my butt kicked by Vikki Schultz and Glenis Freckelton in year eight.'

Adrian's face broke into a smile.

'I suspect you have the qualities that any chap would be glad to have in a companion on such an adventure.'

Will shook his head.

'I am just a kid. What good could I possibly be to you, or David?'

'You have an honest heart and, I believe, are far braver than you give yourself credit for.'

'Maybe if I was 16, or 26, or really old like 36, or something.'

Adrian nodded in agreement.

'What if you were 36, would you come then?'

Will shook his head.

'It would depend; I would have to ask Mum.'

'Good, I will take that as a yes,' beamed Adrian. 'How can we fail the descendants of such a noble family, with an artisan such as a diesel mechanic at its helm?'

Will didn't know what to say. He stared in horror, then he heard the front door bang shut.

'William, are you still awake?'

'It's Mum!'

'That is my cue to leave,' said Adrian, pushing buttons on his *Sainter*. 'I don't think it would be wise for anybody to know that I have been here, Will, given the Grandfather Paradox and all that. And to be honest, I am worried how it would look if I tried to explain any of this.' Adrian swung his arms to indicate the carnage in Will's bedroom.

Will opened his mouth to protest. Adrian pushed the *Sainter* David had worn, against Will's lips. 'I almost forgot to collect your DNA sample.'

Will spluttered as the device banged against his teeth.

'Thank you, Will. It was lovely to meet you, my great, great, grandfather or uncle. And don't worry, I will be back.'

'But?'

'I know,' grinned Adrian, 'it has been really cool.' The air pulsed and Adrian was gone.

'Sorry it took me so long; I lost all sense of time chatting with Wendy next door. Before I knew. It. I-.' Mary Thomas' voice trailed off; her handbag slipped with a thump to the bedroom floor.

# CHAPTER EIGHT

DAVID DROPPED IN AND out of wakefulness. His whole body ached, especially his head and the light hurt his eyes. As he squinted into the brightness, a dirt-encrusted face, with a blackened and chipped tooth smile, looked kindly down at him.

'So, you're awake.'

David shifted his weight, made it to shin height, then flopped back.

'Lie still, you are bound to feel unsteady and a bit sick in the stomach. Don't worry, it will pass.'

David closed his eyes to steady himself as he rocked back and forth to the unmistakable sound of wheels on hard ground. He reopened his eyes to see the smiling face of his companion. Behind the dirt and greying beard were a set of kindly eyes. The man was thin and could have been any age from 40 upwards, dressed like himself in woollen robes and leather sandals.

David tried to rise. He needed to get his bearings, to work out options. His companion leant forward, holding a wooden cup filled with water.

'Drink, you will need to replace what you have lost from the heat of the sun, and what has leaked out of the cut on your head.'

David felt the back of his head. Withdrawing his hand, it was stained with dirt and specks of dried blood.

'Where are we?'

'On a road bound for Tyre. From there, possibly to Rome, or one of a hundred other ports dotted around the great sea where human cargo has value as a commodity.'

'Slaves?' David asked quietly.

'Or fodder for the games.'

'What's the difference?' asked David, leaning against the cage in which he was being transported.

'For me, not a lot, other than the time I have left, and the manner of my death. If I am lucky, some citizen will like the look of my face and purchase me as household staff. If I am less lucky, a landowner will spend a few coins and I will toil in his fields until I drop from exhaustion and die. Most likely, given my age, and less than robust appearance I will be sold for a few coins as entertainment for the masses in one of the big arenas. It might be that I will be promoted as a swarthy African pirate, or a Syrian desert warrior. It doesn't really matter what they call me, the end will be the same, bloody and violent.'

David took in his surroundings. At the other end of the cage, carried on a two-wheeled cart, sat four men in dirty robes sporting dried blood and bruises. The cart was pulled by four oxen, their driver perched on a ledge at the front of the vehicle. Two Roman soldiers escorted the prisoners, walking either side of the cart, carrying spears resting on shoulders. Their shields were tied to the rear of the cart like a pair of decorated doors. The soldiers' spears, or as the Romans called them, *pilum*, were made with a metal spike attached to a wooden handle designed to bend and sag where the metal met the wood when impaled into an enemy. While the tip of the spear may not kill instantly, the weight of the bent weapon could incapacitate the impaled victim, making it impossible to run as the wooden handle sagged and dragged. Neither guard showed any interest in their charges as they trudged alongside the transport.

'Are you certain?'

'As certain as I can be that we are bound for a ship, then either slavery or death. If they wanted to kill me,' David's companion cast his eyes toward the nearest escort, 'I would already be lying in a ditch with my life blood spilt on the ground or nailed to a cross suffering a lingering public execution. I think myself privileged that the Romans have deemed me to be of some value above a public deterrence to dissent.'

'And what do you see in my future?' asked David.

'It's the games for you, I have no doubt. I was witness to your confrontation with our guests from this very transport. I saw you fell three of our foreign friends bare-handed. You would have taken down more if you had not been struck from behind.'

David touched the wound on his head.

'I was wondering how I got this.'

'I gather it wasn't a planned encounter on your behalf. I am afraid the ambush was for my benefit, set and poorly executed by some of my more enthusiastic students.'

'You're a teacher?'

'I am Polykarpos, late of the Academy Polykarpos, where men and boys have come for more than 20 years to study and create new knowledge through contemplative thought, debate and experimentation.'

David extended a hand to Polykarpos.

'David, David Thomas.'

Polykarpos looked steadily into David's eyes.

'That is a noble name. Are you a descendant of the great King David?'

'I wouldn't know about that, but I do know that ending up as a slave is not on the agenda for today.' David pulled back his left sleeve.

'Your bracelet is gone, David Thomas, I witnessed a soldier take it. Was it valuable?'

'To me, it is invaluable.' David reviewed his surroundings then asked, 'What happened to my companion? He looks a lot like me, only taller with lighter hair and rather talkative?'

'There was one amongst my students that I did not recognise. He was, as you describe, though I did not hear him speak.'

'What happened to him, Polykarpos?'

'The last I saw of your friend, he was being led toward the Hill of Kedumim.'

'What does that mean?'

'It means that he is either dead or dying slowly. It is beyond either of us to do anything about that fact.'

David rose to his knees using the side of the cage to pull himself up.

'What about escape?'

'It's been known, but our best hope for survival is that silver will change hands and we will be set upon a life of servitude as the property of a Roman citizen.'

'You don't think that likely?'

'No.'

David weighed up his companion.

'What can you tell me about where we are going? Will we be put onto a ship as soon as we arrive?'

It was now the turn of Polykarpos to conduct an assessment. What he saw was a man in his prime, fit and strong, with a steady eye who had conversed in fluent Greek, much to the surprise of Polykarpos. When Polykarpos noticed David begin to wake, he had spoken in Greek purely by reflex, which he put it down to stress. As soon as the words tumbled out, Polykarpos realised his mistake. He had expected a blank look, but before Polykarpos could change to Hebrew, this man had replied in the educated Greek of Aristotle and Plato. The accent was Athenian, capital city, not from the provinces. Polykarpos changed to Hebrew to see what would happen.

Polykarpos shrugged. 'If they have their quota, they will sail when the wind is right, if they do not, they will wait. Truly, I know little of the ways of the sea; I have made few voyages by ship and I haven't enjoyed any of them.'

David nodded, then replied in Hebrew.

'I wouldn't worry about it, not yet anyway.'

David used the mesh of the cage to pull himself to his feet, turned a full circle to take in the surroundings. What he saw was an expanse of rocky desert broken up by small clusters of thorn bushes and stunted trees. To the left of the cart, the ground fell away in a long gentle slope, terminating in the green sward of a grain crop flanked by a stand of citrus trees. A few sheep, a boy shepherd, along with his dog lying in the shade of a tree, added to the picture. There were no other travellers on the road, nor could David see any structures. He looked down at Polykarpos.

'Would you have any objections in becoming my guide for a few days? I will pay you well for your services.'

Polykarpos smiled.

'Might I point out that we currently have another appointment.'

'Point taken, however, if you were to find yourself free, could you lead me back to where you first saw me?'

Polykarpos dropped his smile and spoke in Latin to see what would happen.

'Alright, if you can persuade our Roman friends to let us go, I will be your guide for as long as you need.'

'Deal,' said David taking Polykarpos by the hand.

Polykarpos didn't know what to make of David. He appeared educated, focused and, from what he could see, not afraid of what fate had in store. He was either mad, or something else. Polykarpos was hoping for something else.

'So how are we to begin our journey?'

David looked ahead of the cart.

'Can you see that stand of bushes on the edge of the road?'

'Yes.'

'Our driver is just ploughing on in a straight line, no deviation around potholes or moving to give room for our escort as we pass trees or thorn bushes.'

'I am not sure he is awake,' replied Polykarpos looking at the driver slumped against the outside of the cage. 'The oxen know the path and are happy enough to plod along.'

'Auto pilot engaged.'

'Sorry?'

'It's not important,' replied David, moving to the side of the cart where the bushes reached out onto the edge of the road. 'If I can get you something sharp, could you cut through the rope holding the door shut, quickly?'

Polykarpos looked at the finger thick rope that linked the doors of the cage together. It had been fed through the bars on the doors four times, then tied with two ugly knots.

'It may not be quick to cut through all the strands.'

'You won't have to cut all of it, if I kick the door hard enough.'

Polykarpos narrowed his eyes. What had he to lose?

'Alright David Thomas, I will do as you ask.'

David nodded his thanks.

'Just one more thing, can I borrow one of your sandals?'

Polykarpos was surprised by the request but took off a sandal and handed it to David.

'Thank you,' replied David, taking off the woven belt which held his robe secure at the waist and tying one end to the sandal.

Polykarpos watched as the oxen cart approached the stand of shrubbery which would either cause the escort to move closer to the cart to squeeze through the gap or walk out and around the obstacle. Realising what was about to happen, Polykarpos moved to allow David to get hard up against the cage.

David hung the belt, with its attached sandal, outside the cage, then watched and waited. His head hurt and he felt like vomiting. None of that was going to matter if he screwed this up. The oxen moved past the thorny vegetation, narrowing the gap through which the legionnaire had to pass. The half-asleep soldier moved closer to the cart to avoid the thorns.

David swung the belt in an arc, aiming at the escort's neck. The sandal shot out on its lead till it reached the end of its travel, then curved on its trajectory when the belt struck the chin of its target, providing a pivot point around which the sandal spun in a downward spiral, coming to rest around the guard's throat. The soldier's eyes widened in surprise, then in horror as David pulled with all his strength, dragging the soldier against the mesh of the cage. David's right arm bulged under the pressure of pulling the belt, his left grasped the pilum near the base of its metal barb, thumping it inwards against the mesh of the cage. The pilum bent, collapsing as it was designed to do in combat.

Polykarpos grasped the wooden shaft of the spear. The weapon almost bent in half as he pulled with all his weight to slide it through the mesh of the cage.

'Cut the rope,' hissed David as he held the flailing soldier.

Polykarpos began to saw the rope with the tip of the weapon. It was more of a short-barbed blade than a razor-like knife, but it was having an immediate effect on the tightly wound rope.

David, seeing Polykarpos get to work, pushed the guard away from the cart. The legionnaire gasped for air, staggered once, twice and fell, his head hit the road with a sickening thud, his back and buttocks followed. Legs bounced in the air then fell to the ground in front of the turning wheel. The oxen cart bounced and crunched across a shin, then an ankle.

Polykarpos heard this happening as he dragged the blade back and forth. His life depended upon this one task, it was slow going, way too slow. One loop parted, Polykarpos struck hard against the second.

Vomit welled up in the back of David's throat. He thought of Jen lying soaking wet in a pool of spreading red and shook it off, swallowed hard and waiting for what was to come.

'Stuff them,' he muttered, his face grim, his eyes black.

Legionnaire Dax was thirsty and tired. He had drunk all his water long ago. As if to emphasise his thirst, salt from his sweat ran from beneath his helmet into his eyes, then dripped off his nose to land on his lips.

Dax was a conscript, like most of the empire's foreign-based legion members, hailing from Tarraconensis, which would become the region of Barcelona in eastern Spain. He had joined the legion to feed himself and if he lived to complete 20 years' service, to be granted Roman citizenship. Dax had survived 18 years marching into the dark forests of the Germanic tribes, living well as a garrison soldier amongst the Gauls and now trudging through the deserts of Galilee. Gaul had been pleasurable with good food, no fighting and comfortable quarters. The Germanic forests had been hell, many of his comrades had died in those forests, Galilee was like living in paradise by comparison. No fighting, no cold and enough food and beer to keep him happy for two more years.

Left foot, right foot then left again, he marched. The belt for his gladius was rubbing him raw and the crook of his arm ached from cradling his pilum. He gazed at his charges; dirty, smelly and lost to their families forever. He, on the other hand, knew that ahead lay a hot meal, beer, a bath and a bed to call his own. In comparison, he might as well be a senator in Rome itself. Dax dropped his head, left foot, right foot, left again, a shuffle of his spear from right arm to left to shift the weight.

Noise. A hard thump followed by a startled yell, then a second soft thump. Yelling, voices in different languages. Dax snapped his head up to see his friend pinned against the cart, flailing his arms in a struggle. Then he was dropping, bouncing arms and legs going up, then down, landing out of sight. The cart rolled forward. It bounced. More noise: crunching, cracking, squelching, then down again and on.

His friend lay on the ground, bent and bleeding. Disbelief, then anger boiled in a rush of emotions. The driver was standing on his seat, yelling at the prisoners. Four were huddled at the front of the cart, wide-eyed with fear, holding up their arms in surrender while mixing their voice with that of the driver. Two were at the rear, fighting with his barrack mate. Dax watched the bent pilum dragged into the cage where the old man began sawing the blade against the rope that bound the door. They were trying to escape!

Dax lunged toward the cage, aiming his pilum at the back of the man attacking the rope. He pushed hard, two-handed through the bars, the thrust stopped short. Startled, Dax looked up to see a younger man gripping the weapon with hands wrapped in the robes he had been wearing. Dax tried to withdraw the spear; the near naked man pushed up hard to the roof of the cage. The pilum bent turning it into a fish-hook shape, trapping it inside the cage. Dax released the weapon and stepped away from the cart which continued to roll forward.

Dax pulled his sword, his gladius, from its scabbard as he hurried to catch up while screaming at the driver to pull the oxen up. The driver leapt from his perch to hold the cattle by their halters. Dax stalked back and forth, just out of reach of the cage; the shields slung on the door prevented him from reaching his target from the rear. He tried from the side of the cage, thrusting the sword and his arm through the bars. The younger man used the pilum as a club, striking the blade and deflecting it to the floor. Dax withdrew the sword just as a second blow fell where his hand had been. Bones could have been broken. He began yelling obscenities.

The old man continued sawing as the young one stood guard until the rope parted and the doors moved slightly apart. Dax stared at the door, then at the old man, then at his companion. The younger one said something in Greek and the old man shuffled behind him.

Dax locked eyes with the younger man. There was no fear, no panic, no doubts. A feeling of anxiety built in the pit of the soldier's stomach; this was not how it was supposed to be. Dax moved backwards in line with the cage doors to give himself room to respond to a charge. He pushed his left foot forward, crouched into a combat position, weapon at the ready, eyes on the enemy, his heart thumping.

The doors swung open, the younger one stepped down, the club held in one hand, the other wrapped in his robes. The old man followed. Dax stood poised on the balls of his feet, his gladius held low in his right hand, his pugio in his left. Words passed between the prisoners and they backed away from the cart and headed downhill toward a grove of orange trees. Dax straightened. There would be no sudden charge, no attack. Dax watched David and Polykarpos flee; he couldn't just allow them to run, but he also had four prisoners to secure.

Without thinking, Dax flung himself at the cage, dragging the cut strands of rope together in an attempt to secure the door. The strands were too short. His eyes fell on the pilum dropped by the old one. Using his foot to hold its metal half on the ground, he worked the wooden handle back and forth until the two halves parted, thrust the metal spike through a mesh square of the cage, then used his weight against the fulcrum to bend the metal into a curve, which he fed through both halves of the door before twisting the ends over each other to form a crossed loop. Dax pulled hard against the cage door; the improvised lock held.

Looking down the slope, Dax found the running fugitives were beyond spear range, even if he had one to throw. If he had a bow, that would be different, Dax was a very accurate archer, even on a bad day. He could try and run them down, use his blades to end their lives.

A noise made Dax turn. His friend was shaking and screaming in pain as he tried to sit up, his legs lay splayed at an unnatural angle; shattered bone appearing white through bloodstained skin. Dax knew the injuries could not be mended, he had seen many such wounds in battle and they all resulted in death. His friend lowered his head in resignation; he knew the outcome as well as Dax did. Dax lifted the weapon slowly, almost involuntarily, he spoke just one word to his friend, 'Sorry.' The weapon struck the base of the skull with a thump. His friend, his drinking buddy, slumped at Dax's feet, twisted and broken as a howl of pain and frustration welled up and burst into the air.

The plan was simple: put distance between themselves and their jailer as fast as possible.

'How are you doing Polykarpos? Can you keep going?'

'I can keep going as long as we must David. The alternative holds no appeal to me.' Polykarpos nodded toward a rocky hill. 'Beyond that rise lies a path used by shepherd boys, it winds its way over a track that finds as much shade and grass as possible between here and Nazareth. Follow it and we should reach the village just on dark.'

'Thank you,' said David, 'I am in your debt.'

Polykarpos stopped to look into his companion's face.

'I feel that the path we are on is not of either of our choosing. The Gods, or God, if a single deity is what you believe in, has brought us together for a purpose.'

David nodded.

'I have a task, a debt of honour I have to fulfil for a friend whom I consider to be closer than any blood relative.'

Polykarpos turned his head slightly. When he spoke, he did so in the tongue of the Nile just to see what would happen. 'You are on a quest? For what, revenge?'

'No, not revenge,' replied David in the dialect of the Pharaohs. 'I am here to find two people who have committed a crime, to make them face justice.'

'Do you mean to kill them?'

'No. Where I come from, we don't kill people for committing a crime, no matter how heinous it might be.'

'I must assume then that you are from a land far from the rule of Rome.'

'You have assumed correctly,' agreed David.

'Tell me David, what is your native tongue? You speak many languages; you must have studied under a great master.'

'Aussie is my one and only language, Polykarpos. I have appalling handwriting, as well. I remember my year eleven English teacher, Mr Young's comment on my report card, *brilliant work, if only I could read it*. It gave my dad a laugh at the time.'

Polykarpos looked confused.

'I don't understand, you speak in Latin, Hebrew and Egyptian and are we not conversing in Greek?'

'What can I tell you Polykarpos? Technology, it's a wonderful thing.'

# CHAPTER NINE

## NORTH ADELAIDE, AUSTRALIA AUGUST 15th, 1975, CE

FOLLOWING THE SHOCK OF finding her son surrounded by the destruction in his bedroom, Mary Thomas had been at a loss to comprehend what could have happened. Her heart lifted when it was obvious he was unharmed, then William told Mary that a stranger from the future had destroyed his room after appearing, then disappeared in a glow of green light. It wasn't the first lie that almost broke her heart, it was the others that followed as the story spread further and further from reality.

At first Mary thought William might have fallen from his bed, then in a concussed and confused state stumbled around in the dark fighting off imagined demons, which caused the destruction of his room. An examination by the family doctor had discovered nothing more than a bruise on his arm, which Will claimed happened when his bed flew through the air and collided with the wall.

The doctor conceded, he was unable to find anything physically wrong with Will, so after a discussion with Mary and Will's father, Colin, who couldn't believe that Will would deliberately smash up his room then invent such a story to cover it up, a referral was arranged with a specialist in Adelaide.

A week later, Mary and William caught the train to the state capital with Mary clutching a written referral in one hand and her heavily overloaded handbag in the other. Her Boho style leather shoulder bag contained all manner of useful items: such as emergency tissues, a rolled compression bandage, phillips head screwdriver, hairbrush and several different shades of lipstick, amongst other essentials.

To Mary, it was unthinkable that William had turned from a responsible child into something which she could not recognise. The destruction of his bedroom was not something she would ever have imagined her son doing. Mary prayed it had just been something William had eaten, something that had fermented in his stomach into some hallucinogenic gas that had poisoned his brain while he slept. She also prayed it wasn't drugs. Anything but drugs.

Mary had married during the 1950s and had her children during the early sixties, while she was in her early twenties. It was the way it was in those days: you left school at 15, found a job, generally something in a shop, found a boyfriend, hopefully a decent bloke, married and had kids. It was what was expected but didn't leave much time between being a child and having a child. At the time, Mary had wished for more time before having to be grown up and responsible.

Though raised in a conservative, religious family, Mary had been at parties where marijuana had been smoked; she had even tried it once. All it did was make her throat sore and her clothes smell. She couldn't bear the thought of her son becoming a drug addict and ending up living in a caravan park surrounded by discarded half-smoked joints and stray cats. She dreaded the thought of William being unloved, unwashed and possibly growing a beard. She would find what was wrong with her son and help him, no matter what the cost.

A train trip would normally have been an adventure for Will, but not today, because today he was off to have his head examined. When Adrian had appeared, it had all seemed real, even when he had been inside Adrian's memories, learning about Cynthia and Emil and the *Cabinet*. A week later, he was questioning everything. Did he go bananas and smash up his room in his sleep like Mum said could have happened? Had he imagined everything else? He could sort of live with that, but not with the look of worry on his mum's face.

The doctor's referral was at a hospital in North Adelaide. They travelled from the train station by taxi, which was a new experience for Will. They had taxis in the Mount, but they were for old ladies going to bowls, or trips home from the pub for those too inebriated to get their keys into the ignition of their car, with concerned bar staff arranging the ride.

Will thought it strange, sitting in the back seat with his mum. He felt a bit like a pretend snob doing it, but Mary treated it as if it was just the right thing to do. He went along with it for his mum's sake but scrunched down to avoid being seen.

When they arrived at the hospital, they were directed down a shiny corridor to a door covered in pictures of cartoon characters and flowers. That was all Will needed, reinforcement that he was about to be treated like a little kid. A nurse took their names, then pointed to a door covered in cartoon fairies which led to a waiting room. Inside were four mothers with their children on wooden bench seats, arranged against two walls. Two of the women were dressed like Will's mum in their finest down-the-street clothes, clutching handbags bursting at the seams with God only knew what, perched on their knees.

One mother was dressed in the shortest of short skirts and a low-cut top covered in gold sequins, which barely held in her boobs when she moved. Will tried not to stare, but it was almost impossible not to look. Mary gave Will such a scowl that he spent the next 10 minutes staring at his shoes.

The last mother wore a scruffy pair of jeans with frayed cuffs, Ugg boots with a hole in the right boot, where some of the wool lining poked out, and a faded black t-shirt with the unmistakable shape of a cigarette packet under the left sleeve. Will studied the kids: two girls, two boys, all sitting patiently as if they knew the drill. The boy directly opposite him looked about Brian's age, using a finger to either widen his right nostril or show everybody in the room where his brain was by pointing at it. His mother gave them a reassuring smile, while gently moving her son's finger away from his nose.

The second boy, who was older than Will, was dressed in dark blue flares, red platform shoes and satin shirt undone to the third button. Under the shirt, Will could see the glint of a gold chain with a star sign medallion attached. The boy was either a Leo or a Fitzroy supporter. He had hair just like Barry Gibb from the Bee Gees. Will thought, *city kid, probably a wanker*, then was immediately glad he lived in the country.

Will also studied the girls. One was about five, clutching the arm of her well-dressed mother. There was nothing unusual about the pair. Then his eyes met those of the girl sitting next to the woman with a cigarette packet stuffed up her sleeve. She was dressed almost as a mirror image of her mother, just without the cigarette packet up her sleeve. The girl was pretty. Not what Will was told was supposed to be beautiful, but to his 14-year-old heart and hormones, she was stunning.

The teenager had long, dark hair that shone when the light from the window struck it from above. Her nose was pointy, but not too long and she had blue eyes that caught the reflection from Gibb Junior's shiny shirt, like fire light on a window at night. Will found himself staring, then looking away just in case she noticed. Then staring again, until he had to look down when the girl turned her head towards him.

Will felt his face redden. He turned back to the kid with the finger up his nose, who was at it again. Up went the finger, then down came the mother's hand to unplug it. The cycle repeated about every 10 seconds. Will couldn't help but watch with fascination; the mother smiled at him, like it was all just so normal. Will had to look away and when he did, his eyes locked onto the pretty girl. She stared back, then winked with a hint of a smile. Now he was seriously going red, Will could feel his face burning.

'Your first time?' asked the girl's mother.

Mary nodded a in reply. What could she say? Yes, it was the first time she had needed to take her son to visit a psychiatrist. Mary was not embarrassed; she was ashamed. Not of her son, it was not William's fault, it was hers, it had to be. What would Ita have thought of her as a parent if she knew?

'Don't sweat it,' the woman advised, while pulling the cigarette packet out of her sleeve, 'we have all been where you are. The trick is not to take it too seriously. Nod like you give a shit and smile when you leave. If you're lucky, you'll get Doc Brown. He's a bit grumpy, but he knows his stuff. Doc Brown can tell the difference between a kid just stuffing up and one that's a fruit loop. If your son has all his marbles, he will give him a talking to and send you on your way. If he figures that your kid is a snag short of a barbie, Doc Brown will do everything he can to sort him out. He's a good egg, Doc Brown.' The mother stopped to pull the plastic off the cigarette package which she stuffed under her seat.

'If you're unlucky, you'll get Doc Elliot. He likes his patients to call him by his first name, that seems odd to me. I mean a doctor is a doctor. I don't like to think about them as ordinary people, especially as a woman who has to have a check-up down there,' she nodded in the direction of the lower half of her body. 'I like to keep that sort of check-up professional, and a little less like after a good night down the pub. It's all nice to be friendly, but if I am having my bits and bobs examined, I would like the bloke doing it to have a certain level of professional distance. I like them to be friendly, just not a friend.'

The woman looked at the door to check if anyone was approaching.

'From what I have heard, Doc Elliot pretty much thinks everybody is mental and has made it his job to cure every kid that ends up in his office using what he calls, the latest *American Methods*, whatever that means? If you get Elliot, just play along, do whatever he wants, no matter how stupid. If you fight the bugger, he will have child welfare all over you.'

Mary didn't know how to reply. She clutched her handbag tighter as if it could protect her from the things this odd woman was saying.

'What's the kid in for?' asked the woman, shaking out a fag, then foraging in her jeans for a lighter. 'Don't worry, we don't go spreading gossip. We are, what Doc Brown calls, a support network. Elliot probably means well, but I don't think he has a bloody clue to tell you the truth.'

She nodded to the woman with the young girl. 'That's Janice and her daughter Lilly.'

Janice smiled. 'Hello.'

'Janice was told that Lilly was a bit slow, you know, behind with crayons and scissors at the kindy. The next thing, she gets referred to Elliot by some well-meaning child support worker. Janice had a think about it and decided it was a lot of nothing and tried to cancel. A big mistake. Doc Elliot put a court order on Janice through child welfare, just because she didn't want to play his game. Janice tried to fight it in the courts, didn't you Janice?'

Janice nodded.

'It nearly cost Stan and me our home trying to fight them. In the end, it was just easier to play along. Lilly is left-handed. The kindy teacher kept trying to make her do things with her right hand, which is why she struggled,' explained Janice stroking Lilly's hair. 'Doc Elliot insisted Lilly was suffering from some mental trauma, from being made to do things with her right hand, instead of her natural left hand. He makes me sit and watch while Lilly draws pictures, colours them in and cuts them out. Then Doc Elliot and I skip around Lilly, repeating over and over that she is a good girl. I have been promised that we need only one more session and Lilly will be adjusted back to what he calls a healthy id, whatever that is. To be honest, it's annoying and embarrassing, way more than you could ever imagine.' Janice looked directly at Mary, almost pleading for understanding. 'I can put up with it for just one more visit to finally get away from him.'

Janice placed a hand on top of Mary's. Mary looked at it in surprise, her knuckles were white where she gripped her bag.

'Just don't fight him and it will be ok,' whispered Janice. 'Don't fight him, not if you love your son.'

Mary was speechless; this was not what she expected.

'That's Margaret and Andrew, all dressed up like a pox doctor's receptionist and her pimp,' the first woman indicated with a nod. 'Another of Elliot's little projects. Tell them your story, Marg.'

The woman in the sequined top leant towards Mary, tears welling in her eyes.

'Please don't judge me by what we are wearing, it's not our choice. My husband is a bus driver, I work part time on the checkouts at Woolworths when the kids are at school. It's just to make ends meet.' Margaret reached into her handbag pulling out a tissue to wipe her face. 'I just want this over and done with, it's just so silly.'

Mary had to grit her teeth not to cry at the distress on Margaret's face. This was wrong, all wrong.

'It started with a teenage boy showing off to impress a girl, and just look at what has become of us,' Margaret said, looking down at her clothing in embarrassment.

Andrew put an arm around his mother.

'It's okay Mum, it will be alright.'

He looked at Mary and Will.

'I didn't mean it to end up like this. Really, it was just a joke. The guys at school were joking around that I looked like Barry Gibb from the Bee Gees. It's not my sort of music. Zeppelin, Purple, Slade, that's what I'm into, head banging rock.'

The boy sadly raised the pinkie and index finger on his right hand in a heavy metal salute, then quickly dropped it, checking the waiting room door.

Margaret gripped Andrew's hand.

'When this is over, you can play whatever music you want.' Margaret turned to Mary, 'It's been hell on our whole family.'

Andrew squeezed Margaret's hand as he continued his story.

'It started the night of the school social; I had asked Bronwyn Gericke if she wanted to go with me. She seemed to like me, so I thought, why not? The guys and I were outside the school hall just talking, joking around with each other while I waited for Bronwyn to rock up and we were going to go in together. It's harder than you think to ask a girl to the social, if she says "no" then the word will get around and none of the girls will say "yes" after that. I've played footy, but nothing is rougher than a gang of girls laughing at you. It makes you feel horrible inside. Anyway, the guys just wanted to hang out together, maybe see if they could meet up with a girl on the night. Girls that won't talk to you during the year, seem to like you a lot more at the social. I like girls, but I don't understand them, not really,' he shrugged. 'They can be nice to you one day, then slag you off in front of their friends the next.'

'Yeah, we are a mystery,' interjected the woman in the black T shirt. 'It keeps you blokes on your toes,' she advised, while pushing her hand under her shirt to scratch an armpit. 'It's all part of the female charm.'

Mary's eyes widened in surprise as a pink bra cup was exposed.

Andrew didn't even seem to notice as he continued his story.

'A couple of the guys called me Barry as a joke, Bronwyn got it and laughed. Then the guys wanted me to do my Bee Gees impersonation. I had been messing around, singing some of their stuff at footy practice, as a bit of a joke. So, I started to sing *Massachusetts*, which is the one Robin sings with that funny sort of wobbly voice. They all loved it. Next thing I knew, Bronwyn pashes me in front of everybody, so I climbed up on top of the roof of the lunch shelter, the one out the front of the school hall and I'm into it. I belted out, *Spicks and Specks*, and the guys are clapping and laughing, and kids came out of the hall like they were coming to watch a fight on the oval. Bronwyn was laughing, I was laughing with her. The guys were yelling for me to sing another one. What could I do? So, I sang *Holiday* and *To Love Somebody*. By then, half the school had come out to watch and sing along.

'Then I lost it; I was being an idiot, showing off for Bronwyn. I started yelling that I was Barry Gibb's other brother and that if they didn't believe me, I would jump off the roof. It was supposed to be funny, then the kids started yelling, "Jump Barry, jump." The thing was, I could see Bronwyn was really into me. I sort of really dig her as well, so it was just great. Then Mrs Boundy, the deputy head, shows up with the cops and a couple of St John's Ambulance guys. Mrs B starts yelling through a megaphone that I should stay where I was and not to jump, as if it was something I would do. I mean why would I?' Andrew wiped away a tear. 'Honestly, it was just supposed to be fun.'

'The police brought Andy home,' said Margaret, continuing the story. 'Andy told us what happened. We had a talk with him and laughed about it the next day. Don, my husband, thought that the embarrassment at school would be enough punishment, and besides, nobody got hurt. We didn't know that Andy could sing, and he can, he can really sing, bless his heart,' said Margaret looked lovingly at her son. 'Before we knew what was going on, a court order from child services came for Andy to see a child psychiatrist. We were allocated to Doctor Elliot and the nightmare started.'

'He is crazy,' whispered Andrew, looking toward the door. 'He wouldn't believe that I was just messing about. Doctor Elliot said I was showing classic signs of *"Juvenile Munchausen Syndrome"*. Doc Elliot said that if I didn't face the reality of my fantasy, I ran the risk of becoming a dysfunctional adult lost in a world of delusion. That's what he told Mum and me and wrote in a report to child services.'

Margaret took up the story again, 'Our family doctor read the report. He said Doctor Elliot believes Andy really does believe he is a Bee Gee and we have to play along until Andy comes to a realisation that he is not a member of the Gibb family, or he could harm himself.'

'Seriously, why would I want to be one of them?' pleaded Andrew. 'They're not even really Aussies. They're Poms that live in Queensland! They don't even play proper footy there, they play rugby!'

Mary gripped Will's hand so tight it hurt. Will couldn't help himself, he had to ask the question, 'What does he make you do?'

Andrew locked his eyes on Will.

'He makes me sing the same songs over and over while Mum has to pretend to be a fan waving her arms in time to the music. Mum has to call out that she loves me and I'm not Andy Gibb.'

Margaret raised her eyes to Mary's.

'It's so embarrassing. I like their music and Andrew sings it beautifully, but when I watch Andy singing I could just weep.'

Mary looked at Margaret's clothing. 'He makes you dress like that?'

Margaret nodded.

'Doctor Elliot picked out the clothes himself. He wears a white suit with flares and dances along to the music with some of the nurses who pretend to be girls at a concert. He has a disco ball and flashing lights set up, just like at one of those dance places in Hindley Street.'

Will didn't want to, but couldn't help asking, 'What does he make you sing?'

'*Run To Me*, then *Jive Talking*. I have to finish with, *To Love Somebody,*' croaked Andrew.

'How do you sing both Barry and Robin's part?'

'Doctor Elliot stands next to me and sings Robin's bit. He sounds horrible.'

Will's mind raced; he couldn't think of anything sensible to say.

'I know,' half sobbed Andrew. 'I have to sing to Mum, like she is a hot chick at a concert. It's just wrong!'

Will felt terrible about thinking Andrew was a wanker before, then his mind raced thinking about what this Elliot guy could make him and his mum do. *God, please no*, he thought, *let us get the other doctor.*

'Why?' asked Mary, with all the connotations that could be put into the word.

'Because Doctor Elliot is crazy!' stated Margaret. 'Because he says the only way to break Andrew out of his fantasy is to use what he calls, aversion therapy. Doctor Elliot said if we show Andrew how ridiculous it is to believe he is one of the Bee Gees, by making him live out the fantasy over and over, his grasp on reality will return.'

Andrew gripped his mother's hand.

'I think he just wants to embarrass me so I will never do it again and I won't. I will never sing, ever again.'

'You weren't hurting anybody, Andy,' said Margaret, looking lovingly into her son's eyes. 'Both your father and I are very proud of you; I couldn't ask for you to be any more grown up than you have been through this whole thing. When this is over, I want you to sing as often and as happy as you can. Just not another Bee Gees song ever again.'

The waiting room door opened, a nurse dressed in pink hot pants, matching satin top and her uniform hat peered into the room. 'Andrew, Doctor Elliot is ready for you now.'

'Come on Andy, you have a concert to give and I for one am going to bloody well enjoy it,' stated Margaret defiantly.

As Margaret stood, the top part of her attire wiggled and shimmered in the light, threatening to spill its contents.

'You know, I actually like this top,' she confessed to the other ladies in the room, 'it has spiced things up at home no end with my husband.' With this, Margaret took her son by the hand and marched with as much dignity as she could through the door.

Once the door closed, a lighter flickered, cigarette smoke began to waft upwards.

'Sorry, do you want a fag?' offered the woman in the black t-shirt. She looked at the no smoking sign on the wall and ignored it.

Mary shook her head.

'Sorry, I should have introduced myself properly. I'm Tracey, this is my daughter Charlene, though we call her Charlie.'

Mary nodded and replied, 'Hello Tracey, my name is Mary Thomas, this is my son William.'

'Nice to meet you Mary,' replied Tracey, extending her hand to shake. 'Up from the country?'

'Yes, Mount Gambier.'

'Nice. My old man used to live there as a kid. Said it rains nine months of the year and drips off the trees the other three.'

'It's not like that,' bristled Will.

'Careful,' advised Tracy, 'in this place it pays not to make too much noise.'

Mary asked, 'Is Doctor Elliot really that terrifying?'

Tracey puffed out a smoke ring before replying.

'He's a bit of alright to look at. If I wasn't hitched, I would have no problems letting him park his slippers under my mattress. The problem is, he is away with the pixies.'

This did not exactly decrease Mary's anxiety.

'But Doctor Brown is a better choice?'

'Yep, nice old bloke, done the right thing for Charlie.' Tracey butted out her cigarette on the arm rest of the seat. 'Charlie had a bit of trouble at school. I know she looks like an angel, but she can be a real tough bitch when she has to be. Can't you Charlie?'

Charlene, or Charlie, was staring at Will. She made him feel very uncomfortable by producing a stunning smile.

'A couple of the well-to-do kids at school took a dislike to one of Charlie's friends, a lovely girl; Fiona is her name. Fiona's mum has been raising Fiona and her sister by herself; her husband died a few years back. Nice woman, works hard. She struggles a bit, so the kids have to make do with clothes from Vinnies and the Salvos. Nothing wrong with that, I told her, the kids are fed, clothed, clean, healthy and at school, so she is doing bloody great.'

Mary pictured a stoic woman, fighting to keep her family together. She hoped she could do the same if it was her.

'The girls were calling Fiona names, picking on how she dressed, what she washed her hair with, where her family lived, the usual bullshit girls can get up to when they get to high school and go through puberty. Charlie warned them off, told them if they picked on Fiona they would have to deal with her.' Tracey patted her daughter's knee in approval. 'The girls didn't listen. They started pushing Fiona about in the corridor at school, so Charlie gets in their face and tells them to bugger off politely. The headmaster told me she didn't even swear, which shows a bit of class when you think about it.'

Mary nodded, looking back and forth between mother and daughter. She noticed the look Charlie was sending to her son, with a feeling of alarm.

'The girls were thinking they had Charlie's bluff, so they start in on her. Four of them, there were. The leader is from one of those very well-to-do families, you know the type: think they are better than everybody and can do what they like.' Tracey looked at her daughter. 'Well, they're not.' Tracey looked back at Mary. 'One of the teachers saw it happen, thankfully, he backed up Charlie's story or who knows where we could have ended up. Anyway, the girl gives Charlie a push, so she pushes back, standing her ground. Well, this sends them all off. They try pulling Charlie's hair and scratching her face, but they picked on the wrong girl. What the little darlings don't know is that Charlie's dad is ex-army. He was an instructor in unarmed combat. Scooter, that's my hubby, had passed a few lessons on to our girls. He drummed it into our kids, that it's for self-defence only.' Tracey patted her daughter's knee again. 'Scooter has seen some horrible things. He wanted to make sure our kids are prepared for what can happen. Life's not all cartoons and happy holiday visits with the grand parents for every kid.'

Mary nodded, thinking of the article she had read in the *Women's Weekly* about orphan children in India. Ita Buttrose had written a heart wrenching editorial on the subject.

'Well,' continued Tracey, pulling out the cigarette packet again, 'Charlie punches the boss girl in the face, breaks her nose and splits her lip. She grabs one girl by her hair and bangs her head into a locker door, which knocked her out for a while. Then Charlie takes the girl, who has hold of her hair by the wrist, and twists her arm until she drops, then drives her knee into her chest, knocking the wind out of her. The fourth little darling comes at Charlie with a drawing compass, trying to stab her. Charlie knows how to disarm somebody with a knife, so she side-steps the girl, grabs her wrist with the compass and twists the arm till it goes up her back, then drives her into the lockers headfirst. A lesson asked for, and given I would have thought, but no, the head bitch has a boyfriend in fourth year who's been watching his girl do her stand-over thing. When he sees his girl go A over T, he's a bit upset and comes in thrashing his arms around like some great boof-headed idiot. Charlie can't run away, so she does what her dad taught her to do when in danger: strike first. Fist to the throat, followed by an elbow to the guts, then a full-blown squirrel grip to the nuts. Down he goes like a bag of shit onto the floor.'

'Oh my gosh,' gasped Mary, 'were you hurt?' she asked with genuine concern for Charlie.

The girl shook her head without breaking her smile at Will.

'Not much more than a couple of scratches and a bruised elbow,' replied Tracey for her daughter. 'It caused a fair bit of crap with the cops being called and a suspension from school for a month. Child services got involved and before we know what's what, we end up here. We got lucky; Doc Brown took Charlie on and, once he heard the story, he figured out she is not a bad kid and was just trying to protect somebody in trouble. Doc Brown knows Charlie is not some violent threat to public safety like the parents of those girls tried to tell the cops. It's a load of crap and the doc knows it.'

'But you have to come here for regular visits, consultations?' asked Mary with concern.

'We got landed with a court order for six months of visits with the doc. We can live with that, can't we Charlie?'

Charlie nodded, while finger twirling a lock of hair and smiling at William.

The door opened. A white-haired doctor in his sixties holding a cup of coffee stepped into the room. 'Charlene you're up,' he grunted.

Tracey and Charlene gave the doctor a welcoming smile.

Doctor Brown nodded in greeting as he sniffed the unmistakable scent of burnt tobacco. 'Tracey, were you smoking again?'

'You want one, Doc?'

'No, I gave the filthy things up years ago,' he said gruffly. Doctor Brown noted Mary and William sitting on the bench. 'You're new,' he said, noticing the referral letter in Mary's hand. 'May I?' he said, taking the note. After unfolding the letter and reading it, he passed it back.

'I am most deeply sorry, Mrs Thomas,' he said apologetically before ushering Tracy and Charlie through the door.

Mary felt nauseous; it had to be Doctor Elliot then. Mary listened as a few words of conversation between Doctor Brown and his patient filtered down the passage.

'Did you beat anybody up this week, Charlene?' Mary couldn't hear a reply. The doctor spoke with laughter in his voice, 'No? That's a pity.'

'William, honey,' started Mary, turning to her son. 'No matter what happens, please know that your father and I love you and we will do whatever it takes to get you through this.'

'It's okay, Mum, I will do whatever Doctor Elliot says. I promise not to cause any more trouble.'

Mary smiled reassuringly at her son.

'And stay away from that girl. No matter how much she smiles at you, William, stay as far away as you can.'

Will noticed when his Mum talked about Charlie, her smile had frozen solid, which meant she was deadly serious. Will thought that was probably a great idea; Charlie had frightened the life out of him.

Ten minutes of near silence ensued in the waiting room, only broken by the rhythmic movement of a boy inserting a digit into a nostril and a parental hand removing it. Will was packing it, his churning stomach told him the worst was yet to come.

Mary was acutely aware that her son was not okay.

'I wouldn't take too much notice of what that Margaret woman said, William. You know what people can be like; they make things up, exaggerate. I am sure Doctor Elliot will be nothing like what she said. After all, this is a top hospital and doctors are very professional people. They spend years at university and medical school and to be a specialist means you are really one of the top people in your field.'

'You're sure, Mum?'

'Of course I am sure,' smiled Mary. 'Doctors are like priests, there is no way a priest would do anything to harm a child, because of the type of people they are and the training they have to go through.' Mary took her son's hand. 'Think about Father O'Leary and all the work he does with young boys from the church. He started the boys' gymnastic club and the swimming club and the photographic club. Does he ask for any help when he is working with young boys? No, he does not! He is such a dedicated man to those children. You know, I have heard that he has offered for some of them to stay at his house if their parents have to travel out of town. That is the type of caring people that doctors are, just like priests.'

'Dad doesn't like him.'

'Your father doesn't believe like I do. He is a good man, a very, very good man, but he isn't inclined to think highly of the clergy.'

'I think Father O'Leary is creepy. He looks at you like Aunt Milly does when she sees chocolate cake.'

'Milly can't help her size; she told me it's something to do with her glands.'

'Dad says it's because her eyes are bigger than her stomach, which is why her bum is bigger than the boot on the Monaro.'

Mary was about to give her son a gentle rebuke and a reminder of how we should treat others, when the door swung inward on its hinges. This was the moment when Doctor Rodney Elliot made his grand entrance into William and Mary's lives.

One look at the doctor and Will could hear his father's voice stating the obvious assessment that he couldn't help making himself. *That bloke looks like an absolute bloody wanker to me.*

# CHAPTER TEN

EMIL WAITED IN THE glow of the *Cabinet's* interface. He knew he should have allowed the machine to be destroyed, but the truth was, he needed it to exist, and not to for the sake of the business or the advancement of science. He needed it for a far more personal reason. He needed the *Cabinet* just in case she called for help and he had to find her.

It had been 15 years since any customer had been given direct access to the *Cabinet*. Now it was a remote experience with a few select Thomases Costumery stores providing access to its products via a secure holographic link to the warehouse. The reason for the change was simple, nobody dared think of the consequences of another incident like Cynthia Horrigan's.

Since the time of the accident, the *Cabinet* could not be operated without Gerald providing access to the warehouse and Emil inputting the operations code and DNA sample. Dwight wasn't required to be present to produce costumes; his security role was to safeguard the recall bracelets. He was, however, present for the monthly operation of the *Cabinet* as the technician who maintained the machine. As the brothers had separate components of the family business to attend to, it was logistical to run the *Cabinet* only once a month when they met for an operational business meeting.

While it was true the brothers could charge practically whatever they liked for use of the *Cabinet*, Gerald had reasoned that doing so could be detrimental. Even amongst the exclusive few who sought that one-off genuine historical garment, price could still be an issue. Counterfeit costumes had surfaced, however, without proof of provenance, a knock off was as valuable as a fake old master painting. They were lovely to look at, but not the real thing.

The night of the fire and the assault on David's friend and partner had changed everything. Gerald was contacted by the police to inform him of the break-in on the night. The stabbing of a police officer and fire was explained as a possible panicked over- reaction to being cornered. He had been assured that no effort was being spared to apprehend the individuals who had attacked one of their own. Crimes of this nature were not to be tolerated.

Gerald had immediately initiated a meeting between the brothers. It had been face to face and it had to be as soon as practical. Dwight and Emil assembled in Gerald's lounge room the next morning.

Before they had even sat, Gerald unloaded about the *Cabinet* and the risk the family was running by its mere existence. He wasn't concerned about the damage to the warehouse, it had been minimal, what was driving his anger, and Emil thought fear, was that the secret they had been hiding could have been discovered, which was a risk not only to the business, but to their families. Emil noted, with Gerald, business had the higher priority.

Dwight had fired back about the lack of security on the building, which he blamed on Gerald's penny-pinching management style. Gerald had coughed and spluttered, then argued that it was decided years ago to hide the *Cabinet* in plain sight and not give it any more significance than any piece of equipment used to run the business.

Dwight had fumed and made the pointed observation that the *Cabinet* was not just any piece of equipment. Emil could see an explosion was fast approaching and stepped in to end the debate by simply asked a pointed question, 'Did the police ask about the *Cabinet*?'

'Yes, they asked about the *Cabinet*,' fumed Gerald. 'One recognised it from an article he had read in a genealogy periodical.'

'What else did they ask?'

'If it had been interfered with. I had to explain that the safety protocols wouldn't allow it to be just turned on and used. They were sceptical, so I demonstrated how the process requires both an input code and DNA scan, then I had to explain the computer interface. A female officer called it cute and rustic.' Gerald slumped into a chair deflated. 'I have never been so stressed in my life.'

'Was there any evidence it had been interfered with?' asked Emil.

'Not that was evident. If somebody had used it to travel, it would have still been running from the computer interface, wouldn't it?'

'Yes,' confirmed Dwight, 'You can't shut the interface down remotely; somebody would have to be at the console to turn it off.'

'Then we are in the clear as far as the police are concerned,' stated Emil. 'The burglars couldn't have used the *Cabinet*, even if they knew how to.'

'I suppose so,' conceded Gerald, 'but the risk still exists, that damn *Cabinet* is still here waiting for somebody to discover what it really is.' Gerald blushed as soon as the words were out of his mouth, he had used the "D" word and was horrified. 'I strongly believe the time has come when the risk to all of us far outweighs any potential rewards of keeping that machine.'

David made a detour home to shower and change before traveling to his uncle's house. He had managed to get very little sleep overnight while he waited outside the critical care ward. The "what ifs" kept returning in his mind. What if he had told Jen what he was doing? What if he had ignored what he knew about the *Cabinet* and just stayed with Jen instead of searching the *Cabinet* room?

David parked in the shadow of a cypress tree where he could watch his uncle's front door without being obvious. The house was pretty much the same as he remembered it from childhood, only the trees in the yard were larger and the street seemed smaller. Two vehicles were parked in the driveway. A search on the registration confirmed they were rentals, driven no doubt by his father and his Uncle Emil from the airport on a summons from Gerald.

David chose not to go into the family business, partially because he thought the whole societal fascination with dressing up was ludicrous. He was doing what he felt he was destined to do; be a police officer, but right now he felt a failure as a protector of society. Then the words of Jen came rushing to the front of his mind.

*How you react when you stuff up is more important than the fact that you have stuffed up. Anybody can throw their hands in the air, sit in the corner and sulk. Well, that's worse than bullshit, it's pathetic. You pick yourself up, fix your mistakes; learn from them and you move on.*

It had made sense then and it made sense now. He had got it wrong and Jen had paid the price and now he had to make it right. The problem was, he couldn't do it without the help of the Thomas brothers and he wasn't sure he would get it.

David opened the window of his car to release a nano surveillance drone targeted to attach itself to the window of his uncle's home. The police utilised such devices under the legal conditions imposed by judges issuing warrants. What David was doing was way outside anything legal. If the family found out, he would probably not be on the Christmas card list, but it was unlikely that it would go beyond that.

David watched and listened as the brothers argued amongst themselves. It was clear that going to them as a group would not bring the cooperation he needed. Uncle Gerald was hell bent on getting rid of the *Cabinet;* he was scared as hell of it for some reason that was not immediately obvious.

Dad was fighting to hang on to the machine. David knew if he approached his father, he would be all for using the device. It would be just another means of collecting data to study its operation. That could be difficult to manage.

Uncle Emil was as he remembered, logical and pragmatic, being the adult in the room, he was also concealing something. If David was reading his Uncle Emil's behaviour correctly, he didn't want to lose this machine, which was something he could use as a way in and David was going to exploit it.

After two hours of often heated discussion, the Thomas brothers came to an uneasy truce. Emil thought Gerald was hiding some greater fear than what he had expressed for the *Cabinet* to be gone, but chose not to explain why? In the end, he begrudgingly agreed to a compromise proposal put forward by Emil and supported by Dwight.

The *Cabinet* was to cease operation while new security measures were put in place. Hiding the *Cabinet* in plain sight was still deemed to be less risky than pretending it didn't exist. Dwight was given the role as the technical director of the company, to oversee this project while the remainder of the costumery business continued as per normal.

Dwight had not got his way either. Disposal of the *Cabinet* was still potentially on the horizon, but he believed Emil was on his side, which gave him hope. Emil was as fearful as his brothers, just on a far more personal level. He understood Dwight's need for the machine, it was a love affair of the mind. He needed to find the *Cabinet's* secret like people needed to breathe air.

Gerald, on the other hand, was scared to death of something which had the *Cabinet* at its core. What Emil feared was that if Gerald felt really threatened, he could break up the business with the aid of any competent lawyer and liquidate its assets, including the *Cabinet*.

After a final nod of agreement, Dwight and Emil made their way to their cars.

'Do you want to head into town and get some lunch before we fly out?' asked Emil.

'No, I will give it a miss. I thought I might catch up with David. I haven't seen him much since he got his promotion to detective. He seems to be doing really well and loving the job.'

Emil nodded in understanding, remembering that his nephew was living and working nearby at Warrnambool where the *Cabinet* was stored.

'I wonder if he had anything to do with the break-in?'

'I'll ask him, maybe he will tell me more than the police told Gerald.'

'He might not be able to say anything if he is working the case.'

'I'll ask him anyway. If he can't say anything he can't.' Dwight stopped beside the door of his car. 'One thing about having David here that I hadn't considered, was that he could at least give us a heads up if the break-in has anything to do with what seems to be eating Gerry. I mean he was really off his game today.'

'It's more than that, he was afraid.'

'Afraid? I thought he was just being the usual difficult Gerald. Seriously, destroy the *Cabinet*?! I thought his accountant soul would implode when I heard him talk of cutting off the biggest currency generator for the family business.'

'Yes, it was strange.'

Dwight slipped into the car seat.

'You know, there is no way in the world that we can let Gerald destroy the *Cabinet*. It's just too damn important, and not just for the family.'

'I know,' replied Emil earnestly, 'I know.'

Dwight started his car, 'I guess that you and I had better make sure common sense prevails. I'll talk to you next week.' The car reversed out of the driveway and headed down the street.

Gerald was at the window watching his brothers. Emil waved before entering his rental car and driving away. As the car departed, Gerald returned to his lounge room where he stood in front of a wooden dresser and opened the top drawer to reveal a leather-bound book decorated with a gold embossing. Inside the cover, printed in bright red ink, were the words, *Gideon Bible Society*. Gerald stared at the object then blurted out a single word cry for help.

'Fuck!'

David followed Emil at a distance; closing the gap once they exited the residential neighbourhood and entered the boutique shop district that ringed the city's centre. Discreet red and blue lights flashed as a signal for the driver in front to pull over.

Startled by the sight of an unmarked police vehicle signalling for him to pull over, Emil steered the car off the road into a parking space. Emil was unsure of the protocol; he didn't know if he should exit the vehicle or if he was expected to remain in his seat being unsure of what he could have possibly done wrong. He watched the rear vision heads-up display. The driver's door of the police vehicle behind opened. The officer was in plain clothes. Maybe this wasn't anything to do with driving, maybe this was about the break-in or the *Cabinet* itself? Emil felt sick to his stomach as he wound down his window.

'How can I help, Officer?'

'Hello Uncle Emil.'

'David?'

'Hi Uncle Emil, we need to talk.'

Emil shook himself out of the memory. It was only a week ago, but it seemed like a lifetime. David had led his uncle to a small late twentieth century themed restaurant near where they were parked, shepherding Emil into a booth at the rear of the eatery. Before they were seated, Emil realised it was not a coincidence that David had pulled him over.

'Am I in trouble with the law?'

'Do you think you are in trouble, Uncle Emil?'

Emil's eyes narrowed.

'Is this an official conversation?'

'I am hoping that it doesn't have to turn into one, but I am quite prepared for it to.'

David sat back as a waitress approached with coffees he had ordered when they entered the establishment. Emil guessed the waitress was aged somewhere around 50, dressed in tight, black trousers with rips across the fabric on one thigh, and a black t-shirt with red lettering, printed to look like blood spelling out *Bite Me.* On her left breast was a badge with the name *Camilla,* and a yellow circle with three black marks representing eyes and a smile. If this fashion choice wasn't bleak enough, Camilla's makeup was of a style Emil recognised as Goth from the late 20th century.

'Thank you, Camilla,' said Emil politely. In return, he received a withering stare, which encouraged Emil to reply with a broad smile. This elicited a look of confusion, and she frowned, almost smiled, then hurried back to the front of the store.

'Camilla is role playing Uncle Emil, just like the customers, who dress up in costumes the Thomas Corporation sells who come here to eat. They like to pretend that they are somebody else, somebody from the past who had a more interesting existence than their own. It's what made the Thomas family business what it is. It's making money from people's boredom with life.'

'Is that a professional opinion?'

'It's a fact, not an opinion.'

'Why are we having this conversation?' asked Emil bluntly.

'Because I care about my family. By family, I don't just mean those I share a genetic bond.'

Emil took a second to register what David was telling him.

'Is she a friend, the police officer at the warehouse last night?'

'Jen is family to me, Uncle Emil,' David paused, his mouth set firm. 'It's only because of our family that Jen is fighting for her life. It's also why we are not having this conversation at my station.'

Emil realised, something far beyond a break-in gone wrong, had occurred or David wouldn't be wasting time talking with him when he could be hunting down the people responsible. *Shit*, Emil thought. *Shit, and shit again.*

'You had better tell me what happened, then tell me what you need me to do.'

Emil checked the screen of the *Cabinet's* interface. Nothing had changed. His mind went back to that meeting with David, which still made his guts churn, but not for the same reasons. Initially, it had been a feeling of guilt. He, Dwight and Gerald may not have stabbed Officer Rostig, but they were responsible for why it happened. Jenifer Rostig was attacked because the Thomas brothers were hiding a secret and his nephew left her without backup because of a misguided obligation to protect his family. *Bullshit*, Emil thought, it was to protect the bloody business on Gerald's behalf, to allow Dwight to chase his scientific holy grail and to fulfil a personal desire that benefited nobody but himself. *That was just crap*, he thought with rising anger remembering what happened to Cynthia in this room 14 years ago and what happened last week.

'Are you 100 percent sure it was him?'

'Yes, it was him. You had a meeting with him at Uncle Gerald's house after Cynthia Horrigan's accident. I remembered him, because I peeked through the blinds and watched him walk to his car. He turned and waved with this huge smile on his face. It was the same wave and the same smile, and he recognised me. He said, *say goodbye to your mother, young David, for me. That's while you still can.*'

Emil was stunned, not wanting to accept the facts in front of him.

'If I was in your position, I wouldn't want to believe it either.'

Emil sat back in the booth as if searching for an answer.

'You are certain it was him?'

David nodded. 'You don't have to just rely on my word.'

'Somebody else saw him?'

'No,' said David flatly, 'but I am wearing this.' David pulled back his sleeve to reveal what looked like an oversized faceless watch.

Emil almost laughed, 'Seriously?!'

'It's not a recreational device.'

Emil dropped his smile.

'Are you telling me that is a police memory retrieval device?'

David nodded, 'It's one of the last produced before all credibility was lost and they started to market them for recreational use.'

'I thought the police had abandoned them; you can't use that in a court.'

'True, you couldn't use one in court,' agreed David opening the device to remove two thin wires with tiny suction cups attached.

Emil stared at the device.

'You don't have to relive it, if you don't want to.'

David passed a lead to his uncle, 'it's for Jen.'

It was dark. Emil felt water fall from his hair to run down the bridge of his nose, before landing on his shirt. There was water on the floor, small puddles reflecting the light that shone from the end of a corridor. Emil recognised the room; he was outside the laundry and the door that led to the *Cabinet*. Emil looked down at his hand; he was holding a handgun, a stunner the police carried. On his wrist was an encrypted radio device, Emil didn't know how he knew this, but then immediately reasoned that if he was in David's memory, he would know things that David knew.

Emil raised the radio; the sound of David's voice filled his head.

'Jen, what's happening?'

There was no reply. Emil felt sick with anxiety, then he was running, looking left then right, the weapon out in front, held in both hands.

'Jen, talk to me Jen, where are you?' David's voice was almost yelling into his wrist.

Emil felt himself drop next to the door at the end of the corridor, he pushed open a gap to peer through the opening. The gun was up leading where he was looking, right to left, starting high then working down to the floor. His hand came up to his head, his glasses changed. Emil could see in the dark and there was a shape on the floor. It was Jen, lying unnaturally on her stomach. One leg was tucked under her hips, the other was bent and splayed out behind.

He was on his feet, running. There was a glow behind Jen, smoke was beginning to billow out a doorway. Emil suddenly realised that it was a fire. He wanted to look at it, just for a moment, but it wasn't his body, wasn't his memory, then he was speaking rapidly into his wrist using David's voice.

'Bravo 34 to dispatch, officer down at my location. Urgent medical assistance required and armed response backup.'

Emil was kneeling, blood oozed into his trousers from a puddle of red spreading across the floor, his heart beat faster with worry. Then the heat hit him. Steam began to pour out of his clothes, his hair dried as the moisture boiled away. Emil could feel his clothes burning against his skin, he had to move Jen away from the fire. Then he was up, grasping Jen's arms and pulling. She was heavy, a dead weight. He pulled, dragged and slid Jen as fast and as far away from that fire as he could. Emil felt his chest heave, his lungs gasping for air as he strained against the weight and the heat, until he came to a stop near the grand front entrance door. It was an impenetrable barrier preventing him, preventing David, from removing Jen from danger. He had loved that door, that grand pompous portal to escapism. Now, in this moment, in this memory, Emil hated every banal thing it stood for.

'Jen, Jen, can you hear me?' Emil felt himself plead with David's voice. Her eyes flickered, then opened. A wave of relief began to flood his chest.

Then the memory changed. He was on the floor, outside the entrance to the *Cabinet* room. Emil felt David's body rise on one knee, look down to check the weapon in his hand, then he was up, moving, swinging left as soon as he was through the entrance. That's where the *Cabinet* was, where they would be.

The *Cabinet* stood out like a torch in a tunnel surrounded by shadows. Why were the lights in the room off? Then he saw the two figures dressed in black jump suits that seemed to almost disappear into the background. For a moment, their heads appeared to be floating, disembodied in mid-air, then they moved to look at each other, the shape of their bodies shimmered as an outline. They were holding hands, a man, and a woman. The woman was holding a backpack by one strap with her free hand, as it sat on the floor at her feet. She was tall, very pretty, with dark hair pulled away from her face. She smiled, then Emil saw him, a face from the past, beaming with an enormous laughing smile.

'Too late, I am afraid. If I were you, I would head home and make the most of your life as it is, as quick as I could. Things are going to change; they will never be the same again.'

Emil knew the voice. It was as full of self-importance as it had ever been. He felt anger well up inside at the betrayal. He had to stop him, he had to stop them. The bastards. The evil self-seeking bastards who had done the unthinkable to Jen.

Emil was running and yelling.

'I know you; I'll find you. I'll stop you; I'll bring you back.'

He fired the weapon. The blast seemed to leap from his hand, banging against the glass of the *Cabinet*. Emil knew it was useless, his finger kept pulling the trigger over and over in some vain hope that the next pull would crack the glass case open and knock that smile right down his throat.

Then he stopped smiling, as if a thought had suddenly disrupted the moment. Emil knew in that instant, he had recognised himself, rather recognised David.

'Well, what do you know? The people you bump into at the oddest of times,' he said turning to the woman conversationally. 'It's young David Thomas, all grown up. You remember, I told you about him? Dwight's son?'

Emil fired again. The man from his past swung his head to stare directly into his eyes, 'Say goodbye to your mother for me, young David. That's while you still can.'

Then there was the bright green glow. It pulsed three times and Emil was alone.

'Shit!' he heard himself yell with David's voice. 'Shit! Shit! Shit!' came the expletives as he spun around, searching for something, anything. His eyes fell on the glow of the computer interface. There it was, right there in green and grey lettering behind that curved glass window.

'Got you,' Emil breathed, 'got you.'

Emil felt sick. Jen, poor bloody Jen, left to die because of that bloody machine. He knew he didn't know the woman, but he had felt what David felt and it had ripped a hole in his heart to see her lying on the floor. Emil saw the pain on David's face. He went to say something, needed to reach out.

David shook his head.

'We have to fix this; the rest can happen later.'

'Shit,' Emil swore under his breath. 'Why? Why now, and how? That's something that I find difficult to understand. The *Cabinet* has to have my codes, my DNA to operate. Not only that, but only Gerald and a few of his very trusted staff have security codes to the warehouse.'

David placed a piece of paper on the table.

'Do you recognise any of these addresses?'

Emil ran his eye over the list.

'Two of the buildings are owned by the Thomas Corporation.'

'Do you ever visit those buildings?'

'Yes, yes, of course I do. Dwight and I have an office in this one.' Emil pointed to an address on the paper. 'We use it when we have to stay over; it has two bedrooms and an attached bathroom on the upper floor. It's basic, clean and quiet and convenient.'

'It is also one of the premises that our bible burglar visited.'

'I don't understand.'

David reached into his jacket and withdrew a book.

'Have you seen one of these recently?'

Emil took the book.

'It's a religious textbook, a bible, we produce replicas for sale and rent.' Emil turned it over, then opened the front cover. 'Who's Gideon?'

'A century or more ago, it was a group which morphed into a corporation associated with a religious organisation that used to distribute free bibles as a recruitment and propaganda exercise. They put these things in motels and hospital rooms.'

'Really?' replied Emil, then he asked the obvious question, 'Why did you ask me if I had seen one of these Gideon books?'

'I'm trying to tie together a link. A Gideon bible was left at the building where you and Dad have an office, after it was broken into a month ago. Nothing was reported stolen at the time, but now I am thinking something that nobody would notice was removed.'

'My DNA.'

'It wouldn't be hard to collect a skin cell or saliva from a toothbrush in the bathroom.'

'Why haven't I heard about the break-in, and if they had my DNA why break into other buildings and leave a bible?'

'This wasn't about theft. If the break-ins are linked with what happened last night, it was about gaining access to the *Cabinet*. The books were probably left to confuse the matter. The question should be why make it so complex?'

'Why go to ancient Israel?' asked Emil touching the book. 'You think it's linked to this?'

'I suspect the woman might be linked to the book; I believe she drove the knife into Jen's back. *No hesitation*, was what Jen said, *no hesitation, just stuck it in*. A professional thief wouldn't do that.'

'What are you suggesting?'

'What comes back to me is what he said, *things are going to change, never be the same again.*'

'Are you suggesting they are going to change the present, by changing the past?' Emil's guts were now doing backflips at the thought of the ramifications.

'Maybe, maybe not. They may have gone to ancient Israel just to throw us off their trail, then jumped forward in time from there. They might have some plan to live like kings using their knowledge from the future to get rich, or it could be on some personal crusade to change world history. I don't need to know the answer, I just know that I am going to hunt them down to face justice for what they did to Jen.'

Emil nodded in understanding.

'I need your help, Uncle Emil,' stated David. 'I need access to the *Cabinet* and you are going to provide your DNA, and the code to make it happen.' Emil understood this was not a negotiation. 'I also need you to stay with the *Cabinet* to make sure nothing is done to stop me.' Emil nodded again. 'Do you understand what I am asking?'

Emil reached across the table and put his hand out to his nephew.

'I understand that what happened, not just to your Jen, but to Cynthia, is on me, Dwight and Gerald and I have to make it right.'

'No matter what the consequences,' stated David accepting the handshake like a sworn oath.

'No matter what the consequences,' replied Emil.

Emil's thoughts drifted back to the meeting in the café. Once the commitment had been made, the conversation turned to practical matters. Emil could provide access to the *Cabinet* and guard the machine for David. He would barricade the entrance if need be.

They agreed not to include Dwight in their plans. David knew his father would insist on a long-drawn-out process of testing, running trials and monitoring every piece of equipment. Any hope of secrecy and quick action would disappear.

David was overdue to visit his parents, where the recall devices were stored in a safe in his father's workshop. Dwight used the same security code for everything, NCC1701, which had some unknown reverence to his father, so gaining access would not be an issue.

Having sorted travel through the *Cabinet,* and the return home, the problem was how to access the machine in the first place. Approaching

Gerald was immediately discarded. Emil knew talking to Gerald would force the issue in the wrong direction.

David asked, 'Who else has security access to the building?'

Emil began to run through the list, 'The warehouse manager and the assistant warehouse manager.'

'Could we use either of them to get to the *Cabinet,* without drawing attention?'

Emil shook his head.

'I would be able to talk my way into the room, but I would be hard pressed to explain your presence.'

'But it could be done?' pressed David. 'If we had no other alternative?'

'Yes,' agreed Emil, 'but it would be a break with standard practice.'

'Would this be a problem?'

'The risk is too high that Gerald would be told. He would want to investigate.'

'It's still an option, if you can keep the machine operating until I return?'

Emil shook his head.

'I could do my best to stop anybody shutting it down at the controls, but I have no idea what the effect would be if power to the building was shut down. Dwight might know the answer, but I don't.'

David nodded.

'I don't want to involve Dad; I would rather take the risk.'

Emil shook his head.

'You might want to take the risk, but I won't. We must have better options than this.'

'What about cleaners or maintenance staff?'

Again, Emil shook his head.

'The warehouse has automated maintenance robots to keep the facility in order.'

'Who else has access? It can't just be Gerald's handpicked crew.'

Emil clicked his fingers.

'You know who else has access to the warehouse and is unlikely to make a fuss?' Emil stood and started to make his way out of the dining booth. 'How long would it take you to prepare, could you be ready within a few days?'

David rose to follow. 'Who?'

'I don't know why I didn't think of him first?'

'Who?'

Emil walked briskly toward their cars, 'it's obvious now that I think about it, somebody that has access to the warehouse for legitimate reasons and is unlikely to read anything sinister into being asked to let us into the *Cabinet* room.'

'Who?' asked David, running to catch up with his uncle.

Emil stopped next to his car, then clasped David by the shoulders. 'Your cousin, Adrian.'

'Adrian?' replied David in surprise.

'Yes, uncomplicated, trusting Adrian. Gerald brought him into the business a year ago, in an attempt to instil a sense of responsibility into him. He has access to the warehouse day and night to collect special orders for our more demanding customers, Adrian is very good with the customer relations side of the business. Happy to talk and listen, non-threatening and always eager to please. And way too trusting for his own good.'

'I haven't really spoken to Adrian in years, not since we moved away, apart from Christmas a couple of times.'

'Will that be a problem?'

'It shouldn't be, we were great friends as kids. Thinking about Adrian makes me feel guilty for not making contact for so long, and now I need to rekindle our relationship, especially since we are both living in the same city again.'

Emil dropped his hands.

'That sounds like something you should do for the good of the family.'

'Re-establish old family bonds, maybe do some of the things we promised each other we would do when we were younger.'

'Would any of those things revolve around the *Cabinet*?'

David nodded. 'We used to talk about travel through the *Cabinet*. I remember learning about movie theatres at school; I wanted to go back and see what it was like for fun.'

'Did Adrian fantasise about time travel?'

'Well, the idea of doing safe things, like going to a punk rock music venue, Adrian has always been into classical music. You know, Metallica, ACDC, that sort of thing.'

Emil shuddered at the thought. 'Way too highbrow for my taste.'

Emil and David stood silently in thought for a moment, then Emil had an epiphany.

'Could you use the memory retrieval device?'

David frowned.

'Could I convince Adrian to give us access to the *Cabinet* by filling his head with childhood memories to make him want to help us? For Jen, yes, I could.'

'For Jen and Cynthia,' said Emil.

'Agreed.'

David opened the car door for Emil.

'I'll make contact with Adrian later today, but first I need to get some sleep, then do some research at the station into who the woman is. Officially, I'm on compassionate leave. I am not cut off, but I will need to be careful.'

'Okay, be careful.'

'What are you going to do, Uncle Emil?'

'The first thing I am going to do is to ask you to stop calling me Uncle, just plain Emil will do. I need to give you the respect you deserve, not only as a police officer, but as a man of integrity, which I know you are.'

'Okay, Emil,' nodded David in agreement.

'Then, I am going to make arrangements for my second in charge to run things while we get ready for what we need to do.' Emil climbed into his car. 'Contact me after you speak with Adrian, then we can make firm plans on how to proceed.'

'Agreed,' said David, closing the car door.

David watched his uncle drive away, then sat in his police vehicle.

'Bravo 34, computer data base link.'

A computer-generated voice issued from a hidden speaker, *'Computer link established Detective Thomas.'*

'Get me contact details for one, Adrian Thomas. Last known employer, Thomas Costumery Warrnambool, Victoria.' A holographic image of Adrian, smiling for his driver's licence, flashed above the dash of the car along with rows of text. 'Forward that to my personal data link.'

*'Transfer completed.'*

'Ok, cousin, let's see if you are up for a walk down memory lane.'

Emil awoke from his thoughts when the machine beeped. There was a whoosh of air followed by a flash of green light as something solid landed in the *Cabinet.*

'Hello Uncle Emil, I think you owe me an apology.'

Emil didn't reply, there was no sign of David.

Adrian didn't notice his uncle's distress and carried on, 'I get the feeling that you and David haven't been totally honest, which is not the sort of thing a chap expects from family. Well not close family. Second or third cousins maybe, but not with your favourite uncle.'

'Where the hell is David?'

'Really Uncle Emil, really! I am beginning to think that good manners evaporate everywhere I go today, it's becoming exhausting.'

Emil stepped back from the *Cabinet*.

'FUCK,' he yelled while looked to the ceiling for an answer. He took a deep breath and offered his hand to Adrian, 'I am sorry, let's get you out of there. Do you need a drink?'

'I am quite parched, that's probably why I have a headache all of a sudden.'

'Dehydration can cause headaches,' said Emil, handing Adrian a Pimms and lemon. 'So can stress, believe me, I know about stress headaches. I'm having one now.'

'This is nice, what's it called?'

'It's a Pimms and lemon' said Emil trying to remain calm.

'I must remember that,' said Adrian, making an entry in his note pad. 'I have been a bit of a silly sausage; I should have realised that you and David were up to something. Shame on you, Uncle Emil, and on me for being so gullible.'

Emil sat beside his nephew.

'This is not a game, Adrian, it's deadly serious. I need to know what happened and if David is safe.'

'I agree it's not a game, which is why I have started on a rescue plan to bring David home. In fact, I have already recruited an assistant, a great young chap, salt of the earth-type with bags of wisdom passed down from his elders.'

'What?'

Adrian tapped his hand on Emil's leg.

'It's a long and exciting story with lots of interesting characters. One chap I met; Peter, had breath that I swear could -'

Emil grasped Adrian's hand to stop it pounding on his leg.

'We don't have time for this, I need to know if David is alive?'

'Why wouldn't he be?'

'David wouldn't just abandon you, not unless it was the only way to keep you safe.'

'Well to be honest, I am not sure exactly where David is now, or should I say, then? I am not really sure on the time travel protocol.'

Emil gritted his teeth and squeezed his nephew's thigh hard to gain his attention.

'Adrian, I need facts. Can you tell me what happened in short concise sentences? Can you do that Adrian?'

'I can do better than that, Uncle Emil.' Adrian rolled back his sleeve to reveal the recall device attached to his wrist. 'David added a memory retrieval device to the *Sainters* before we went on our little excursion.' Adrian paused, 'I should probably explain that a *Sainter,* is the new name for these. I can't take the credit for it; it was William's idea. He named it after his football team in the twentieth century. Apparently, they beat Collingwood with a one-point win after the final siren off a dodgy free kick to win a premiership. It was an important historical event.'

'What?'

'I know, I had no idea either.' Adrian opened the device to withdraw the cables. 'David said it was an insurance policy, I didn't understand at the time, but it makes sense now.'

Emil took a cable from Adrian without a word, placing a cup on the end of a lead against his temple.

'You do know how this works?' said Emil.

'I have to remember.'

'You have to do more than that, you have to show me everything as it happened, no hiding anything or pretending how you wish it had been.'

'I understand, Uncle Emil. If part of the price to bring David home is some embarrassment over my memories, then that is a very small price to pay.'

'Ok Adrian, show me what happened.'

Emil closed his eyes, Adrian closed his, there was a flash of green light and Emil found himself lying on top of a group of men in the dirt somewhere far in the past.

# CHAPTER ELEVEN

POLYKARPOS AND DAVID ARRIVED at a rise overlooking the village of Nazareth just on dark.

'As promised, David, we are back where we started.'

David, placing a hand on his companion's shoulder, said, 'I owe you a great debt for your help Polykarpos.'

'You made that sound like a farewell.'

'I can't ask any more of you.'

'You saved my life, David, that is a debt not easily discharged. I think I must accompany you a bit longer on your journey.'

'Are you sure?'

'Yes, I am sure.'

'Then, I need you to do exactly what I say, when I say it. Questioning my orders could get us killed, which is something I would like to avoid.'

'Agreed,' replied Polykarpos thinking David was a man accustomed to leadership, but then again, maybe he was something else.

'I didn't get a chance to get my bearings when I arrived in the village,' stated David.

'You would like me to take you to where I first saw you, and my foolish students this morning?'

'If you could, please.'

'The Romans don't normally patrol at night, but today I think they will want to make their presence felt. We will need to tread lightly. Follow my lead and do as I do, David.'

David nodded. 'Lead on Polykarpos, this is your town.'

Polykarpos led David through the fruit trees that ringed the settlement, paused to listen then quietly crossed the gap to the first building. David followed, first checking his flanks, then to the rear, before crossing.

'We must travel down this alley, then turn right at the granary which will take us to the road that runs through the village. We need to cross to the other side. The Romans will be watching the road from the roof of the temple.'

'Is there a blind spot you can't see from the roof?'

'The north wall of the building casts a deep shadow; you can only see a cubit or two of the road, if you were looking in that direction.'

'Then we need to make sure they're not looking.'

Polykarpos nodded, then went to step into the alley. David stopped him. There was a noise, a rhythmic slap of leather on hard soil, approaching.

David placed a finger to his lips, then indicated for his companion to move into the shadow of the building. He peered around the corner; it was a legionnaire slowly walking a patrol beat. David couldn't make out his face but heard the unmistakable sound of yawning as the soldier approached. The legionnaire was not on high alert but would pass within a metre of where they were hiding.

David searched for a something to use as a weapon. The only thing in abundance were stones on the ground of the alley. They could hear the legionnaire moving closer, then a significant brassy note as he broke wind in a series of short blasts, coinciding with each hobnailed footstep. He picked up a pebble. When he gauged the legionnaire was close enough, he hurled the stone to land behind the soldier. The pebble bumped against a wall in the alley, the sound echoed in the still of the night. Fear of the unknown in the dark came rushing to the fore, the legionnaire swung his pilum from his shoulder and turned to face the noise.

David hurled a second stone. The legionnaire tightened the grip on his weapon and made a cautious approach toward the sound. Once he had taken five steps, the soldier increased his pace. David and Polykarpos removed their footwear, then tiptoed across the gap of the alley behind the legionnaire and on towards their destination.

Polykarpos led David to the base of the synagogue. It was the tallest building in Nazareth, sitting adjacent to the Roman road that bisected the village. It commanded a view of, not just the road they needed to cross, but in daylight, most of the township. Like the other buildings in Nazareth, it was made of stone with a flat roof from which the glow of a warming fire could be seen.

For David, the fire was a blessing. It would disrupt the guard's night vision and be a focus of attention. Still, a distraction was needed to ensure the guards were looking the other way. David would have preferred to walk around the village to approach the other side, the risk of extending their time in the dark and being discovered, swayed his decision. The sooner he found his bag, the earlier he could search for Adrian.

Polykarpos drew a map in the sand indicating buildings and an alley across the Roman road. He drew a figure of a man next to a building, pointed to David to indicate where he had first seen him, then an ox cart, indicating to himself. To one side of the mud map, he drew a series of crosses with stick figures attached.

'Adrian?' mouthed David.

Polykarpos shrugged a maybe.

'Okay,' whispered David holding up one finger to indicate first, then pointed to the location on the map where his effigy had been drawn, then two fingers while pointing to the crucified men, to show this was the second priority.

Keeping to the shadows, David looked toward the roof of the building. He caught a glimpse of two uniforms and what he thought was the shadow of a third soldier. Next, David crawled to the edge of the building, peering right, then left, along the road. The far side was in shadow, as was the base of the synagogue. There was, as Polykarpos explained, a gap without shadow he would need to traverse to get to the other side. Anybody looking in that direction would see them cross.

David returned to Polykarpos, who stood waiting with pebbles in hand. David moved to take the rocks, but Polykarpos shook his head then waved his hand for David to move into position.

'Are you sure?'

'Go,' whispered Polykarpos moving to a position to launch the stones.

David removed his sandals, inched as close as he dared to the end of the shadows and waited. Clink, clink, thump, thump. There was a murmur of voices above, then the sounds again, clunk, clunk, clink, followed by louder voices. A third round of noise echoed in the dark. The shadows cast from the roof top fire grew shorter as the men above moved to the far side of the structure.

David moved, two quick steps out of the shadow, three more into the dark across the road. He pressed against a wall, listening, heard no obvious alarm, then hurried away to commence a grid pattern search. If he was to survive and track down the fugitives, he had to find the bag and its contents. The *Cabinet* would have transformed it into a container from this time period, which might have kept it safe or piqued the curiosity of somebody to look inside.

It took David less than two minute to find the site of the fight, scuff marks where steel shod hooves had bit into the compacted surface and the remains of broken sticks, used as improvised weapons, were all that remained. There was no evidence of his bag. Logically, it could have been picked up by the Romans. If it was, he and it were probably lost forever, that was unless Adrian had escaped and he and Emil came looking for him. The problem was, he could be dead long before they found him. A minute at the costumery, could be years in the past.

He was alive and had found an ally but couldn't continue to put him at risk. Grandfather paradox, notwithstanding, Polykarpos had done enough.

He could try a house-to-house search of the village but come first light, he would stand out as a stranger and the Romans could react badly to his presence. He could give up on the bag and carry on without it, but the fugitives had a bag of their own when he saw them in the *Cabinet*. David was certain it didn't contain just a change of underwear. They would use technology from the future to make a life for themselves in the past and it didn't necessarily follow that this time period was their final destination. They could well have jumped forward in time, in which case he was stuffed. *Bugger landing on top of those men and ending up in a fight before Adrian and I even had a chance*, David thought. It was probably caused by a simple three-dimensional navigation error, something to do with the machine's perspective of where the surface of the earth was in its time frame, compared to where it was in the past. David had nearly landed on the roof, remembering bouncing against the wall on the way down. Then he looked up.

Polykarpos knew about throwing stones. Had not David of the Israelites used a stone to kill Goliath? He waited until David was in place, then launched two projectiles, held his breath and listened for the sound of pebbles landing. There were three voices talking, the noise stopped one.

Polykarpos launching two more missiles. The collisions were fainter and further away, all three voices stopped. Polykarpos heard footsteps moving to his side of the building, time to repeat the trick. He changed the angle of the throw and used three stones. The effect was immediate, all three voices began to speak at once. Polykarpos didn't know if David had crossed the path, but if he hadn't, now was the time to act.

A head appeared over the lip of the roof. Polykarpos pushed into the shadow of the wall; he doubted he could be seen but it was time to move. Sandals in hand, Polykarpos tiptoed into the adjacent alley. He could hear the thump, thump, thump of hobnails descending from the roof, not one, but two heavy bodies. Polykarpos watched as the legionnaires reached the bottom of the steps. One soldier headed toward where he had flung the stones, the second made a direct line to where he was hiding. It was probably a manoeuvre to approach the noise from two sides. It didn't matter why the soldier was heading in his direction, he just was.

David spotted a calfskin bag dangling from the roof by a leather thong wound around the opening, attached to which was a plastic buckle that shouldn't exist. David breathed a sigh of relief; it was his bag. He searched for a means to bring the bag down. Finding nothing, he launched himself into the air but couldn't reach.

There were stone steps leading to the roof on the adjacent building. He climbed to the roof, making way too much noise in his own mind. With luck the residents would be too scared to check as death had already come to the village once today.

David mentally measured the distance between buildings, it was further than he wanted to jump, then he thought of Jen and ignored the risk. David braced one foot against the lip of the roof, took three deep breaths, pumped his arms to gain momentum then leapt forward as fast as he could. In three bounces, he was at the end of the roof, up and forward he jumped, trying to gain height to aid with distance.

His torso colliding in a sickening thump onto the edge of the far building's roof, knocking the air out of his lungs. David folded at the waist, his knees smacked into the stone below causing pain and removing skin. His hands struggled to gain a grip as he started to slide backwards.

'Shit,' he gasped, digging his fingers into the roof surface.

His left hand gripped the wooden frame that held the roof together, his body swung to the left and slowed. David brought his feet up to grip against the wall. The leather soled sandals slipped; more skin came from his knees as they scraped against stone. The fingers on his left hand were burning, his shoulder felt like it was about to be pulled from his body as he hung there, not able to go up, not wanting to fall down. It was only a few metres, but that was more than enough to break a leg, or worse.

Breathing deeply, he used his right hand to grip the edge of the roof as he levered himself up, while trying to use his feet to gain a hold. David's left sandal dropped to the ground, toes dug into the wall and gave some purchase as he used the last of his strength to pull himself up. David's chest was back on the surface of the roof. It dug into his ribs and spread the pain into his torso, the timber frame beneath his left hand crumbled, he slid backwards again.

David scrambled to slow the slide, but there was nothing he could do to stop the fall. Panic, then logic, interceded. He tried to go limp to minimise the impact. He used his fingers to slow his momentum, then he stopped sliding as one foot, then the second, found something solid. Gasping for breath he looked to the heavens as if to yell a thank you as a voice came from below.

'Daddy, what is that man doing on our roof?'

David froze.

'I don't know, Milcah. It's an odd thing to find a man trying to jump from our neighbour's roof to ours. If it was me, I would have used the ladder.'

David looked down; he was standing on a ladder. At the base was a husband and wife with two children; the youngest, an infant cradled in the arms of a woman, David guessed to be, in her mid-thirties.

'Hello,' said David, exhausted, but relieved. 'Thank you. I assume you put it under me?'

'He doesn't sound like a thief, Daddy,' said a young girl holding the hand of a bearded man.

'I'm not sure I know how a thief was supposed to sound, Milcah,' replied the father. 'Maybe they are polite when cornered? Maybe this man is not a thief, he could just be a man who likes to jump from house to house in the middle of the night. People have strange hobbies, think of your Uncle Levi.'

'Uncle Levi is funny, Daddy.'

'Well, to you he may be funny, to others he seems strange. To Levi, he is just Levi.'

The woman looked up at David. She had red hair and freckles spread across her nose. 'I think he is a thief; we should call the Romans.'

The father placed an arm around the woman.

'I don't know about that, Mary, they may not be in the best of moods.'

Mary gave a sigh, then testily said, 'Yes, you are probably right, let's not wake the Romans. Though I don't know how anybody could sleep with the noise our thief was making. I will hear all about it from her next door in the morning. She thinks she is special ever since her father died and left her two goats. She likes to make a big deal of the fact that she has goat shit to shovel and we don't have any.'

'Mary, I promise to buy us a goat as soon as we have enough shekels saved.'

Mary calmed, then kissed her husband on the cheek.

'I know you are doing the best, Joe.'

'Thank you, Mary,' said Joe, kissing his wife gently on the lips, 'I will be inside with Milcah in a few moments, we should all get back to bed.'

'Don't be long, I have laundry to do in the morning and if I sleep in, all the best rocks at the stream will be taken.'

'We won't. I promise.'

'Good night, thief,' said Mary glancing up at David as she hurried inside.

'How will we know if he is a thief or not Daddy?'

'Perhaps we should ask him? That would be the polite thing to do.'

Milcah was pleased with the idea.

'Yes Daddy, we should ask if he is a thief.'

'You heard my daughter,' said Joe looking up the ladder, 'are you a thief?'

'No, I promise you I am not a thief.'

'Then what are you stranger? Why are you jumping on our roof in the dark?'

'My name is David. I am sorry if I frightened your family; I meant no harm.'

Joe squatted next to his daughter.

'See Milcah, he is not a thief. He is a man named David who said he means us no harm.'

'That's good, isn't it?'

'Yes, it is good that he has not come to rob us in the night.'

'Did you think he might have wanted to Daddy?'

'No, I think I have seen this David in front of our home earlier today.'

'Was he one of the men fighting with the Romans?' squealed Milcah in excitement.

'Shall we ask him if he was one of the men silly enough to attack Roman soldiers, then return after curfew, making so much noise that he could attract Romans to our house?'

David slid down the ladder.

'I meant what I said, about meaning you no harm.'

'What you mean to do and what actually happens could be two very different things. Do you know what the Romans would do to us if they found you here?'

'I am sorry,' repeated David. 'I never meant to get involved. It was just a mistake.'

Joe shook his head in disbelief.

'I saw you from the carpentry shop; they took you away with Polykarpos.'

'Yes, that did happen.'

'Did you escape?'

David nodded.

'And you came back here. Why would you do that?'

'I left something behind.'

'Is it worth your life? Is it worth the life of my family?'

'No, it's not worth anybody's life,' answered David, looking up at the bag, 'but it is of great value to me.'

Joe looked up the ladder.

'It's on my roof, this thing that is of great value, but not worth a life?'

'Yes. I dropped it and I need it back.'

'You dropped it on my roof?'

'Yes.'

Joe addressed his daughter, 'You see, Milcah, if you ask, people will tell you. This man, David, dropped something on our roof and he was trying to get it back.'

'I think he is silly, Daddy. Why wouldn't he use the ladder to get it down? You would lend it to him, wouldn't you?'

'If he asked nicely, I probably would.' Joe faced David. 'Are you a man who is likely to ask?'

'Yes, under normal circumstances.'

'Will you let him use it, Daddy?' asked Milcah.

'Shall we find out?'

David looked from the father to the daughter and back to the father.

'May I borrow your ladder please, Mr Joe and Miss Milcah?'

'What do you want to retrieve with my ladder, David? I think a reasonable person should be given an explanation under the circumstances.'

'I could, but time is against me.'

'I don't understand,' said Joe moving between David and the ladder. 'You do realise the risk I am taking just talking to you.'

From off in the distance came the sound of shouting.

'*Polykarpos,*' muttered David looking towards the noise.

'Polykarpos is here? asked Joe in surprise.

'We escaped together; he is keeping the Romans distracted so I can get what I came for.'

Joe stared at David, then squatted next to his daughter.

'Milcah, tell mummy she needs to put out the lamp and hide.'

'Yes, Daddy,' Milcah replied without question.

'And tell her that Polykarpos is not dead, not yet anyway.'

The girl turned and ran as fast as her little legs could carry her around the building.

'Polykarpos is you friend?'

'He was my teacher.' Joe turned to face the noise. 'My son also went to the school of Polykarpos. It's because of him that I dream of my own carpentry shop and goats to shit in the street for Mary.'

'I can help him, if I can get to my bag.'

Joe replied, gripping the ladder to steady it, 'I don't know why, but I am going to help you David who claims not to be a thief. I just hope Mary is wrong about you.'

David nodded his thanks then scaled the ladder. Thoughts of Polykarpos overrode the pain and fatigue. He knelt beside the bag and removed a two centimetre long and half a centimetre thick lozenge-shaped hydration tablet. Pressing his thumb into the centre caused two chemicals to mix in a fizzing reaction, which dragged water vapour out of the surrounding air, reducing its temperature to its dew point to form liquid water.

David held the tablet above his open mouth. Within moments, water droplets formed, raining down on his face. Dry as the desert air might be, it still contained a percentage of water vapour; technology was allowing David to harvest it. Each tablet could produce up to four litres of water, depending on the temperature and relative humidity of the atmosphere surrounding it. When the tablet stopped fizzing, David dropped it. Reaching back into the bag, he picked out three more hydration tablets, tucking them into the woollen underwear under his tunic.

David next retrieved a first aid kit. He had cuts and bruises to various parts of his body and now he was cooling down, he could feel their presence. He swallowed an anti-biotic pill then searched for pain relief; it came in the form of a sticky pad which he attached to his abdomen, allowing the chemical to slowly release into his blood stream.

Next, David retrieved a stimulant. It went against his better judgement to take the mixture of artificial adrenaline and other stimulants, but he was stuffed, physically exhausted. David inhaled the contents of a vial, the effect was immediate, but not overpowering. In his fatigued state, it just made him feel near normal again. The effect would only last an hour or two, after that he would crash back into exhaustion. An hour of feeling fit and alert might be all he needed to get himself and Polykarpos out of danger.

David found the service weapon he had drawn from the police armoury as he would on any normal work shift. It had been scanned, recorded and checked through all of the required procedures and processes. Now it was in his hand, centuries before it had been invented.

Finally, David withdrew his surveillance glasses. He had three pairs in the bag. Not being a weapon, they were not subject to the same level of controlled access. He activated the night vision and scanned towards the approaching voices. Polykarpos was moving rapidly between buildings, not far behind six legionnaires were walking the narrow alleyways in an extended line search. The outer two were on the edge of the village, positioned to look both into the town and out to the surrounding fields. As the line moved, the soldiers would halt at each crossroad, then sound off, left to right, reporting on what they could see. Polykarpos was being funnelled toward David and beyond to an open plain, where he could not hope to hide.

David slid down the ladder, then handed the bag to Joe.

'Could you hold this for me, Joe? I won't be long.' David went to move away then stopped. 'I wouldn't look in the bag, some things are best not seen.'

'Sorry?'

'If I don't come back, burn it or bury it someplace a long way away from your home and it will be okay.'

'I don't understand.'

'I don't have time to explain. Please, just do what I ask, Joe,' said David moving off toward the noise.

Joe was stunned by the change in David. He was full of energy when moments before, he had been struggling to climb the ladder. He had something in his hand that looked like a tool. It wasn't anything Joe had used or seen before, and what was David wearing on his face?

As Joe watched, David pointed the tool in his hand down and to his side. Wind, light and noise exploded. Dust flew in the air then blew backwards after bouncing off a wall.

'Jehovah,' whispered Joe in surprise, 'definitely not a thief.'

Mary loved her husband, but there were times when Joe's kind nature was not an asset. She feared it would end up killing him one day. Take the thief. Here Joe was helping a stranger who, earlier today, had been fighting with the Romans in the street. Just being suspected of helping the thief could get them killed.

The problem was, Mary had loved Joe ever since the day she turned 16 and Joe had become her boyfriend. Joe stuck by her when she found out she was pregnant, despite the fact they had not lain together in that way. They had come close when kissing. Joe had gotten over-excited and the passion had leaked out of him, much to his embarrassment and her amusement, on more than one occasion. Mary thought it wise not to talk about Joe's brother, Cleopas, who had been less circumspect about her honour.

Joe thought it was a miracle of their love. Mary had expected Joe to accuse her of being a liar who had been unfaithful. Instead, Joe had smiled, told Mary he loved her and wanted to marry her. So, they had and were happy living in their three-roomed home, even if they couldn't afford a goat yet.

Mary put Milcah and baby James to bed. Her oldest son was not in the village, having been sent on an errand for Issac his employer. Mary loved all her children, but her 17-year-old first born was being particularly difficult of late. Mary had heard her son speak about the injustices the poor suffered and while she could not disagree, these words were dangerous. She tried to make him see the reality of the world in which they lived, but the righteousness of youth was difficult to battle. Mary believed her son needed to concentrate on his apprenticeship. Everybody had need of a carpenter at some time and you could earn enough to marry and buy goats and even a cow, if you did well. Imagine the shit you could collect from a goat, and a cow, what vegetables you could grow with that added to your garden.

'Mary!' called Joe from the door. 'Hide this and don't look inside, no matter what.'

'What is it, Joe?'

Joseph dropped the bag behind the door, then covered it with a sheep skin. 'Please don't ask, I don't know if I could explain it.'

Mary looked to the lump behind the door, then at Joe who was flushed with excitement.

'It's the thief's, isn't it?'

'Yes, it's David's. But he is definitely not a thief.'

Mary pointed at the lump; it stood out like a camel hiding behind a lamb.

'Seriously, Joe!'

Joseph looked to the bag, then back to his wife.

'What?'

Mary gave a sigh of exasperation.

'Joe, we don't know this David. Think what could happen to the children.'

Joseph felt as if his wife had slapped him.

'I didn't think, Mary. David said he could save Polykarpos. I believe him and I know I have to help him. He performed a miracle, Mary. David commanded light and wind from his hands as he ran towards the Romans.'

'Really, a miracle, Joe? Are you willing to risk everything for this man you don't know?'

'No. Yes. I don't know, Mary?'

'Well, you had better know, husband. If you tell me to hide this bag and

111

risk everything, then I will do it. Just be sure, because if the Romans kill us all, I will never speak to you again, husband. I mean it. And you can forget about early morning wrestles before the children wake up, there will be none of that either.'

'Yes, Mary,' replied Joseph feeling justifiably reprimanded.

'Well husband, what's it to be?'

Joseph looked at the lump behind the door, picked up the bag and put it at Mary's feet. 'I love you, Mary,' he said and kissed her on the forehead.

'Go,' said Mary, giving Joe a push toward the door. 'I can see it in your face that you want to help this David, just don't get killed.'

'I won't, I promise,' said Joe as he slid through the door.

Mary grasped the calf skin bag to move it somewhere less obvious. It was really heavy. Mary was small, but strong; even so this was more weight than she would normally lift by herself. She dragged the bag toward the door. It could be buried under the goat shit next to her neighbour's home. If the Romans didn't come, she could retrieve it in the morning without anybody being the wiser. As she strained to drag the bag, the strange black buckle, attached to the leather drawstring, caught on the doorframe. She pulled to free it. The buckle let go, sending Mary sprawling on her backside and spilling its contents at her feet. Mary swore, then sat up in wide-eyed surprise.

'Shit Joe, what have we done?'

# CHAPTER TWELVE

DAVID TEST-FIRED HIS WEAPON as he jogged towards the noise. Dust blew along the street, the stunner worked as it should. He counted six soldiers in pursuit of Polykarpos, banging their gladius against shields as they paced forward. If Polykarpos left the cover of the streets for the open desert, those on the outside of the line would see him. The problem was, he was running out of buildings to hide amongst.

David ran the length of the alley until reaching the desert. Once well clear of buildings, he turned at right angles and jogged until in line with the Romans. Only the closest soldier should be able to see him from this position. With luck, he could get very close without being noticed. What worried David was their wooden shields, which may well deflect a shot from the stunner. If they did, the Romans had two pilums each which they could hurl in his direction.

David waited for the line to advance, then moved on his target, stunner up, safety off, finger inside the trigger guard with a two-handed grip. He fell into a rhythm with the shield banging, using the noise to cover the sound of his footfalls. When he was within 10 metres of the outside soldier, the line halted. The Roman turned to line up with his companions and David shot him in the back twice: a double tap. Green light filled the space between buildings, the rush of wind and dust bounced along the alley.

David rushed past the collapsing legionnaire, firing twice more, hitting the torso and buttocks of the next in line. The soldier straightened, shook in a convulsion of rapid nerve pulses and toppled unconscious.

Flying dust further reduced visibility in the alley. The green glow came and went in a blinding flash, shocking the third soldier in line. *It was about to get interesting,* David thought grimly. He had only seconds to act before he lost the advantage. He ran towards the next target, arms extended firing multiple blasts. The first shot bounced off the wall near the soldier's head, showering him with mortar and rock dust. Training and muscle memory kicked in, the legionnaire's shield rose to cover his head and torso, legs and ankles were exposed, the next two blasts were aimed at ground level.

The first struck the alley floor, stone chips and dirt impacted the Roman's feet and legs. It must have stung like hell as the target staggered backwards.

The second shot hit legs full blast, knocking the target off his feet. David heard a skull encased in a metal helmet, hit the ground, bouncing up and down with a sickening thump. Three down.

David knew time was up for his shock tactics when a pilum slid off the wall near his face showering him with stone dust. The soldiers couldn't see him through the dust and darkness in the alley, but there was a chance a weapon thrown in the confined space could find a target. He retreated, found the first turn to his right and ran one street parallel to where the remaining soldiers were rallying into a defensive formation, using their shields to form a wall as they moved along the alley.

David found the next crossroad and lowered himself to the ground to observe the soldiers' approach. The men on the flanks turned to face the side roads as they proceeded. The formation paused, then seeing no obvious threat, moved on. David needed to get behind the shields but didn't fancy tackling three soldiers at once. He could fire as rapidly as he could squeeze the trigger, but the odds of getting three debilitating shots before they hit back was too large.

David looked up. Hit them from above as well as behind, was the answer. Knock one or two down, then change the angle of attack. He moved closer, searching for steps or a ladder to get to the roof tops. Bingo! Two houses on was a set of steps leading to a roof, which David scaled then dropped to his belly and crawled to the edge.

David used his glasses to find Polykarpos. The teacher was huddled against a wall, hiding behind a pile of something warm. Polykarpos had buried himself in the discarded straw and manure from an animal pen.

David watched the Romans using their locked shields as a wall, providing minimum body exposure. With their body armour and shields, it was going to be difficult to get three effective shots. Legs and faces were the only soft target if a single shot take- down was going to work. What David needed was a distraction to break their formation. Searching for something to throw, David rolled over. Something jabbed him in the buttock. Reaching down he found the unmistakable diamond shape of a hydration tablet in his underwear.

Joe saw the flash of green light. How was this David doing this? Who was he really? Green flashed twice more. Joe could feel the wind and dirt swirling out of the alley ahead as he reached the entrance. Flash, flash, flash, green flared bright showing two men on the ground and David, with his arms outstretched and light coming from his hands. A Roman launched something into the air; the green light flashed; the soldier fell as if suddenly dead.

Joe watched David sway as a spear clanged against the wall of Ephraim, the rope -maker's home. It clattered and slid along the ground, coming to a halt at Joe's feet. He looked down in surprise, jumping to avoid being hit. When Joe looked up, David had disappeared into the dust swirling between the buildings. He moved cautiously, risking everything to follow a man he knew nothing about.

Joe stopped as he reached the first Roman on the ground. The man was asleep, not dead. How could this be? Joe moved to the second Roman; this one was also asleep with one leg tucked up behind his back on an impossible angle.

'STOP WHERE YOU ARE!' screamed a voice.

Joe froze. Three Romans were approaching behind raised shields, Mary would never talk to him again. He was a dead man and he knew it.

David needed the legionnaires to pass his position to expose their backs to attack. They were moving with purpose, keeping in formation which could work to his advantage. The shields might protect from a frontal assault, but any shots fired from behind would rebound on the three carrying them. A distraction to break their concentration was the first priority before he exposed his position.

Suddenly, something was different, their pace quickened, the soldier in the centre of the formation raised his pilum above his head into a throwing position.

'STOP WHERE YOU ARE' came the command.

David rose to his knees. Shit, it was Joe. The Romans would kill him the moment they found their friends.

David squeezed the hydration tablet, then threw it as hard as he could. He wasn't usually a very accurate shot with a stone, so he aimed at the centre of the men's backs in the hope he would hit one of the targets. The tablet went high and slightly wide striking the inside of the centre soldier's shield with a *whack,* rebounded off armour, then fell to the ground.

Felix, the senior legionnaire, looked down in surprise at what he thought was a stone thrown from the darkness.

'Halt,' he commanded, 'this might be a trap.'

The soldier on the right swung behind his companions to cover their rear.

'Shit,' said David lying flat on the roof, this was not what he intended. 'What can you see, Titus?'

'Nothing.'

'Check the roofs, there could be a dozen armed bastards waiting to stone us.'

'I can't see anything, Felix.'

'There must be something. Where did this come from then?' asked Felix picking up the hydration tablet. It activated; water bubbled out of what he had assumed was a stone cast from a sling.

'What sort of trickery is this!' Felix exclaimed, dropping the tablet to the ground where it fizzed creating a pool of water.

The Romans broke formation as they backed away from the growing wetness. David shot them rapidly in succession, starting with the furthest on his left, firing twice because of the distance, then once each to the centre and right soldiers, striking each in the buttocks and upper thighs, dropping them to the alley floor. David then stood to scan the surrounding streets. Polykarpos was covered in shit where he had last seen him, Joe was at the entrance of the alley on his knees, there was no other movement on the streets. His night vision picked out faces peering through windows and around the edges of doors. Nobody was leaving the safety of their homes. Good, the fewer witnesses, the less interference with history, the better. God only knew what he may have already done to the timeline.

David slowed to a walk as he approached a pile of manure pushed up against a stable wall.

'You can come out now, Polykarpos. The Romans won't cause us any more trouble for hours.'

Polykarpos stood and shook himself.

'Have you saved my life again David?'

'I don't know about that,' said David helping Polykarpos up, 'I think we saved each other.'

'Perhaps David, perhaps we have.'

Both men grinned, David held onto his companion's hand.

'Thank you, Polykarpos, for everything you have done, but if I were you, I would get the hell out of town and forget you ever met me.'

Polykarpos shook his head.

'No, you have saved my life twice, I must remain at your service, at least for a while longer.'

David wanted to argue, but he needed help and Polykarpos was willing.

'Okay, but very shortly my body is going to need rest, I will fall asleep wherever I am and not be able to wake up for around eight hours. There is nothing I can do about it, so we need to act fast.'

Polykarpos nodded.

'What is it you need me to do?'

'Help me find Adrian. You said he would be taken to a hill somewhere near.'

'The Hill of Kedumim,' Polykarpos gestured to the open desert, 'it is this way.'

David hesitated, 'I assume Adrian will be in a bad way?'

'He would have been tied to a wooden cross and exposed to the sun without water or shade. If he is strong, he may still be alive.'

'Okay, so we free Adrian as fast as possible, provide first aid, then get both of us to a hiding place until tomorrow morning. Can we do that Polykarpos?'

Polykarpos nodded, 'There is a cave, I could carry you there if need be.'

'Will there be a guard at the hill?'

'A soldier will be present to prevent relatives from trying to save the crucified.'

'Will there be water at this place?'

'Only what the guard carries in his water skin.'

'Then I will have to make water, but we need something to put it in.'

'You can make water?'

'If we have to, but don't worry it's not magic, it's just technology.'

'Is this the same as you telling me the Romans will not wake for hours?'

'Pretty much.'

Before Polykarpos could ask how, the sound of running feet approaching, made him turn. David drew his stunner, 'Get behind me.'

Polykarpos did as he was told as David flicked the safety on his weapon then tucked the stunner back into its hiding place.

'It's okay, it's a friend.'

Joe had seen David kneeling on the roof with light and wind coming from his hands. It was like the stories told of angels smiting the wicked from above. He fell to his knees in fear, then David stood, looked all around as if surveying his dominion, before disappearing from the roof. Joe inspected the Romans on the ground, they were asleep just like the others, then turned and ran towards Mary and home before suddenly stopping.

What was he doing? Had he not just witnessed a miracle with David having saved his life? It couldn't be an accident that David had left his bag on the roof of their home and returned to get it back. Could it? Joe turned and ran to find David, not because he wanted to, but because he suddenly knew he had to.

Polykarpos watched the running figure, it was Joseph the carpenter.

'Hello, Joe,' Polykarpos called.

'Polykarpos!' exclaimed Joe. 'You're alive, thank Jehovah.'

'Yes, despite the efforts of the Romans and your old classmates.'

Joe hugged his teacher, 'I am so relieved to see you, but you do stink.'

'I am afraid I do. I suggest you clean yourself off before you go home, Mary wouldn't appreciate you dragging what I am covered in through her kitchen.'

David watched Joe and Polykarpos embrace, overjoyed at their reunion, but time was running out.

'What are you doing here, Joe? I asked you not to follow me, mate.'

Joe dropped to his knees.

'O Great One, please forgive me. I beg you not to smite me, or my family for my disobedience.'

'I don't have time for this, Joe. I need you to go home and stay safe with your family.'

Joe stole a glance at David.

'I am sorry, Great One, if I had recognised you earlier, I would never have broken my promise. I ask for forgiveness.'

David turned to Polykarpos, 'Help me out here, please?'

Polykarpos took his old student's hand.

'Stand up, Joe. Perhaps David can explain who he truly is and put both of our minds at rest.'

Joe got to his feet but kept his eyes downcast.

'Joe, I am a man, just like you, but I come from a place far from here. My people have tools, something we call technology, which might look like magic to you, but it's not. They are just things we use to make life easier, like using your ladder to get on a roof.'

Joe looked unconvinced, so David took off his glasses and passed them to Joe. 'Put these on. It won't hurt, I promise.'

Joe looked up and reluctantly took the glasses.

'It sits over your ears and on your nose and you look through the round bits.'

Joe hesitantly put the glasses on. David touched the frame to activate the night vision.

Joe staggered as the image filled his eyes. He could see the Romans on the ground where he could not see them before and faces at doors and windows peering from houses along the alley. Joe dropped to his knees.

'Please, Great One, I never meant to do any wrong.'

David took the glasses from Joe's face.

'This is just a tool, Joe. It's no different to a saw or a hammer where I come from. It's not magic, it's just technology.'

'I don't understand, I am not worthy to understand.'

David turned to Polykarpos, 'We don't have time for this.'

Polykarpos nodded.

'Perhaps, Joe doesn't need to understand, he just needs to accept you for who you are, to be of help.'

'I don't want to get anybody else involved Polykarpos, Joe has a family to think of.'

'I think Joe's destiny has already set him on a path to join us, plus, if you fall asleep as you say you must, then two sets of arms to carry you to safety would be better than one.'

David had to admit that logistically it made sense.

'Alright, Joe, I am going to ask a favour, and you have every right to refuse if you don't want to do it.' Joe nodded his understanding. 'Would you be available to help Polykarpos and me for the next hour. We are going to look for my cousin on some hill or other.'

'The Hill of Kedumim,' confirmed Polykarpos.

'I won't lie, Joe; it could be dangerous and I need you to promise to run away and not look back if I tell you to.'

Joe nodded again.

'Yes, Great One, I promise to do as you ask.'

'Then the first thing I ask is for you to call me David.'

'David,' repeated Joe.

'Then I will call you Joe, or Joseph if you prefer.'

'Only my mother calls me Joseph, and Mary, when I upset her.'

'Joe it is, then.'

Polykarpos gestured towards the nearby hill, 'Shall we go?'

'Joe, could you find something to hold water in?' David moved his hands to show a rough size. 'Something around this big?'

Joe nodded.

'I have a bucket at the carpentry shop, I can run and get it, then return to the Hill of Kedumim for you, David.'

'Good man, I appreciate the help.'

Joe stood with a grin on his face.

'Off you go then,' said David with a shake of Joe's hand, 'and thank you Joe.'

Joseph took the hint and tore off down the alley.

'Joe was a good student,' said Polykarpos. 'He is a good husband and a good father.'

'Will he be back?'

Polykarpos nodded, 'Joseph of Nazareth is a man of his word. He will be back.'

Dax ended his chase on a rise overlooking Nazareth. His mind and body were feeling the effects of a lack of water and his armour was killing him. *Not that this mattered*, he thought as he stopped to catch his breath. Something must have drawn them back to this village, when all logic should have told them to run anywhere but here.

A flash of green light lit up the sky above the town. It flashed again and again. Something told Dax if he found the source of light, he would also find his quarry.

Maximus had a promise to keep. To kill in battle was one thing, to make men suffer as an example to persuade others to conform, was something less. Maximus didn't like the pettiness of it; it was not honourable.

It had been a strange day. First, there was the attack by a group of local idiots trying to free the Greek school master who had been preaching dissent. Maximus hadn't witnessed the attack, being occupied auditing the local grain store at the time. His men had reported that two fools had leapt off a roof to attack them, with one, an unarmed Jew called David, knocking three of his young soldiers senseless before he was captured.

Then there was the Jew, Adrian, who talked in ridiculous riddles, then seemed to vanish in a green light. His young soldiers had been crying about witchcraft and magic. Maximus had needed to slap one to regain order. It was none of these things, it was a trick, a potion the Jews had slipped into their water or the wine. These things could make you imagine sights and sounds that were not real.

Maximus had once eaten mushrooms in Gaul which had done the same thing. The chieftain who served him the meal, swore it was the work of forest spirits. Maximus found removing the chieftain's head and sticking it on a pole in the middle of the village had vanquished these so-called spirits. If he ever came across this Adrian again, he would receive the same treatment.

Maximus found the sentry on the Hill of Kedumim awake and alert. He snapped to attention as the Centurio approached.

'Any trouble, soldier?'

'No, Centurio. The prisoners are all still alive, but they have been quiet since sundown.'

Maximus nodded; he wasn't expecting trouble, all the local troublemakers were here on the hill waiting to die.

'Lend me your spear, soldier, I will stand your guard and wait for your relief.'

The young legionnaire did as he was bid. It had been a long day and he was looking forward to bread, cheese and a beer, along with an early night.

'Remind your relief to be on time lad, my generosity only stretches so far.'

'Yes, Centurio,' replied the young soldier as he made his way down the hill.

Maximus hefted the weapon. The blade was sharp, the shaft well-balanced and the suffering had gone on long enough. He walked to the first pole. It was leaning on an angle, the face of its occupant pointing directly into the sky. Maximus wondered if the sun had already blinded the man.

Maximus tapped the pole.

'Are you alive, Jew?' Maximus didn't want to spear a man who had already gone to meet their god.

'Hello? Is that you Uncle Phillip?'

'No.'

'Um, is it Ephraim the rope -maker? You sound like Ephraim.'

Maximus looked at the form on the cross, it was a young voice.

'No, it's not Ephraim.'

'Are you sure?'

'Yes.'

'Peter, who do you think it sounds like?'

'It's the centurio come to stab us all to death, you idiot.'

'No, I don't think it is. It might be Silas from the grain store. He is very good at doing voices.'

'It's not bloody Silas, John.'

Maximus looked to the next crucifix; the angry one, named Peter, was glaring at him.

'Go on Roman, do as you promised. Just stab John first if you really want to end our suffering by shutting him the hell up.'

'As you wish.' Maximus raised the spear aiming the blade just below John's ribs. It would pierce his heart, stopping it instantly. Maximus drew back the blade, but as it began to thrust upward, a bright, green flash of light struck him full in the back.

David called Adrian's name as he ran from cross to cross.

'Your cousin is not here; these men are all from my school. There is Peter, James the son of Alphaeus, John, Andrew, Bartholomew, James the son of Zebedee, Judas and Thaddeus.' Polykarpos moved along the line of crosses. 'See, here is Matthew, Phillip and Thomas.

David stopped running; Adrian had not been crucified. He picked up Maximus' spear, then used it to cut the ropes on Peter's arms. Peter toppled forward. David held him off the ground while Polykarpos cut his feet free.

'Thank you,' said Peter, as he gripped Polykarpos by the hand. 'It is good that you are still alive Master Polykarpos.'

'I am glad to see you alive as well, my friend.'

'How?'

'It was David that saved us, he is not what he first appears. He might be the one we have been waiting for.'

Peter watched David move from cross to cross, cutting down his friends. He was taller than most, clean-shaven like a Roman but that was all that looked different.

Peter looked at the unconscious centurio lying in the dirt.

'How?'

'David calls it technology; he claims it is a tool no different than a saw or a hammer. If we had such tools, we could throw the Romans out of Judea and Galilee.'

'Why didn't he kill the Roman?'

'Where David comes from, they punish the guilty, but do not take life. Not even the lives of thieves or murderers.'

Peter pondered this.

'What does he want? Why is he helping us?'

'David is seeking to capture two criminals from his land and bring them to justice, his helping us is purely accidental.'

'And he doesn't want them dead? These criminals he is chasing?'

'No, David has made it clear he is to do no harm while he is in Galilee.'

'Do you believe him?'

'Yes, he is a man of his word. He has saved my life twice and has asked for nothing other than I act as his guide in return.'

'Do you trust him, Polykarpos? It's one thing to believe a man is telling the truth when he has no need to lie, another to trust a man without reservation'

'I think that I must. David may have a great part to play in the story of our people and he doesn't even suspect it.'

Joe ran to Isaac's carpentry shop, found the bucket, tucked it under his arm and rushed out to the street where he came face to face with Mary.

'Mary!'

'Joe,' replied Mary, blocking her husband.

'What are you doing on the street? It's too dangerous.'

'I need you to put that thing down Joe and come home.'

'What?'

'Joe, Joseph. I need you to listen to me, to think about your children and do as I ask.'

'Mary?'

'I saw what was in the bag, Joe. I went to hide it and I tripped and it spilled on the ground right outside our door.'

'No, Mary,' said Joe horrified, 'you didn't take anything from the bag, did you?'

Mary opened her hand to reveal gold and silver coins.

'He is a thief; he has to be. No ordinary person would have this much gold and silver. These are Roman coins, not shekels. If we are caught with this, we are all dead.'

Joe felt a flood of relief.

'Thank Jehovah, this is only money, Mary. I thought that you might have found one of David's technologies.'

'Only money, Joe?! There is enough to buy half the houses in Nazareth and have some left over to buy a cow, a dozen sheep, two goats and a donkey to pull a cart. We could have a pile of shit as high as the granary with what it could buy.'

'I love you, Mary, my wife.'

'What?'

'I want you to go home and hide the bag as David asked, then kiss our children and go to bed. I don't care what noises you hear, or what you see, just don't go outside until I get home.'

'What?'

'You are wrong about David; I think he is not a man; I think he is something else in disguise.'

'Joe, he is a thief, a trickster. Look what is in this bag he wants us to hide. He will get us killed.'

'David saved my life, Mary. The Romans were going to kill me outside of Ephraim the rope-maker's house. I saw it in their eyes, they were going to shove a spear right through my body. Then David raised his hands,' Joe extended his arms and clasped his hands together in front of his body, 'and light and wind came and the Romans dropped to the ground asleep. It was a miracle, Mary. I witnessed a miracle right outside Ephraim's house.'

'A miracle, Joe? David is a thief; he is tricking you.'

'No, Mary, he is not a thief. David has this thing; it's like a mask you put over your eyes, he put it on my face and it turned night into day, I swear it. I could see people in the dark hiding in their homes as if I was standing at their doors.'

'Joe, you're talking nonsense, no man can turn night into day. It has to be a trick with a mirror and a lamp, the sort of thing Levi does with his magic show, it can look real but it's just a trick. This David is a thief with lots of tricks. Miracles are just stories told by the priests to make us pay their wages. You've heard it before, believe in Jehovah and pay his messengers on earth or be forever damned. You don't see any of the priests going hungry.'

'What about our son? Wasn't it a miracle that you became pregnant when we had never lain together as man and wife, not even once? You told me the pregnancy was a miracle, I believed it. I believed you.'

Mary didn't know what to say.

'Isn't our oldest son a miracle?'

'Yes Joe, our son was, and is, a miracle,' replied Mary quietly.

'Then you have to believe me when I tell you that I witnessed a miracle.'

Mary couldn't see how she could say anything else.

'If you tell me you witnessed a miracle, then I believe you. I have always believed in you as a good and honest man.'

'I love you, Mary, but I have to do as David asked. He said he needed my bucket and I am going to bring it to him.'

'Why?'

'David said he could make water and he needed something to hold it in.'

'David said he can make water?'

'He said he needed a bucket about so big.' Joe moved his hands to show a size.

'I assume he is not talking about, you know,' Mary spread her legs and mimed a male urinating, 'make water Joe.'

'I don't think that's what he means, not for a bucket this big.'

'It could be another trick.'

'No, it will be a miracle. One of David's technologies.'

Mary was silent. Joe believed in the good in everybody, maybe today it was going to get him killed. She sighed and touched the face of her love.

'Come home, Joe.'

'Mary, I love you, but I can't.' Joe took his wooden bucket and ran toward the Hill of Kedumim.

Dax counted 16 men, some on the ground, some tied to the crosses and one was using a spear to cut them down. One was a centurio lying face first in the dirt.

He edged closer, recognising the old man who was talking with a Jew on the ground, an easy target from this distance. The young warrior was the one using the cavalry spear, he had his back turned, another easy target.

Dax had collected spears from the soldiers he found lying on the streets of Nazareth. He had thought them to be dead, but they were asleep and he could not wake them. Dax drank their water, ate their bread, collected four spears and headed up the hill to where he saw the green light flash.

Dax shuffled forward on his knees to reduce the range; a pilum would not necessarily kill, but it would make it easier for him to finish the job with his gladius. He would take their heads and present them to his centurio in the hope of being forgiven. His right arm drew back, the pilum extended behind his body, his left arm stretched toward the target to aim the strike and balance his body. Dax lined up the young one, steadied his breath to launch the weapon.

'David, I have it,' came a breathless call from behind. Dax swung toward the noise. Joe's bucket collided with the back of his neck and everything went black.

'Sorry, I didn't see you,' apologised Joe.

David answered Joe's call, 'Bring it here please, Joe.'

Joe hesitated, looked at Dax, then ran to David.

'Are you alright?' asked David.

Joe nodded and held up the bucket. David placed it on the ground, squeezed a hydration tablet and dropped it in the bucket then, seconds later, passed the bucket back to Joe.

'Can you make sure all of the men drink please, Joe? When the bucket is empty, bring it back and I will make some more.'

Joe's eyes widened in joy at witnessing another miracle. Any doubt he might have felt about David, evaporated as fast as the bucket had filled.

'Yes, David,' said Joe in a whisper.

'You are a good man to know,' said David putting a hand on Joe's shoulder, he felt blessed by the touch. If only Mary could have witnessed what he had just seen, it was a story for the whole family, one he knew his oldest son would just love to hear.

David was suddenly incredibly tired; the effects of the stimulant were almost gone. He stumbled to Polykarpos and dropped to the ground.

'I am done, Polykarpos. I'm about to fall asleep and won't be able to wake until morning.'

Polykarpos reached out to steady David.

'Peter and I will get you to the cave and watch over you, it is the least we can do for saving so many lives.'

'Just doing my job,' slurred David, struggling to keep his eyes open.

'Peter has news of your cousin, he was not killed, he vanished in a flash of green light.'

Peter nodded. 'He disappeared like an angel of Jehovah in the scriptures.'

'You can thank the brilliant work of my father for that,' murmured David as he slid into darkness.

'Polykarpos, did this David just say he was the son of Jehovah?'

# CHAPTER THIRTEEN

EMIL DISCONNECTED HIMSELF FROM the device. If what Adrian remembered was true, David was injured and alone and no longer had a recall device. What a bloody mess.

'Did it make sense, Uncle Emil? I did my best to remember everything. I didn't exactly cover myself in glory during the scuffle, I'm afraid. By the time I got myself sorted, it was all over. Then I tried to explain to the officer in charge, but as you saw, it didn't go well. Still, I did manage to find Will Thomas. He is family and as Will said, you will do anything for your family, because they are your family, and so you must.'

Emil didn't have a choice; he would have to contact Dwight and tell him what had happened.

'We need to put together a rescue plan, gather supplies and such like, and we will need currency, I gather it is fairly important,' added Adrian.

Emil nodded. 'Yes, we will need money, as well as rations, first aid supplies and additional *Sainters*, as I gather, we are now calling them. And weapons.'

'Weapons?'

'Yes, something to disable a threat as quickly as possible.'

Adrian smiled. 'It does sound exciting when you say it like that.'

'This is not a game. David could die, you could die if I send you back.'

'Oh, I am going back. I promised David, and I promised Will.'

Emil shook his head. What choice did he have? If he went through the *Cabinet*, who would keep Gerald from screwing everything up? It was unrealistic to expect Adrian to put himself between the wishes of his father and loyalty to his uncle and cousin.

'Alright, but I need technical assistance with the *Cabinet* and you are going to need a partner. The one advantage we have, is that time in the past is able to be paused from our perspective. The disadvantage is that time here is ticking away. Come tomorrow, the warehouse will be full of Gerald's people and we can't be here if we are to keep this secret.'

'We're not going to tell Father?'

'We can't, you do understand that, Adrian?'

Adrian nodded.

'Yes, I understand, but Father wouldn't, which is why we can't tell him.'

Emil had to admit that perhaps he had underestimated Adrian.

'William Thomas is the man I choose as my assistant. He struck me as the sort of chap you would like as a wing man when the chips are down.'

'He was a teenager when you met him, Adrian. He could have grown up to be homicidal criminal, for all we know, he might not have even lived to be an adult.'

'I know what I saw and I saw a true and dependable Thomas. I have met thousands of people working front of house for the business, you get to see personality types, how they behave, how they react when things go wrong. Some people are just the wrong type of chap, some are the right type. I believe William Thomas is the right type.'

'You will be betting yours and David's life on him. Are you prepared to risk everything on a 14-year-old boy you have only met once in your life?'

Adrian looked from his uncle to the *Cabinet*.

'He wasn't always 14, Uncle Emil. I can investigate his life and see what sort of a chap he grew into.'

Emil shook his head. Perhaps this William Thomas could be the dependable objective -focused team member to send with Adrian. People from the 20th century had a reputation for sturdiness, and when called upon, the ability to use force or guile to survive. These were the attributes that David had and Adrian sadly lacked. *Send a David to rescue a David*, he thought.

'You can make the final decision, Uncle Emil, conduct a job interview, ask Will to give an example of the time he had to sort out a conflict between work colleagues, you know the usual silly questions people ask. I have no idea why; you might as well just say make up a story that makes you look good, so I can tick it off the selection criteria.'

Emil nodded.

'Dwight would have to agree, as well as the two of us.'

'You are going to tell Uncle Dwight?'

'Dwight is the only other person I feel we can safely involve, though he is just likely to try and go through the *Cabinet* himself to find David.'

'He can't though, can he? That's why David made contact with me, why we went through the *Cabinet* together, David needed my access to the building?'

Emil nodded. Adrian was smarter than everybody assumed.

'Yes, that's right, no one or two of us can use the *Cabinet* without the third.'

Adrian stood.

'Then it's settled. I will research the life of Will Thomas and you will talk with Uncle Dwight to sort out the thingies we will need to take with us, which sounds like a plan.'

'It sounds like a potential disaster.'

'What choice do we have, Uncle Emil? As you said, we are running out of time, and besides, a chap is very much looking forward to the adventure.'

# CHAPTER FOURTEEN

WILL LAY ON THE lounge, pretending to watch the television while having a moment of reflection. Following the *incident*, as his mother called the events in his 14th year, things had basically turned to shit. First, Adrian appeared and destroyed his bedroom. Will wasn't sure if this really happened or he imagined it, then his parents accidentally put him in the clutches of Doctor Rodney Elliot.

Will spent two months under Doc Elliot's supervision, forced to re-enact that night over and over again in a mock-up of his bedroom in the hospital ward. Doc Elliot played the part of Adrian, carried into the room with arms extended as if on a cross to the soundtrack of *Jesus Christ Superstar*. There was a wind machine and lighting effects, with nurses acting as stagehands, upending his bed, throwing clothes and comic books in the air to replicate the carnage. Mary had been made to participate under the threat of Will being forced to undergo electric shock treatment to reset his brain. She played the game and waited it out, just as Margaret and Janice had told her to.

Mary would wait outside the bedroom, knock to enter, sit on the bed, hug her son and explain her absence, then leave before Doctor Elliot entered to play the role of Will's conscience in the guise of Adrian, demanding that Will confess the secret he was keeping from his parents. Between re-enactments, Will had sessions with Doc Elliot in his office. These were more stressful than the weekly pantomime. Will's parents had raised him to always tell the truth, so he did, repeating the story of Adrian and his visit over and over again. Doc Elliot accused him of lying, of hiding a secret and questioned if his father had done something to make him feel sad, or frightened. Will was having none of this; his father was the best bloke in the world.

To Will's embarrassment, Doc Elliot asked how he felt about girls. Yes, Will liked girls, no, he didn't have the same feelings about boys, not even secretly. No, that was not why he smashed up his room. No, he was not acting out in frustration because he couldn't tell his parents the truth. Talking with Doc Elliot made him sad, that was a truth. It also made him ashamed of what he was doing to his parents.

Eventually, Will gave in and told the lie, he had smashed up his room and invented Adrian to cover it up. Doc Elliot smiled, then accused him of lying for not telling the real truth. Will didn't know what Rodney Elliot wanted to hear. Not the truth, that was obvious.

Will's Dad, Colin, locked horns with the doctor in a battle of wills, which was exactly what Doc Elliot wanted to happen. For Elliot it was entertainment, for Colin Thomas it was infuriatingly frustrating. With the law on the doctor's side, Colin was forced to comply, under the threat of legal action.

In the end, it was the friendship of Tracy Wilson that rescued Will. Tracy was appalled with what Mary confided to her and used Charlene's visits with Doctor Brown, to force him to confront what his fellow physician was doing. Doc Brown witnessed one of Will's re-enactment sessions, standing beside Colin, watching via a closed-circuit television relay under the watchful eye of two huge hospital orderlies. Doc Brown apologised, then sent for the hospital administrator to witness what would fill the front-pages of newspapers if he didn't act and end Rodney Elliot's game. Will was discharged that afternoon and Tracy received the biggest hug from Will's parents one could imagine.

Thinking back, while watching the Countdown Christmas music special, Will turned red with embarrassment and anger.

Mary poked her head into the room.

'William, could you take the vegetable scraps down to the chook house? And remind Brian to change, Bruce and Beryl will be here any minute.'

Mary was in her annual flap over Uncle Bruce and Aunt Beryl coming for dinner on Christmas Eve. She had spent the day baking, preparing the roast lamb and scrubbing the house from top to bottom, even though it had been spotless.

Colin wasn't home from work yet. Will knew his dad would be hoping to miss the grand entrance of his in-laws. Uncle Bruce had a big mouth, Aunty Beryl, a big bum and Will knew his dad had to fight hard not let them know how he felt when they really started to annoy him.

'Okay, Mum,' said Will, happy for the distraction. 'I'll feed the chooks and tell Brian to get changed.'

Mary smiled. William always did what was asked and never complained. She loved both her sons, but William was definitely the easier of the boys to live with.

Will smiled back at his mother. It was way too little for what she deserved, after what his parents had gone through for him. Even before Will returned from hospital, rumours had done the rounds. Most of what people said was ridiculous, but when his family tried to set the record straight, it just seemed to make it worse. The general consensus of the rumours was that Will had smashed up the Thomas home in a fit of deviant sexual frustration and Mary found him naked, *doing it* to pictures from a pornographic magazine. It had been confirmed, by people in the know, that he couldn't be stopped until the police handcuffed his arms behind his back.

How could you fight this? How would telling people what actually happened, make things any better? It couldn't, so the Thomas family refused to talk about it and life settled to a different form of normality. As Dad said, 'It's not what people do to you, but how you react which is the measure of the strength of a person.'

The church community, hearing the stories, were either drawn to Mary with their good books in hand, to provide solace, comfort and above all, moral advice, or they shunned her as the parent who raised a deviate miscreant who was but a small step away from worshipping Satan. Mary was appalled by the behaviour of both sides of the moral divide and thought of locking the whole lot out of her home as a sign of solidarity with her son. Colin had been the voice of reason.

'Let it go,' he had said, 'Eventually there will be somebody else's life to poke around in, and they will lose interest.'

Colin had been right, but it took a toll on Mary's faith. Will was powerless to fight the tide of condemnation and let it crash about him until the outrage and hatred subsided into a murmur of disgust at his presence. At least when they focused on him, they tended to leave his family alone. Will learnt quickly that people were quick to judge without knowing the facts, which even he questioned as it all seemed so ridiculous, apart from his time in hell spent with Doc Elliot, who was an absolute bloody wanker. Then thinking of the W word made him feel nauseous. W, the letter W, was what people called him behind his back. Sometimes it meant *weirdo*, sometimes it meant *wrong*, as in he was just wrong as a person. Mostly it meant *wanker*, in the hobby sense.

To Will, it was simply his fault, he could never make it up to his family. What he could do was be a good son and brother. It was a tiny thing, but at least it was something.

Will went to his bedroom. Brian was lying on his bed reading a comic, still in the same clothes he had been wearing all day.

'Mum wants you to get changed, Uncle Bruce and Aunt Beryl will be here in a minute.'

Brian ignored his brother.

'For once, how about stop being a drop kick and help a bit. Mum's stressed enough without you doing bugger all to help.'

'You can bugger off *W*, I don't take orders from you.'

Will stared at Brian. It no longer hurt when strangers abusively called him *W*, it had become normal, like breathing. Having your brother do it was entirely different.

'What did you call me you shit head?'

'You heard me, *W*. You're the biggest *W* in the world and can't tell me what to do.'

Will closed his fists in frustration. He felt like slapping Brian, but he couldn't, just like everything else he couldn't do anymore.

He couldn't play football. Nobody on his team would pass him the ball and the other teams double and triple tackled him, sinking in elbows and knees whenever they could. It got so bad, the coach had to keep him on the bench because he had become focus of the game rather than playing the game itself.

Will and Colin talked about it and Will decided to quit playing. He didn't give up because of what was happening to himself, but because of what was happening to the people Will thought of as mates. If being on the footy team was turning them into bad people, then that was unacceptable. Will loved the game, but he would never be able to play again.

While losing his mates was devastating, Will didn't even want to think about girls. None of them wanted to be seen talking to Will, much less dance with him at the school social. His mate Gary still talked with him, but not if there were girls nearby. It was too big a risk.

'Fuck you, Brian. Mum can just sort you out herself.'

'Fuck you, *W*, with knobs on,' replied Brian giving his brother a two-handed double finger salute. 'I wish you were dead, then at least the rest of us could have a normal life.'

And there it was, right there in those few words spoken by his own brother. Will was the problem, not the rest of the world. He couldn't argue, because it was what he knew to be true.

Will walked the concrete path that led to the chicken enclosure at the back fence. He wasn't thinking, he was just doing. As he trundled along, music drifted across the neighbour's fence. The Sullivans had a window open to let some cool air in on a hot summer night. Countdown was still on, Molly Meldrum, the host of the national institution was introducing Kate Bush singing Babushka. Will liked the way Kate danced, nobody called her names for being different. He stopped to listen, it was getting dark and he didn't think anybody would see him standing in his back yard. A light came on in the Sullivan's house, the curtains were open. Mrs Sullivan, who at age 25, insisted that Will and Brian call her Wendy, entered the room with her two-year-old daughter Skye on her hip.

Will liked Wendy, she was friendly and funny, she was also pretty without being up herself. Wendy always waved and talked to Will down the street which made him feel normal, she didn't give a stuff what people said about him.

Wendy sat Skye on a bed to dress her in pyjamas then started to dance to the music. Will hadn't expected this, he knew he shouldn't watch but Wendy was just so good at it.

There was a free-standing coat- rack in the room and Wendy grabbed hold of it with one hand, mimicking the swing and sway of Kate Bush in the music video, pretending the hat stand was the double bass used as a prop in Babushka. Wendy was laughing, Skye was laughing and Will couldn't help but smile. It was a moment of pure joy and Will just wanted to feel some of the warmth, if just for a moment.

Feeling happier than he had in ages, Will started to walk away, then Wendy dropped the skirt she was wearing and kept on dancing. Will froze to the spot, mouth open, he knew it was wrong to watch but his legs wouldn't move. He tried to walk away, but Wendy kept dancing to Kate, right there over the fence.

'No,' he said out loud and turned away because it was the right thing.

'What are you doing?'

Will spun around in surprise at the voice of his Auntie Beryl.

'Nothing, Aunt Beryl, nothing.'

Beryl looked at her nephew, then to the light coming from the window next door. Wendy was in the midst of putting on a pair of jeans, she had her back turned and had finished dancing. The light went out and Wendy walked from the room holding Skye by the hand.

'What have you done?'

'It was an accident; I didn't know Mrs Sullivan was going to...' Will trailed off in embarrassment. 'It's not my fault, the music was playing and she started to dance, like Kate Bush and I...'

'William, don't even think about trying to shift the blame for this. I think you are a dirty little pervert, yes that's what you are. It's not just your mother and father who have suffered because of your behaviour, Bruce and I have been affected by it as well. It may prevent your uncle from getting his next promotion at the bank, did you know that? Did you even think about it before you started on this horrible little obscene obsession of yours? It's disgusting, William, there I have said it, and I am not sorry.'

Will knew he had done nothing wrong, that was the frustrating thing, but he couldn't do anything about it.

'Please don't tell Mum,' Will said finally. 'She doesn't deserve to be hurt anymore.'

'You should have thought of that William, you should have controlled yourself like a decent human being. If you were a dog, I would have you fixed, straight down to the vet you would go, and then see how you behave.'

'I am not a pervert, Aunt Beryl. I didn't plan it, it just happened,' said Will getting angry. 'It was an accident; I was just in the wrong place at the wrong time.'

'An accident!'

'Yes, it was an accident, Aunt Beryl, I swear it was.'

'It might be an accident that you were out here when that woman next door...'

'Mrs Sullivan.'

'When Mrs Sullivan was taking her clothes off, but you shouldn't have been watching her. It was disgusting William, if you keep up this behaviour you will end up in jail where all the perverts and homosexual left wing communist sorts go, mark my words you will.'

Will didn't know how to respond. What could he say that would make any difference?

'I will have to tell your father. There is no choice in the matter if you are ever going to stop this sort of behaviour. My parents would have used the strap if any of my brothers behaved the way you do and they would have deserved it.'

Will thought about his father. He would hear him out then he would decide what to do. Dad would understand, Mum would just be hurt again.

'You're right Aunt Beryl, you should tell Dad. I deserve to be punished if I had done something wrong, but I haven't. You are just over -reacting for the sake of it, just like the rest of them. William Thomas is a pervert, William Thomas should be locked up because he is crazy, William Thomas is evil, I am none of those things, Aunt Beryl. I never have been and you can't make me believe I am. So go ahead and tell my dad, I can live with myself, can you?'

Beryl was enraged.

'If Bruce heard you speaking to me like that, he would box your ears. Yes, I will tell your father and you will be punished.' Then a light went on in her eyes. 'However, I think you should apologise to Mrs Sullivan first. It can be a lesson in humility.'

Will was horrified. If he had to tell Wendy he had been watching her undress like a pervert peering through her window, their friendship would be over and Will would be even more alone. Then Will thought of what it would do to his mother's friendship with the Sullivans. He almost wept in frustration at the thought.

'William, you are going to march next door and apologise to Mrs Sullivan, then you are going to tell your parents what you have done. Then you will apologise to me, and your Uncle Bruce, and God help you if you don't do exactly what I say.'

'You can't make me, Aunt Beryl, you can tell my dad, I agree to that but not to anything else. It's up to my parents to decide if I have done something wrong, not you.'

'You rude arrogant lout, William Thomas. You are worse than a pervert, you are bad all the way through. You deserve to be sent away to a home for delinquents.'

'And you have a fat arse, Aunt Beryl. You're a rude woman who thinks she is better than everybody else just because your husband works in a bank.' Will immediately wished he hadn't said what he was thinking. It was the truth, but what good had telling the truth done him in the last two years.

Beryl clutched her chest as if having a heart attack.

'How dare you speak to me like that! I'll call the police and report you for being a dirty pervert spying on women getting undressed in their own homes. How do you think that will go down with your reputation? They will lock you up with all the other perverts.'

Will glared at his aunt, she glared back.

*Shit*, Will thought, *Aunt Beryl was likely to do what she said out of spite.* He didn't care about himself; he was thinking of his family.

'Okay then, I am up for it if you are.'

'You haven't the guts,' spat Beryl.

'It's this way,' said Will storming off, Beryl hurried along behind, pushing

Will in the back as if she was the one forcing him to move. Will wanted to grab her arm to stop her but he couldn't. Instead, he ran to make her hurry, this seemed to infuriate her more.

Will stood at the front door of the Sullivan's home contemplating what to say, until the pokes in his back forced him to ring the doorbell. The chime echoed, the porch light flicked on and the door was opened by Wendy, eating chicken leg, with Skye sitting on her hip.

'Hi Will, Merry Christmas,' said Wendy with a happy smile before noticing Beryl, 'Hello?'

'Hello, Mrs Sullivan, I am William's Aunt, Mrs Caruthers. You might know my husband; he is the local branch manager of the Adelaide Bank.'

'We don't bank with them, but I have heard of your husband.'

'I thought you might have; he is an important man in business circles.'

'Yes, I have been told he is bit full of himself and his own self-importance.'

Beryl glowered at the description but held it together. She was here to humiliate her nephew, not to get into an argument with this obviously rude woman.

'We are here on a serious matter, Mrs Sullivan. My nephew has something to tell you. I apologise for what he is about to say, but it is of such grave concern that it cannot wait.'

Wendy shifted her gaze.

'Is there something wrong, Will?'

Will shook his head.

'It can't be that bad.'

'I saw you. I saw you through your bedroom window when you were dancing.'

Wendy looked at Will's aunt and saw the triumph on her face, she was here to embarrass Will and enjoy his humiliation.

'What happened?'

Will looked at Wendy with a tear just beginning to form in one eye.

'I'm sorry, Wendy; I didn't mean for it to happen. I was walking in the yard, I could hear Kate Bush singing, I stopped to listen and then you turned your light on. I looked over and...'

'It's me that needs to apologise Will, I couldn't help myself.' Wendy looked over Will's head, 'I am sorry; I can see how Will could get upset, I practically destroyed Kate's choreography.'

'That is not why we are here, Mrs Sullivan. We are here because my nephew was spying on you while you were disrobing. It's the act of a deviate and he should be held to account for what he has done.'

'Sorry, who are you?'

'Mrs Bruce Caruthers is my name, Mrs Sullivan.'

Wendy handed Will the partly chewed drumstick, then extended her hand to Beryl.

'Nice to meet you. It's not often you meet a woman named Bruce. I like the way you own it; it suits you.'

'My husband's name is Bruce, Mrs Sullivan.'

'That must get confusing, you both being called Bruce.'

Beryl glared hatred at Wendy, but before she could clarify that this was the socially correct way to be addressed, Wendy had turned her attention back to Will.

'Was I really that bad?'

'No, you were great.'

'Did I upset you?'

'No, I just wasn't expecting it to happen. When you took your skirt off, I had to walk away. I didn't want to be a perv, I wouldn't do that to you.'

Wendy knew Will was telling the truth, he had been through hell and she wasn't about to add to his misery.'

'I believe you, Will.'

'Thank you, Wendy.'

'No. This is unacceptable, Mrs Sullivan. If we don't act, he will continue down the path of deviance that he is on.'

Wendy eyed Beryl with disgust. 'Will, did you see my boobs?'

'No.'

'Did you see my bum?'

'No.'

'Are my undies any more revealing than the bathers I wore when we went to the beach?'

'No, I don't think so?'

'Right, that's settled then. Nothing bad or wrong happened other than I forgot to close the curtains. Bruce, I promise not to do it again, just in case I scare the cows and they stop giving milk. Are you okay with that Will?'

'Yes, Wendy.'

'Good, then I will get back to my dinner, I might even throw Kate on the stereo later and do some dancing with my husband. If I do, I solemnly swear to keep the curtains shut just in case I cause a riot or the fall of moral standards in the Mount.'

Will beamed at Wendy and mouthed a 'thank you'.

'Nice to meet you Bruce, send a Merry Christmas to Mary and Colin and Brian for me, Will.' With that Wendy Sullivan closed the front door to her house and turned off the light.

'Unacceptable. That woman has no moral standards.'

Will loved Wendy even more now, the way she stared Aunt Beryl down and put her in her box was possibly the highlight of his year. Will had no fear of what Aunt Beryl could do now. *Please tell Dad*, he thought. Then let him talk with Wendy and it would all be sorted.

'William, I want you to go to the lounge room and wait there. I am going to the kitchen to talk with your parents. I make no apologies for what is about to happen, you have brought this on yourself.'

Will nodded in reply. What else could he do? He would sit on the lounge and stare at the Christmas tree covered in its plastic balls and tinsel with the brightly wrapped presents under it, waiting for tomorrow morning. It was all very peaceful just sitting there, then it happened again.

# CHAPTER FIFTEEN

THE NEEDLES ON THE Christmas tree shook and the baubles rattled in a breeze. Will looked at the doors and windows, they were shut. An awful feeling of premonition hit him. Will tried to stand, to brace for what he knew was coming, but he was too late. First came the burst of light, fluorescent green rather than dull like nature, followed a micro- second later by the pressure wave which burst across the room, throwing everything into disarray. Will watched his arms and legs fly up and away as he and the lounge were propelled across the room.

Something red materialised in front of the old fireplace, which now housed a smoke-stained glass fronted oil heater. Colours erupted from the green of the Christmas tree, which levitated and rotated at speed flinging decorations to all corners of the room.

Will's journey ended when the brown vinyl lounge struck the wall, flipped in the air and landed across the front door entrance. Will felt pain as his left arm smacked into the wooden frame of the door. Just like the last time, he felt his brain register.

Green light flashed twice more and the room returned to still silence as suddenly as it had erupted into motion.

'Shit!' said Will knowing what must come next.

'Will, is that you over there under the furniture?' It was the same voice; friendly, polite, apologetic and smiling at the same time. 'Sorry for the lack of notice, I would have given you a call, but unfortunately the only option was to just call around and hope you were at home.'

Will pushed against the lounge to wriggle out through a gap; the room was a bigger mess than he could have imagined. Wrapped Christmas presents had been torn apart and their contents spread across the room, along with the family photos from the mantel above the old fireplace, their glass and frames scattered and broken.

Adrian saw Will's head emerge, pulled down the false beard covering his face and grinned in delight.

'It's wonderful to see you, William. My, you have grown.'

Will looked up from the carnage.

'Why are you dressed as Santa Claus?'

'It is rather eye catching,' beamed Adrian twisting in a half pirouette to highlight his costume. 'When I saw it in the *Cabinet's* database, I just couldn't resist. Loved the colour, and it's a perfect disguise given the time of year. Plus, it adds a level of dignity, and I would have thought, trustworthiness to my appearance.'

Will shook his head, it was ridiculous, but Adrian was deadly serious.

'WHAT'S GOING ON IN THERE?' came the unmistakable baritone voice of Uncle Bruce from behind the door leading from the lounge room.

'Crap,' said Will, wriggling to get free.

'Who's that?' asked Adrian, letting go of his false beard.

'It's Uncle Bruce,' groaned Will.

'He doesn't sound very friendly.'

'You don't know the half of it. He has his head so far up his bum, it's not funny. If he wasn't Mum's brother, I doubt Mum or Dad would even to talk to him.'

'He has what?'

'Can you give me a hand?' asked Will struggling to free himself.

Before Adrian could react, the door shook and rattled. The Christmas tree lay hard up against the door, holding it closed. Bruce was on the other side, puffing in indignation at the boy daring to bar his passage.

'OPEN THE DOOR, BOY. Do what I say or you will rue the consequences.'

Adrian grasped Will's outstretched hand.

'He isn't the violent type, is he?'

'Dad reckons Uncle Bruce likes to throw his weight about because he is making up for the small size of his thing and suffering from an enlarged sense of self-importance.'

Adrian looked confused. Will wiggled his index finger, then pointed at his crotch, Adrian frowned at the thought.

'Dad reckons it's a bit like buying a red Monaro rather than a beige Kingswood as the family car. It's not particularly practical, but it makes him feel better about being sold short as a bloke. Dad says it's what you do and how you behave that's important as to what sort of a bloke you are, not the size of your dick.'

Adrian nodded, immediately regretting not bringing his notebook. Will wriggled free of the lounge, then half fell over as he regained his feet.

'You really have shot up since I saw you last, it suits you,' said Adrian surprised at the change.

Will didn't know how to react; it seemed an odd thing to talk about for a self-conscious 16-year-old, especially to Santa.

The door rattled again.

'Open the bloody door boy, my patience is wearing thin.'

'Is he always that assertive?'

Will looked at the door.

'If Uncle Bruce could meet you, they will finally have to believe me.'

Will had tried to talk to people, to explain. That hadn't worked so he had followed the advice of his dad and simply laid low. Time, Colin had explained, healed most wounds. In time, most things could be forgotten, or at least allowed to fade in people's minds. But now, Adrian was here as proof that he had been telling the truth.

Adrian took a reluctant step in front of Will.

'I'm sorry, but I don't think that's a good idea.'

'No, you can't just turn up and expect me not to tell anybody.' Will pointed to the destruction in the room. 'I am not going to be blamed for this again.'

'I am very sorry Will, but there are things, deadly serious and dangerous things you need to know. Firstly, you were right, I was a dupe in a far larger adventure than even I could have imagined.'

'What?'

'When we last spoke, you asked if David was chasing down a time travelling villain.'

'I don't remember that.'

'Well, you did ask, and you were correct. David was pursuing two criminals in the past.'

'Why should I care, Adrian? Have you any idea what you have done to my family, how you have hurt my dad and my mum?' Will went to push past, but Adrian moved to block him again.

'Get out of my way, Adrian, or I swear I will knock you on your arse.'

'I can't Will, I really can't,' said Adrian in a whisper. 'This is too important, it's about our family, the Thomas family and possibly every other family on the planet. Things are about to happen, things you and I may not want to happen and only you and I can stop it.'

'You can't seriously still be expecting me to go running off with you, not after you've wrecked my home again and destroyed our Christmas, not to mention that Uncle Bruce is about to rip into me for something I didn't do because Aunt Beryl believes I'm a pervert.'

'Will, the people that David is chasing are dangerous. They stabbed his friend, a police officer and set fire to the Thomas warehouse to cover up their crime. They know David recognised them and was going to follow them into the past.'

'Isn't that David's business as a cop? Isn't that what he is supposed to do?'

'Yes, that's what David did. The problem is, he did it unofficially, secretly, to protect the family. How could he do it any other way without telling the whole world about the *Cabinet?* Which could be a good thing or really bad. One thing for sure, it wouldn't be good for the family, for our family, Will. On top of this, Father wants to dismantle the *Cabinet* which would strand David in the past and could result in a giant grandfather paradox event.' Adrian started to do finger wiggles but stopped to avoid a harsh stare from Will.

'What's it got to do with me if David has gone all Dirty Harry?'

'Dirty Harry?'

Will rolled his eyes.

'Bloody hell, Adrian, haven't you heard of Clint Eastwood? You know, *do you feel lucky punk? Well, do you?'*

Will spoke with such anger that Adrian truly regretted not bringing his notebook, he would have to look Clint Eastwood up in the Great Wikipedia Data Base.

'Will, the criminals knew about the *Cabinet*, they broke into the warehouse to use it to travel back in time. They have the ability to change the past, our present and our future, to alter the timeline so that the Thomas family ceases to exist. The Grandfather Paradox and all that nasty sort of thing are in play if David doesn't stop them.'

'William, William, are you alright?' called Will's mum from beyond the passageway door.

'Of course he is alright, Mary. The fool has probably just thrown a tantrum at being caught out by Beryl. That deviate son of yours has probably destroyed the room and blocked the doorways to stop us from catching him in the act. That boy is a bloody disgrace to the family, Mary, you should have sent him away to a reform school years ago.'

'William could be hurt, the noise we heard, it sounded like an explosion. Fumes from the oil heater could have come in contact with electricity from the Christmas tree lights and blown up.'

'Mary could be right,' replied Aunt Beryl from behind the door. 'It was too loud for somebody just throwing things around, the whole house shook.'

There was silence for a moment.

'You could be right, Beryl, maybe the pervert isn't responsible. Maybe there was an accident. Call for an ambulance, just in case, I will go around to the front to see if I can get into the room from there.'

'Shit,' said Will in a whisper, 'Aunt Beryl is going to call an ambulance; the police will probably come as well.'

Adrian paled.

'Alright Will, the truth is, only four people, other than David and the criminals he is chasing, know what's going on. They are Uncle Emil, Uncle Dwight, myself and you. Father has to be kept in the dark because he could disrupt everything, stranding David in the past and allowing the criminals to change history. The consequences could be, and I apologise for doing this,' Adrian made air quotes, "catastrophic". We don't know how the police would react if we involve them, and just convincing them of the truth could take too long. What we do know, and I am quoting my uncles, is that while David might be in the distant past, the changes that occur will be relative to the time it takes in the past to appear in the future. If it takes a day for something to change for David, then the ripple effect through time will occur one day after in our future. Don't ask me why because I don't understand.'

'What are you trying to tell me?' whispered Will.

'Will, you and I are David's best hope for rescue. David, as a trained police officer is our family's best hope to stop a potential disaster occurring. Your parents, your brother, your uncles, aunties and cousins could cease to exist, or nothing may happen at all. The problem is we can't take the chance. We have to act and I need your help.'

Will understood what he was being told, but it seemed ridiculous that he was needed to save the world.

'Shit, you can't just rock up and lay all this on me. It sucks Adrian, the whole thing. My life, school, what's happened to my family and what you are asking me to do.'

Adrian nodded sympathetically. 'I understand, but doing nothing could *suck* even more.'

The front door to the house made a scraping noise as somebody tried to push it open.

'Your Uncle Bruce?'

'Yes, that will be him.'

'He can't see me Will, I doubt he would recognise me in my disguise, but we have no idea what it could do to the timeline.'

'Shit,' breathed out Will, 'no, I guess not.'

'Good chap, I knew you were made of the right stuff the moment we met.'

'Boy, are you hiding from me? Open this door, boy, or I will have to break it down.'

'Ok, what do you want me to do?' asked Will. His life was already shitty, so how could helping Adrian possibly make it worse?

'Spiffing, Will,' beamed Adrian. 'I just need to tag you so Uncle Dwight can tune the *Cabinet* into your location in the future.'

'You have to do what?'

Adrian withdrew a syringe from his Santa sack.

'I have to insert a tracking device under your skin; it's the same technology used for pets, apparently it's mostly painless.'

'You are going to stick something inside me using that?'

'Yes, it's the latest thing, no messy shaving of fur required.'

'I can hear you boy, open this door now.'

'When your Uncle Bruce is on a theme, he sticks to it,' whispered Adrian.

Will watched the front door bulge inward. Adrian was genuine in what he believed, and he believed in Will. Apart from his parents and the Sullivans, nobody had believed in him for a very long time, Adrian was trying to do the right thing for his family, that's what Will wanted too.

'Ok, do it, then disappear before Uncle Bruce sees you.'

'Good show, Will,' beamed Adrian. 'Turn around and lean forward so I can inject the tracker in the back of your neck under your hair to hide it.'

Will turned and leant forward.

'WHAT THE HELL IS GOING ON IN HERE?' bellowed Bruce Caruthers, all puffed up in righteous indignation, seeing his nephew bending over with Father Christmas pushing up hard behind his back.

'Shit,' said Will, looking up to see the anger on his uncle's face.

'Golly,' squealed Adrian.

'What in the name of God are you doing?'

Will ignored his uncle.

'Do it, then go. Heaven help me, but I will deal with Uncle Bruce.'

Adrian pressed the injector against Will's neck. It did hurt, but not as much as Will thought it would. Adrian dropped the injector into his Santa sack and stepped away from Will.

'Who the hell are you?' demanded Uncle Bruce while placing a steadying hand on the lounge suite. The exertion of breaking into the room and bellowing in outrage had fairly drained the breath from his body.

'It's me, Uncle Bruce,' replied Will, moving to block the view of Adrian.

'Not you, boy. Him, Santa.'

'There is nobody here but you and me, Uncle Bruce.'

'Don't be absurd boy. Him, Father Christmas behind you.'

Will turned to look, 'Sorry, I can't see anybody else.'

Adrian's startled eyes darted back and forth between Will and Bruce.

'Don't play funny buggers with me, boy,' Bruce spluttered, 'I can clearly see Father Christmas standing behind you. He's looking at me right now.'

Will turned to Adrian and mouthed, '*Go.*'

'You're looking right at him, the tall skinny man in the red suit with the white beard. Don't tell me you can't see Santa; he is right behind you.'

Will turned to face his uncle. 'Sorry Uncle Bruce, I stopped believing in Santa when I was seven. Thanks for trying, but honestly, I am too old to believe in Father Christmas.'

'What are you playing at boy, he is right there, behind you? He's just pulled a toy out of his sack; don't tell me you can't see him.'

Will needed Adrian to disappear in front of Uncle Bruce, then it would all be up to his uncle to try and explain what he had seen. Will knew how well that had turned out for him.

'Stop where you are you, you .... Santa pervert.' Bruce pushed past Will and made a lunge at Adrian.

Will tried to stop his uncle but momentum and an additional 40 kilograms in weight saw him pushed aside.

Bruce almost laughed at the look of terror on Adrian's face, then everything changed. His knees buckled and his body convulsed in a great tingling shock of pain, he lost bladder control and warm ammonia scented liquid filled his trousers. Then he was on the floor shaking uncontrollably with dribble running down his chin and liquid oozing from his nose. Then it all went black.

'What have you done?' whispered Will.

'Defended myself,' replied Adrian holding a taser in his hand. 'This is more effective than I thought it would be. Well done, Uncle Dwight.'

Will looked his uncle. He had wet his pants and, from the smell, had done something else embarrassing, but he didn't appear to be physically injured.

'Will he be alright, you haven't caused brain damage, have you?'

'Not that I am aware of.' Adrian held up the taser. 'This is a copy of a non-lethal defensive device for personal protection from your time period. I'm surprised you don't recognise it?'

'No, I have never seen anything like it.'

'Ah, probably best not to mention it, then.'

Uncle Bruce's body convulsed then settled back motionless.

'You had better go, it's going to be hard enough to explain without somebody else seeing you.'

Adrian extended his hand to Will.

'It's been a pleasure, Will. I just know you and I are going to make a great team, us two Thomas boys.'

Will shook Adrian's hand.

'What happens next?'

'I report mission accomplished, then we prepare what we need to track down David. I will drop in to pick you up, we go back to home base for a final briefing and then it's off to rescue David, catch the crooks, of course, and save the world as we know it. We should be able to pull it off with a bit of the old pluck, and push on attitude. Mind you, it could be slightly dangerous, but what good adventure worth having isn't.'

'William, are you alright?'

Will turned to see his mother and Wendy push through the gap between the door and the lounge. Mary's face was white and Wendy's eyes wide as dinner plates. Wendy stared at the destruction in the room, then at Bruce lying in a puddle of his own making on the floor.

'What happened?' asked Wendy, narrowing her gaze as she noticed a tall skinny Santa standing behind Will.

Will dropped his head. How could he explain this?

'Hello,' said Adrian, waving in greeting. 'It's my fault I am afraid, as it was last time. My name is Adrian, Adrian Thomas.' Adrian stepped over the prostrate Bruce to greet Mary and Wendy with a smile.

'Adrian? *The Adrian*?' questioned Mary in shock.

'I don't know about being *the Adrian*, but I am, *an Adrian*. There is no point pretending to be Santa; Uncle Bruce saw through my disguise which I was slightly surprised by. I guess you live and learn these things.'

Wendy looked between Will and Adrian, then took another look at the destruction in the room.

'You did this?'

Adrian nodded.

'It's a draw back from time travel. There is a shock wavy thingy every time you materialise. It got myself and my cousin David into a spot of bother when we landed in Galilee; we upset a protest rally which I believe was something to do with the misuse of livestock and a lack of proper democratic government. Awfully embarrassing at the time.

Ended up a bit of a misunderstanding all around. David was carted away by the constabulary on the erroneous assumption that he was part of something called the *Jewish Resistance Movement*.' Adrian used the quotation mark finger wiggles, realised what he had done and dropped his hands to cover what was probably a major social faux pas. 'It was an incorrect assumption by the officer in charge. Unfortunately, the chap wasn't in the mood to listen to reason, so when the opportunity arose, to put it in your local vernacular, I did a runner.'

Adrian turned to Will. 'Did I get that right?'

Will nodded as he watched his mother's growing concern and Wendy holding a hand over her mouth to hide a smile of amusement.

'Anyway, as I was saying, it's all my fault, nothing to do with Will. I just dropped in to wish Will a Merry Christmas. In fact, a very Merry Christmas to all of the Thomas family and friends.' Adrian grinned at Wendy to include her in the greeting. 'Nice to meet you by the way. Adrian Thomas,' said Adrian extending his hand for Wendy to shake.

'Come here, William,' commanded Mary. 'Come and stand behind me.'

'Mum?'

'Just do as I ask.'

'Mum?'

Wendy shook Adrian's hand.

'I don't think he's dangerous, Mary; he might have just had too many pre-Christmas drinks. My name's Wendy, by the way.'

Adrian smiled.

'I think at this point I am supposed to inquire if you have been naughty, or nice?'

Wendy laughed, 'I like you Santa, and yes I am nice most of the time.' Wendy dropped her voice, 'I have been known to be naughty as well, but only with my husband.'

'Oh,' replied Adrian, 'well, I assume that's alright, given it's consensual?'

'Bloody oath it is, Santa,' winked Wendy. Adrian and Mary blushed at the admission.

'A pleasure to meet you, Wendy, you are the first friend of Will's I have actually met. And to answer your inquiry, the answer is no, I am not much of a drinker. I don't like the taste, to tell you the truth.'

Adrian turned to Mary.

'You would be Mary, Will's mother. You do a lot of charitable work; I was most impressed when I looked you up. Your husband Colin is a tradesman, an artisan of his time and a man of great wisdom and thought. You must be very proud of your family.'

Mary grabbed Will's arm and pulled him behind herself.

'What do you want with my son?'

'Sorry, didn't Will explain? Will is going to assist in saving the world as we know it by helping rescue my cousin David from the clutches of a gaggle of Roman soldiers in ancient Galilee. Obviously, it's not going to happen today, what with it being Christmas. I just dropped in to touch base and confirm the arrangements etc.'

'My son is not going anywhere with you. I think you have done enough damage; I need you to leave right now Adrian, or whatever your real name is.'

Adrian was stunned by Mary's tone; she was obviously upset.

'My most sincere apologies, Mrs Thomas, it was never my intention to cause harm or distress to Will, yourself or any other member of you family.'

'I think you are a bit past the point of saying sorry,' said Wendy kneeling beside the semi-conscious Bruce. 'What did you do to this bloke?'

'It's a temporary effect, I assure you. I had no choice; the chap was threatening physical harm to Will and myself. I used a defensive device to sedate him as a last resort.'

The sound of a siren approaching could be heard, Mary kept her eyes locked on Adrian.

'You are out of time Santa; the police will be here shortly. I hope you have a better story for them than the lies you have been telling my son.'

Adrian addressed Mary calmly, 'I should not be telling you this, but I will, to put your mind at rest, and as proof that I and Will have been totally truthful with you.' Adrian looked to Wendy, 'are you the sort of friend who can be trusted to keep a secret which, if exposed, could endanger their future?'

Wendy looked at Mary and Will as she answered, 'Of course, I will keep a secret if it is to keep them safe.'

'You are definitely on the nice list then,' said Adrian. 'What I am about to tell you is public record in my time. I offer it as proof of who I am and my sincerity of action toward you and your family, Mary.'

Adrian let the gravity of the situation build, then spoke, 'According to the Great Wikipedia Data Base, Bruce Caruthers was taken from your home via a medical retrieval team. He will make a full recovery, return to his place of work and fail in his bid for further promotion. According to the records, the chair of the promotions committee considered him to be, and I quote, *overblown, self-opinionated and only moderately competent in his role.* He was deemed to be unsuited for further advancement, *having risen beyond his intellectual capacity.* It was also noted that he had an eye twitch which made him appear to be winking in a conspiratorial manner which was deemed to be a disadvantage when dealing with customers.'

'Uncle Bruce doesn't have a twitch,' said Will.

Wendy looked at Bruce on the floor.

'He does now.'

Adrian continued, 'According to the records, his condition was attributed to a fault associated with electrically operated festive decorations, causing a flash ignition when mixed with fumes from a hydrocarbon-based heating appliance. The one oddity surrounding the report was the lack of ignition residue which was not able to be explained at the time.'

'What about William?'

'According to the records from the *Border Watch,* Mary, Colin and Brian Thomas along with Mr and Mrs Caruthers are named as being present. Will and Wendy are not mentioned.'

The noise of the siren was growing closer.

'Why would I believe you?' asked Mary.

'Because it's the truth, Mum, I told everybody, but nobody believed me.'

Mary looked at her son; Mary hadn't believed William then and look what happened.

'Alright, let's just say this is all true, that you are this long lost relative from the future who just happened to crash into our house and turned our lives upside down by accident.'

'Yes Mum, it's all true.'

'If it's true, what do we do now?'

'According to the historical records, Will and I were not present,' stated Adrian. We just need to make that happen. I can leave and Will could go with Wendy, if that is agreeable?'

Wendy took Will by the hand.

'Skye needs a babysitter while Mike and I put her presents under the tree.'

'Bye Will,' called Adrian to their departing backs, 'a pleasure to meet you, Wendy.'

'Are you going to leave now?'

'Yes, of course, Mary. But I must apologise again, I never meant for any of this to happen.' Adrian put his hand on the *Sainter,* then hesitated. 'It is all true Mary. Will might be the key to keeping, not just your family safe, but he could save society as we know it.'

'And what happens if William doesn't go with you?'

'I don't know, Mary; we may shortly have never existed, that's the problem with the Grandfather Paradox.'

'I don't understand.'

'No, neither do I properly, which is why we need Will.'

The door scraped against the lounge suite as Colin Thomas pushed into the room.

'Mary, there is an ambulance in our driveway, what the hell is going on?'

'It's Father Christmas, I am afraid,' said Mary turning to face Adrian. 'He had a little accident in our lounge room, it happens from time to time, some sort of shock wave thingy apparently.'

'Who the...?' started Colin seeing a tall, skinny Santa Claus surrounded by carnage.

'I am afraid he has to be going,' said Mary. 'Lots of presents to deliver to children all around the world.'

'Thank you, Mary,' said Adrian with a final wave, 'you are definitely on the nice list.' With this, Adrian touched a finger to the *Sainter*, the air pulsed green three times, folded in upon itself and Santa Claus disappeared.

'What the hell?'

'It's okay, Colin, it's all okay,' said Mary moving to squat beside her brother. 'You know, next Christmas I think we should go away someplace, maybe to the beach. Somewhere that we don't have to invite Bruce and Beryl. I think that would be nice for a change, don't you?'

# CHAPTER SIXTEEN

## WARRNAMBOOL, JULY 26TH 2117 CE, 18:04 HOURS

THE *CABINET* BOOMED AND Adrian materialised.

'Hello Uncle Emil, Uncle Dwight, mission accomplished.'

'Did you implant the tracker?' asked Dwight opening the *Cabinet* door.

'That went very smoothly, I didn't feel a thing.'

'Did he agree to help us?' asked Emil.

'Will was reluctant to begin with, Mary was particularly doubtful about the proposal initially.'

'You interacted with his mother?'

'I didn't have a choice, Uncle Emil, not after Uncle Bruce broke into the room acting aggressive and shouty. Before I forget, Uncle Dwight, thank you for the taser; it worked wonderfully.'

'You used the weapon on the boy's uncle?' questioned Emil with growing concern.

'I don't think Will was too upset about it and Mary didn't seem majorly concerned. He had been rather rude to her only moments before, besides, Wendy checked on his welfare and he didn't appear to be permanently injured.

'Who is Wendy?'

'Wendy is a neighbour. Oh, and I saw Colin Thomas, Will's father, but I didn't get the chance to interact with him.'

Emil was aghast, imagining the consequences of Adrian's interaction with not one, but five individuals in 1977.

'Tell me about the taser,' asked Dwight taking the sack from Adrian. 'Is the voltage sufficient, or do we need to increase the output?'

'Dwight, for once consider the big picture,' snapped Emil.

'Adrian, did you interact with anybody else?'

'Nobody else, Uncle Emil. Just Will, Mary, Uncle Bruce, Wendy, who is very nice but can be naughty with her husband in a consensual manner, and Colin Thomas, whom I only saw for a second or two.'

'Who saw you materialise?'

'Only Will, I made a bit of a mess unfortunately.'

'Are you certain of this?'

'Absolutely, Uncle Dwight's landing coordinates were spot on.'

'Who saw you leave Adrian, how many people?'

'Only Mary and Colin Thomas.'

'What about this Uncle Bruce?'

'I don't think so, the chap was out like a light.'

Emil paced.

'Maybe it is not as bad as it could have been. Your interaction with people, other than William Thomas, may have only had a negligible effect on the timeline.'

'I don't feel any different, Uncle Emil. In fact, I feel quite upbeat.'

'I haven't noticed anything different,' replied Dwight watching his brother pace. 'I think we should assume any impacts have been minimal.'

Emil nodding in agreement.

'Okay, given the lack of anything to indicate that Adrian has caused a significant change in world history, the plan stands.'

Emil turned to Adrian.

'How was William Thomas? Was he physically sound? Were there any signs of mental fragility? Importantly, had he matured sufficiently to understand what we are asking of him?'

'He has certainly grown Uncle Emil and more forthright than when we first met. He threatened to knock me on my arse not long after I arrived.'

Emil furrowed his brow in concern.

'Why?'

'It was my fault; it seems our first encounter caused considerable stress to Will and his family.'

'Have we interfered with the Thomas family to the point where they won't help us?'

'No, I think letting Will's parents see me may have helped.'

'How?'

'I got the impression that proof of my existence may have relieved the tension somewhat. That's what upset Will the most, the fact that nobody believed him about our first encounter.'

Emil nodded then asked, 'The boy's mother understood what we're asking of her son?'

'I believe so. I explained the situation and Mary knows what could happen if we don't act to help David.'

'And she agreed for her son to go with you? She understands the risks?'

'Well, Mary didn't forbid it. I think it was all a bit of a shock initially, plus, Uncle Bruce behaving as he did wasn't a help. Apparently, he is concerned about the smallish size of his penis which makes him aggressive and boorish.

If you have this physical characteristic in the late 20th century, you can overcome the stigma by purchasing something called a *Red Monaro*. I gather it is a sort of automobile.'

Dwight snorted in laughter, which caused Emil to glare at his brother, then at Adrian, who was being serious, which elicited another laugh from Dwight.

'What about the father, Colin Thomas?'

'I think my disguise may have fooled him. Mary carried on the charade that I was Santa, telling Colin that I had presents to deliver and needed to be getting along. Perhaps my disappearance could be explained as simply as that.'

Dwight stopped sniggering. Emil stared at his nephew in awe of his naivety.

'Like I said, mission accomplished.'

Emil sat and thought.

'Let's consider what we know. William Thomas is of sound body and mind, that is confirmed?'

Adrian nodded.

'We have the tracker in place, so we can locate him when we need to.'

Dwight and Adrian both nodded.

'The situation has been explained, along with the potential consequences of not acting.'

'Just as you asked me to,' said Adrian.

'We have agreement from William Thomas to help retrieve David.'

Adrian nodded again.

'We know where and when David arrived, so we have a point to commence the rescue mission from.'

Both Adrian and Dwight nodded agreement.

'Dwight, can you prepare a rescue kit?'

'I have already started.'

'Adrian, you now have a partner, albeit one who is still a teenager.'

'Will is a Thomas, he will do splendidly.'

'Be that as it may, I would like to wait until he has matured and gathered some life experience before we contact him again.'

'If Adrian can research the Wikipedia Data Base and select a suitable contact date, I can program the *Cabinet* around a specific physical address at a particular time of day, which should allow for a less chaotic arrival by Adrian,' suggested Dwight.

'Find an event, Adrian; a wedding or a funeral, where it is confirmed that Will was present. It should coincide with him being in his physical prime during his mid-twenties to early thirties, but it needs to be before he settles into a permanent relationship, which could prevent him from agreeing to accompany you.'

'Understood, Uncle Emil, I will search the records of the local newspaper in the town where Will and his family lived.

'Make that your highest priority.'

'Roger.'

'Dwight, we need to be ready to send Adrian no later than 1800 hours tomorrow.'

'That won't give me much time.'

'We may not have any more time,' said Emil holding up his phone which displayed multiple text messages left by Gerald, all referencing the need to urgently meet about the *Cabinet*.

'Shit,' said Dwight.

'Shit indeed,' said Emil putting the phone in his pocket.

# CHAPTER SEVENTEEN

DAVID OPENED ONE EYE. His body ached, his head hurt and his mouth tasted of something disgusting.

'So, you're awake. I don't know how you could sleep, I couldn't, but then I have a conscience.'

David raised his head.

'Hello Mary, do you have my bag?'

'Yes, I have your bag, thief,' she hissed in anger.

David sat up. The movement made him nauseous, he had to close his eyes before replying.

'Mary, I'm not a thief. I am here to find two people who have committed crimes in my land and take them home to face justice.'

'So, you are a liar as well as a thief. You may have fooled my Joe, but you can't fool me.'

Mary emerged from the shadows dragging the calf skin sack across the floor of the cavern. 'Take your bag and go. If you don't, I swear by the life of my children, I will turn you over to the Romans.'

A shadow filled the cavern as three entered the cave.

'He is awake!' called Joe in joy.

'How do you feel?' asked Polykarpos laying a hand on David's shoulder.

'Good,' lied David. 'I'm a bit dry, but other than that I'm pretty good.'

'David needs water, Mary,' said Joe, 'can you find the blessed bucket of David?'

'The what?'

'The bucket David used to make water. It was a miracle, Mary. The bucket was empty then David waved his hand and it filled with the sweetest water I have ever tasted.'

'It was a trick, Joe, nothing more. This David is a thief. You've seen what he's hiding in his bag, Roman gold and silver. No honest man could earn so much in five lifetimes.'

'A thief would not have risked his life to save me and all of my students, Mary,' stated Polykarpos.

Joe could not contain himself; he was bursting to tell his story.

'The Romans were going to kill me, Mary. I was on my knees next to

Ephraim the rope- maker's house when David performed a miracle and saved me.'

'Yes Joe, you told me last night. I didn't believe it then and I don't believe it now.'

'It's true,' said Peter, 'I saw David shoot green light and wind from his hands, the centurio they call Maximus, was knocked to the ground unconscious in an instant.'

'So, what are you three wise men are trying to tell me, is this David, whom none of you had ever laid eyes upon before yesterday, is what, a god like the Romans worship, or perhaps an angel? Or is he Jehovah himself in disguise?'

'No,' said Polykarpos seriously.

'Yes!' beamed Joe.

'I don't know,' replied Peter looking first at David, then at Mary's angry stare.

'Polykarpos is right,' said David kneeling, 'there is nothing supernatural about anything you have seen. It's just technology, not magic.'

Peter helped David to his feet.

'Thank you,' said David extending his hand. 'I assume you helped Polykarpos and Joe bring me here.'

Peter nodded.

'Thank you. I am in your debt,' said David, taking the man's hand in his own.

Peter was confused, he should be the one thanking David for saving his life.

'I ... I ... ' Peter stammered.

'What Peter is so inarticulately trying to express is, it is we who are in your debt,' said Polykarpos.

'You don't owe me anything, I am just sorry for the trouble I've caused. If I could have some water, I can be on my way.'

'Mary, where is the bucket?' Joe asked.

Mary glowered at the men.

'You have got to be joking. I don't know how many ways I can say this, David is a thief.' Mary emptied the bag. Gold and silver coins spilled on the dirt floor. 'Do you know anybody in the whole of Galilee who has such a fortune?'

Peter and Joe were dumbstruck, they had never seen so much gold. Polykarpos looked at David in curiosity.

'Are these coins truly yours?

'Actually, they belong to my family. My father is an engineer, a cross between an inventor and a builder is probably the best way to describe him. He created the coins and my Uncle Emil put them in the bag. I assume it's more than I actually need?'

'This is more gold than a man could earn in many lifetimes,' stated Polykarpos. 'Are you truly unaware of the value of this wealth?'

'To be honest, currency, sorry money, doesn't have that much importance where I come from. My father taught me that how a person behaves, how they treat others, is the true measure of a person's worth, not what they own, but how they live.'

David looked from face to face. Mary was tight-lipped in disapproval, Peter looked confused, Joe was smiling as if in love for the first time and Polykarpos had one eyebrow raised in thought.

'Take the coins, if they can help you. Just leave what I need to pay for transport, accommodation and food for say, a month. Its only money, it's just a means to an end.'

'Your father, the creator, he taught you not to value wealth but to value people?' asked Peter staring at the coins.

'Yes, he did,' nodded David. 'Don't get me wrong, Dad is no angel himself, he gets so focused on his creations that he forgets to think about people. I'm the opposite, I can't stop thinking about Jen, who was hurt by the people I am chasing. That's why I have to hunt them down and bring them to justice.'

Polykarpos spoke in Persian just to check what he was thinking. 'What do you want in exchange for this wealth that has no value to you, David?'

David replied in the accent of an Assyrian nobleman. 'Some water would be nice, other than that, I just need my bag and I will hit the road.'

'What did David say? What did you say to him?' asked Joe.

'I asked David what he wanted for his gold and he said he would like some water.'

'Where is the bucket, Mary?' interjected Peter staring at the coins, 'David needs water and he needs it now.'

'Don't dare order me about, Peter. If Joe ever tried that tone on me, he would be sleeping with her next door's goats for a week.'

'Mary, my love, please, where is the bucket?' asked Joe politely.

Mary gave a sigh of exasperation and pushed past the men.

'Don't worry, I'll get the *Blessed Bucket* though it's empty. Peter's revolutionaries drained it before skulking away to find a place to hide.'

David watched Mary disappear through the cave entrance.

'I like Mary. Joe, you are a lucky man to have her as your partner.'

'Partner?'

'I meant wife.'

'Yes, Mary is a very good wife, she sews and weaves very well, and I have yet to see another woman as good at washing clothes in the river.'

'Mary's your wife, Joe, not your servant.'

'I don't understand. It's Mary's obligation to bear children, cook and clean and do for her husband, just as it is my obligation to protect and guide her. That is the way it has been ordained by Jehovah.'

David raised an eyebrow.

'Have you considered that how you treat women is as big a reflection on your character as how the Romans treat you?'

'Sorry?' said Peter in surprise. 'Are you suggesting that we treat our women the same as the Roman's treat the people of Galilee? That's absurd. Our women are respected, we don't beat them, well, not unless they deserve it. We don't steal their possessions; what they own belongs to their husbands or fathers and we don't forbid them from going to temple. They sit in the back and listen to the priest and can join in the prayers if they are not too loud. It's very different.'

'So, you're saying that women are like a possession that you protect because of its value to your lifestyle and economic well-being. Isn't that the same as owning a slave?'

'Women are nothing like slaves, we don't pay for our wives, well, apart from the wedding dowry.'

'Are your women free to make their own decisions? Could Mary, for example, open a carpentry shop, or buy a house, or, I don't know, a herd of cattle if she wanted to? Could she choose to divorce Joe if she didn't like him anymore, or go to a day spa while Joe stayed home to look after the children?'

'No, that's unnatural. Why would a woman want to open a carpentry shop? Why would a man want to look after their children like a woman does?'

'I like looking after my children,' said Joe, 'and I help Mary with the housework where I can, she works so hard that some nights I send her to bed and I cook and feed the children. Mary looks after me and I look after her. We are partners, like David said, it takes the two of us to raise our children working together.'

Peter was startled.

'You do the washing?'

'Yes, Mary taught me, she was very patient.'

Polykarpos laughed, 'See Peter, I told you David was different. What other man could convince a husband to admit he helps his wife with her work and to do so proudly?'

'It's not natural.'

'Come on, Peter, you cannot say that you have never helped your mother with her chores?' said Polykarpos.

Peter blushed.

'I thought so, only a fool would treat his mother, or his wife, the way we pretend is the natural order of things.'

Mary entered the cave carrying the wooden bucket. Peter moved to take it from her.

'Let me, Mary, it looks heavy.'

Mary scowled and swung it away.

'My husband asked me to fetch this bucket, that's what women do; get things done.'

Joe placed a hand on the bucket's handle.

'Thank you, Mary, my love. I don't know what I would do without you, I really don't.'

'What?'

'Joe is a lucky man to have you as his wife' said Polykarpos bowing to Mary.

'What?'

'Thank you, Mary,' said David, taking the bucket from Joe.

Mary was confused. What had happened to these men since she left the cave?

David opened his first aid kit and withdrew a hydration tablet which he squeezed and dropped into the bucket. Mary's eyes widened in surprise.

'What sort of a trick is this?'

'It's not a trick, Mary, it's technology. Water is always in the air, just not in liquid form most of the time. All I am doing is cooling the air so the water can turn from a gas into a liquid. It's the reverse of turning water into steam when you boil it.'

Mary touched the water. *How could David be creating such an illusion?*

Joe dropped to his knees. 'Are you okay?' asked David.

'Is this a miracle David?'

'No, it's science.'

David opened a jar of electrolyte supplements from the first aid kit and removed a red tablet. 'Do you like raspberries, Joe?'

'I don't know what "raspberries" is.'

'I think you will like it; most people do.'

Joe nodded as David dropped the tablet into the bucket, then he scrambled backwards in surprise until he collided with Mary's legs.

'It's okay, Joe,' reassured David. 'Do we have a cup we can put water in?'

Mary found a wooden cup; David filled it to the brim with red liquid.

Peter blanched at the sight.

'It's blood, he has turned the water into blood!'

David lifted the cup to his lips and gulped down the contents. He felt better instantly as the water increased his hydration and the supplement replaced the sodium, calcium, potassium and chloride lost from his body.

'It's not blood, Peter. It's an additive designed to allow my body to recover from the effects of last night. It's medicinal, not magic.'

'It's blood. Look how it has run down the sides of his mouth!'

David stuck his tongue out and licked around his mouth.

'No, it's definitely a raspberry -flavoured energy drink.'

Mary pushed past Joe and Peter to stand over the bucket.

'It doesn't smell like blood; it smells like fruit mixed with honey.' Mary took the cup and dipped it into the bucket, then lifted the cup to her face, sniffed the contents then raised it to her lips and drank.

The taste was very pleasant, it was almost cold enough to make her teeth hurt, then the effects of science, from far in the future, kicked in and Mary began to feel better than she could ever remember. Her head felt clearer, her body lighter on her weary legs as energy charged through her small frame. She took another sip, then downed the remainder in a long swallow.

'It's a sweet wine that gives you back your energy. How did you do this David? How did you turn water into wine?'

David shrugged.

'It's just technology, nothing more.'

Polykarpos took the cup from Mary, gestured to David for permission to fill the vessel and dipped it into the bucket. He stood erect, drank deeply, then passed the half full cup to Peter. Peter hesitated, then put the cup to his lips and sipped. His eyes widened at the taste as he looked to Mary, Polykarpos, then David, for reassurance.

'It can't harm you, Peter; unless you drink too much, then it could give you the runs.'

'It will make me run?'

'No, it could give you an upset stomach.'

'My stomach will become sad?'

'Polykarpos help me out here. It's like if you eat too many dates, do you know what I mean?'

Polykarpos nodded his understanding.

'What David is trying to explain is that too much of this wine may cause your bowels to act up.'

'I still don't understand?'

'For Jehovah's sake, David is saying it could give you the shits,' explained Mary.

Peter spat the drink on the ground.

'That is a dangerous thing, David. I have friends who died from the shits.'

David nodded. Dysentery could be a life-threatening medical condition.

'You would have to drink multiple buckets before that is likely to happen. In fact, what you are all drinking is commonly used to ease the symptoms of dysentery, which is what my people call the shits.'

Mary looked at the jar of electrolyte tablets.

'It's a medicine?'

'Yes, it can be, though it's primarily designed to help you recover from excessive physical exertion. It can help with other causes of dehydration, such as dysentery or excessive vomiting and helps with a fever as well.'

'Could it help a sick child?'

'If they were dehydrated, it won't cure the problem, but it can help with recovery.'

Mary contemplated what she had been told.

'What will you trade for your magic potion, obviously not gold, you have enough coin to last an honest man a lifetime. Maybe, there is something else you want, or need as a man who may not be a thief after all.'

'Mary, you can't ask such a thing.'

Mary looked angrily at Joe.

'This man who saved your life would not have needed to if he hadn't tried to jump on the roof of our home to retrieve his bag full of coins that he claims are not stolen.' Mary next swung her gaze to Peter. 'Would you have been crucified if David, who swears he is innocent of everything, had not fallen off our roof on top of you in front of the Romans?'

'David saved my life and the lives of your friends,' said Polykarpos.

'Donkey shit, Polykarpos. I say we have helped him as much as he helped us, probably more so. The Romans would have hacked off David's head and put it on a pole in the village if we hadn't hidden him.'

'Mary is right,' said David, 'my coming here has not helped your situation. The best thing I can do is leave as quickly as possible.'

'I want my trade, David; I think it is only fair given the risks we have taken to help you.'

'Mary, I don't know...' started Joe.

Mary placed a finger across Joe's lips for silence.

'Joe, you know I love you dearly, but I need you to trust your wife and let me do the negotiation. Can you do that for me and our children?'

Joseph nodded, wide-eyed, then took a pace backwards.

Peter went to say something; Polykarpos cut him off with a shake of the head. Peter shrugged and remained silent.

'Okay, I understand it is your cultural need to haggle over a trade, so let's do it.' David had already decided to leave most of the coins and as much of the medical supplies as he could spare. He picked up a jar of electrolyte tablets for Mary to see.

'What will you trade me for this?'

'I will trade you a goat, one that gives lots of milk.'

'We don't have a goat,' said Joe.

Mary glared at her husband.

'We can buy one to trade, Joe.'

'It doesn't matter, I am lactose intolerant,' replied David wanting to cut the goat discussion dead.

'If you don't want a goat, how about a donkey?'

Joe went to state the obvious about not owning a donkey, Mary cut him off with an upright finger.

'I am too big to ride a donkey, and how am I to feed it on my journey?'

Mary looked at Joe seeking inspiration. Joe smiled the smile he kept just for Mary and their children and Mary had an epiphany.

'Are you married, David?'

'No, I am not married,' replied David cautiously.

'Has your family pledged your betrothal to somebody in your village?'

'No, I don't have a girlfriend and I am definitely not engaged. I thought we were discussing a trade?'

'We are. My sister is yet to be betrothed, she is taller than me, strong and with a pleasant, some say, pretty face and she is not dull or boring. If you meet her and you find her unsuitable as a wife, then she could act as your servant while you are travelling through our land. Though, if you are not to be betrothed, then this must be a purely business arrangement. Anything else would bring down the wrath of Jehovah and our family on your head.'

David didn't know what to say. He had once been convinced by the guys at his station to try speed dating and found the whole experience embarrassing. It wasn't that he hadn't wanted to meet somebody, it just seemed so forced and desperate at the time, and now he was being offered a wife for a jar of raspberry-flavoured electrolyte tablets.

'Yes, a wife David, a man like yourself in possession of a fortune must be in need of a wife.'

David was shaken by what sounded like a quote from Pride and Prejudice.

'Her name is Hannah,' blurted our Mary.

Peter and Polykarpos gave an audible gasp. They had been convinced Mary was talking about her other sister, the kind, pleasant and dutiful Salome.

'Joe can fetch her now.' Mary turned to Joe and mouthed a plea for him to, *please just do it.* 'Tell Hannah that her sister needs to see her right away.' Mary moved closer to her husband and whispered in his ear. 'When she tells you to *bugger off* and threatens to slap you for being an idiot, go and see my mother and explain that we may have found a match for Hannah. Tell her it's not a joke, that I am deadly serious. Now, please hurry, Joe.'

Joe looked startled.

'David saved my life, Mary. Surely you can't mean Hannah?'

'Joe, if you love me and our children, make Hannah come. You never know, she may just do as I ask for once.'

# CHAPTER EIGHTEEN

DAX WOKE. HE SQUINTED into the sunlight, the shape of a man was leaning over his body with something long in its hand, a spear! Dax rolled away from the weapon.

'Don't be a fool, soldier,' snarled a voice. 'If I had wanted you dead, I wouldn't have bothered to wake you.'

Dax stopped and struggled to one knee, his pugio gripped in his right hand, his left hand shading his one eye not swollen by bruising. Standing in front of him was a centurio, the officer was glaring at Dax, daring him to make a false move.

'Sir,' replied Dax, lowering his weapon.

'What happened to your face, soldier?'

Dax raised a hand to feel the bruising.

'I was hit with something hard made of wood,' he replied, pulling a splinter from the cut above his eye.

'Where are you from? You're not one of mine.'

'Tenth Cohort of the Sixth Legion Ferrata, Sir. Originally, I am from Tarraconensis.'

'I served there for two years, it grows good wine and even better fighters.'

Dax nodded in agreement. The wine was good and the local tribesmen could be fierce, which was one of the reasons the Romans had been eager to have them in their army.

'What's your name, soldier?'

'Dax, Sir.'

'Why are you here, Dax? Your cohort are on road building duties between here and Tyre.'

'Yes, Sir, most of my barrack is and some are maintaining patrols in the villages.'

'But you are not doing either of those things, Dax. You are here with a head wound, leagues from your cohort. How do you explain this?'

Dax doubted the centurio would understand, but he gripped his pugio tighter and told the truth. It was better than lying, even if it showed you in a bad light.

'I was on prisoner escort to the port of Tyre. I have to report an incident that resulted in the death of my escort partner and the escape of two men who were my responsibility to deliver to Tyre.' Dax looked directly into Maximus's eyes. 'I am in pursuit to kill them and avenge the death of my barrack mate.'

Maximus studied Dax. The man was a veteran, the scars from camp punishments and battle wounds, along with the tan line where the chin strap of his helmet sat, all gave witness to his years of service. His presence was an anomaly, just as it was that he had not been discovered by his own men. This was wrong. It had been wrong since he laid eyes on that odd beardless Jew yesterday.

'And you followed the prisoners to this hill?'

'Yes, Centurio. I was about to spear the prisoner called David when I was knocked down.'

Maximus' eyes widened.

'Where did you collect this David from?'

'From Nazareth, Sir, along with a thief, a man accused of defiling his sister, a boy pickpocket and an old man named Polykarpos, who escaped with David. It was said he was a dangerous heretic that Annius Rufus himself wanted removed because of the risk of unrest from the Nazarenes.'

Could it be the same David, the one Octavian had kept alive because of his value in gold?

'How did this David and the old man escape? Tell the truth, I will know if you are lying.'

Dax explained the heat and tedium of marching beside the ox cart and the sudden noise that woke him from his stupor. He spoke of how the narrowing of the track had drawn his friend within striking distance and how the sandal and the belt were used to ensnare his fellow guard, the noise the cart wheel made and the crunch of breaking bones. Dax spoke of his anger and attempt to kill the men who caused the death of his friend. He explained the frustration of being outwitted and having his weapon taken, then the dilemma of whether to pursue the fleeing prisoners or secure the prison cart. Dax maintained a steady eye when he spoke of ending the pain of his friend, then moved on to his pursuit and the green light that drew him to the hill. The stealthy approach, the raised pilum, the blow to the face, then nothing until being awakened by Maximus.

Maximus believed Dax was speaking the truth. There was more to this David than Maximus had first thought. He understood tactics and displayed courage; the man could be a deserter, possibly an officer with training and skills that had gone native because of a woman or disillusionment with army life, it had happened before.

'Tell me of the green light.'

'I saw it from the rise above the town,' said Dax pointing. 'There was no flame, just a bright green light that flashed, then went out.'

'Could you see what was making the light?'

'No, Sir. I ran to where I had seen the flash, there I found three legionnaires asleep on the ground.'

Maximus had goose bumps; it was as if something evil had been hunting his men in the dark.

'What did you do when you found these men?'

'I couldn't raise them, so I left them as they lay. The light flashed at the top of this hill, so I followed it and found the old man Polykarpos and the warrior David freeing the men on the crosses. I raised my pilum to throw it; the next thing I remember was a pain in my side as you woke me.'

Maximus pondered what he had learnt. There had to be a link between the attack on his troops, the disappearance of the mad, beardless Jew and the attack on Dax and himself in the dark. If this was the beginning of an uprising, it was poorly organised. They should have killed both Dax and himself when they had the opportunity. Had the rebels panicked and run away when Dax appeared, thinking he was a scout ahead of a larger force? Maybe this David, this possible deserter, had perceived the danger and made a strategic withdrawal, but what was the green light and how was it being used as a weapon? None of these thoughts explained why troops from the garrison had not found him and Dax before now.

'I am not in a position to pass judgement on your actions, Dax; however, I find your dedication to recover the prisoners commendable.'

'Sir,' said Dax, loosening the grip on his weapon.

'As I am short of soldiers, I am requisitioning you into the third cohort until such time as I deem it appropriate to return you to your unit.'

'Sir?'

'And now we are going down to that shit hole of a village called Nazareth and find out what the hell my soldiers have been doing all night. Then we are going to saddle some horses, find where this David and Polykarpos are hiding and remove their heads.'

# CHAPTER NINETEEN

DAVID WANTED TO END Mary's matchmaking as quickly as it started, but he couldn't afford to upset the people whose help he needed if he was going to find the fugitives and get home.

Peter and Polykarpos followed Joe out of the cave. David could hear them talking without making out the words. Mary, in the meantime, was putting together something for him to eat.

'It's goat,' said Mary holding out a pita bread wrap.

'Thank you, Mary, I can't say I've ever eaten goat before.'

Mary raised an eyebrow in surprise.

'It's the white meat from the entrails. I wash it, then dry it with salt in the sun. Joe likes it with bread and cheese, I don't have any cheese, so it's just on bread.'

David bit into the offal sandwich; it was a little salty but very edible. Mary watched David eat, nodding in satisfaction as he took extra bites.

'Tell me about your family, are you really so wealthy that you carry around Roman gold as if it was silver shekels?'

'My family is well off, but I work for a living, just like Joe. My job is to protect people and enforce the rule of law. That's why I am here, Mary, doing my job.'

'Does your family live in a home with lots of rooms like the wealthy Romans? It is said that Herod sleeps in a bed stuffed with the feathers to make it soft. Do you have a bed stuffed with feathers?'

'No, my bed is not stuffed with feathers.'

'What of your home, David? How many rooms does it have?'

'I have a two-bedroom apartment.'

'Your home has two rooms?' asked Mary thinking of her own house. 'Do you cook and store your food in one and sleep in the other?'

'No, the bedrooms are just for sleeping, and I have a kitchen where I cook with an attached pantry for storing food.'

'Your home has four rooms?! Two for sleeping, one for cooking and one to store your grain?'

'I also have one and a half bathrooms and an entertainment area.'

'What is a bathroom?'

'That's a room where you wash your body. My home has a separate laundry for washing clothes.'

Mary looked sceptical.

'Nobody has a room just to wash in, and why would you need a room to wash clothes? You would have to cart water to your house to do that.'

David didn't know how he could explain his world to Mary, but he didn't want her thinking he was lying to her either.

'Mary, I know you find it hard to believe what I am telling you.'

'Why would you think that, David? Is it because everything that comes out of your mouth sounds like a lie? What I don't understand is why Joe and Polykarpos can't see it.'

David sighed, 'Alright Mary, would you believe your own eyes if I could show you my home?'

Mary's brow furrowed.

'How?'

'I can use technology to show you moving pictures of my home. It will seem like you are actually there in the house. If it gets too much, I can stop it, if it frightens you.'

'So, now you are trying to frighten me into believing your stories?' bristled Mary in indignation. 'You can't scare me, David.'

'Good, that has never been my intention.'

'Don't even try,' said Mary, balling her hands into fists. 'If I have to, I can defend myself.'

'I believe you can, Mary, I just don't want you to have to.'

David removed a data storage device from his bag which contained three-dimensional images of the ancient cities of Galilee and Judea for use on his man hunt, along with his personal photo album, including a video shot at the house warming party held at his apartment. David hadn't wanted the party, it wasn't his style to be the centre of attention, but Jen had pushed the point that he needed to play the game and suck it up for the good of the team, so he had invited his work colleges to join him in a night of team bonding.

At the end of the evening, only two guests remained. Jen, who had stayed to help clean up, and Constable Leticia Bradbury from the traffic division. Leticia had been very attentive to David for the entire evening, sitting next to him on the lounge, sharing food from her plate and taking every opportunity to monopolise his conversation and make body contact. Jen didn't need to be a detective to recognise what was going on. When the trash had been binned, the dishes washed and stacked away, they congregated in the lounge room. David seemed oblivious to the looks from Leticia at Jen, who hadn't taken the hint to go home. Jen wasn't taking the bait.

'Dave, I need a hand with one final thing in the kitchen, Leticia you can go now if you want.'

Leticia didn't move.

'I don't mind staying, if David doesn't mind the company.' This was accompanied with a twirl of a finger in the hair, a slight tilt of the head and a rather hungry smile.

'Right,' said Jen deadpan, 'Dave in the kitchen, Leticia can make herself comfortable here, can't you Leticia?'

'Yes, I can, Jenifer,' she replied without taking her eyes off the somewhat confused David.

Jen placed a hand on David's elbow and ushered him to the kitchen at the rear of the apartment.

'Are you interested in Leticia?'

'Sorry, what?'

'Do you want a relationship with Constable Leticia Bradbury? It's a simple question.'

'What made you say that?'

'Well, she wants to know you, Davey boy and I don't mean in a platonic manner.'

'She told you that?'

'Jesus, Dave, call yourself a detective. She's been coming on to you like a hooker working a sales convention all night.'

David blinked in surprise, 'Seriously?'

'Leticia has her heart set on feeling the thread count on your sheets with her bare arse, then seeing what you make for breakfast in the morning.'

David leant against his kitchen sink.

'No, I am not interested in Leticia. It's not that she isn't attractive or nice, the problem is if it goes wrong, we end up working together with a failed relationship nagging away in the background.'

Jen nodded. 'Okay, if you just want to shag each other tonight, that's your business. Leticia obviously has her heart set on it and if that's what you want too, I can bugger off home with nothing more said. If it's something more she has in mind and you don't, then don't even start it.'

David shook his head.

'Sex without emotional commitment doesn't really do it for me.'

'Okay, then,' said Jen taking David's hand, 'don't say anything stupid or read anything into what I am about to do. This is purely to avoid any potential embarrassment and cut this thing off tonight. Do you understand David?'

'No, not really, but I can follow your lead.'

'Good, just don't overreact.'

Jen led the way to where Leticia was reclining on the lounge with her shoes off and an additional button on her blouse undone. Jen slipped her arm around David's, inserted her fingers into his hand, rested her head on his shoulder and faked a small yawn.

'I don't know about you, Leticia, but it's been a long day and I imagine you have an early start with the traffic division tomorrow.'

Leticia's brow furrowed, *what was going on?*

Jen continued, 'I am fairly knackered, Dave. I might just have a quick shower before bed.' She let go of David's arm, placed her hands to either side of his face and planted a slow kiss full on his lips.

'Thanks for coming, Leticia, I know Dave appreciated it.' Jen removed her shoes then turned and headed toward the bedroom, pulling her blouse out of her skirt as she went. 'Don't forget to lock the door and don't be too long, if you're quick you can hop in with me.'

Leticia watched Jen walk away, stood, did up the errant button on her blouse and red-faced, made her way toward the door of the apartment.

'Thanks for inviting me, David,' she said through a forced smile.

'Thanks for coming, Leticia,' replied David, looking over his shoulder toward the bathroom. Jen's shoes and blouse lay on the floor outside the door making an obvious territorial claim.

Leticia hesitated, leant forward and planted her lips on David's cheek.

'If it doesn't work out with Jenifer, you can always give me a call.'

David was even more confused by this second kiss.

'Constable Bradbury nicked off then?' asked Jen, popping her head out of the bathroom, as David closed the door.

David nodded.

'Good. I'll be off home in a minute and catch you in the morning.' She claimed her shoes and blouse off the floor.

'What just happened?'

'I saved your arse from a potentially difficult few weeks and, by luck, you did me a solid at the same time.'

'How did I do that?'

Jen put a hand on David's shoulder to steady herself while she slipped on her shoes. 'Do you know Constance from records?'

'Yes, I know Constance.'

'Yeah, well Constance has somehow come to the conclusion that I bat for the other side. She does apparently, which is 100 percent her own business, and good on her. Anyway, given that I am not in a relationship and we get on well together at work, Constance has been doing what Leticia was doing towards you tonight, only she has been less subtle and frankly more persistent. I like Constance and it's flattering, but I prefer blokes, and you know my rule about office romances.'

David nodded.

'So, this was as much to send a message to Constance as to scare Leticia off.'

'And I was beginning to doubt your powers of deductive thinking Dave. We'll make a decent copper out of you yet.'

'Am I to deduce that Leticia will spread the word, saving you from having a difficult conversation with Constance?'

'Bingo, you got there in the end.' Jen stood upright and headed to the door. 'See you in the morning partner. Bring coffee, it's your buy seeing as you owe me one.'

'Good night, Jen,' said David as the front door to his apartment closed. God, he loved having Jen as a partner, she really did have his back.

# CHAPTER TWENTY

POLYKARPOS AND PETER WATCHED Joe disappear.

'I told you he was like no man I have ever met.'

Peter nodded in agreement.

'If I had not seen the miracles, I would not have believed it possible.'

'It is more than that, David is as brave as a lion, yet refuses to kill those who would have no hesitation in ending his life.'

'Is he really just a man, Polykarpos?'

'He claims to be.'

'Do you believe him?'

'The truth is, I don't know who or what David truly is.'

'Do you think he is the one sent to lead our people out of servitude?'

'No, I have always thought the stories to be metaphors, rather than factual.'

'But you have seen David do things.'

'I have seen David do incredible things with the tools he calls technology and technology is just the practical application of science. We Greeks invented science.'

'David called his father a creator, is that not another name for Jehovah?'

'I don't think he is the son of God, but I see how you could draw that conclusion.'

'It doesn't matter does it? What we tell people to believe, will be the truth.'

Polykarpos nodded. Peter was right, it didn't matter who David was. What was important was who people believed him to be.

'David has asked for my help, Peter, and I am obligated to go with him, but that doesn't mean he can't perform more tasks that others may view as miracles on the journey.'

'Just as it won't hurt if people rally to our cause as a result of these miracles,' said Peter soberly.

'You don't feel right using him?'

'I don't feel right about the Romans trying to kill me and my friends, Polykarpos.'

'If David is not inclined to join us, we can still use his name to rally the people. If he disappears, we can say David had to join his father the creator and we won't be telling a lie. We can tie his eventual return to some great event and tell everybody that those who live good and honest lives will be saved, while everybody else can go to some other place,' the old man replied.

'Some place worse than living in Nazareth,' said Peter, pondering Polykarpos's proposal. 'It all sounds fanciful and ridiculous.'

'The best lies often are. If it sounds like a little lie, people are more than happy to see it for what it is. If you speak a massive, unbelievable lie that couldn't possibly be true, but say it often enough with enough conviction, it grows its own truth.'

Peter was about to reply when a cacophony of sound burst from the entrance of the cave.

# CHAPTER TWENTY-ONE

DAVID PLACED THE DATA device on the cave floor, then activated it using voice commands.

'Display personal files.'

A holographic file index filled the space above the data device. David used his hands to wave, swipe and pinch until he found what he was looking for. Mary stared wide-eyed.

'What is that?'

'This is how my people store some of their memories.'

'How can you capture a memory?'

'It's like making a drawing, just instead of using paper and ink, it's done by copying light and sound. Where I come from, we have clever machines built by people like my father that can record moments of your life, then store them in a machine like the box on the floor.'

Mary was dumbstruck.

'This is not witchcraft?'

'It's just a tool, Mary. It's not magic.'

'What are you doing with your hands?'

'The machine understands certain hand signals and words. I tell it what to do by using the right words, or by moving my hands in a way it recognises.'

'You truly are not a thief?'

'I am the exact opposite of a thief, Mary. My job is to catch thieves and stop people hurting others, which is why I am here.'

David found the file he was looking for and paused to explain, 'This particular memory was collected at celebration called a house warming party. You may find it a bit scary, it will be noisy, there will be strange music and some of the people's clothing may offend you.'

Mary raised her hands and spun in a circle to indicate the hologram that filled the cave, 'If this doesn't scare me, the inside of your home won't.'

'Okay, Mary, to open the memory say the words, *play file.*'

Mary didn't understand, but said, '*Play file.*'

Mary jumped in fright. A man's face appeared, talking and laughing in a strange language. The vision swung to show a second man, who was holding the recording device, laughing with the first face. The view returned to the first man, which waved for Mary to follow, but before she could lift a foot her vision moved to a door as if she was already walking.

'David?'

'It's okay. What you are seeing is another person's memory from their point of view. If you stay still, the memory will flow along and you can just watch. If you try to walk inside the memory, you could hurt yourself, the cave walls are not that far away.'

'It feels like I am in a dream and have no control.'

The door opened, light and noise spilled out. Mary shielded her eyes as the image moved through the opening. She felt slightly giddy and had to face the direction of travel to avoid feeling she was being dragged sideways. As Mary turned, the noise volume began to rise, the man leading the way stopped, smiled widely and began talking rapidly.

'What does this man find so funny?'

David hesitated. 'Dylan, the funny bugger leading the tour, is making a cutting remark about my work wife and whether she would approve of my bachelor pad.'

'Work wife? You said you were not married?'

'I'm not married, Mary.'

'Then what is a work wife? Is it a prostitute like the women who follow the legions? If it is, then I was right about you all along.'

David sighed. 'What these two clowns are not very subtly joking about, is my partner, Jenifer Rostig. We work together, that's all.' David thought about it, then continued, 'That's not true, Mary, Jen is far more than a partner on the job. She is my teacher, my confidant and my best mate. I trust her with my life and she trusted me with hers. There is nothing I wouldn't do for Jen and nothing she wouldn't have done for me.'

Mary saw the pain in David's eyes.

'Is Jen the one who was hurt?'

'Yes.'

'This woman is somebody you trust with your life?'

'Yes.'

'Do you love her?'

David had never thought of his relationship with Jen in such a simplistic way.

'Yes Mary, I love Jen.'

Mary nodded in understanding.

'Is that why you came to Nazareth, to seek revenge for this woman you love?'

David put his hand into the light, *pause*, the memory froze.

'No, what I am going to do is catch the crims and bring them in to face justice.'

'What if they don't want to come with you?'

'I have ways to persuade them.'

'With something like this?' Mary withdrew the stunner from her robes.

'I was hoping somebody picked that up.'

'Joe said you could make a wind with this that knocked the Romans from their feet and put them to sleep. Is that true?'

'Yes, it's a weapon designed to incapacitate.'

'Can it kill?'

David nodded, 'If it is used incorrectly. '

'Do those you are chasing have such a weapon?'

'I don't think so, not given that they stabbed Jen with a knife because I wasn't there to protect her.'

'You blame yourself for this, David?'

'I put my family's needs above my duty as a police officer, for that I can never forgive myself.'

Mary could see the emotion in David's face.

'You wanted this Jenifer for your wife?'

David was surprised by the question.

'No, even if I had romantic feelings for Jen, she wouldn't have felt the same. Jen is my best friend in the world, I loved her for just being Jen, that's more than enough for me.'

Mary nodded in understanding. Joe was her best friend, as well as her husband and the father of their children.

'Can I have that please?'

Mary handed over the weapon; David checked the safety then tucked it into his underwear. Mary looked at this man in front of her, surrounded by a picture made from light. Joe and Polykarpos were right, David was something else. Then she asked a question.

'What do you want from me, David?'

'I want you to believe me, Mary,' replied David simply. 'I need your help. I need the help of Polykarpos and maybe Peter and his friends if I am going to find the people I am after.'

'Surely Peter or Polykarpos would be easier to convince?'

'Yes, I could probably get Peter to help me for the coins, Polykarpos would do it out of a sense of obligation and, I suspect, curiosity. Joe would do it out of some misguided sense of, I don't know what.'

'Joe thinks you're an angel.'

David laughed.

'Well, that's wrong on so many levels, and a reason not to involve Joe.'

'That doesn't answer my question, why me?'

'Because I think you are the one person in Nazareth smart enough to get it. What I am going to tell you may seem like bullshit, please just hear me out before making a judgement. If you couldn't possibly believe anything I tell you, I will leave as promised. If you do believe me, I will ask for your help. If what I ask is too much, or too dangerous, please say so. No matter what you decide, I will leave as many coins as I can and the medicine as promised, no trade will be needed.'

'You swear this by Jehovah?'

'I don't believe in gods, Mary; I believe in people.'

'Now who is being gullible.'

'You believe in Joe?'

'Of course, I believe in my husband,' said Mary taking the point. 'Then I want you to swear on your love for Jenifer Rostig.'

David held out a hand.

'In my culture, if you are meeting somebody for the first time, or about to commit to a deal with a person, you take their hand.'

Mary looked into David's face and took his hand.

'Don't think you get to touch any other part of my body, David, no matter what happens in your land.'

'Fair enough,' David said with a smile. 'I swear as a gazetted officer of the law to tell the whole truth and nothing but the truth by my love of Jenifer Rostig and in the sight of Mary of Nazareth's god, Jehovah.'

Mary shook hands.

'All right then, tell me your story.'


'I don't know what to think?'

'It's the truth, Mary.'

'It makes less sense than Joe's idea that you're an angel.'

'I don't have wings, and I can't perform miracles.'

'But you can turn water into wine.'

'That's technology, Mary. It's no different than the memory I have just shown you.'

'Can you show me your Jenifer Rostig? Have you a memory of her in your box?'

David nodded then used his hands to fast forward the file.

'What is that noise?' yelled Mary.

'Sorry,' David pushed his arm out and said, *'Music.'* Holographic words appeared in the image with a picture of the artist Michael Bublé, performing *Haven't met you yet.*

*'Volume down,'* ordered David.

The hologram had moved to a room filled with people eating and drinking. There were men dressed in brightly coloured clothes, some of which were covered with writing and pictures. Some of the women were dressed like the men, others had gowns of fine cloth that hugged the curves of their bodies. Some had lots of flesh showing, some had none. Two women were holding hands, two bearded men were doing the same with one sitting on the other's lap feeding him morsels of food. Mary's eyes widened in surprise.

Then Mary saw David in the memory, sitting on a long-padded chair with a young woman on one side and an older woman on the other. *The younger was very pretty, the older was attractive in her own way*, thought Mary. The older woman's face wasn't coloured like the younger one who had painted lips and glowing cheeks. The younger one wore a red gown that showed off her legs up to her thighs, the top half hugged her figure such that when she moved, her breasts seemed to strain against the cloth. Mary's eyebrows rose in disapproval.

The older woman was dressed like the men in the room, wearing trousers and a long sleeve top held together in the front with buttons. Mary tried to guess her age, thinking she was older than her looks would have you believe. She was muscled under her clothes, but exuded femininity. Mary noted the older woman was watching the younger woman with a look of disapproval.

Mary watched the younger woman lean across David's body when there was no need. She touched him when they talked, then flicked her hair and smiled that smile.

Mary stuck her arm into the light and said, *'Pause.'*

David, who had been watching Jen, was surprised.

'Are you okay?'

Mary pointed at the younger woman, 'Is this your Jenifer Rostig?'

'No, that is Leticia Bradbury.'

'Is she a prostitute?'

'What makes you ask that?'

'She wants to lie with you, David, not as your wife but for her pleasure and no other reason. Did you lay with her David?'

'No Mary, I did not have sex with Leticia. I like her as a person and respect her as a work colleague, but that is all.'

'Good, she is not right for you; she would break your heart.'

Mary pointed at Jen.

'This one can see what I see.'

'Yes, she warned me about Leticia and basically showed her the door that night.'

Mary nodded.

'Is this your Jenifer?'

'Yes, that's Jen.'

Mary looked into David's eyes; it was all there.

'I believe you now, you are not a thief, or a trickster. You are here because of your love for this woman who is like a mother to you. That I understand.'

'Thank you, Mary,' said David, relieved to be believed.

David put his arm in the light, *'Close file,'* The hologram disappeared.

Mary turned. Peter was on his knees as if scared for his life. Polykarpos was standing behind Peter, wide-eyed in awe at what he had witnessed.

Peter looked at David, 'I am unworthy to stand in your divine presence.'

'Jehovah, give me strength,' said Mary, giving Peter a slap across the top of his bowed head. 'Get off your knees. David needs our help.'

'Oww!' exclaimed Peter looking daggers at Mary.

David extended a hand to help Peter up.

'I won't bite, I promise.'

Peter took the proffered hand and rose to his feet.

'You truly are not an angel?'

'No.'

'Are you a prophet of Jehovah?'

'No.'

'Weren't you listening?' said Mary in frustration. 'David is a police officer.'

'A what?'

'It doesn't matter what you call David,' chimed in Polykarpos, 'what matters is how we can help.'

'Thank you, Polykarpos,' said David graciously. 'What I need is get away from here as quickly as possible so that I don't put you in any further danger.'

'Peter's cousin buys horses from the desert tribes and sells them to the Romans; I am sure he could supply as many swift mounts as you need.'

'Could you arrange that Peter, without putting yourself in danger?'

Peter nodded.

Mary glared at Peter. 'Don't tell me you are talking about your cousin, Simon?'

Peter was instantly offended.

'I know Simon's loyalty lies with coin and not causes, but he is not going to cheat me.'

'Simon would sell his mother if he could turn a profit,' bit back Mary.

David looked to Polykarpos.

'Can this Simon be trusted?'

Polykarpos answered thoughtfully, 'Mary is right, as is Peter.'

David accepting the advice, said, 'Make a deal with your cousin please, Peter. I need two horses, that is, if you are willing to come as my guide, Polykarpos?'

'I made a promise and I will keep my word. As for Peter's cousin, buy three horses. We should take at least one other with us. The Romans are looking for two men, if we are three, it may confuse them.'

'Alright then, three horses.'

David picked up a fortune in gold and silver from the cave floor.

'Will this be enough?'

# CHAPTER TWENTY-TWO

'AUNTY HANNAH, WHY DO women grind wheat to make flour and men don't?'

Hannah paused winding the handle on the grindstone she was using and sat her niece on the table that held the basket of grain.

'Because, Milcah, men can't be trusted to do it properly. When you get older, you will realise that while men think they make everything important happen, it is actually women that get things done.'

'Why?'

'Well, men have that thing between their legs that women don't. Some people think it makes decisions for the man without thinking of the consequences. Men go to war because they want to prove that their thing is bigger or better than other men's, or chase after women who clearly don't want anything to do with them.'

'Is that why Peter keeps coming to see you, even though you don't like him?'

'You've noticed that have you?'

Milcah nodded.

Hannah carried on, 'Or it can persuade a man to race another man with horses so fast that they fall off and injure themselves.'

'What if the horse doesn't want to race, I don't think that is fair?'

'Lots of things in life aren't fair, my lovely Milcah, which is why I'm grinding grain and a man isn't.'

'What else does the thing that men have, make them do?'

Hannah considered this as she poured grain into the top of the grindstone. 'It makes men drink wine until they fall down or climb trees just because a tree is there.'

'Trees can't tell you if they want to be climbed.'

'No, they can't.'

As Hannah turned the handle, flour spilled out of the mill into a clay pot. She looked at the contents.

'Not enough yet,' she said disappointedly.

'Aunty Hannah?'

'Yes, Milcah.'

'Is the thing that men have, why you call some men dicks?'

'You have heard me say that, have you?'

'You were talking with Mummy and you said Peter's friends were acting like a bunch of dicks. Mummy laughed and then you said that Peter was probably the king of the dicks, given the way he is behaving. Then Mummy said that if they continued to let their dicks do their thinking, they were likely to end up dead. Mummy wasn't laughing when she said that. Why did it make her sad?'

Hannah stopped grinding.

'Your mother and I were talking about a very grown-up thing, Milcah. Peter and his friends' things have been whispering in their ears that they can rid us of the Romans, but they don't have experience with war or the money and weapons to do it, they only have their things whispering in their ears.'

'I don't see how their things can beat the Romans. It can't use a bow or throw a spear or drive a chariot that could trample the Romans into the dirt.'

'No, it couldn't.'

'Is Daddy a dick, like Peter? I don't want his thing to tell him to fight with the Romans.'

Hannah placed her hands gently on her niece's shoulders.

'Your father is a good man; the problem is he has a thing that whispers in his ear like other men. Unlike Peter, your father has someone that can talk sense into him, do you know who that is?'

Milcah thought about this.

'He has Mummy?'

'Yes, Joe has Mary to drown out the sound of his thing whispering and he is smart enough to listen to your mother when it really counts. All men can be dicks, but the difference between Peter and your dad is that he has Mary and you to stop him from behaving like one.'

'And that is why women grind flour and men don't?'

'That's right Milcah, men can't be trusted not to listen to their things, women don't have one so they can get things done, like grinding wheat to make flour.'

'Hannah, Hannah,' called a voice.

Milcah looked up to see her father.

'That's Daddy yelling for you, Auntie Hannah. He is running and waving his hands.'

Hannah didn't look up.

'I assume he can see us.'

'Yes, Aunty Hannah, I waved and Daddy waved back.'

'Hannah, Hannah,' came the call again.

'Why do you think he is calling my name, even though he knows we can see and hear him?'

Milcah looked towards her father.

'I think it's because his thing is whispering in his ear and he can't think properly.'

Hannah wiped her hands and looked towards Joe. He had stopped running and was bent at the waist trying to catch his breath. Joe raised a hand of acknowledgment that he had been noticed at last.

'Let's wait and see what your father has to say, then we can decide.'

Joe walked the last 20 paces.

'Hannah, thank Jehovah, I found you.'

'I didn't know I was lost?'

'You're not lost, Aunty Hannah; you are here with me.'

Joe seemed not to notice the repartee between the two women and launched into the message he had run so hard to deliver.

'Hannah, Mary needs you to come with me right now.'

Hannah looked quizzically at her brother-in-law.

'Is Mary injured?'

'No.'

'Have the Romans taken her hostage after what happened?'

'No, it's nothing like that.' Joe hesitated for a moment. 'Well, it is linked to last night, but not in the way you might think. Mary said I was to run and fetch you; she needs to see you right away.' Joe held out his hand for Hannah to take and follow him.

'No Joe, once I have ground the flour I need to make the dough, then while it is resting, before going in the oven, I have an appointment with my favourite rock and a load of washing. After I tear myself away from that enthralling task, I need to light the oven and put the dough in to bake; after that I have to clean the shit out of mother's goat pen. When that's done, I will probably have a few minutes to consider Mary's invitation.'

'Then you're not coming?'

'No, I have bread to bake.'

'Yes Daddy, I like Aunty Hannah's bread.'

Joe looked at his daughter.

'Milcah, can you go and keep your grandmother company, Hannah and I need to have a grown-up conversation.'

Milcah shook her head, 'I can't Daddy, Alte Bobeh has taken James to

184

see the shepherd boys, she said it wasn't safe for men or boys to be in the village today. Mummy said that I should stay with Aunty Hannah, so I am.'

Joe nodded understanding.

'Your mother was right; I hadn't thought what the Romans are likely to do.' He looked back to Hannah. 'You really do need to come with me.'

'No, Joe, you can bugger off if you can't come up with something better than Mary needs to see me now.'

'Mary thinks she's found you a husband.'

Hannah looked incredulously at Joe.

'You can definitely bugger off then.'

'It's not what you think, this is not like Peter.'

'I should hope not.' Hannah was about to tell Joe exactly what she was thinking when she noticed Milcah listening to their conversation.

'Milcah, take the flour inside, add the water and salt then work it like I showed you. Remember to wash your hands before you mix it together.'

Milcah understood.

'You and Daddy need to say things that you don't want me to hear?'

Hannah lifted the nine-year-old from the table and handed her the bowl of flour.

'Do you remember what we were talking about?'

Milcah nodded and wiggled her little finger.

'Yes, this is one of those times when a woman needs to say things to drown out the whispering in a man's ear. Off you go and make sure you wash your hands.'

'Yes, Aunty Hannah,' replied Milcah running off to complete her task.

'What's whispering in my ear?'

'Don't worry Joe, it's just a secret we women keep between themselves.'

Joe didn't get it so carried on, 'Hannah, you really need to come with me please.'

'Well, that makes all the difference, you saying, "please". No Joe, I am not coming.'

'Mary said if you didn't come, I was to go see your mother.'

'Really Joe, you can do better than that!'

'I don't think she is serious about finding you a husband, I think she needs your help to trade with David for some medicine. It could save the boys and Milcah's life if they get a fever or come down with the shits.'

'What exactly did Mary promise in exchange for this magic medicine, Joe? Don't tell me my sister promised me as a wife.'

'Well no, not at first.'

'That's a relief,' said Hannah sarcastically. 'I would hate to think I was the very first thing that Mary tried to barter with.'

'Mary said she would trade a goat for David's medicine.'

'You don't own a goat.'

'Mary said we could buy one, but David didn't want a goat, he's lactose intolerant which means he can't drink milk.'

'Fair enough,' said Hannah continuing the sarcasm, 'what did my loving sister offer up next?'

'A donkey.'

'Where were you going to get a donkey if you can't afford a goat?'

'I didn't ask, you know how Mary can be.'

'Let me guess, this David didn't want a donkey.'

'He said it would slow him down in his mission.'

'His mission? Is this David one of those prophets promising the coming of the Messiah, provided we hand over our silver?'

'No, David said he is not a prophet; besides he has more gold than I have seen in my life.'

'This David that Mary needs me to meet, has money?'

'And he has technology. David used it to save my life and the men the Romans were going to execute on the Hill of Kedumim.'

'I know I'm going to regret asking, but how?'

'David brought forth light and wind that knocked the Roman soldiers down and put them to sleep, then he made buckets full of water using his hands and a small stone which he turned into wine. We watched David do it. I drank the wine and it made me feel strong. David has promised to give the secret of this wine, which is a medicine, to Mary.'

'And Mary wants me to marry this David, who can turn water into wine?'

'I don't' know, but I do know that Mary needs to see you now.'

'Sorry Joe, I'm not buying it and I don't understand why Mary would believe what sounds like the work of a clever trickster.'

Joe nodded.

'You're right, Mary thought David was a thief, but now she doesn't.'

Hannah was surprised, Mary was not a woman easily fooled.

'Why are you so enamoured by this stranger?'

Joe relaxed. While Hannah had told him to bugger off twice, he felt her resistance softening.

'Well, David is friendly, he speaks a lot of foreign tongues, and though he is from a faraway land, he doesn't have a strange accent, and he says please and thank you, even when you don't expect him to.'

'That's fascinating, Joe. I will just drop everything to meet this David who speaks well and has good manners. I couldn't think of anything more important in a prospective husband.'

'Are you being sarcastic, Hannah? I don't think it's helpful if you are.'

Hannah gave a sigh and composed herself.

'Go ahead, Joe, I am listening with interest.'

'David has enough gold to buy the entire village and all the surrounding fields.'

'You believe it's his money?'

'Yes, I believe David, but Mary didn't at first.'

'Mary has to be cautious, Joe; she has a family to think of, as do you.'

'I am thinking of my family, Hannah. I think David was sent to meet us for a reason.'

'So, who is he then? What do you really think?'

Joe shook his head and said, 'I can't. You will tell me to bugger off again.'

Hannah almost laughed. 'You said Mary thought he was a thief.'

'Polykarpos, Peter and I know David is not a thief.'

'Using Peter as a character reference isn't going to convince me.'

'Forget what Peter thinks, I'll tell you what I know.'

'Alright, give it your best shot.'

Joe took a deep breath and played the card he believed would sway Hannah.

'I could tell you that David is brave, handsome and smart, but I don't think that will change your mind.'

'You forgot to mention if my future husband is young or a wrinkled old man. He is old and wrinkled, isn't he?'

'No, I believe David is around your age.'

'You still haven't convinced me, Joe. All you have told me is that this David is not ugly, has gold and is polite and brave, which sounds like any of the Roman officers that prance around Nazareth. None of which impresses me.'

'What I wanted to tell you was, what David said. It made me realise how important Mary is in my life.'

'Okay Joe, tell me, I am quivering in anticipation at the thought of his wisdom.'

'David said, how we men treat women is as big a reflection on our character as how the Romans treat us.'

'What did he mean by that?'

'David said Mary should be my equal partner in making decisions and raising the children.'

Hannah's eyes widened in surprise.

'He said that men and women should be equal?'

'David said women should be free to make their own decisions and open a carpentry shop or buy a house or a herd of cattle if they wanted to. Then David said women should be able to change husbands if they don't like the one they have. This made Peter splutter, then David said something about going to a day spa, I don't know what that is, but apparently, it's something women do where David comes from, while their husbands stay home and look after the children.'

Hannah was stunned.

'He said this to Peter, the man who believes women are only here to bear children and cook and clean for their husbands?'

'And Peter listened, and then offered to help Mary carry a bucket, like he was apologetic for asking her to fetch it.'

Hannah shook her head.

'Peter apologised for ordering a woman about?'

'Well no, he asked Mary if he could carry it for her.'

'I bet Mary told him where to go.'

'Well yes, she did.'

'Good on Mary.'

'David made me realise that I was taking Mary for granted. I felt embarrassed, to be honest.'

'This David said all of this to you, Peter and Polykarpos?'

'Yes, he did.'

Hannah picked up the bag of grain and bustled past Joe.

'You're definitely not coming then?' asked Joe in despair.

'Oh, I am coming all right, Joe, I want to see if this David is all you say he is. I'll just send Milcah to stay at her friend's house and I'll be back.'

Joe let out a sigh of relief.

'Thank you, Jehovah,' he whispered, 'thank you for sending the angel, David.'

# CHAPTER TWENTY-THREE

WILL SAT ON A fold-up chair in a corner as far from the stage in the Compton Soldiers' Memorial Hall as he could. The rectangular limestone building contained the compulsory 1960s portrait of the Queen and an honour roll of those the building commemorated.

Will read the list of names, noting two Thomases and was relieved that neither had a little black cross next to their names, which marked those who had not survived conflicts from the Great War to Vietnam.

Will's eye moved to the focal point of the hall. On the stage sat four black speakers linked via a mass of cables to twin record players and a massive CD player operated by the DJ for the night, the bearded and slightly rotund, Brad.

Brad had made up for his lack of musical talent with an abundance of enthusiasm, endeavouring to radiate disco chic in an era of Bon Jovi and Midnight Oil, where music had evolved to a grittier form and the mullet replaced the afro. He found his DJ calling in the era of Gloria Gaynor and KC and the Sunshine band. The music moved him and he believed that it would be a great way to meet women.

A decade later and aware of his increasingly middle-aged looks, he still believed the one was out there, somewhere on a dance floor. She would look to the stage, see the inner groove of his soul and recognise that fate and the rhythm of disco had brought them together. Tonight could be his Dirty Dancing moment, tonight a Frances, a Baby, would notice the Johnny Castle inside him.

Putting aside his Swayze fantasy, Brad believed he could play just the right track at just the right time to make every performance magical. Fortunately, most audiences he entertained were generally well and truly pissed by the end of festivities and couldn't remember much if anything of his DJ skills.

Will's gaze moved to a banner above the stage, *Congratulations Brian & Lonica On Your Engagement* was the headline message. A second smaller banner, highlighting the week's other momentous event, was attached beneath, *Tony Plugger Lockett 1987 Brownlow Medallist*. A third hand-written note was pinned below this simply stating, *Go SAINTS*.

Will raised his glass of coke in salute.

'Go Saints, and good on you Plugger, at least it's something to celebrate for the year.'

Mary Thomas was in her element, bustling about in the kitchen at the back of the hall, directing the arrangement of sausage rolls, potato salad and sliced beetroot into the various bowls and platters. She had wanted a sit-down meal at the Barn Palace to celebrate the engagement of Brian and Loni. Colin had refused to spend so much money when a barbeque at home, with drinks in the garage, would do the same job. He even conceded moving the Monaro for the event.

Mary had given Colin a withering look and a compromise was reached. They would hire the Compton Hall, Mary would make the salads and the engagement cake, Colin would pay for a keg, soft drinks and provide a spit roast lamb. Brian and Loni had offered to pay, Mary and Colin had refused. This was going to be the first of their children to marry and, if they were brutally honest, it was likely to be the last.

Will's life wasn't Mary's only worry. Brian was flitting from job to job as if he was standing on hot coals. Loni had work with the railways but the writing was on the wall that the line could be shut by the government at any moment. Besides, Mary wanted grandchildren. If Loni had to work just to pay the bills, it was unlikely to happen anytime soon. Colin and Mary would pay for the engagement party, Brian and Loni could save their money towards a home deposit.

Mary removed her apron then headed out the rear of the hall to find Colin. He was standing beside the gas heated rotisserie watching the lamb rotate with a glass of beer in hand.

Colin had hired the roaster from George, their local butcher, where he had purchased the lamb along with the sausage mince that Mary mixed with herbs and chopped onions to make sausage rolls. When Colin explained it was for his son's engagement party, George had made a great show of looking up bookings in a ledger, running a finger down the list of dates then silently shaking his head. Colin said it was for his son Brian's engagement, just in case that was the issue. Almost immediately, the shake turned to a positive nod and the booking was pencilled in. Colin paid for the meat and waited until out of earshot before muttering, *absolute bloody wanker,* under his breath.

Mary and Colin watched the lamb rotate, drops of liquified fat dripped from the carcass to splutter and flare as they struck the burning gas below.

'It looks good,' Mary said, slipping one hand into the grip of her husband's.

Colin nodded, took a sip of beer and sliced off a sliver of meat which Mary took between forefinger and thumb. The meat was just the right colour, just the right texture and held just the right level of moisture to be perfect.

'It's ready,' said Colin, cutting a slice for himself.

'Well done,' said Mary, putting both arms around Colin and kissing him gently.

'What brought that on? You don't normally get all romantic out in public?' asked Colin.

'I think we are alone; Brian's friends are all standing around the keg and Lonica, sorry Loni, I keep forgetting that is what she likes to be called, is sitting with the girls discussing wedding plans.'

'It sounds like our engagement party.'

'The music was probably better,' said Mary with a smile.

'I can't argue with that, though Brad was cheap and dead keen when I told him that Loni was inviting half a dozen of her girlfriends over from the west.'

'Talk about desperate and dateless,' Mary felt ashamed the moment the words left her mouth.

Colin handed Mary his beer to finish.

'We have a lot to be thankful for, Loni is a better woman than I ever thought Brian would marry. She is intelligent, funny and smart enough to know when to put her foot down with him. Loni may even make Brian grow up.'

'Do I hear a note of disapproval, I think she's lovely.'

'No, I am convinced Loni will be great for Brian. I'm just not convinced Brian will be good for her.'

Will had a view of all that was going on. Brad was head down concentrating, a headset of earphones firmly in place, Brian was by the keg channelling Don Johnson from Miami Vice in a cream-coloured linen suit, cracking jokes with his entourage of Spandau Ballet clones, mullet haircut bogans and muscle-bound footballers in body shirts.

In the opposite corner was Lonica and the girl friends seated in a circle. The women clung together as if held by some invisible force forged by something primitive. Firstly, the circle formed a defensive shield against the males who were fuelling their testosterone driven urges with liquid stupidity and group bravado. Nothing was more powerful at blunting unwanted advances than the combined strength of female scorn. A withering look of disgust, accompanied by the verbal taunt of, *in your dreams mate* or, *I have never been that drunk,* or the simple *piss off loser,* could deflate egos in an instant.

Secondly, it was a defence against attack from within, as the presence of testosterone and alcohol could bring out the bitch in even the most gracious of feminine compatriots. The fear was that if one left the circle, they would be subject to attack by a member of the cohort who needed to shore up their position. Something along the line of, *I don't know what she was thinking with those shoes,* or, *Janine is such a slut.* This behaviour, while being counter to social standards, was unfortunately often the reality at such events.

The accepted convention was that if one had to leave the circle, you must be accompanied by a close associate. It had been long surmised that the accompanying female was present to aid in case of an attack from one of the males drawn to the female who had wandered away from the defensive formation. The escort could equally defend against the unwanted attention of a rival female. This practice, theorised to be the inspiration behind the author of *The Art of War,* Sun Tzu's idea, if it was best to keep your friends close, it was as important to keep your enemies closer.

Loni, with her hair in a half up, half down style with some curls, was one of the few in the group not sporting a hairdo inspired by the *Charlie's Angels* television series. Will could see five Farrah Fawcetts, a sprinkling of Molly Ringwalds from *Pretty in Pink,* two Madonnas from *Desperately Seeking Susan,* a Kate Jackson, two Jaclyn Smiths and a Bonnie Tyler, or was that a Rod Stewart? It was hard to tell the difference.

Will's study moved to the dance floor. It held a small crowd of young children and teenage girls who had yet to graduate to the older female circle. It was, at least, keeping the older ones from sneaking outside for a furtive cigarette, or a pilfered glass of beer.

In the last corner of the hall, were gathered the aunts and uncles, the work colleagues, neighbours and friends. The men were universally clutching a beer, holding dull conversations about next week's football final. The women had congregated in the kitchen, some like Wendy Sullivan genuinely to help, others because of the memories of being a younger woman in a circle and the lingering fear of being talked about if not in the room.

Loni spotted Will hiding in the corner. She liked Will, he was smart and funny when he wanted to be. Brian had warned Loni not to associate with his brother early in their relationship. She had received the same advice from people at work, Brian's friends and his Uncle Bruce and Aunt Beryl, which had her thinking there must be something seriously wrong with him.

Mary was lovely, Colin was serious, but a big softy underneath. Brian made her laugh and was a little childlike in some ways. Will, however, was an enigma. When Loni had invited Will to join in activities he would politely decline. Brian was furious when Loni had suggested they take Will down the pub for a meal; she hadn't wanted to push the issue because it wasn't worth getting into a fight over.

Then last Christmas, Loni had found herself alone with Will at his parents' home. She discovered that Will was not some strange deviate or wanker, as Brian had described him. He could hold an intelligent conversation and didn't say a bad thing about anybody. Will also didn't stink, nor was he creepy, as her work colleagues had suggested. Loni couldn't understand what people had against him. Then Bruce and Beryl had arrived laden with Christmas gifts, Will stepped into the street and disappeared without a word. To Loni's surprise, Beryl rushed through the door to check that she was unharmed, Bruce had puffed himself up and stood in the doorway to block Will from returning. It was bizarre behaviour.

Loni gestured for her maid of honour to stay put. She didn't need an escort as all eyes in the hall followed her to where Will sat on his own.

Brad noticed nobody was listening to his music, much less raising an eye to the music master. There was only one thing to do, he would have to play his "get the party going" song.

It started with a finger running across a piano keyboard from right to left, followed by four multiple finger plunges on the ivories, which started, not only the rhythm of the song, but also the mass gathering of females to the dance floor. By the time the vocals of Anni-Frid Lyngstad and Agnetha Fältskog had bounced out of the matt black speakers with the opening bars of *Dancing Queen,* Loni and Will were lost from view behind a wall of dancing shapes.

'Hi Will.'

'Hi Loni' replied Will.

'Can I sit with you?'

Will looked to where Brian was holding court.

'Why?'

'I just wanted to see how you are doing.'

'I don't think that's a good idea Loni, I don't want to cause trouble for you.'

'How can you cause trouble? I don't see you hogging the beer and you aren't causing a nuisance on the dance floor. Thinking of that, why don't you come and dance with me? It could be fun.'

Will was horrified at the thought.

'I don't dance Loni.'

'Neither do I really, but I get better the more wine I have.' This made Will almost laugh.

'Come on Will, just one dance, I don't see any men getting up, you could set an example.'

'No thank you,' said Will politely. 'I appreciate what you are trying to do, but the moment I go over there,' Will pointed to the mass of gyrating bodies, 'everybody will run away and you and I will be left looking like a pair of idiots.'

Loni admitted defeat and sat next to Will.

'If you won't dance with me...'

'I can't dance with you, there is a difference.'

'Okay, can't dance with me, then you can at least talk with me. I need to talk to somebody who doesn't want to talk about wedding stuff for a while. I know what I want, so everybody else should just shut up and listen and then it will all just go smoothly.'

'Mum causing issues?'

'Mary is fine, it's my family that's being a pain.'

'Is Brian helping?'

'He does what I tell him to, that's the important thing. Sometimes I think Brian is way too focused on his car racing, but I have got him under control.'

Will contemplated this thought. Loni might make something out of his brother after all.

'All right, what do you want to talk about?'

'I want to ask you a question, well, a couple of questions.'

'Okay, ask.'

Loni sipped her wine, 'why do they call you *W*?'

How could he answer this?

'I have been told a lot of stories; they are never the same. I heard you went crazy and destroyed your parents' house, then I was told you spent years in a mental home for killing every cat in the neighbourhood. Then I was told that you are some sort of a pervert that was caught having sex with a sheep in a church. Somebody even told me you were caught about to sacrifice a baby in some sort of a devil worship ceremony and was only stopped by the police at the last moment, then you spent years in a mental home.'

'None of that is true, well apart from wrecking the house. It happened twice, once in my bedroom, and once in the lounge. I was in a children's mental ward for a couple of months after the first time, which nearly did send me nuts.'

'You did bust up your own house, then got put in a loony bin?'

'No, I was there when it happened, but it wasn't me. You know, wrong place, right time.'

'If you didn't do it, who did?'

Will let out a sigh, 'I can't tell you.'

'Because you will have to kill me afterwards?'

'No, I can't tell you, because you won't believe me, and if I did tell you I will become the strange brother of the man you almost married. I don't want to mess this up for you and Brian.'

'It can't be that bad.'

'It's toxic Loni, and it's coming back, I just don't know when.'

'What's coming back?'

'A relative.'

'What, like a long-lost uncle who has made you promise to go away with him to someplace sweaty in Africa to find some lost treasure that will make you rich and famous? Wouldn't that be funny?'

Will smiled.

'You're closer to the truth than you know. It's not an uncle, it's my great, great, great, great, great grandson or grandnephew, that depends if I ever have kids or he is descended from you and Brian. I am thinking he is one of yours. His name is Adrian and there is no treasure, just the fate of society as we know it in the balance.'

Loni laughed, then asked, 'Why don't you have a girlfriend, Will?'

Now it was Will's turn to laugh, 'Who would want to be the boyfriend of the *W*?'

Brian's eyes narrowed in anger; Will was up to something with his fiancée. It wasn't that he expected anything to happen, Loni wasn't that sort of girl and Will didn't have the guts. The problem was the snide remarks behind his back that he knew were coming if he didn't do something about it. People were watching Loni laughing with Will. This had to stop.

'Grubs up,' called Colin carrying a platter covered in chunks of roast lamb.

Mary followed, leading a procession of women carrying bowls and platters filled to overflowing with finger food and salads.

'Eat, everybody,' Mary said, indicating for Brian to lead the procession to the table.

Brad took the hint and rummaged through his CD collection for Kenny G's *Gravity* Album. Nothing held a candle to Donna Summers *Last Dance* or the Bee Gees *You Should Be Dancing* but Kenny G was soothing to eat by. Having set the volume, taken a sip of his free beer, Brad studied the room. Two of the women seated in the circle looked his way, giggled, then looked away to carry on a conversation. One was a Molly Ringwald look alike; the other was sporting a Madonna coiffure. Brad didn't recognise any of this, to him they were upright, breathing, over 18 and had smiled in his direction. Maybe tonight was the night.

Brad made his way to the floor of the hall, wondering if he should go and ask them to help select the next set of songs, that was always a good way to get close to a girl at a gig. After two false starts, one toward the keg, the second toward the food line, Brad put his self-doubts to one side and decided to walk over and say 'hello'. He would be John Travolta playing Tony Manero strutting to the beat of *Staying Alive*. He breathed in, hoped his gut hadn't popped over his belt and marched to the beat in his head.

Brad was six paces away when Molly Ringwald nodded to Madonna.

'You're right, he does look like that old guy who played Father Christmas at the Panel Board Christmas show.'

'Yes,' replied Madonna, 'and his fly is down like you said. How gross is that?'

'He's not coming over here?' replied Molly Ringwald in mock horror. 'God no, yuk.'

Travolta deflated, looked to his open zip, heard voices giggling, pulled up his fly and moved to the end of the food line. Maybe tonight wasn't the night after all.

'Finally,' said Loni. 'If I don't eat shortly, I will end up hangry.'

'Hangry?'

'Hungry angry,' replied Loni, dragging Will by the hand, 'come on, the lamb won't eat itself.' Loni looked for her fiancé. 'Can you see Brian?'

'He might have gone to the loo; all of that beer has got to go someplace.'

'I guess so,' said Loni, contemplating driving Brian home. 'I told him to behave. If he gets drunk, he will be for it.'

Will smiled at the idea of Loni giving Brian a dressing down, then the sound of a car engine revving, followed by tyres squealing, disrupted his thoughts. Will looked at the keg. Its guard of honour had vanished, along with

Brian. There was a bang of metal colliding with something solid, followed by massed cheering of drunken voices. The engine revs rose again, along with the unmistakable squeal of rubber being dragged sideways. *Shit*, Will thought, *one of Brian's dickhead mates was doing donuts in the carpark.* Then a horn sounded, it was the unmistakable alarm call of his own Toyota Corolla.

Will pushed through the crowd to see his orange sedan slide sideways into the wooden boundary fence of the carpark. The Spandau Ballet clones, the mullet haircut bogans and the muscle-bound footballers, all yelled encouragement, Brian in the driver's seat, grinning and laughing with each spin of the wheel. Will wanted to get to his car and beat the living shit out of the arsehole. Arms held him still, as a glass of beer, followed by a second and a third, was tipped over his head with more cheering.

'Let go,' demanded Will. This brought a fist in his gut.

'That's what you get for putting the moves on our mate's girlfriend.'

'Fucking *W*, who the hell does he think he is?' said a second beer breath voice.

'Let him go!' came a command from behind.

The crowd turned. Colin had his left fist closed tight in plain view, his right behind his back wrapped around the shaft of a shifting spanner.

'Let go of my son and move away.'

One of the t-shirt wearers pointed a finger at Colin.

'You don't get to tell me what to do, old man.'

'I think I just did, or are you too stupid to notice?'

The footballer swung an open hand at Colin's face to slap him into submission, he had done this many times to assert his dominance. If that didn't work a closed fist would follow.

Colin avoided the open hand. Fighting full of beer wasn't the same as fighting sober. As soon as the hand had passed, Colin swung the 12-inch chrome-plated Kingcraft shifter. The footballer swayed backward, easily avoiding what he thought was the danger with a grin; he could now justify bringing his fists into play. Colin had been around a lot longer than his opponent; the swing was a distraction as he drop kicked Brian's friend full pelt between the legs. The top of his foot squashed the intended targets against their owner's pelvic bone. This was followed by an exhaling of breath and a thump as the owner of the bruised appendages dropped to his knees in agony.

Two more amateur athletes stepped forward with angry intention. Colin didn't hesitate. He landed the shifter between neck and shoulder breaking the clavicle and putting the owner down in agony. The third tried to push past his two mates but came to a bloody halt as the fist of Wendy Sullivan's husband met his nose at pace. Brad appeared brandishing a chair over his head.

'Come on then, let's see how well you can dance,' he said, waving the weapon from side to side. The aggression stopped; the crowd stepped back in surprise.

'Go home, the lot of you,' commanded Colin. The group muttered, picked up the wounded and made their way to their cars. Girlfriends, who had moments before been watching from the hall, disappeared into the dark to find their rides home.

Beryl moved to intercept Mary.

'How awful, if I was Lonica I would put the wedding off. The way Brian behaved.' Beryl shook her head at what she had been forced to witness. 'It was probably the beer, but it's not Brian's fault alone, he was provoked after all those years living with the disgrace in your family. I know it's hard to think about, but it's the other one that caused this.'

Mary placed the platter she was holding on a table.

'Beryl, there are times that I am duty bound to turn the other cheek,' Mary straightened her skirt and clasped her hands in front of her chest, 'but I am more than just a Christian woman; I am a wife and a mother to two children. One is a gentle soul, who through no fault of his own has been subjected to spiteful torment since he was just 14 years old. William has never harmed a soul in his life. He is a good son, a good man and an example of restraint and patience.' Mary let the point sink in.

'Brian has suffered as well, just not to the same level as William. What happened tonight was stupid and irresponsible. It is disappointing, but I am not going to disown Brian for it and besides, it's a family matter, and by family, I mean people who support each other in good times and the bad.'

Beryl turned up her nose.

'Are you saying you don't consider me to be real family?'

'No Beryl, I don't consider you at all, and before you say anything else, I think I should warn you of what I am thinking.'

'What? What are you thinking Mary?' hissed Beryl.

'I am thinking, what would Ita Buttrose do in my position?'

'I don't understand.'

'Ita would have an intelligent and sophisticated way of expressing her feelings, the problem is that I'm not Ita, I can only be me.'

'What has that got to do with your son's behaviour? This sort of thing is unacceptable Mary, you should be ashamed.'

'Ashamed, Beryl? You have no idea how close I am to knocking you on your arse right now.' Mary felt herself blush at having used the "a" word.

'You wouldn't dare.'

'But I would,' said Wendy Sullivan. 'I wouldn't be averse to a bit of girl-on-girl action, invite Bruce as well if you like, though it might be a bit more of a fair fight if you let him have his balls back for half an hour.'

Beryl fumed, turned on her heels and yelled across the hall.

'Bruce, we are going. Don't even think of finishing that beer.' She strode to the table holding the engagement presents, collected her gift and marched to the exit.

Wendy put an arm around Mary.

'Are you okay?'

'I am ashamed for letting Beryl get to me.'

'I would have slapped her and called her a bitch.'

'I am embarrassed enough about swearing.'

Wendy pointed at Beryl wobbling her way to the exit.

'What do you see there Mary? I bet even Ita would be forced to think it.'

Mary sighed, 'Yes, I am afraid that Beryl does have a rather big arse.'

Colin helped Will to his feet. He didn't think anything was broken but he felt awful for what he had done to his family again.

'I'm sorry, Dad.' Will looked at his car. One headlight was broken, a taillight hung from its mounting and the driver's side was dented along its entire length. It would take more than a cut and polish to fix.

'Your brother's an idiot, Will. I hate to say it, but if Loni doesn't reconsider marrying him, I will lose a bit of respect for her.'

Will looked at Brian standing on the edge of the light emitted from the hall.

'I think Brian has more things to worry about than my car.'

Colin followed Will's gaze. His younger son, head bowed, was being addressed by his fiancée. Loni had her arms crossed, one foot tapping up and down on the ground while she was speaking angrily at her betrothed. Brian looked as if he was being beaten by a dozen men wielding cricket bats. *So that's what* hangry *looks like*, thought Will.

'Are you right to drive home?'

'Yes Dad, I'm fine.'

'Okay, go home and get some sleep, we can sort out everything tomorrow.

Brian is going to pay for your car to be repaired, or he will be buying you a new one. That won't be negotiable.'

'I can stay and help clean up.'

'No, those idiot friends of Brian are just as likely to come back and nobody needs to be involved in more stupidity because off a bruised ego or two. Besides, Brad can help, I am paying for music until midnight. That doesn't mean he can't wash dishes at the same time and I don't think he is in a hurry to leave.'

Will looked through the hall door. To his surprise, Brad was happily engaged in conversation with Madonna who, only minutes before, had considered him too gross to talk to. Maybe, getting out from behind the mixing desk was what he needed, rather than hiding behind the music. *Good on you, Brad*, Will thought.

'Okay, Dad.' Will started to walk toward his car and stopped after two paces. 'Thanks for saving my arse.'

'Don't think anything of it, Will. I just thought, what would Plugger do. A kick in the nuts seemed the right answer.'

# CHAPTER TWENTY-FOUR

WILL WAS HOPING TO sneak home and avoid being spotted by the police for driving a defective vehicle. The car was probably a write-off, but things could have been a lot worse. At least he had gotten away without a beating for being the *W* again. While Brian had been the catalyst for tonight's excitement and his father and friends, his saviour, the disappointing part was he shouldn't have needed saving.

Colin and Mary had urged Will give up and leave the Mount to start a new life where nobody had heard of the *W*. He had been tempted, anybody who knew Will wouldn't blame him, but the problem was he didn't have that choice to make. Call it destiny, or bloody stupidity, which is what it really was. Will was stuck because Adrian was coming back and if the tracker in his neck didn't work, he might not be found so he would be putting his family at risk, even his idiot brother.

Will stuck to the speed limit, driving as inconspicuous as he could. There was only 500 metres to go, one more turn into Bond Street and he was home. Red and blue lights flashed from behind, lighting up the interior of the Corolla.

Will looked for his car's side mirror, it wasn't there.

'Shit!' he realised it must be lying in the carpark at the hall.

Will turned into the kerb, slowed to a stop, turned off the engine and removed the key from the ignition. In a moment, a defect sticker would be attached to the windshield and he would be walking home.

Will looked in his rear-view mirror. The red and blues and headlights shining through his rear window made it impossible to clearly see details. It looked to be just the one uniformed officer exiting the patrol car; the blue uniform stopped just behind the driver's door.

'Are you aware you have a broken taillight and a non-functioning head light, Sir?'

Will swung his head in surprise, it was a female officer.

'Yes, I am aware of that,' replied Will politely.

The officer moved to the passenger side shining a torch across the damage. The beam of light then swung to the rear of the car, where it focused on the registration plate before the officer moved back to her position behind the driver's door.

'Is this your car?'

'Yes, Constable, it is my car,' replied Will, now resigned to more than a walk home.

'Driver's licence please, and it's Brevet Sergeant, not Constable.'

*Shit.* From Will's understanding, a sergeant would not normally be on the street randomly patrolling for traffic violators.

'My licence is in my wallet. Is it all right if I hop out of the car to get it out of my pocket?'

The officer moved back a pace.

'Alright, just keep your hands where I can see them.'

Will nodded, then pulled the door handle. The panel damage had caused the door to jam shut. He pushed hard, nothing moved.

'The door's stuck,' Will said through the open window.

The officer used her torch to inspect the door and saw a deep bend in the metal.

'I can see this might be a problem. What I want you to do is drop the key out the window where I can see it.'

Will did as he was told.

'I am going to the passenger side of the vehicle. When I tell you to move, slide over with your hands where I can see them, I wouldn't want there to be a misunderstanding between us when you move.'

'Okay,' said Will looking ahead, hoping the Brevet Sergeant wouldn't over-react.

The passenger door rattled, creaked, then sprung open. Will wasn't game to look, just in case this was deemed to be a mistake.

'Move to this side of the car.'

Will shuffled over, making sure that his hands were in plain sight.

'Place your hands out of the vehicle, then exit.'

Will did as he was told, standing with his arms half raised. He wasn't sure if he was supposed to raise them above his head or keep them where they were. Torch light shone in his face.

'Turn around slowly.'

Will rotated slowly right to left, until he had completed a full circle.

'You can lower your hands.'

Will kept them in place, just in case.

'Licence.'

Will lowered his hands to reach into his pocket to remove his wallet, found his licence and passed it to the police officer.

'Is this your current address?'

'Yes, it's up the hill, off Shepherdson Road, you turn right at the deli.'

There was silence as light moved from the licence to Will's face and back again.

'Mr Thomas, can you explain why you are driving your vehicle in its current state?'

Will raised a hand to shade his eyes.

'It was in an accident about an hour ago, my car collided with a fence.' Will couldn't sense a reaction from the behind the light. 'It was my fault; I wasn't paying attention. I intend to contact the owner of the fence to pay for repairs in the morning. I couldn't find anybody to talk to where the accident happened, where I hit the fence.'

Will didn't want to lie, but he also didn't want to cause trouble for his family, and besides, how much more trouble could he be in?

The police office turned off the torch and moved under the streetlight. She was shorter than Will, with black hair tied in a bun behind her police cap. She wore no makeup and didn't need to; it was an attractive face. The sergeant had brown eyes, a small straight nose that curved up slightly at the tip, lips that seemed to turn upwards at the ends as if preparing to smile and a very small cleft in her chin. There was something familiar about her. Will risked a glance at the officer's name badge which said Wilson. He had gone to school with a Tony Wilson. She didn't look like Tony.

'Mr Thomas, we have a problem.'

Will remembered his father's advice, *if you have nothing positive to contribute, then don't.* Then, without thinking, failed to follow it.

'Please call me, Will. Mr Thomas sounds like you're talking to my father.'

Brevet Sergeant Wilson tilted her head, considering the request.

'Okay then, Will. First things first, I can detect a strong smell of alcohol about your person. How much have you drunk tonight?'

Will felt the stickiness in his hair.

'I haven't drunk any alcohol, Sergeant Wilson. What you can smell is beer that was spilt on my head.' Will could see a look of disbelief forming. 'That happened before the accident with the fence.'

'Go on,' said the sergeant taking out her notebook.

'I was at my brother's engagement party, at the Compton Hall.' Will pointed in the direction of the hall. 'Some of my brother's friends were a bit enthusiastic with their celebrations and they poured beer on my head.'

'Was this before or after you had an altercation with three males at the party?'

Suddenly, Will really didn't want to talk.

Brevet Sergeant Wilson read from her notebook, 'At approximately 20:20 hours this evening, three males aged 23 years; all residents of Mount Gambier, presented at the casualty department of the Mount Gambier Hospital. The second most seriously injured has a broken clavicle.' Brevet Sergeant Wilson pointed to her collar bone. 'The cause, blunt force trauma,' the notebook was referenced again, 'according to the duty doctor, *it looked like he had been belted with a hammer or something similar*. The second gentleman has damage in the genital area. He may lose a testicle.'

Will couldn't have spoken even if he wanted to.

'The third gentleman has a broken nose, it is the doctor's opinion, caused by a blow from something solid, like a fist.' Brevet Sergeant Wilson closed her notebook. 'Do you have any comment to make, Mr Thomas?'

'No,' said Will, expecting to be cautioned, or handcuffed, or whatever the official process was for arresting a person.

'Mr Thomas, Will, I have a problem with the gentlemen in question, not the least of which is how they received their injuries. Perhaps you can be of some assistance.'

'How can I help?' asked Will dreading the answer.

'You can start by telling the truth. We have witness reports that you were not the driver of this vehicle when it collided with the fence at the Compton Hall. We have statements from the injured parties that you were,' Brevet Sergeant Wilson referenced her notebook, '*doing donuts, because you are a mad wanker.*'

Will nodded. He would confess to anything short of murder to keep his family out of trouble.

'The injured parties allege you assaulted them with a tool, in fact a 15-inch Sidchrome shifting spanner.'

'It was a 12-inch Kingcraft,' replied Will flatly. 'I was defending myself after they poured beer on my head and the one with the broken collar bone punched me in the stomach.'

Brevet Sergeant Wilson's pen scratched at the notebook.

'That corroborates some of my information but doesn't clear up why my constables have several different accounts of the event.'

Will waited for the next question.

'Why do you think your parents and a husband and wife by the name of Sullivan confessed to assaulting the three injured parties? Then there is Bruce and Beryl Caruthers who claim the three injured parties were trying to restrain you from attacking your brother when you assaulted them. Then we have a statement from a Brad, the disc jockey,' the notebook was referenced, '*he didn't see anything, but if he had, it was probably not Will's fault,* and *he is available for hire if the cops were planning any sort of end of year party. Especially if it has a disco theme.*'

Will felt sick.

'It was me. I hit the bloke with the shifter, I kicked the other bloke in the groin and I punched the last one in the face. It was self-defence, nobody else was involved.'

'Are you prepared to swear in a written statement and in court that the injuries were sustained in self-defence and that the gentlemen involved were intent on doing you serious bodily harm?'

'Yes,' said Will resigned to his fate.

'Good,' said Brevet Sergeant Wilson closing the notebook.

'I don't understand.'

'The seriousness of the alleged assaults are one reason I am here; those involved is another.'

'Because it's me?'

'No, not primarily.' Brevet Sergeant Wilson provided an explanation. 'There have been a number of assaults in the city at night around licensed premises involving your brother's friends. Up until tonight, none of the victims have been willing to make a formal complaint. Thanks to you, we can bring them in for questioning and hopefully convince some of the other men assaulted to make an official complaint.'

'You think they were going to beat me up at my brother's engagement party?'

'No, I think they would have waited until after the party, then kicked you near to death in the carpark. Your brother did you a favour by getting them to tip their hand early.'

'I guess I will have to thank him.'

Brevet Sergeant Wilson placed a hand on Will's arm and moved him towards her patrol car.

'I am sorry Will, but for your evidence to be used, this will have to be done by the book.'

'Okay.'

'William Thomas, I must caution you that having identified that your motor vehicle is unroadworthy as per the South Australian Road Traffic Act of 1961, that I have cause to believe you may have been operating said vehicle on a public road while under the influence of alcohol. I have detected a strong smell of alcohol about your person and I am directing you to undertake a blood alcohol breathalyser test. You may refuse to undertake this test if you have a valid medical reason that prevents you from doing so, in which case, I will escort you to an appropriate medical facility for a blood sample to be taken for the purpose of testing your blood alcohol levels. If you refuse to submit to the taking of a blood sample, I will place you in custody until the blood sample is forcibly taken. Do you understand what I have just explained to you Mr Thomas?'

Will nodded.

'I need you to say the words, Will.'

'Yes, I understand. I am happy to undertake a breath test.'

'I am also going to defect your car, which means it cannot be driven on the road until it passes a road worthy inspection. Are you clear on that, Will?'

Will nodded. 'I'll get it towed tomorrow.'

Brevet Sergeant Wilson opened the police vehicle's boot to find her breathalyser. 'The gentlemen of interest are not the only person who grabbed my attention.'

'You came because the *W* was mentioned.'

'I was told all about the *W* on my first day in the Mount nine weeks ago, you're a bit of a local legend. I read the files from when you were 14, then 16 and the unsolved random assaults. Opinions at the station range from you being some sort of Damian from the Omen, to just one of life's shit magnets. I asked if you were dangerous, all I got was laughter. Apart from one senior constable, who thinks you are the son of Satan walking the earth. I am keeping an eye on that one. The thing is, it didn't shock me. It couldn't, I already knew some of the story.'

Will looked up in surprise.

'We have met before, Will; you probably won't remember.'

'I went to school with a Tony Wilson, is he your brother?'

'No, it was in Adelaide. I was 14 at the time.'

Will wracked his brain, then it dawned on him, the girl who had smiled at him while twisting her hair. Tracey and Scooter Wilson's daughter.

'Charlie Wilson?'

'Charlene Wilson, only my family and closest friends are allowed to call me Charlie. Just like only your mum calls you William, right?'

Will nodded. 'My mum writes to your mum, cards at Christmas, phone calls on birthdays.'

'Mum made me promise to make contact and send her love when I was transferred.'

Will thought he saw Charlene Wilson colour slightly.

'I suppose you have been busy; Mum will understand.'

'I was hoping it would be in different circumstances.'

Charlene pushed a button on the breathalyser, it flashed red.

'Bugger.' She bent at the waist over the luggage compartment of the car in search of batteries.

Will was confused. Should he call her Sergeant Wilson, or Charlene, since they had met before and their mothers were good friends? Then it happened again.

# CHAPTER TWENTY-FIVE

IT STARTED AS A barely discernible breeze that grew in intensity, picking up leaves and dust that swirled around Will and penetrated the open luggage compartment causing Charlene Wilson to close her eyes and sneeze. Will's nerves tingled, *surely not*, he thought, *not now*. He braced but it was too late.

Green light flashed into existence. The blast flung Will's arms and legs toward the rear of the police car, his torso followed as if being pulled rather than pushed from behind. His feet arrived first, striking the rear bumper either side of the bowed torso of Charlene. Will had been on target to strike the vehicle in an upright plane, legs against the rear bumper, head into the extended boot panel. Instead, his body pivoted forward and down at the hip, his thighs collided with the back of Charlene's legs. Will had just enough control to thrust his hands down either side of the blue uniform beneath him, but still ended up lying on top of Charlene as if in some intimate embrace. This lasted less than a second.

'Get the hell off me.'

Will was very aware of his hands, spreading them wide to avoid contact with the front of the blue shirt. He felt the roundness underneath him pushing up, which almost caused Will to hyperventilate in panic and bang his head against the inside of the boot lid as he stumbled backwards, raising his hands in surrender to prevent being shot.

'What the hell do you think you are doing?' hissed Charlene with a hand on her revolver in its holster.

'It was the shock wave, it knocked me off my feet,' replied Will in panic. 'I swear, it was an accident.'

'Bullshit. I don't know what's going on in your head but assaulting a police officer is totally unacceptable.'

'Why would I do that? It makes no sense.'

Charlene shook her head. 'There is something seriously wrong with you.'

Will sighed in exasperation. 'I'm really sorry, but I have no control over any of this.'

'Turn around and place your hands on the car, spread your legs and keep looking forward.'

Will did as he was told.

'I read the file, so don't try any of that "Adrian from the future did it" rubbish.' Charlene put a hand in the middle of Will's back and pushed. 'William Thomas, I am arresting you for the assault of a police officer during the execution of their duties. I am going to caution you, as is required under the law in South Australia. You do not have to say or do anything in response to questioning, anything you say or do may be used in court. Do you understand what I have just explained to you?'

Before Will could reply, a familiar voice spoke from the darkness.

'There you are, Will. I was worried that I had come to the wrong place, at the right time, or the right place, at the wrong time.'

'Hello Adrian,' replied Will.

Charlene turned to face the voice in the dark.

'This is official police business, please move along.'

'Sorry, I didn't realise you were still engaged, Will.' The voice paused, 'It is now, Will, to be absolutely clear, tonight. We will need to be off as soon as you have finished with the police officer.' The voice addressed Charlene, 'It is Brevet Sergeant Wilson, isn't it?'

Charlene unclipped the strap on her holster before turning back to Will. His left hand was on the roof, the right hung at his side with one half of the hand cuffs closed around the wrist.

'Both hands on the roof,' she ordered.

There was a clang as the handcuff made contact with the roof.

'How do you know this man, Will?'

'You know who he is, you read the files.' Will turned his head, 'Adrian, this is Charlene Wilson, she is an armed police officer.'

'A pleasure to meet you, Charlene,' replied Adrian.

'Are we likely to have a problem?' asked Charlene, addressing both Will and the voice in the dark. She swivelled her hips to highlight her hand resting on the butt of her weapon.

'No,' said Will emphatically, 'not from me.'

'No,' said Adrian, 'though we are rather on a bit of a timetable Sergeant Wilson. If you could have Will sign whatever document you need him to and we will be on our way. The fate of the world as we know it, is at stake.'

Will almost groaned.

'Adrian, just go away, you can catch up with me later.' Will looked at Charlene, 'I assume you will let me go home after you charge me?'

'No, I can't just let you go home after assaulting a police officer. You will be arraigned in custody until Monday morning when the magistrate can set bail conditions. Your friend can visit you at the station tomorrow.'

'Apologies, Sergeant Wilson, but I don't think I can. Tonight is a point in time that we could definitely confirm where Will would be. I used the archives from your local paper, *The Border Watch,* to pinpoint a place and time. You both make the front page on next Tuesday's edition.'

Charlene looked at Will.

'Is he dangerous?'

'No, he's not dangerous.'

'Is he mentally challenged?'

Will frowned.

'I don't think so, though we have only talked twice in the last 12 years. Well, 12 years for me, God only knows how long for him.'

Charlene looked blankly at Will.

'Father is causing issues. Uncle Emil and Uncle Dwight have to keep him away from the *Cabinet,* they can't come with me to find David, so we need you, Will,' said Adrian.

'Will is under arrest, you can visit him at the station tomorrow.'

'Sorry, but that won't do,' replied Adrian, 'the fate of the world is at stake.'

Charlene kept her hand on the butt of her service weapon. She would have to get a lot more direct with this clueless member of the public who was enabling Will's fantasy.

'Come over here where I can see you,' she said. 'Do it slowly, we wouldn't want any mistakes to happen.'

'All right, Sergeant Wilson,' replied Adrian happily.

The first thing Charlene saw emerging from the shadows, was the matt-black barrel of a long gun. It had four longitudinal slots cut in the metal behind the hole that marked the exit point for projectiles. Charlene recognised the muzzle flash suppressor for what it was, and what it belonged to. Ex-Warrant Officer Scooter Wilson, her father, had been in the army a long time, Charlene had cradled this weapon in her arms more than once.

The man in the dark was holding a General-Purpose Machine-Gun Model 60, or M60. It was the poster weapon of Vietnam war movies; mounted on vehicles, in the doors of Huey choppers and carried by the biggest and ugliest grunts as a section support weapon. It fired 7.62 rimless NATO rounds at a velocity of 2800 feet per second, had a cyclic fire rate of between 550 and 650 rounds per minute and spat steel-jacketed projectiles in a cone of fire rather than striving for pinpoint accuracy. The M60 was designed for one thing: to kill and maim people.

Charlene risked a glance over her shoulder, noting the houses on the opposite side of Shepherdson Road next to the Army Reserve Depot. They would be directly in the line of fire. Adrian took another step forward, the glow from the overhead streetlight shone off a belt of rounds attached to the breech of the weapon. A second belt of rounds was draped over his right shoulder and across his body to the left hip. He was dressed like Sylvester Stallone in his role of John Rambo, wearing a ragged cut sleeve olive drab shirt, army trousers, military GP boots and a dirty strip of cloth tied around his head, hanging like a tail over his right ear. It would almost be laughable if it wasn't for the weapon itself.

'Where did you get that gun?' demanded Charlene.

'From the armoury,' replied Adrian pleasantly. What he didn't say was that it was a replica weapon from the prop armoury at the costumery. 'I think it adds a level of authority, menace in fact.' Adrian addressed Will, 'My last disguise didn't work out the way I had envisioned it would.'

Will remembered Uncle Bruce had not behaved well towards Santa; he would have gone on the naughty list for sure.

*What armoury?* thought Charlene, then she remembered they were across the street from an Army Reserve Barracks.

'Put the weapon down.'

'I would like to, but I can't Sergeant Wilson. If I did, you won't allow Will to come with me and Will has to come with me,' said Adrian losing his smile.

'I am ordering you to put that weapon to the ground and step away from it.'

'No, Sergeant Wilson, I can't do that.'

'If you don't lower the weapon, I will be forced to fire on you. I don't want to do that.'

'I don't want you to either,' said Adrian. 'Is this what they call a Mexican standoff?'

Will shook his head. 'You need three people pointing guns at each other for one of those.'

'Is that how that works? Thank you Will.'

'Lower your gun,' repeated Charlene.

'No, mine is bigger so it should take precedence.'

The bloke was nuts! Charlene weighed up her options. She could draw this out, hope somebody noticed and called it in, which could end up in a hostage standoff, or worst-case, a gun fight. She could draw her weapon and call his bluff, that's if she got that far before being cut in half by the smiling Rambo. Then again, if he really wanted to kill a cop he could have already done so. If she gave up her revolver, he might just take Will and run for it. That would remove the immediate danger posed by the automatic weapon pointed at a group of residential houses.

Against all her training and better judgement, Charlene opened her hand and lifted it up and away from her gun.

'Thank you, Sergeant Wilson,' said Adrian. 'I believe we would all feel more comfortable if all the guns were put away. I know I would.'

'You first.'

'Ladies first, I think,' said Adrian politely.

Charlene used one hand to undo her gun belt with the intention of dropping it at her feet.

'No,' said Will, 'I think that would be better out of everybody's reach.'

Charlene glared at Will, 'What do you suggest?'

'In there,' Will pointed toward the open rear of the police vehicle.

'I'm not getting in the boot,' said Charlene defiantly.

'Just the gun,' said Will apologetically, 'I didn't mean anything else.'

Charlene looked at Adrian.

'Is that what you want?'

'If you think it's a good idea.'

Charlene was a bit stunned that this nutter was asking how she should be disarmed.

'All right then, I am going to drop my gun in the boot.'

'Thank you, Sergeant Wilson,' said Adrian. 'Please close the lid once it's in place.'

Charlene lowered the gun belt into the opening and closed it with a solid thump. Will took his hands off the roof and faced Adrian.

'Now what?'

Adrian lowered the M60 before tossing what looked to be a digital watch to Will. 'It's a *Sainter*. All you have to do is push the big button when I say so. Once we get back, Uncle Dwight has a bag of technical thingies and survival supplies to help on the mission, then we're off to Nazareth in the age before deodorant and dental hygiene. Once we arrive, all we have to do is find David, help him track down the two fugitives, capture them, attach a *Sainter* and return them home to face justice.'

Charlene tried to follow what seemed to be a confused ramble.

'Who's David? Why is it so important that you take Will to find him?'

'David is my cousin,' replied Adrian helpfully.

Charlene took a step toward Adrian, the M60 came up, pointing at her middle. Adrian didn't seem to notice the weapon was aimed at the police officer.

'It's a somewhat tragic story, Sergeant Wilson, involving deceit, theft, missing persons and the stabbing of a police officer who was David's partner at work. These events preceded my trip with David to Nazareth.'

'Nazareth, in Israel?' questioned Charlene.

'Yes, Nazareth is in Israel in 1987,' replied Adrian with a smile.

'Your cousin David is a serving police officer?'

'Yes, he is. David was in pursuit of the fugitives that stabbed his partner, Jenifer Rostig. Uncle Emil and David were the only two in the loop on the mission, I was unwittingly duped into helping. I thought we were on a tourist adventure, you know the sort of thing, take in the sights, collect a few souvenirs, sample the local cuisine then be back home for work on Monday, but it all went terribly wrong.

'We literally landed on top of Peter and his companions while they were ambushing some Roman soldiers. We were captured, David was left behind, I escaped which led to my surprise visit with Will 12 years ago. I'm afraid I rather made a mess of Will's bedroom on my first visit,' said Adrian remorsefully. 'Long story short, after a bit of a discussion, I discovered that we are related. Will promised to come with me to rescue David when he was older and now that he is 26, we found a definitive record of where he could be contacted again.'

'Let me guess, from the front page of Tuesday's *Border Watch*.'

'Well done, Sergeant Wilson,' replied Adrian in admiration of Charlene's deductive powers.

'And here you are, dressed as *Rambo* carrying a machine gun so I would be intimidated into giving up my weapon and let you escape with Will.'

'Well done again, Sergeant Wilson.'

Charlene lowered her arms; the idiot was acting out the fantasy from the original police statement taken in 1975.

'Is that a real gun, Adrian?'

'Lord no! I wouldn't carry around a real gun, people could get hurt. This, Sergeant Wilson, is an imitation weapon.'

Charlene took rapid strides toward Adrian.

'Give me that weapon.'

Adrian unslung the M60 and held it out two-handed for Charlene to take.

'Hands on the vehicle,' Charlene ordered as she took the weapon, opened the breech, removed the ammunition belt, then cleared the gun. Will turned back to face the roof, placing his hands and feet in the required position.

'Shit.'

Adrian thumped against the vehicle to Will's right. Charlene grabbed the open half of the handcuffs and slammed it around Adrian's wrist chaining him and Will together.

'Isn't this exhilarating?' said Adrian, his face split with a huge smile.

'Shut up,' said Charlene patting Adrian down. 'What is your real name?'

'Adrian Thomas is my real name. I haven't lied, Sergeant Wilson. Why would I?'

Charlene used her leg to push Adrian's feet apart and removed what looked like a digital watch from his back pocket.

'Alright, Adrian, if you insist on continuing the charade, I am going to now formally caution you.'

'Are you arresting me, Sergeant Wilson?'

'Yes, I am arresting you, for threatening violence to and the unlawful detention of a police officer in the course of their duty. I am now going to caution you as is required under the law in South Australia. You do not have to say or do anything in response to questioning, anything you say or do may be used in court. Do you understand what I have just explained to you?'

'Absolutely, Sergeant Wilson, you are very good at this.' Adrian looked at Will. 'In fact, I believe Sergeant Wilson would be an absolute asset on a missing person's search.'

'No!' mouthed Will emphatically. 'Absolutely not, Adrian.'

Charlene held the watch device in the gap between Adrian and Will.

'What is this? It looks like a watch, but it reads like a calendar, is it what you passed to Will?'

'Yes, it is.' Adrian held up his wrist to show the *Sainter* he was wearing. 'Will, show Sergeant Wilson yours.' Will held up his wrist in embarrassment. 'As you deduced Sergeant Wilson, it is not a watch, it is in fact a *Sainter*.'

That word *Sainter* meant something, Charlene had read it in the file from 1975.

'Are you telling me this is your time travel device?'

'Well yes, and no, Sergeant Wilson,' replied Adrian.

'If you are going to be relying on a mental health defence, you should save it until you meet with your lawyers.'

'I should explain,' started Adrian. 'Technically, the *Cabinet* at the costumery warehouse is the actual time travel machine. The *Sainters* are personal devices which allow the *Cabinet* to be activated remotely.'

'Get in the car, Doc Brown, and you too, Marty McFly,' said Charlene opening the door of the patrol vehicle. 'We can pretend it's a DeLorean if it makes you feel comfortable.'

'Wait,' said Will, turning to face Charlene. He had to duck and twist his arm because of the handcuff link with Adrian. 'This all sounds ridiculous, I know it, you know it, and if Adrian had any concept of the reality, he would too. But the truth is, it's all true, the whole thing. You were at the hospital the day I became Doctor Elliot's patient; you must have heard what happened, what he did to me, what he did to my parents.'

'I heard the story. It was probably enough to push you over the edge but that doesn't explain Doc Brown here.'

'Is that going to be my official police alias, Sergeant Wilson?' asked Adrian. 'I wouldn't be averse if it was. Adrian Thomas, aka, *Doc Brown.*'

'Shut up Adrian, you are not helping,' said Will before turning to Charlene. 'It followed me, what Doc Elliot did and said about me. Why do you think those idiots were going to beat me up? Nobody would have objected; some people would probably have cheered them on. I am the *W,* Charlene. You said you knew all about it.'

'This is a conversation you should be having with your lawyer.'

'There won't be any lawyers, there won't be a court case because Adrian and I are leaving. I know it sounds ridiculous but it's all true, I swear it.'

'You're under arrest, Will, you are not going anywhere.'

Will held up his hand with the *Sainter.*

'Why would I make any of this up? Why would I torture myself and put my family through hell if it wasn't true?'

'Probably because you are suffering post-traumatic stress from Doctor Elliot?'

Will lowered his head in resignation.

'Yep, I am nuts, I am the *W,* everybody believes it, even I think it's true some days.'

'Will, get in the car.'

Will stood his ground. 'Before we go, can I ask a favour?'

'What?'

'Tell my parents that Adrian came and I had to go with him.'

'They can see you at the station in the morning.'

'Promise me you will tell them.'

'All right, I promise. Will you get in the car now?'

Adrian spoke, 'Are you ready, Will?'

'Yes.'

'On the count of three. One, two.'

Charlene took Adrian by the arm.

'It's late and I have lots of paperwork to complete.'

Adrian held his ground.

'Please, Sergeant Wilson, indulge us. I promise, if you let Will and I activate our *Sainters,* we will be as compliant as possible. It's not much to ask.'

'You really are going to keep doing this right to the end?'

'We have our mission, Sergeant Wilson; the fate of society is at stake.'

Will interjected, 'Just let him push the button. If nothing happens, we'll do anything you ask without complaining. We promise, don't we, Adrian?'

Adrian nodded. 'It will only take seconds.'

Charlene looked at the *Sainter* she had taken from Adrian; it had a large red button with the word *Engage* present in raised script.

'Let me guess, if you push this, the time machine will activate back at your secret lair and you will disappear in a puff of smoke?'

'A flash of green light, there isn't any smoke involved,' said Adrian.

'Seriously!' said Charlene as she pressed *Engage*. Instantly, Charlene was surrounded by a bright green aura, the centre of her body and the surrounding air seemed to fold in upon itself, pulsed three times and she was gone.

'What the hell!' exclaimed Will.

'That went rather well,' said Adrian stretching through the open car door to release the boot latch. 'I believe the key to these handcuffs is with Sergeant Wilson's belt. Be a good chap and see if you can find them.'

'Shouldn't we go after her?'

Adrian shook his head.

'Uncle Emil and Uncle Dwight are expecting Sergeant Wilson. We should give them a few moments to talk.'

Will rounded on Adrian in disbelief.

'You didn't just come to collect me, you planned to kidnap Charlene all along. What the hell are you thinking? She could kick both of our arses and hand them to us on a plate if she wanted to. Do you really think she is just going to go along because your uncles back in the bat cave talk nicely to her?'

'No, Will, I knew Sergeant Wilson was coming with us to the warehouse, beyond that, it's up to the persuasive skills of Uncle Emil.'

'What do you mean, you knew she was coming?'

Adrian withdrew a folded piece of newsprint from inside his shirt.

'This is a copy of the front page of next Tuesday's *Border Watch* in your timeline.'

Will read the headline.

'You lied to Charlene, you lied to me, Adrian.'

'I did tell her this was a tale involving deceit and missing persons, Will.'

Will stared at the newspaper. In the centre of the page were two grainy head and shoulder photos: one of Charlene in uniform, one of Will from his driver's licence. The banner headline read, *Police Officer & Local Man Mysteriously Disappear Without Trace.* On the second line in smaller print, *Police car and missing man's vehicle found abandoned on Shepherdson Road.*

'Shit,' said Will.

# CHAPTER TWENTY-SIX

OCTAVIAN DISMOUNTED, HANDED THE reins of his horse to Asher, his servant, then made his way up the steps of his villa. Ahead lay a bath, food and rest, but before any of that, Octavian had to meet with his business partner, who was not his lover, despite what the gossips said about the woman. As Octavian trudged up the steps, he reflected on the woman waiting to hear his news from Nazareth.

Octavian had first seen her on the road outside his villa months before. His eye had been drawn to a woman at least a head higher than the bustle of Jews on the street. She had looked directly at him, not intimidated, more curious than anything. Octavian noted her looks. She was the equal of the noble women of Rome, not their better, but at least their equal. Maybe she was a new girl from the brothel that catered for those with power and gold, not the brothel where girls could be paid for with a single silver coin.

She had simply walked up and told Octavian that she could offer him more wealth than he could acquire in a lifetime if he gave her half an hour of his time. Then she had placed five gold aurei coins in his hand, as a sign of good faith and a bond that she was not here to do him harm or waste his time. How could Octavian refuse such an offer? He invited her to his villa for the 30 minutes she had purchased of his time.

The woman had introduced herself as simply Julia, like the daughter of Emperor Augustus, who had been banished to the island of Pandataria for her scandalous behaviour. Then she told Octavian that Julia, the daughter of Augustus, the widow of Marcus Vipsanius Agrippa and divorced wife of Tiberius Caesar Augustus, would die within the week and that news of Julia Agrippa's death would arrive on a ship from Rhegium in 10 days. Julia then handed Octavian a parchment sealed with wax which he should read when the news of Julia Agrippa's death arrived in Tyre. If it was of interest, Octavian should come looking for her.

Octavian had little doubt this Julia was one of the false prophets that preyed on the wealthy with fortune-telling and visions of the future. It was a risky occupation. If they were convincing and their patron gullible enough, then they could live a very wealthy life, at least for a while.

Octavian didn't know whether to be flattered or insulted. He took the parchment and had Asher escort Julia from his home. The parchment went into the drawer of his desk. What could it contain that could be of interest to the *Praefectus Castrorum* and de facto governor of the port city of Tyre? Then Octavian felt the weight of gold pulling on his belt. *Why not?* he thought and summoned his secretary to issue orders for the captain of the next ship to arrive from Rhegium to be brought to him. Maybe it was worth the five gold aurei Julia paid.

# CHAPTER TWENTY-SEVEN

A SHIP FROM RHEGIUM arrived as predicted, 10 days after Julia's meeting with Octavian. The vessel had sailed within an hour of the death of the daughter of the late Emperor Augustus, carrying the news beyond the inner circle of the empire. The ship's captain was summoned into the *Praefectus Castrorum's* presence the moment it had touched the wharf. As a precaution, guards were placed on the vessel. No one was to leave or board the ship upon pain of death until Octavian rescinded the order.

The ship's captain had no idea why he was marched under military escort before the *Praefectus Castrorum*. He was no threat to the empire, being just a poor ship master plying his trade between ports. He had never crossed the line into smuggling. On his own admission, he was too cowardly to take such a risk. Deposited at the feet of Octavian, the captain waited nervously.

'Tell me Captain, what news is there from the city of Rhegium?' asked Octavian quietly.

Breaking the seal, Octavian read the scroll. It contained the date and time of Julia's death and the fact that she had died from starvation, even though there was a record harvest where she lived. The document named the ship and its captain, as well as a list of the contents of the hold. How could this woman have known so far in advance of Julia Agrippa's death and of the ship which would carry the news to Tyre? It had to be a trick, but how was beyond Octavian, who called for his horse and an escort of two Immunes, his senior clerks, to make his way to where his spies told him Julia had her villa.

Julia did not seem surprised to see the *Praefectus Castrorum* at her door. 'Did you find the scroll interesting?' she asked without preamble.

'How could you know not only when and how she would die, but also the manifest of the ship that would bring the news? That was a touch of genius.'

'I am not trying to deceive you, Praefectus Flagelon. I want to be your business partner, nothing more.' Julia gestured for Octavian to enter her home. 'I needed a way to prove what I am about to propose is not a sham. I am not a prophet or a visionary, I collect information, and information is the most valuable commodity available.'

Octavian agreed, information was valuable. On it hung the fate of battles, fortunes and empires. It could also get you killed, if you were not careful how you used it.

'You didn't answer my question.'

Julia gestured towards two facing seats.

'Please make yourself comfortable, Octavian. It is alright to call you Octavian? If we are to be partners, we should dispense with some of the formalities.'

'I think you are getting ahead of yourself, Julia. Don't presume that I am here because of the display you arranged this morning, which I will admit was impressive.'

Julia smiled, 'Then why did you come?'

'Let's call it curiosity. I am hoping you are not going to disappoint me, that could be fatal.'

Julia smiled before replying.

'I am not pretending to be anything other than what you see: a woman who has a business proposition to put to you. I have some resources, you have others, put them together and I believe we can both get what we want. You can decide to work with me, or kill me, or just walk away forgetting we ever met. That's a gamble that both you and I must take.'

Octavian sat; it was an interesting approach if this was a fraud.

'Alright, tell me your proposal. Let's see if we are both gamblers or just you.'

Julia sat and smiled at Octavian.

'Let me start with a demonstration of the type of information I have access to. Some of what I am going to tell you, a person could learn from others. Some of what I am going to reveal only you should know.'

The door to the room opened. Julia gestured for a servant to approach.

'I haven't had breakfast. I hope you don't mind if I eat while we talk, please feel free to help yourself if you're hungry.' A plate of dates, olives, cheese and bread was placed on a table between the seats. Julia waited for the servant depart then began to speak.

'Octavian Drusis Flagelon, you were born in the third year of the reign of Gaius Octavius known as Augustus, the first Emperor of Rome. Your parents are Felix and Domitia, your father served with Augustus' great uncle, Gaius Julius Caesar's army, which earnt him citizenship and the right to own land. Your father purchased a farm near Capua when he left the legions and married his childhood sweetheart, Domitia. Their estate was large enough to support them and their children, but not large enough to divide amongst four male heirs. Being the youngest son, you needed a career to provide for yourself, and support your parents as they grow older.' Julia paused to spread olive oil on a slice of bread, topping it with goat's cheese and two pitted olives. 'Where I come from, the benefits of a Mediterranean diet are well recognised, but I do crave something made with cocoa and sugar.' Julia placed the bread on a plate and offered it to Octavian, who placed it on the table between himself and Julia.

'Men your father fought with had brothers and sons in positions of importance. A word to the right people secured you a position in the legions where you completed six months as a *tiro*, a new recruit, then moved up the ranks. You have been a loyal soldier serving wherever the empire has needed you. In fact, you should command a legion of your own, to the surprise of many you have chosen not to accept this promotion when it has been offered.'

Julia poured wine and offered it to Octavian, who placed it on the table next to the plate of bread and cheese.

'You have chosen to remain an administrator, a manager of business for the legions for want of a better description. Some would ask why, but you and I both know that you are exactly where you want to be.'

'So far, all you have told me is a matter of public record, which shows you know how to collect information, but you stretched beyond facts in assuming you know my mind. I would be careful with what you say next.'

Julia didn't flinch.

'You wish to remain the *Praefectus Castrorum* because you are good in the role and it provides certain opportunities.'

Octavian placed a hand on the hilt of his pugio.

'Is this where you attempt to blackmail me over some imagined abuse of my office?'

'No, you are not corrupt Praefectus; if you were, we wouldn't be having this conversation. I need a man of his word as a business partner, which is why I chose you.'

'What are you trying to say, Julia? While this has been an interesting distraction, I think you should get to the point?'

'I think I will stick with the facts first, then we can discuss my proposal if you are interested in what I can offer.'

'Alright, just do it quickly.'

Julia pointed at the platter of bread and cheese she had prepared for Octavian.

'Do you mind? As I said, I haven't had breakfast yet.'

Octavian removed his hand from his pugio and passed the plate.

'I have already eaten.'

'Thank you,' replied Julia with a momentary smile. 'As I was saying, you are not corrupt by the standards of your age. You are a good and honest administrator, a stickler for the rules who does his duty for Rome. However, in your position, you get to know when there is to be a glut of wheat and prices will fall and when the empire needs timber or stone for construction, which will drive up costs. This allows you to provide information to your family in Capua on when to purchase goods that will be in demand, then sell them on at a profit when the empire goes to the market. This month, it might be rope for an expansion of the fleet, next month, concrete to build a new aqueduct. Where I come from, this is called insider trading. Here, it is just good business sense.'

Octavian put his hand on his pugio.

'If your story were true, some may perceive it as corruption.'

'Some may, but given the minor nature of your investments, it is unlikely to be investigated. It certainly would not be worth the trouble for a person, such as myself, to raise the issue. What would I have to gain? I have no proof, only knowledge and knowing something to be true isn't the same as being able to prove it.'

Julia was right. Octavian did use his family to make a profit from the empire's logistical needs. There was opportunity for corruption on a grand scale in his position but he had never been tempted to stray from the path of honour as he saw it.

'Alright, I concede that your information is sound. I am helping my family, there is no crime in that.' Julia waited for Octavian to continue; she would let Octavian raise his doubts then seal the deal with her trump card. 'All that you have told me could be learnt from a spy in my office. That would not be in the interest of Rome, or yourself Julia.'

'I can't speak for Rome's enemies, but I don't have a spy in your office, Praefectus.'

Octavian studied Julia's eyes, there was no hint of deception. Either she was telling the truth or was exceptionally good at this game.

'For the moment, let's say you don't have a spy amongst my staff, let's assume you have other means of collecting information. You still haven't explained how you knew about Julia Agrippa.'

'It's a secret that I am not going to share with anyone. That would be dangerous, not just to me but ultimately to you and your family.'

Octavian shook his head in anger and began to rise.

'I don't like people who play games. Maybe it's time I just removed this threat to my family. I find that dead people tend to be less troublesome than the living.'

Julia stood. It was time to play her trump card and see if she had read the man right, or wrong.

'You wed in secret to a woman from Germania seven years ago when you were serving as a centurio at Moenus. Your wife's name is Adalburg; she is the niece of Arminius, the warrior chieftain who defeated the army of Publius Quinctilius Varus in the Teutoburg Forest, which makes her a very important person in the eyes of the Germanic peoples. You wed Adalburg to bring peace by joining Rome and the Bucinobante tribe in a bond of marriage. It may have been a marriage of convenience to begin with, I don't know that as a fact, but I do know you love your wife and children. You have a son named Berard, and a daughter Eadgyo, if my information is correct.' Julia paused to let this sink in. 'They are living in Gaul in the town of Autricum. The money you make through your family is supporting them as well as your family in Capua. You cannot bring Adalburg and your children to Rome while you are still the *Praefectus Castrorum* of the Sixth Legion because, what you did is against the rules. You knew that when you took Adalburg as your wife, which leads me to believe you are willing to accept a level of risk to keep her as your wife.'

Octavian was stony-faced quiet. Maybe Julia had guessed right about his motivation. 'While you were at Moenus, married to the chieftain's niece, peace reigned. When you left with your family, hostilities between Rome and the Bucinobante re-emerged. You could have left Adalburg and the children with her family, instead, you secreted them away from the eyes of your superiors and her family with the help of your oldest and truest friend, Maximus. I believe he is still under your command.'

Octavian bristled. 'Have you spoken to Max?'

'No, this needs to be an understanding just between the two of us, a secret arrangement of mutual benefit.' Julia then spoke quietly and very carefully. 'I mean you no harm, Praefectus. What would that gain me? Why would I care who you marry? I am not Roman, I hold no loyalty to any side in your wars, or your empire building, I simply need somebody in your position to help me with a personal project. I chose to ask you because of your position and level of authority in Galilee, which I would find useful in my quest when the time comes.' Julia could see Octavian's mind spinning. 'I am not interested in anything military or the politics of Rome, my needs are far smaller,' Julia paused. 'The obvious question you have is what do you get out of helping me, and what do I want you to do?'

Octavian was unconvinced of the benefits or the threats posed by continuing to listen to this woman.

'Why should I listen to anything that comes out of your mouth? Maybe I should just remove you as a potential threat.'

Julia sensed the moment had come when she would know if her gamble had paid off. If she had it wrong, she would push the button on the recall device and jump forward in time to start again.

'I promise not to do anything to threaten your position, your family, or your empire. I need history to play out the way it was intended, with one small exception. In exchange, I promise you wealth and the security it brings. That is the business arrangement I would like to secure with you, Praefectus. You need money to keep your family safe and eventually bring them home to Capua. I offer you gold to buy land, build a home and secure the future of your children. And let's be clear, if I do this with you, I will be as much under threat as you are.' Julia took a sip of wine. 'Please sit down, Praefectus, you are making me feel uncomfortable.'

Octavian remained standing. Part of him wanted to dispose of the threat Julia posed. The logical part of his brain understood he was going to need more gold than he could raise playing the market with his salary.

'If you betray me, I will kill you, Julia.'

'I wouldn't expect anything less. I assume it is alright to call you Octavian now?'

Octavian didn't reply. Julia smiled as the soldier sat.

'You will need money, to reap the benefits of our alliance.' Julia rang a small brass bell and two female servants entered carrying sacks, which they placed on the table, then left the room. 'A gesture of good faith, Octavian, I would like you to invest this in our future.'

Octavian opened the nearest sack. The gold and silver contents glittered in the light. 'Your money?'

'Think of it as working capital for our partnership. What I would like you to do is invest this money, use the information I supply to increase its value, we will split the profits 50-50. I am providing the initial investment and market information; you will use your contacts to buy and sell goods that we can legitimately turn a profit from.'

Octavian felt the weight of the sack.

'This is a fortune, why do you need more?'

'I will need to maintain this villa as a base of operations for several years. That will require more money than I brought with me. I have a trusted housekeeper to manage my staff and this villa, but when I am away, she will need a man to be the public face of my household for the benefit of appearances sake. Could you help me with that?'

'I can approach one of my men nearing the end of his service who has proven to be honest and hardworking. They may be happy to take on the role, if the pay is good and the duties not overly taxing.'

'Your man will need to be discreet, as well as trustworthy.'

'I will be careful who I consider,' replied Octavian dryly.

'Good,' said Julia producing her smile again. 'Now that we have agreement on that part of the enterprise, I have a gift for you.' Julia handed Octavian a parchment. 'This is a list of significant events, including the major players involved, dates, locations and outcomes that will occur over the next year. Some of the events may be of no economic benefit to our business arrangements, but I think that forewarned is forearmed.'

Octavian unrolled the parchment. Listed were both civil and military building projects that were to commence, the dates of rebellions within the whole sphere of the Roman world and some beyond its boundaries. There were notes on weather events that could disrupt shipping, fires and floods that ravaged cities, predictions of bumper harvests in some provinces and crop failures in others.

'You are certain of this?'

'Some of the dates may be a few days or a week out, but they will happen.'

'You said you were not pretending to be an oracle?'

'That's right, I just have access to information that others don't.'

Octavian tucked the parchment in his armour.

'If what is written comes to pass, we have a business arrangement, Julia.'

Julia smiled broadly and thrust her hand across the table for Octavian to shake. He was surprised by the gesture, but gripped Julia's forearm with his hand holding it in a vice- like grip.

'A partnership,' he said with a nod of his head.

'A business partnership, Octavian,' agreed Julia.

'If that is all for now, Julia, I have business to attend to,' said Octavian standing.

'It's not quite all Octavian. I haven't told you of the task I need your help with.'

Octavian hefted the sacks of coin.

'The personal project you mentioned?'

'Yes, and no. I think it's only fair that you see how my list works in the next say, three weeks. If you are happy, then I will provide you with the names of some people that I need you to find. One is associated with an event on the parchment that is going to occur in Nazareth. This person must be apprehended, and I think the word most appropriate to use is, neutralised.'

Octavian nodded, 'Consider it done.'

'If you don't mind, there is one other thing, I would deal with it myself, but I think I should defer to your expertise in this case.'

'What is it?'

'I think it will be easier to show you than explain the problem. Before I do, can I ask if your assistants can be trusted to be discreet?'

Octavian tilted his head slightly as he studied Julia before replying. There was something dark in those blue eyes, something cold that no amount of smiling could hide.

'They can keep their mouths shut.'

'Good, then bring them along, it might save two trips.'

# CHAPTER TWENTY - EIGHT

DAMIAN DIDN'T KNOW HOW long he had been a prisoner. It could be two weeks or three. Having no window in his prison, he had no way of gauging the passage of time.

He had been wrong to trust Julia. She was the one who wanted only women in the household; they would be easier to control, she had argued, Damian had gone along with Julia's wishes, which in hindsight, had possibly been for all the wrong reasons.

He had been totally surprised when the assault came. Julia had seemed happy; everything was going to plan. They had intended to stay a few weeks using the currency they brought from the costumery to establish a temporary base of operations.

Julia said she wanted to follow her heart, to see the man as he truly had been, unfiltered by the passage of time. She wanted to sit at his feet and listen to him talk. She had vowed not to interfere in his life; it had to happen just as it said in the book. Nothing must change that.

Damian wanted to build an empire, one that created wealth as they jumped forward in time, to the point where their money could buy the type of influence to mould the future the way they wanted it. That had been his plan and he thought it was Julia's as well. Now, in the dark of his cell, in pain and hunger, he knew he had been manipulated all along. Julia told him what he wanted to hear and while he had been a fool, it was not his fault. It was always them, never him. It was the one truth he still believed, even after it had gone so wrong.

The girl, Sapphira, the pretty one, must have said something. It would be easy enough to explain, she had just over- reacted. The problem was, Julia had refused to talk with him. Then it happened. The house had been silent and he had finally fallen asleep, which was just one of the things he had found so difficult being locked in the dark. Julia led the women down the steps, arms pinned him face down on the stone floor. Julia said nothing as she straddled his back, putting her weight on his torso, then pinned his arms with her knees. It had hurt, the bones of her legs pushing into the flesh of his body. He had tried to reason with Julia, to explain. He struggled, begging for her to get off until he ran out of breath and lay still.

'Me too,' whispered Julia.

'What? What does that mean?'

Julia hit him in the back of the head with something solid.

Sapphira came into his view, holding a lamp in one hand and club in the other. Damian could see the shadows cast by the wom him on the floor by the flickering light. Julia dug her knees int making him writhe in pain. The shadow made it look as if Julia w from his back like a parasite.

'I am sorry, Sapphira,' he called in a gasp, laced with terror.

'Me too,' said Sapphira.

'I don't understand, what does that mean, Julia?'

'I thought that you were a student of history, my love.'

'What?'

Pain as the club collided with the heel of his foot. He tried Julia pulled his head back so violently he struggled to breathe speak. Something glinted, shone in the flickering lamp light. I the coldness of the blade against his skull before he saw its shar

'What's that?' he almost screamed, knowing exactly what it

'It's a much-loved heirloom my love. Surely you remember those years ago when you met Cynthia.'

'I don't understand. Do you want me to apologise? Do you say sorry to Sapphira?'

'What about Atarah? Does she deserve an apology as well?'

'Yes, yes, of course, I apologise to Atarah. It was a misunder we can talk about it, I can explain.'

Damian's head was pulled to the left so he could see Atarah a

'I am sorry, Atarah. I never meant to upset you. It won't ha I give you my word.'

Atarah had a gentle, kindly face, burnt brown by the sun and There was no emotion in her eyes as she walked, swinging a like a whip.

'You're not going to let this happen, Julia. This is not part You wouldn't be here if it wasn't for me. You need me.'

'Yes, I did, but I don't need you anymore.'

'Yes, you do. You need me more than ever; you need a man Galilee is not like home. Women can't just do what they war to be a man.'

Julia eased her grip just enough to take the strain off Dami

'Maybe you're right, but the point is, I need the right man for the job. That doesn't mean I need you.' Julia pulled Damian's head back to the point where his throat stretched tight, then laid the flat of the blade against flesh.

'You can't do this, Julia, it's wrong. I helped you, surely that means something?'

Julia hesitated, 'Maybe you are right, maybe we should look to local custom. When in Rome, as they say.'

'This is not you, Julia.'

Julia smiled, 'Damian, you have absolutely no idea who I am.'

'Tell me then, help me understand.'

'No, there have been enough lies. Sapphira, Atarah, Cynthia, Tonya, me, all of the women who have listened to your lies have heard enough. I hate to think of the pain you caused with your words.'

'Please, Julia. I am begging you to listen to me.'

Julia turned the knife so the edge of the blade sat against Damian's throat. He held his breath.

'No, not yet.'

Damian gasped in pain, as the leather strap whipped across his buttocks.

'Me too,' said Atarah.

Julia dropped Damian's head.

'I don't think you ever understood anything that women have tried to tell you. It goes in one ear and out the other, as if our voices are just meaningless noise.' Julia thought about this. 'Maybe the punishment should be that your words are just noise to women. Wouldn't that be ironic?'

'What are you going to do?'

'I am going to take away your words so you can't use them to hurt another woman.'

The point of the knife pushed into skin and scraped against bone behind Damian's ear. He screamed as blood ran down the blade. The knife cut, then flicked an object, the size of a watch battery, onto the cellar floor. Julia took the lamp from Sapphira and searched for the object which she crushed with the heel of her sandal.

'That will do for tonight ladies,' said Julia. 'Once I have found the right man, we will continue this conversation, Damian.'

'I don't understand what you are saying, Julia,' pleaded Damian.

'Isn't that ironic, my love?' Julia replied in Hebrew. Damian's words would never hurt another woman, not without his translation implant.

Damian thought if only he had some inkling of what they were planning. He should have known, but then how could he? Julia, the deceitful, scheming, treacherous bitch had lied to him right from their first meeting. He couldn't admit, it had been brought it on by his own arrogance. It was all her fault.

Normally, women came to him. On occasions he had had to send out signals, use his charms, his looks and his words. Women just loved being with him: the pretty ones, the ugly ones, the married and the single. It was a cross he had been forced to carry ever since puberty marked him out as the one women had to have. Still, it had its moments, and it wasn't all one way. They got far more from him than he ever received in return.

He should have walked away after that first night at the genealogy club meeting. He should have realised the moment Julia ignored his opening smile. It happened occasionally; you couldn't always tell who was a lesbian or a man-hater. It would be so much simpler if they had a badge, or something to identify their preferences. Then there were the women who were blindly loyal to a partner. While commendable, it lowered their attractiveness in his eyes. There were also the few women afflicted with the same curse as himself. It was customary to nod in recognition of a fellow hunter, then let them get on with their own game.

The trap was set at the meeting. It was procedure for three or four members to present a 10-minute talk on their family history. Normally, it was used as an opportunity to bask in the achievements of some long-lost relative. Damian listened to the dissertations. If the speaker was a woman of interest, he would take notes, it was an easy way to break the ice with a target. Repeat the boring facts over after-meeting drinks and he was half-way to their bed and often to their fortunes.

When Julia stepped up to the podium, she captured all of Damian's attention while relating the life story of a country reverend who had lived an unremarkable life and died an unremarkable death. It was bland in its content, dull even, if he was to judge it by the standards of the other histories he had forced himself to listen to, but it wasn't to Julia. She had been passionate about the priest and his life, then it struck him, Julia wasn't attracted to his charms, because that's exactly what they were, charms. Then Julia smiled at the audience. Damian smiled back with the crowd. He couldn't help it, this tall, dark-haired woman had them all in the palm of her hands with a simple story and a smile. If only it was so easy for him.

He had been captivated by a clever, calculating plan of subtle seduction. He should have recognised that he was the prey and not the predator. Julia had used his own skill set against him; she had made him chase her, deceived him into thinking she was in love with him. The truth was, all Julia wanted was his knowledge of that damned *Cabinet*. It had all been a ruse, a trick to gain access to that bloody machine.

Damian made a plan. It needed to be subtle in its application if Julia was to come to him. First, he needed to gather intelligence. To understand his target, he needed to know her motivation, what drove her to be Julia. Damian liked to think of this as following the five P principle. This being, *prior preparation prevents piss poor performance.* It wasn't a statement of rousing motivation, but it was the way to success.

Julia hosted Sunday afternoon gatherings in one of her family's grand homes for believers of one of the archaic religious cults. It was called a bible study class. Damian knew about the bible; it was a book written centuries earlier containing stories of mythical beings, magic, sex and gratuitous violence. It contained a doomed hero sent to change the world by his father, who was killed because he didn't take into account local politics, and the fact that the people with power thought his left-wing politics a pain in the arse.

Getting invited to a group meeting wasn't difficult. Damian simply befriended one of the more gullible members who was bursting for Damian to come and hear the word when he had shown the tiniest spark of interest and not run away laughing.

When Damian attended his first Sunday gathering, he was stunned by the opulence of the home where the meetings were held. The wealth and the privileges it afforded radiated from the very masonry of the structure. The second thing that negated the absurdity of the gathering in Damian's mind, was Julia.

Julia was genuinely welcoming to all as she met the faithful with a smile and handshake. If she recognised Damian, she didn't show it. Refreshments were served in the reading room of a grand library stacked with floor to ceiling bookshelves. White bread sandwiches cut into delicate triangles served with tea and coffee on silver platters were circulated amongst the gathering. This was followed by a prayer delivered by a bearded gentleman sporting a wooden cross on a silver chain around his neck. Damian realised that this man must be the priest who led the group in its studies.

Once the prayer had been spoken, the gathering retired to a room filled with sofas and leather wing-backed chairs, where the priest intoned another prayer which ended with a massed ah-men. Damian followed the herd, lowering his eyes during the priest's dissertation and muttering the ah-men with a slight delay once he realised it was the required response to every speech the priest gave. Julia smiled at his embarrassment, then touched Damian on the arm in a show of reassurance. That was the point, the exact moment, Damian now realised he had become the hunted without realising that Julia was the predator.

The meeting ended with a prayer, followed by an ah-men, after which the crowd began to drift away with more handshakes and warm words from Julia. It had been an odd experience. Damian half wanted to walk away, the problem was he was used to getting what he wanted, and he wanted Julia, especially now he had seen the wealth her lovely body came wrapped in.

Damian planned to be amongst the last to leave. This should give him time to talk with Julia as she said goodnight and imprint him more firmly in her memory. As he waited for the others to have their farewell moment with Julia and the priest, Damian studied the display in the grand entrance hall, which included holographic images of Julia, her parents and two older brothers collected over time. They started with a 20-something military officer arm in arm with a woman who could have been Julia's twin, followed by their marriage, the officer in dress uniform and his bride in white. Next came children recorded over time until finally Julia was graduating in a cap and gown from university.

Photographs of relatives from previous generations covered most of the wall. Hidden lights highlighted each image as the observer approached, making it seem to be the most interesting object in the room. The moment your eyes began to wander, another image beckoned. It was all very clever the way each succeeding photograph drew you into its world.

Damian paused as long as seemed respectful, before moving to the next image. He would let Julia lead the conversation, ask two thoughtful questions, then depart with a smile and a promise to think on what he had learnt. He wanted to leave an impression that he wasn't convinced but might be persuaded to adopt the cult's beliefs. If Julia took the bait, then the game was truly afoot.

Damian used his peripheral vision to check the length of the line, then moved to the next display, a glass fronted cabinet set into the wall. Inside were objects and images dating back to the dawn of the photographic image. Nine shelves covered the lives of nine previous generations. Damian glanced at each shelf in turn. The family resemblance moved backward in time, slowly changing as different genes were introduced. The story was much the same: military officers, military officer's wives and husbands, medals and awards. Pictures from battle fields in foreign lands along with posed family groups.

At the middle shelf, the backgrounds changed from an Australian landscape to the shores of the American continent. An ancestor had emigrated from the United States at the end of the Second World War. The pictures showed a marine sergeant with a pregnant bride standing outside of Melbourne's Flinders Street Railway Station. A war bride and a change of country as a result, Damian assumed.

The higher the shelf, the further back in time they went. Damian was interested in the story as it pertained to Julia, the target. Here were levers he could use, the five Ps at play. He found the priest from Julia's presentation on a lower shelf than the marine sergeant; a second, or third son who had not followed the military tradition. The top two shelves held sepia images and objects from the nineteenth century, men in high collar coats with braid and bright buttons, long swords and an array of facial hair. The women and children, dressed in their best clothing, were gathered around a seated military man like decorations on a Christmas tree. They were adornments to the central figure, rather than a critical part of the main narrative.

Then he saw her on the top shelf. It was not the Cynthia who had gone into the *Cabinet*, this was the dark-haired woman who had emerged after Emil had pulled her back. At first, Damian didn't believe what he was seeing, then he read the description inserted into the picture frame. *Cynthia Horrigan and son Michael. Holy Cross Episcopal Mission January 1st, 1891.* Damian read on further, *two days after surviving the Wounded Knee Massacre.* It was all true, time travel, the *Cabinet*, Cynthia's story, here was proof he could not deny. Anger rose as his mind raced back to Gerald and the way he had paid him off with a pittance. *The bastard!* he thought.

'Did you enjoy the reading, Mr Treffer?'

Damian was lost in thought, staring at the brown and white photograph. It was definitely Cynthia rugged up against the cold of the snow visible in the background. Her hair hung each side of her gaunt face, resting upon shoulders white with snowflakes. The boy was almost as tall as his mother, rugged up in a soldier's long coat. Cynthia had that knife hanging at her waist, the boy looked sad, as if somehow broken.

'Mr Treffer?'

Damian composed himself then turned to face Julia.

'I'm sorry, I was lost in my own thoughts for a moment.'

'That's quite alright, Mr Treffer. After a reading, I too, am sometimes lost in thought.'

Damian nodded in understanding.

'I think I owe you a further apology. I was lost in thought about the picture in your display, not the wisdom of the bible study class.'

Julia smiled slightly.

'Don't be afraid, Mr Treffer, I wouldn't dare presume that an intelligent person would embrace our beliefs in a single session. That would be unrealistic, untrue to the teachings, which need time and reflection to be understood.'

Damian nodded. It all sounded very reasonable when explained by Julia. She was a good salesperson, very good at customer relations. It was just a pity that Julia was selling tickets to join a cult.

'Thank you, I will think about what you have said.'

'That's all we can ask, Mr Treffer.'

'Julia.'

'Yes, Mr Treffer?'

'Could you tell me about the people in your family display? I used to work for the Thomas Costumery Corporation and recognise some of the clothing worn by your ancestors. I have a particular interest in the American Wild West and find it fascinating to see artifacts and to hear stories from the real history of the period.' Damian pointed to a photograph. 'Could you tell me the story of this gentleman? He is a major, I believe, in the 7th Cavalry Regiment?'

Julia stood next to Damian.

'Yes, that is Major Silas Howard. He had a long and bloody military career. Silas was too young for the Civil War but made up for it being involved in the systematic destruction of a number of Native American nations. He received a medal for his tireless dedication, a century later he would have been charged as a war criminal. I am a descendant of Silas Howard in a direct line of male heirs, that's how my family likes to think of the glorious chain of military service, father to son, the eldest boy, preferably. Many women in our family have also served with distinction, you just don't see their faces in this display.'

Damian pointed to the photo of Cynthia.

'She doesn't seem to fit that story.'

'No, she doesn't.' Julia opened the cabinet, removing the sepia image for Damian to hold. 'Cynthia Horrigan is the one truly selfless hero on display. After the massacre at Wounded Knee, Cynthia and her son were all that was left of her family. Those that didn't die on the day had already perished due to war, disease and starvation.'

'Do you mind telling me her story, Julia?'

Julia paused, 'If you decide to join us again, Mr Treffer, we can discuss Cynthia after class.'

'Yes, of course,' replied Damian, hiding his disappointment. 'Thank you for today.'

'You're welcome, Mr Treffer,' replied Julia, leading Damian to the exit. At the door, Julia hesitated as if about to say something, then shook Damian's hand before he walked away.

'Mr Treffer,' Julia called catching him as he reached the street. 'Did I hear correctly that you worked for the Thomas Costumery business?'

'Yes, I worked at the costumery in Warrnambool quite a few years ago.'

'Did you know a Mr Emil Thomas? I believe he is one of the owners?'

'Yes, I knew Emil. We worked closely together right up until the time I left.'

'Then perhaps our meeting tonight was more than just a lucky encounter.'

'I don't think I follow?'

'I think you know exactly what I am saying, Mr Treffer. Come next Sunday and we can talk about Emil and Cynthia after the class.'

'I am not sure I understand.'

'I didn't either, Mr Treffer, until I discovered Cynthia kept a diary of events in her life. They are remarkable documents, Mr Treffer. All handwritten in six leather-bound journals. Two tell a harrowing tale of the demise of her family at the hands of the military that my family holds so dear. The earliest journal reads like a work of science fiction. It is very much a page-turning record, full of interesting characters and events. There is even a person mentioned with your name, Mr Treffer. Isn't that an interesting coincidence?' Damian didn't dare speak. 'Come next Sunday, Mr Treffer, the reading is from the book of Matthew, a passage about betrayal and forgiveness. *For if you forgive others their trespasses, your heavenly Father will also forgive you, but if you do not forgive others their trespasses, neither will your Father forgive your trespasses.*'

'I don't understand, Julia.'

'Cynthia forgave her Damian Treffer his betrayal. Maybe I should accept her wisdom on the matter.' Julia turned and headed back to the house. 'Next Sunday, Mr Treffer, let's see if Cynthia was right to be so forgiving.'

# CHAPTER TWENTY-NINE

JULIA WAITED FOR OCTAVIAN to join her on the floor of the cellar where a man was bound at the wrist and ankle by a chain attached to the wall.

'Is this your personal problem, Julia?' asked Octavian with disapproval.

'Yes, it is. I would be grateful if you could assist with the matter.'

'I am not a hired cutthroat who you can use to dispose of a man for a handful of silver.'

Julia smiled. 'Octavian I am not asking you to kill anybody, well, not without good cause. No, what I want is your wisdom in a matter of law.'

Julia addressed Damian in English.

'This is Octavian Flagelon, the Praefectus Castrorum. He is the town's governor and arbiter of Roman law. I have asked him to help decide your future.'

Damian struggled to his feet.

'You can't trust these people; they won't take orders from you. I know you don't want to hear it, but you will be lost if you don't have a man beside you. You can call the shots, I won't fight your decisions, it can just be for show, but you need a man, Julia, you need me.'

Julia addressed Octavian.

'I am afraid that Mr Treffer doesn't speak Latin, or even Hebrew, not anymore.'

Octavian looked Damian's wound.

'What happened to him?'

'I was forced to remove a piece of metal from under Mr Treffer's skin. If I hadn't, it could have proved fatal to him. Unfortunately, the surgery also removed his ability to understand anything other than his native tongue, which I speak and can interoperate if you have no objections. I'm sure Mr Treffer won't mind.'

Octavian looked from Julia to Damian.

'How did he come by this metal in his head? Was it a battle wound?'

'No, Mr Treffer has never served in the military. It was inserted as a cultural practice, like having your ears pierced.'

Octavian nodded.

'I have seen similar things in my service with the legion.'

'Some people are slaves to fashion,' replied Julia.

Octavian furrowed his brow.

'What did you tell him?'

'I introduced you, Octavian, as an arbiter of the law, here to help decide his fate.'

'What was his reply?'

'He expressed an opinion that I could not trust you, or any local man, and that I should set him free because I needed his help to survive in this land.'

Octavian looked to Damian and indicated with a raised hand, *come closer*. Damian looked to Julia.

'He wants to get a better look at you.'

'Doesn't what we had mean anything to you Julia? I thought you loved me.'

'Mr Treffer is happy to answer your questions.'

Octavian frowned, 'It didn't sound like it.'

'Mr Treffer thinks he can sway me to forgive him by appealing to my emotions. He is incorrect.'

'Why is he chained to the wall?'

'Mr Treffer made unwanted sexual advances towards a young woman in my household staff and a threat against the safety of the family of another. He is guilty of betrayal of their trust and mine.'

'Are your servants slaves?'

'No, slavery is abhorrent, and that is beside the point. All women have the right to be treated with respect and dignity, which includes not being subjected to unwanted sexual advances.'

'Were any of the women raped?'

'No.'

'Were they beaten?'

'No.'

'I don't see that a crime has been committed by this man. He may ask a woman for sex, but he may not force a free woman to perform a sexual act. That is a crime.'

'Sapphira is 15, Octavian. He threatened to have her cast into the street if she did not do what he wanted.'

'Fifteen is the age of a child,' said Octavian turning a hard stare towards Damian.

'He told Atarah that if she wasn't willing to do what he wanted, then perhaps her children should learn to eat a lot less often.'

'So far, I have only your word on this matter. Justice demands more than that.'

Julia gestured with a wave of her hand to the top of the steps.

'This is Atarah, she manages my household staff.'

A woman with a pleasant face descended the steps to a stand next to Julia.

'I am Atarah,' she said quietly. 'My husband died from a fever a year ago. He was a good man. I don't know that I will ever have a place for another in my heart.'

Octavian's features softened.

'I am sorry you lost your husband.'

'This is Sapphira. She is the oldest of nine children in a family that struggles to provide food for half that many. Her wages help feed the children still at home. I have been told that one as young as her could be easily sold to the brothels. I wouldn't like to be in her parent's situation where they may have to sacrifice the future of one child to feed others.'

Octavian nodded in understanding.

'I am going to ask questions; I want you to translate all that is spoken without prejudice Julia. Let's call it a demonstration of good faith.'

'Agreed Octavian.'

'What have you to say about this man, Sapphira?'

Julia translated as each person spoke.

Sapphira glanced at Damian, 'I can only tell you what he did when we were alone.'

'How did this man behave?'

'In the beginning he was kind and funny. When I mopped the floors, Master Damian would sit and talk with me. He seemed more like my father, listening to what I had to say than the master of the house. Sometimes he gave me a present, nothing big, just a wedge of honeycomb or a cake from the baker. He didn't ask anything in return. Then he changed.'

'How did he change?'

'It happened on a day when there was only Master Damian and me in the house. I was changing the linen in Mistress Julia's bedroom; he was sitting on a chair next to the bed. I thought was going to ask about my family like he normally did.'

'Did he touch you?'

'No, he just talked to me.'

'What did he talk to you about?'

'My family, and how hard it must be for my parents to feed so many children, and that it was lucky I had my position in the household. Then Master Damian said that if I lost my position, my father could be forced to make an unhappy choice and that I might have to do things with men for money for the good of my family.'

'Did you know what he meant?' asked Octavian.

'Yes, I knew what he meant Praefectus Flagelon,' said Sapphira sharply. 'He meant that my father would have to sell me to the brothel so that my brothers and sisters could eat.'

Octavian shuffled uncomfortably under Sapphira's glare.

'What he did, Praefectus Flagelon, was to say that a smart girl would make the clever choice to keep my job and continue to live a nice life, then he kissed me on my cheek, dropped his robes and lay naked on the bed.'

'What did you do when this man made his suggestion and lay on the bed naked?'

'I finished mopping the floor. What else could I do?'

'What did this man do while you were mopping the floor?'

'He smiled, and played with himself as he watched me work.'

Octavian turned to Julia.

'What does this Damian of Treffer have to say?'

Damian spoke, Julia translated, 'He admits to talking to Sapphira as she said he did, but claims it was a cultural misunderstanding, nothing more.'

'Pity I can't hear him speak for himself. I cannot judge a man solely on the word of this girl who admits he did not touch her. So far, no crime committed under the laws of Rome.'

Julia translated. Damian nodded solemnly at the judgment.

'Atarah should tell you her tale of Mr Treffer,' said Julia.

Atarah spoke, 'He tried his charms on me for about a week, I wasn't having any of it, so he left me alone. It's a game to men like Master Damian, they don't care who they hurt.'

Octavian watched Damian as Julia translated. A smile formed at the corners of the 'defendant's' mouth. He believed himself to be safe.

'Did this man touch you?'

'No, he is too clever for that.'

'Then what are you accusing him of?'

'Of threatening my children.'

'He threatened to harm them?'

'After I confronted him, he said that if I didn't value my place in this household my children might have to get used to going hungry.'

'When did this happen?'

Atarah took Sapphira's hand.

'After I found Sapphira crying in the kitchen, I asked her what was wrong. She wouldn't tell me at first because she was afraid. When she did tell me, I had a word with Master Damian.'

'What did he say?'

'He denied it. He said Sapphira was mistaken, that it was a misunderstanding.'

'Did you believe him?'

'No, he was lying.'

'How do you know he was lying?'

'He tilts his head to the right when he lies.'

Octavian touched Julia's arm before she translated and said, 'Wait.'

Julia understood that Octavian didn't want Damien to hear what Atarah was about to say.

Atarah continued, 'I've seen him do it before, when he lied to me.'

'How do you know he lied to you?'

'Two weeks before that day, Julia asked if I had taken coins from her room for the market. I said I hadn't.'

Julia put her hand on Atarah's. 'I wasn't accusing you.'

'I know, just as I know Damian took the coins. I saw him put them in his purse as I was walking past Julia's room. I didn't think anything of it at the time, not until Julia asked about the money. I didn't want Julia to think I lied to her, so I asked Master Damian to talk to Julia about it. He tilted his head and lied to me, saying he hadn't taken the money; he was happy to let Julia believe I had taken the coins from her room.'

Damian interrupted, 'What is she saying Julia?'

Octavian held up a hand for Damian to be silent.

'What did you do, knowing he had taken the coins?'

'I am a servant; he was the master of the house; I couldn't risk my position, so I said nothing.'

Damian interrupted, 'I have a right to hear the evidence, Julia. You have to tell me what is being said.'

Octavian nodded to the closest Immune who slapped Damian.

'The Praefectus wants you to be quiet, my love,' said Julia, 'I hope you understood the translation.'

Octavian continued, 'What did he say when you questioned him about Sapphira?'

'He said it was a fantasy, dreamt up by a silly young girl and that maybe

241

Sapphira wasn't suited to working in the villa. He said Julia needed servants who didn't go around making up stories and that Sapphira and I would have to prove to him that we wanted to keep our employment. Master Damian said if Sapphira changed her attitude and showed she understood what was required, then he wouldn't have to talk to Julia about letting her and me go.'

Octavian touched Julia's arm.

'Continue the translation.'

Julia translated Atarah's last words.

'What happened next?'

'I told Master Damian that I had seen him take the coins from Julia's room and put them in his purse.'

'What did this Damian of Treffer do when you accused him of lying?'

Atarah faced Damian, 'He said, *you know it and I know it, but who is Julia going to believe?* Then he laughed and walked away.'

Octavian searched Damian's face, he looked mildly amused.

'Did you question him, Julia?'

'Yes.'

'Did he deny taking the money?'

'Yes, he did.'

'Did you believe him?'

'No. Damian Treffer has a history of lying and using women for his own gratification.'

Octavian nodded, then paused before continuing. 'I am going to ask a question. I need you to translate and repeat the reply exactly as spoken.'

'Alright.'

'Ask if he will accept my judgement as the arbiter of law.'

Julia asked the question, Damian looked directly into Octavian's eyes and said, 'Yes.'

'Ask if he loves you.'

Julia hesitated, until Octavian gestured for her proceed with the translation.

'Do you love me, Damian? Do you truly love me?'

Damian looked surprised, then tilted his head slightly to the right before replying. 'Yes, I do love you, Julia.'

'Ask if he feels guilt for taking coins without consent.'

Julia asked the question.

Damian tilted his head again before speaking, 'I didn't take the money, Atarah was mistaken.'

Octavian asked a question of Julia.

'Is this man related to you? Is the coin in question shared by an agreement?'

'No, the money belongs to me. Mr Treffer has no money or property of his own.'

Octavian gave a directive to his men, 'Release him.'

The Immunes broke open first the ankle and then the wrist manacle.

'You're letting him go after what he did to Sapphira and Atarah?' asked Julia in disbelief.

'He committed no crime in that regard. If he had forced himself upon Sapphira, or harmed Atarah or her children, he would answer for it.'

'Thank the Praefectus Castrorum for his wisdom please, Julia,' said Damian rubbing his wrist where he had been shackled.

'I want you out of my home, you evil bastard.'

'There is no need for that, Julia. I told you, these women were lying. I never touched the girl, Sapphira admitted it. Atarah set Sapphira up, filling her head with a story to cover her stealing.'

'Take him for the next slave auction,' commanded Octavian

An Immune grabbed Damian's right hand, pushed it up his back and marched him towards the stairs.

'What the hell?!' bellowed Damian, 'I didn't touch the girl, I haven't broken any laws.'

'Wait,' said Julia.

Octavian held up a hand.

'I assume Damian is to be sold in compensation for my stolen gold?'

'Theft is a crime,' replied Octavian, 'the only thing he has of value to provide you with restitution, is his body.'

'What would be the punishment if he had forced Sapphira to have sex with him?'

'If Sapphira was your slave, you could ask for compensation to the value of your damaged property. As Sapphira is a free woman, a virgin, then the punishment would be severe, especially as she is a child in the eyes of the law.'

'What exactly does that mean Octavian?'

'Death. I don't see child rapists who reoffend, in my court.'

'You are to be sold as a slave,' Julia snarled at Damian.

Damian shook his head.

'No, you need me, Julia. Don't let emotions get in the way of what's best for both of us.'

'It's Octavian's judgement that you are sold in compensation for theft.

The irony is, if you had just asked for the money, I would have given it to you. I guess Cynthia was wrong to forgive you after all.'

'You can't let this happen, Julia. You know in your heart that I am not evil, all men are sinners, the book says so, just as it says that you need to forgive those sins.'

Octavian was growing impatient.

'I have business to attend to.'

'Just indulge me a few moments more, Mr Treffer is about to have an epiphany and tell the truth for the first time in his life.'

'Do it quickly.'

'Damian, if you admit your sexual harassment of Sapphira, I will drop the charge of theft.'

'What happens if I confess to asking Sapphira for sex? What's the punishment for that?'

'I don't know, maybe it's a fine,' Julia paused, 'no, on second thoughts, a life of slavery is what you deserve.'

'I won't accept that; I didn't do anything wrong.'

'What do you want to do?' asked Octavian. 'Am I getting your compensation or do you want to sort this out yourself?'

'Take him, give the money to the poor, just get him out of my house.'

Octavian indicated to his Immunes; Damian was forced up the stairs.

'Stop!' yelled Damian, 'Alright, I confess that I suggested to Sapphira that she might enjoy some intimate time with me. Most women jump at the opportunity.'

Octavian raised a hand.

'Do we take him to the slave market?'

'No, not yet,' replied Julia. 'I need more, Damian; I need you to tell the truth.'

'Ok, I admit that I suggested that it could be to her advantage if she agreed to us having sex together. She needed a bit of encouragement to admit that she wanted the same. The problem is, that unless you ask, you never know.' Damian paused, considering his words. 'It was a misunderstanding, cultural differences, that's all.'

Julia translated. The cellar fell into silence. Octavian nodded and Damian was pushed up the steps.

'No, Julia,' yelled Damian struggling against his removal.

Julia laid a hand on Octavian's arm.

'Can I buy him right now?'

Octavian shrugged, 'The sale will need to be formalised. There will be a transaction fee to be paid for the purchase of livestock. I will supply you a receipt for taxation purposes.'

'Tell me how much and I will pay you in gold.'

'I thought you despised slavery?'

'I do, but Damian must receive his just rewards.'

Octavian clicked a finger. 'Put him back.'

Damian was marched down the steps.

'You can't just leave me in this dungeon,' roared Damian in anger.

Julia turned to Octavian.

'He is becoming tiresome.'

'Ask him to quieten down,' commanded Octavian.

The Immune holding Damian punched him in the ear. Damian dropped to his knees; the second Immune attached the manacles.

Julia took Octavian's arm as they ascended the cellars steps.

'I guess I am about to find out what it's like to be the owner of a eunuch.'

# CHAPTER THIRTY

CHARLENE MATERIALISED WITH A thump, as her police issued boots landed on the floor of the *Cabinet*.

'Hello,' said Emil raising a hand in greeting.

'Hi,' said Dwight.

'Please don't be alarmed,' said Emil, 'we mean you no harm.'

Charlene studied the room; the lighting was low. She couldn't see all the way into the corners.

'My name is Emil; this is my brother Dwight.'

Charlene pushed on the glass of the *Cabinet*.

'Allow me,' said Dwight, 'the *Cabinet* doesn't have a door handle on the inside. That's something I will fix.'

Charlene conducted a scan of the room, not finding anybody lurking in the shadows, she snapped her attention back to Emil.

'Do you know how much trouble you are in?'

'I can only apologise for what has happened, Officer Wilson. This must seem disturbing and frightening.'

'It's Brevet Sergeant Wilson,' said Charlene with an edge to her voice. 'I don't think you or your nephew have a bloody clue. Adrian is your nephew, right?'

'Yes, Adrian is our nephew.'

'Well, your nephew tricked me into holding this thing,' Charlene held up the *Sainter*, 'right after he committed a myriad of offences, including threatening an officer of the law with a firearm.'

'It wasn't a real gun, Sergeant Wilson,' said Dwight, 'it's a replica.'

'Did you lace this thing with a sedative?' growled Charlene holding the *Sainter*. 'Is that how you put me out so that you could get me here to your ridiculous bat cave?'

Both Emil and Dwight seemed perplexed.

'I am sorry, Sergeant, but this is real,' said Emil calmly. 'The *Cabinet*, the glass box behind you, is really what it seems. Surely Adrian explained it to you?'

'Bullshit, do you really think I would believe anything that deluded man said? And whose idea was it to dress him up like Rambo, I could have shot him, then where would you be?'

246

'In serious trouble,' said Emil, 'in fact, the whole world is in peril.'

'Bullshit,' said Charlene, 'is this where you spin me a story of time travel with some villain having gone into the past to change the fate of humanity? You know the worst thing about the whole sorry joke is what you have done to Will Thomas. It's screwed him up, made his and his family's life a living hell.'

Emil and Dwight were perplexed. This was not how they imagined the police officer would behave.

'Sergeant Wilson, I assure you that this is not a deception,' stated Emil. 'You really have travelled through time to the year 2117.'

'Bullshit. The best thing you can do is show me to the nearest phone, so I can call my station and let them know where I am and that I am safe. The last thing anybody needs is the armed response squad turning up looking to put holes in people.'

Emil turned to Dwight, 'Can I borrow your phone?'

'This is pointless, we should just send her back.'

'Phone,' demanded Charlene

'Dwight, please,' said Emil, maintaining eye contact with Charlene.

Dwight handed a thin ceramic rectangle to Charlene.

'What's this?'

'It's the equivalent of a mobile, or cellular phone.'

'Seriously? You are going to play this right out to the end, aren't you?'

'Yes, we are Sergeant,' said Emil with a deferential smile. 'Assuming that to be the case, you might as well humour us. What's the worst that can happen?'

Charlene furrowed her brow.

'Do you want to get arrested? Is this a crime and punishment fantasy you are playing out?'

'No Sergeant Wilson, please call your station.'

Charlene looked at the object offered by Dwight. It seemed iniquitous, but then so had the *Sainter* thing.

'The phone is voice activated. Just ask for the person or the number you want to contact,' explained Emil.

Charlene looked confused.

'Just say the word, *call,* to bring the phone out of hibernation,' said Dwight helpfully.

Charlene frowned then said, *call*. A holographic display shone up from its surface, projecting smiling images of Dwight, David, a girl whose name was Elizabeth and an older woman identified as simply, *The Boss*. A friendly female voice asked, 'Who would you like to talk to Dwight?'

'Fuck,' said Charlene in surprise.

'Sorry,' said the voice, 'my name is Penelope, how may I help you?'

Charlene looked at Emil.

'Penelope is the phone's artificial intelligences personality; you can interact with her like a person if you want.'

Charlene stared at the holographic display in confusion.

'Penelope, please connect with the Mount Gambier Police Station,' instructed Emil.

'Can I ask if this is an emergency call?' asked the phone.

'No, I don't think it is, not anymore,' replied Emil.

The telephone rang twice before a hologram of a woman in a police uniform appeared.

'Senior Constable Twilley, how may I help you?'

Charlene couldn't speak.

'How may I help you?' repeated the officer.

'I would like to talk to the duty sergeant.'

'Who may I say is calling?'

'Brevet Sergeant Wilson.'

'From which station Sergeant?'

'Mount Gambier, I was transferred nine weeks ago.'

The senior constable looked annoyed.

'Brevet Sergeant Charlene Wilson, is it?'

'Yes.'

'Seriously, let's have a look at you! Period uniform, the hair, the badge, shame on you. Is Charlene Wilson even one of your ancestors, or are you just trying to claim her because she was lost in the line of duty?'

'What?'

'Hang up, and don't call again or I will have you charged with wasting police time.'

The hologram disappeared. Charlene was ashen-faced.

'Take me outside, show me.'

'Please follow us, Sergeant,' said Emil.

Dwight led the way.

'We don't use this facility as a costumery anymore, well not since the accident with Cynthia. It's now a warehouse where we hide the *Cabinet* from prying eyes.'

Emil spoke, 'This is where we hid our family secret, unfortunately, not well enough.'

Charlene followed Dwight to a huge, ornately decorated entrance hall filled with crystal chandeliers and surrounded by three stories of glass-fronted rooms.

'This was the heart of the old costumery. It throbbed with customers during its day, making the Thomas family very wealthy, which allowed us to shut this facility when we had to.'

'Because of Cynthia Horrigan? I read about her in Will Thomas's police file.'

'Yes, because of what happened to Cynthia. We can't ignore that fact, Sergeant Wilson.'

Charlene could see shame, contrition and embarrassment written large in Emil's eyes.

'Show me outside.'

Dwight opened the great double-doored entrance of the costumery and Charlene stepped into the street, to come face to face with the 22$^{nd}$ century.

'Ok,' said Charlene, back in the *Cabinet* room, 'you can try explaining this again.'

'Do you know why William Thomas suffered, Sergeant Wilson?' started Emil.

'I only know what's in the records from the investigating officers and statements from witnesses of cousin Adrian's visits.'

'It happened because of greed and the foolishly arrogant notion that we could keep our family safe. We should have destroyed the *Cabinet* the day we discovered what it truly is.'

'The day of Cynthia Horrigan's accident?'

'That was the first mistake, but not the worst. A police officer was stabbed because people wanted to use the *Cabinet* for a purpose I can only guess at. We know that part of their motivation is to change the world because one of the fugitives told David as much, as he watched him disappear into the past.'

'I didn't know a cop had been stabbed. You had better tell me the whole story.'

*What a bloody mess,* Charlene thought after hearing all the details.

'Why am I here?' she asked.

Dwight unfolded a page of newspaper.

'This was how we knew where and when to find William Thomas.

Charlene read the headline and saw her and Will's photograph.

'What does this mean?'

'We don't truly know, Sergeant,' replied Emil, 'but after reading the article we assumed you may somehow end up here.'

'Adrian handed me a *Sainter*. He basically dared me to push the button. Did he plan to kidnap me?'

'No,' said Emil, 'you being here could just be the result of bad luck, or interference with the timeline, we just don't know.'

'Or because your nephew is an idiot!'

'That is a possibility,' agreed Dwight.

'You can send me back? Can't you?'

'Yes, we could,' replied Emil, 'but we don't know what the consequences would be. According to the records you and William Thomas disappeared without a trace. Returning you now could significantly change history or have minimal effect. We just don't know.'

'You're not trying to spin me the time travel grandfather paradox thing, are you?'

'Yes, we are,' replied Emil and Dwight in unison.

'At the moment, you are alive, safe, and in command of your future from this point in time forward,' continued Dwight. 'We believe Mr Treffer and his accomplice have gone back in time to change history, including removing the threat David poses to their plans. They could accomplish this by eliminating one or more of our direct ancestors, thus ensuring that we never existed in a changed timeline.'

Emil took over.

'William Thomas and his family could cease to exist, which would have a direct impact on the life of the parallel timeline, Charlene Wilson. You interacted with William as a child and as an adult and your parents were friends with Colin and Mary Thomas. The question is, what would have happened if you never met? Would you have become Sergeant Wilson of the South Australian Police, or for example, Charlene, the hairdresser.'

'Maybe you didn't reach adulthood,' said Dwight solemnly. 'Maybe alternate timeline Charlene Wilson dies tragically in a vehicle accident, or drowns at the beach, or overdoses on heroin while working as a prostitute?'

'Okay, I get it,' replied Charlene angrily, 'you're blackmailing me into helping you.'

'No, we are not,' replied Emil, 'we are asking for your help.'

'So far, the best help we have been able to offer David is the assistance of my nephew Adrian, who bless him, hasn't a clue, and William Thomas, whose life is a mess,' continued Dwight.

'You need a team leader and you are asking me because I am already involved, plus if I don't, the mission will probably go arse up.'

'I doubt I could put it more succinctly,' replied Emil.

'If I commit to making sure Doc Brown and Will don't die in the first hour, I'm the boss and I make the call to pull the pin if it goes to shit, is that clear?'

'Thank you,' said Emil in obvious relief.

'Please save my son,' pleaded Dwight taking Charlene's hand.

'It's okay,' nodded Charlene feeling embarrassed.

'Now that's settled,' said Emil, 'Dwight has put together a number of items to help with the mission.'

Dwight collected three backpacks from the corner of the room.

'Emergency rations, first aid supplies, currency and the last of my *Sainters*.'

'Weapons?'

Dwight brightened, 'Well, Sergeant, to start with, I have manufactured three handheld electrical stun devices.'

'Tasers?'

'Yes, electrical shock inducers, based the on the Nova XR-5000 model which you would be familiar with in 1987. I improved their performance with a longer-lasting battery and quicker recharge.'

Charlene picked up the taser, turned it on and pulled the trigger. Electricity arced and buzzed.

'What else have you got? I don't want to be dirty dancing with somebody before I can disable them.'

Emil nodded. A number of costumery customers had wanted to live out the Swayze fantasy from the classic movie.

'My father was in a shooting war,' he said. 'There is no such thing as a fair fight, only survivors and the dead. I don't want any of my team ending up in the dead column.'

Dwight smiled and produced a long gun with a folding stock from a backpack.

'This is a directed energy weapon, built from a replica police issue riot gun from your century, which I thought it would be relatively familiar to you.'

'It's a toy, what good is that?'

'It is a replica, Sergeant, not a toy,' replied Dwight flicking the safety off, cocking the weapon and aiming at the far corner of the room. 'I've modified the design, quadrupling the power input and focused the recoil and blast energy in one direction, thus creating, what I think you will agree, is quite an impressive defensive weapon.'

Dwight squeezed the trigger. A massive rush of air burst from the weapon, smashed against the far wall of the room, then rebounded, knocking Dwight and Emil off their feet. Charlene had the sense to duck behind the protection of the *Cabinet* before the weapon was fired.

Charlene took the gun from Dwight and flicked the safety to on.

'It will do,' she said. 'What else have you got in those bags?'

'There is a data storage device containing all the data available from the Wikipedia Data Base from the historical records of the time, including the holographic maps that David took with him. Adrian can show you how to access the information.'

'It sounds like I am going to be relying on Doc Brown, I mean Adrian, a lot.'

'Don't underestimate him,' advised Emil. 'Adrian may come across as frivolous, but he is very bright and good with people.'

'Does he speak Latin like the Romans. I don't and I doubt Will does either?'

'Yes, you will all need to communicate in Latin and Hebrew. Dwight can help with this.'

Charlene looked at Dwight who was holding a large syringe like device.

'What's Q planning to do with that?'

'Q?' questioned Emil, then the light went on behind his eyes. 'Very clever, Sergeant Wilson, yes Dwight is our Q. As an aside, I believe Daniel Craig was the equal to Sean Connery's original interpretation of the Bond role.'

'Who's Daniel Craig?' Charlene asked.

'This,' said Dwight, ignoring the question, 'contains a sub-dermal language translator.'

Emil pointed to a slight bump behind his right ear.

'I have one, as do all of the front of house Thomas Corporation staff. It's a basic business need when dealing with customers from across the planet. David had one as an officer of the law, and Damian Treffer had one because he worked as a costumier for the business. I would assume that his accomplice must also have a translator fitted.'

'What's the side effects?'

'Well, nothing physical, Sergeant,' replied Dwight. 'Some people find it distressing, understanding what an Italian waiter is actually saying when taking your order, and it can be removed, but it's more painful coming out than going in, I have been told.'

'All right, do it,' said Charlene, pulling her hair back.

The room vibrated, followed by a flash of green from inside the *Cabinet*.

'Does it do that every time?' asked Charlene.

'It also produces an outflow similar to the down draught below a thunderstorm. The walls of the *Cabinet* are shielding us from the effect.'

'Oh, I've felt the effect,' replied Charlene feeling the bruise on her shin.

'We're back,' said Adrian grinning.

'You two owe me an apology,' said Charlene pointing a finger.

Adrian's grin disappeared; Will hung his head.

Emil opening the *Cabinet* door.

'I am Emil, this is my brother Dwight.'

'G'day,' said Will, taking Emil's hand, nodding at Dwight then addressing Charlene. 'I am so sorry, I never meant for you to get tangled up in this mess.'

'Come over here,' directed Charlene, patting the seat alongside herself. 'Q over there is going to stick something behind your ear, it's like a universal translator on Star Trek.'

'Okay?' queried Will taking a seat. 'Q, like in Bond, James Bond?'

Adrian laughed, 'That is very good, Sergeant Wilson.'

Dwight put the syringe device behind Charlene's ear. There was a hiss of gas as the sub-dermal translator was pushed through skin. 'I don't get it?'

'Don't worry, Uncle Dwight,' laughed Adrian, 'it's a compliment and very apt.'

'You, Doc Brown, I want a briefing on what to expect when we get to Nazareth, where you last saw your cousin and anything you can remember about the Roman garrison.'

'Of course, Sergeant Wilson,' replied Adrian.

'Shit,' said Will reacting to the sudden pain behind his ear.

'Suck it up princess,' said Charlene bluntly, 'there is going to be a lot more than that to worry about, shortly.'

# CHAPTER THIRTY-ONE

HANNAH TOOK CAREFUL STEPS, guarding her dress against the thorns that hid the cave.

'If we hurry, we can get there before David has to leave,' encouraged Joe.

'What's the rush Joe? Are you worried about missing another miracle?'

Joe looked over his shoulder in frustration. 'If you had seen what I have, you wouldn't be making fun of David.'

'I'm on my way to meet my future husband, Joe; you wouldn't want me to show up with my best laundry and flour grinding dress in tatters.'

Joe waited for Hannah to catch up.

'Peter would marry you.'

'But I don't want to marry him.'

'Why not? Peter can read and write; he earns a good living and he owns two goats.'

'As tempting as that sounds Joe, no.'

'But Peter loves you?'

Hannah put a hand on Joe's cheek.

'Joseph, you see the good in everybody, which is why my sister married you, and the fact that she was knocked up at the time.'

Joe went red.

'Look Joe, I couldn't marry Peter for more reasons than you could understand.'

'But Peter wants to marry you when nobody else does.'

Hannah sighed, 'Peter stinks of fish.'

'I have noticed,' admitted Joe.

'We live in a hot desert. How much do you think a man like Peter sweats?'

'A lot?'

'Yes, Peter sweats a lot. We all do, living in Galilee, it's just that most of us don't smell like rotting fish when we do.'

Joe looked disappointed.

'It can't just be because he smells.'

Hannah stopped.

'Joe, it's because he wants to be the husband of a good Jewish wife. Do you know what that means?'

Joe looked confused.

'It means that Peter wants me to cook, clean, give him children and spend my life dedicated to fulfilling his wishes and obeying his commands.'

'But that's what wives do, that's what the priests teach in temple.'

'No, that's a lie designed to keep women living a life of servitude. If you read the laws of a marriage contract, the *Mibtachiah*, a wife must have equal rights with her husband, including the right to own property, make her own decisions and divorce her husband if she wants to.'

'Peter doesn't want that?'

'Do you remember when I was Peter's girlfriend?'

'You argued a lot.'

'Yes, we did. Peter is not the man for me.'

Joe watched Hannah walk ahead.

'David is not Peter,' he said quietly. 'Maybe Mary is right, maybe David is here to meet Hannah?'

Hannah entered the cave. Mary was sitting with a man who had his back turned, Hannah assumed it was John because he was wearing John's cloak.

'Did we rob somebody?' Hannah asked seeing the pile of gold and silver on the cave floor.

'So, Joe managed to convince you to come,' said Mary, looking up

'Joe said you found me a husband, so what else could I do?' said Hannah sarcastically. She pointed at the coins. 'Is that what the gold is for, to pay somebody to take me off father's hands?

'Where's Milcah?' asked Mary with concern.

'I left her and James with Bilhah, and don't worry about them, the Romans are hiding behind their walls and won't come out.'

'They are afraid of David,' said Joe

'And where is my betrothed?' asked Hannah. 'Don't tell me Peter has whisked him away before I even have a chance to lay eyes on him.'

'Peter isn't back with the horses yet,' said Mary, getting to her feet.

'Then where is my intended?' asked Hannah putting on her best pout.

'Hello,' said David, rising to face Hannah and extending his hand, 'I'm David.'

'Oh shit,' gasped Hannah in surprise. 'I thought you were John; you're wearing his cloak.'

'John left it for David to wear. He ripped his shirt last night,' explained Mary

'How?' asked Hannah, unable to take her eyes off the handsome, well-muscled, and not overly smelly man in front of her.

'Falling off Joe and Mary's roof.'

'Why were you on their roof?'

'David tried to jump on our roof from Bilhah's house to retrieve his bag,' said Mary.

'Why didn't you use a ladder? Joe would have lent one to you?'

'I did,' said Joe, 'then David saved me and Polykarpos and all the men on the Hill of Kedumim from the Romans.'

'Are you the one who has the Romans hiding like scared children?'

'Joe and Polykarpos helped,' said David with a smile for his new friends.

'David is not like other men; he has powers,' said Joe.

Hannah shook her head in disbelief, then pointed at the coins on the cave floor.

'Is this your money?'

'No, that belongs to Mary, Joe, Polykarpos and Peter.'

'But it was your money in the bag on the roof?'

'Yes.'

'So, you're a thief who has convinced Joe you are a god or an angel with magic powers, and for the less gullible, it's gold to shut them up.'

'David is not a thief,' said Mary.

Hannah pointed to the pile of coins.

'No honest man has this much money in Galilee or Judea. He has to be a thief or a trickster.'

Mary placed a hand on her sister's.

'I swear on the life of my children, David is a good and honest man who needs our help.'

'Seriously, Mary, I didn't think you would fall for the lies of a trickster.' Hannah pointed at Polykarpos. 'And never would I have imagined that a teacher would be sucked in to something like this.' Hannah looked at Joe and shrugged, 'I can believe it from Joe.'

'Show Hannah your technology,' said Polykarpos.

David shook his head. 'I don't want to frighten her.'

'Oh, you won't frighten me,' said Hannah looking at Mary. 'Did you promise me to this man for his gold?'

'No, you need a husband, and David has medicine that can stop people dying when they get the shits. It's not like you have had any other offers since you rejected Peter.'

'You know I can't marry Peter.'

'Because he smells? I know that's not the reason, it's because you wouldn't be able to control him.'

'What, like you don't have Joe's balls in a jar under your bed, Mary. You only married him because you had to. His brother wouldn't have you, so you took second best.'

Mary slapped her sister.

The noise echoed around the cave, then, 'Stuff you Mary,' spat Hannah as she launched herself at her sister.

David stepped between the women.

'You take it back,' hissed Mary. 'You're just jealous because I have the best, the kindest man in Nazareth for my husband.'

'I'm not jealous, I'm pissed off with you constantly trying to marry me off to any man with a goat or a handful of silver. Don't you think I should have a choice of who sleeps in my bed? Why should I have to settle, just because you did?'

David held the women apart with his arms, then looked over Hannah's head to Polykarpos and Joe.

'Do you guys want to help?'

Joe skipped around Hannah to wrap his arms around his wife, who continued to struggle as she was dragged away.

Polykarpos copped the back of Hannah's head on his nose, then a flurry of elbows to his midriff, before pinning Hannah's arms to her side and carrying her backwards.

'Let me go!' roared Hannah. 'Let me go or your balls will end up in the same place as Joe's.'

David looked surprised, then turned to address Mary.

'I think that I will respectfully decline the offer of matrimony to your sister at this point in time.'

Hannah stopped struggling.

'What, am I not pretty enough? Am I too quiet for you? Is my bum too big?' she said, putting her hands on her backside to emphasise the point.

David blushed in embarrassment.

'It's not what you think, Hannah. I am sure you would make the right man a wonderful wife.'

'Is this where you say it isn't me, it's you?' replied Hannah sarcastically.

'Have you been told that as well?' asked David.

'Yeah, I have heard it before,' replied Hannah now also blushing.

Mary addressed her sister, 'Well done, Hannah, you've driven another potential husband away.'

Hannah stopped wriggling.

'Good, he is too pretty and I still think he is a thief.'

'You are pretty,' said Mary. 'Don't worry, it doesn't make women fall in love with you, or make you a good husband.' She pushed her way out of Joe's arms. 'Not like my Joe. He is what a husband should be.'

'Our deal stands, Mary,' said David redirecting the conversation. 'The coins, the medicine, it's yours to keep, all I ask is that Peter supplies transport and Polykarpos continues to act as my guide if he is still willing?'

'Our fates are linked, David; I will be your guide for as long as you need me,' replied Polykarpos.

Peter entered the cave, saw Hannah and looked down at his feet.

'Hello, Hannah. You look nice today.'

'Not now, Peter,' spat Hannah angrily.

'You purchased the horses?' asked Polykarpos practically.

'Yes, they are as good as any Roman officer would want to ride.'

'Thank you, Peter. Did you have enough currency, I mean money?' asked David.

Mary interceded, 'Peter had enough, in fact, he brought coin back with him,' she said holding out a hand.

Peter looked blankly ahead. 'The resistance has expenses Mary, they cost silver.'

'That sounds fair,' said David, 'I appreciate the risk you have taken to help me.'

'It was nothing,' muttered Peter, embarrassed by the coins in his pocket.

'I have one final favour to ask,' said David. 'Nazareth was a fixed point where I knew the criminals had visited. It could have been a day ago, it could have been a few months, I was hoping to find a lead on where they are.'

'What do they look like?' asked Mary, 'There are no strangers other than Romans in Nazareth.'

'I can show you,' replied David. 'Hannah, this might be frightening but I promise it can't hurt you.'

'You can't frighten me,' retorted Hannah glaring at David.

David activated the data storage device on the floor of the cave.

'Access files dated July 18th, 2117. Display images, rotate slow speed to the right.'

'Jehovah!' gasped Hannah as two life sized holograms, one a man, one a woman, appeared.

Joe dropped to his knees. Mary grasped Joe by the shoulder and pulled him up.

'It's ok, Joe,' she said quietly.

'These are the fugitives,' began David. 'The male is Damian Treffer. He is 43 years old, has, or had, blond hair, blue eyes, and as you can see, is what many would describe as classically handsome. Damian Treffer is a conman, what you would call a trickster.'

'The woman is Julia Howard. She is 23 and has demonstrated a capability for violence. Julia stabbed Jen.'

'Would they be dressed like that?' asked Mary.

'Change image,' instructed David, 'Display subjects in the costumes selected from the Thomas Costumery Data Base files.' The images changed, Damian and Julia were now garbed in the attire of wealthy Jewish merchants.

'I have seen the woman,' said Hannah, 'she was here with the Roman they call Praefectus Castrorum.'

'Are you sure it was Julia Howard?' questioned David.

'Yes, it was her,' replied Hannah without hesitation. She reached out to touch the images, the light of the hologram flowed over and around her arm. 'How are you doing this?'

'It's not magic, it's just science and technology,' said David. 'What you are seeing is light being used to paint a picture.'

'The Greeks invented science,' stated Polykarpos proudly.

Hannah glared at him.

'You didn't invent painting with light though, did you?'

'Tell me about when you saw Julia Howard.'

'She stopped at the bakery to buy bread, to make something she called a sandwich. She asked where she could buy cheese, olives, cucumber and something green and leafy. I pointed her towards the market and she seemed happy.'

'Do you know where she had come from, where she was going?'

'She came from Tyre. I know, because she liked the cheese that old Ada makes with pieces of date, pistachio nuts, almonds and raisins in it.' Hannah pointed towards the rotating Julia. 'She paid Ada for all the cheese she had, to be sent to her home in Tyre. She said it wasn't fruit and nut chocolate, but it was better than salted fish any day. I didn't understand some of the things she was saying, but she was friendly and paid far more than she should have.'

'This woman was with the man?' asked Polykarpos.

'Yes, but not like they were a couple, it was more like they had business together.'

'What makes you think that?' asked David.

'She pointed out the carpentry shop and the alley next to Mary and Joe's house. She said something about it being the location.'

David looked at Polykarpos and Peter, 'I am sorry.'

'I don't understand,' said Peter.

'David believes this Julia had the Roman Octavian Flagelon, the Praefectus Castrorum, deploy soldiers to Nazareth for the purpose of apprehending him,' said Polykarpos. 'Am I right David?'

'Yes.'

'It also wasn't a coincidence that the Romans arrested me yesterday.'

David nodded, 'You were a potential distraction.'

Peter stiffened.

'Are you saying the Romans arrested Polykarpos just so we would be drawn out into the open for the Romans to attack us?'

David nodded.

Peter shook his head.

'We were all nearly killed because we might get in the way of this woman Julia's desire to kill David, because he is chasing her for stabbing this Jenifer from a far-off land?'

'Yes,' replied Polykarpos. 'I think that is likely.'

'She is a dangerous woman,' said Peter, 'you need to stop her, David.'

Mary hit Peter across the arm.

'That's why I told you we have to help him.'

'Oww!' cried Peter, 'I understand that now.'

'Why would the Praefectus Castrorum form an alliance with these people?' asked Polykarpos.

'Damian Treffer and Julia Howard know things about the future. They know what is going to happen in Roman politics, where and when natural disasters and wars will occur and where the Roman Empire is going to invest its wealth. Information like this can make you powerful, rich or simply keep you safe.'

Mary spoke angrily, 'This Julia stabbed your Jen and now she has plotted for you to die at the hands of the Romans?'

'It's not personal. I am an inconvenience to her plans.' The group was silent waiting for David to continue. 'We now know Julia has a residence in Tyre where she is having goods sent to.'

'Julia wrote the address on parchment for Ada to give to Centurio Maximus for the cheese to be sent to Tyre,' said Hannah. 'If Ada could read, she could have told you the address, but women aren't permitted to learn to read and write in Galilee, did you know that, David?'

'No, I didn't.'

'Are women permitted to read and write in your land?'

'Yes, it's compulsory for all children to receive an education.'

'Isn't that against the rules, like it is in Galilee?'

'No,' frowned David, 'it's against the law to prevent any child from going to school.'

'Do people have to pay in silver to learn how to read and write?'

'No, basic education is free, no matter who they are.'

Hannah glared at the other men in the cave.

'I think I've changed my mind about marrying you, David. You can take me away to your land which sounds a lot fairer than Nazareth.'

Polykarpos shrugged, Joe smiled happily and Peter had anger in his eyes. David changed the subject.

'Julia has a known associate in Tyre who shouldn't be difficult to locate. I can watch this Praefectus Castrorum and he will lead me to Treffer and Howard. All I ask is that Polykarpos guides me to Tyre, points out this Octavian Flagelon and I can do the rest.'

'I don't think so,' said Hannah, 'this Julia wanted you dead and she still will.'

'Hannah is right,' said Polykarpos. 'Word will reach Tyre that we escaped, the Praefectus Castrorum will instigate measures to recapture you.'

'Which means I need to act quickly.'

'Octavian knew what you looked like,' said Polykarpos. 'Julia must have given him a drawing of your face.'

'I will just have to be careful then,' said David.

'I am coming with you,' said Hannah abruptly, 'I know what Octavian, Julia and this Damian look like and they don't know me, and I am a woman, which means I will be invisible to the soldiers looking for you.'

'No,' said Peter, 'you are not going.'

'Is that because I am only a woman, Peter?' said Hannah dangerously. She switched her eyes to David before Peter could reply. 'Would you have tried to forbid your Jenifer from coming with you?'

'Jen would have told me to pull my head in.'

'Well, I am not your Jenifer, but I understand her.' Hannah looked directly at Peter.

'Are you sure?' asked David.

'Yes, I am.'

'All right, I could use your help, but there are rules if you come with me and Polykarpos.'

'Tell me the rules, I will see if I agree to them.'

'Number one, you follow my directions at all times, this is not negotiable.'

'Alright, but I won't be silent if I have something to say you have to listen to me.'

'Agreed, but I have the final say, is that clear?'

'Yes,' said Hannah.

'Yes,' said Polykarpos,

'Yes,' said Joe and Peter.

David shook his head.

'Joe, I'm expecting my family to make a rescue attempt. I need a man to meet them in Nazareth, I can't think of anybody else I would trust with this.'

Joe looked crestfallen, then tightened his mouth in determination.

'Yes, I can do that.'

Mary touched David's arm. *Thank you,* she mouthed in relief.

'I am coming,' said Peter.

David shook his head.

'No, Octavian and his men know you by sight and with Polykarpos as my guide, who is going to be here to lead your people?'

'If Hannah is going, so am I,' said Peter forcefully.

'I don't want you to come, Peter,' said Hannah bluntly. 'If you think acting as some sort of bodyguard is going to change my mind about marrying you, you are wrong. I don't love you and I can't and won't be your wife.'

The light seemed to drain from Peter's eyes.

'You're the one who is wrong, Hannah. We could be great together.'

'No, we wouldn't, you have to see that, Peter.'

'Rule two,' said David breaking the tension. 'If it goes wrong, just turn and walk away.'

Polykarpos and Hannah nodded in silent understanding.

'Good, thank you,' said David. 'I guess then you had best introduce me to the horses.'

# CHAPTER THIRTY-TWO

MAXIMUS AND DAX REACHED the gate of the legion outpost.

'Sentry, to your post,' called Maximus. There was no movement inside the wall.

'The garrison may have deserted,' said Dax.

'Or they're dead, or asleep,' replied Maximus pushing the gate. 'Try the barrack block, I'll go to the office. If they're alive, come and get me.' instructed the centurio.

The post's dormitory door and shutters were closed.

'Salve,' Dax called, 'is there breakfast on offer for a weary soldier? My name is Dax, I am here with Centurio Maximus.'

The door to the barrack opened, a shield was pushed into the gap.

'Are you a man, or a witch?' came a call from the building.

'I am what you see brother, a soldier of the legion,' replied Dax.

'We don't know you.'

'You should have called me,' said Maximus approaching from behind.

'They are afraid, Centurio. They are not thinking clearly.'

'Men,' called Maximus, 'I don't know what happened last night, but it was a Jewish trick not the work of magic.'

The door closed with a bang.

'I don't think they believe you,' said Dax drawing his gladius.

Maximus gripped his pugio.

'Men, I am ordering you to form up on the parade ground now.'

Dax moved away from the barrack, taking up a combat stance.

Maximus nodded in agreement with Dax's move.

'If they won't come out, we back away and find ourselves a horse.'

'Yes, Sir,' said Dax quietly.

Maximus tried again. 'I am giving you a direct order to form up.'

The door of the barrack was flung open. A pilum flew through the air, passing within a hand's breadth of Maximus's chest.

Dax slid backwards keeping his eye on the door.

'You're not Centurio Maximus,' yelled a voice. 'I saw the centurio struck by the green light and fall down dead.'

Maximus recognised the voice. It was the young soldier he had relieved on the hill; he must have seen the light strike him and fled in fright.

'Is this true, were you struck by the green light?' asked Dax.

'Yes, a Jew used something with the same light to escape earlier in the day. It scared the young soldiers then; it seems to have driven sense from them now.'

Dax pointed his gladius at the centurio's belly.

'Prove you are not a witch.'

Maximus eyed Dax, 'It is known that if steel cuts a witch, their blood will boil.'

Dax nodded.

Maximus pressed his pugio on his forearm until it drew blood.

'Are you satisfied?'

Dax nodded, then started withdrawing keeping his eyes on the open door. Five men pushed through the opening, locking their shields together as the formation moved forward.

'Kill them before they can use their witchcraft,' came the call from inside the building.

'Move to your right,' directed Maximus.

'Let's head to the gate,' said Dax sliding sideways to spread the target.

'Agreed, go to the gate house, find weapons while I keep the lads occupied.'

Dax moved using the centurio's body as cover. There was a metallic clang as a pilum clattered to the dirt on his right. The Maximus must have deflected it with his pugio. That showed, not just skill, but a strong nerve. A second thump, a pilum went over Dax's head. If the formation was clever, it would throw at the same target together. No man, or a witch, could deflect five darts at once.

Dax turned and ran to the guardhouse beside the gate. A dozen pilums and as many cavalry spears stood upright in boxes. On the wall hung three bows with full quivers resting on the floor beneath. Taking the closest bow and a quiver, Dax ran out on an angle from the guard house, his appearance made the five hesitate. Maximus quickened his pace backwards. This brought the flight of another pilum which grazed the centurio's thigh. Blood flowed from the glancing blow.

Dax dropped, aimed low as shins and ankles were exposed below the shield wall. His first arrow struck with a solid thump, hitting bone. The shield wall broke, the central column dropped to the ground, exposing the *pteruges*, the skirt made of leather strips that protected the buttocks, groin and upper legs of the next in line. Dax fired again, the arrow punctured flesh passing from one side of a thigh to the other. A second shield dropped, but remained upright as it should with a well drilled soldier. The remaining shields closed around the wounded in a defensive triangle. Dax could see Maximus moving through the gate, now he was the exposed one.

'Move,' called the centurio.

Dax dodged left, then left again, expecting steel to strike him in the back. 'Drop.'

Dax fell on his face. There was the sound of iron striking wood on the palisade that formed the fortification's wall. He rose to his feet and ran on. Iron passed through the air to the side of his face as the centurio launched a cavalry spear at the shield wall.

'Help me close the gate,' ordered Maximus.

Dax put his shoulder to the effort. The wood and iron reinforced structure swung easily on its greased hinge. He picked up a spent pilum, bent the soft steel into a hook then slid it through the brackets used to lock the gate. Dax twisted the iron just as he had on the prison wagon.

Maximus nodded his approval. 'Good work.'

Dax stepped away from the gate. 'Horses?'

'The stable is inside the wall; we will need to go elsewhere.'

Dax was almost too hungry and weary to think much beyond the immediate.

'Where?'

# CHAPTER THIRTY-THREE

MILCAH WAS HELPING MARY hide the coins from David. She was smart enough not to ask why.

'Is Daddy alright?'

'Yes, he is fine.'

'Is Auntie Hannah alright?'

'Hannah is fine.'

'Why are the men hiding? Is it because Daddy helped David the thief?'

Mary looked down at the nine-year-old who was pouring flour from one jar to another to make space for the coins.

'David is not a thief, Milcah, I was wrong. David is a man who came to Nazareth to catch bad people.'

'How were they bad? Were they thieves?'

'Yes, they stole and they hurt a woman.'

Milcah deliberated then asked, 'Is David going to marry Auntie Hannah?'

'No, David can't marry her.'

'Is he promised to marry the woman that was hurt?'

'No, he said he wasn't promised to anybody.'

'Then why shouldn't he marry Auntie Hannah? You said she needs a husband.'

'Yes, Hannah needs somebody in her life, but David isn't the right person, well not right now. Sometimes a woman can meet the right man and she just isn't ready and sometimes a man can meet the right woman, and he isn't ready. You can't plan when you are going to fall in love.'

'But Auntie Hannah isn't happy; I don't like it when she is sad.'

Mary was surprised at the insight of her daughter.

'Did Hannah say she was sad?'

'No,' said Milcah seriously, 'but I can tell when she is sad, sometimes it makes her angry.'

'And you think Hannah is sad a lot of the time?'

Milcah nodded. 'Except when she is really angry, that's mostly when Peter talks to her.'

'Peter doesn't want to make her angry,' said Mary. 'He just doesn't understand why Hannah doesn't feel the way that he feels about her. Being an adult can be very complicated.'

'Is it because Peter smells like fish?'

'Partially,' smiled Mary, 'the problem is Hannah wants something Peter can't give her.'

'What can't Peter give her?'

Mary wiped her flour- covered hands before taking a jar from her daughter.

'I don't know that I can explain it, but you will find out soon enough what is expected of women. It is best to be prepared, so you can avoid the pitfalls and traps that women have to navigate.'

'Auntie Hannah said you would tell me how babies are made, is that what you are going to tell me? If it is, I already know. Babies are made when a boy and a girl sleep in the same bed and wrestle with no underpants on.'

This made Mary laugh.

'There is a bit more involved; we will have a talk about it after supper.'

'Auntie Hannah said you were the best mother in Galilee and I couldn't hear about babies from a better role model. I said I didn't know what a role model was and she said that should be on my list of things to find out about.'

This stopped Mary in her tracks.

'Well, if Hannah said I know about these things, we will definitely have that talk tonight.'

'I look forward to it,' replied Milcah.

There was a knock at the door. Nobody knocked in Nazareth.

'Milcah take James to Bilhah's house. Go out the back and wait until I come and get you.'

'Yes, Mummy,' said Milcah running to do as she was told.

Mary watching her daughter disappear, poured water on the flour on the table, then plunged her hands into the mixture to make it look as if she was making dough, before opening door. There was a woman dressed like any other in the village. Mary looked the woman up and down. Her toenails were painted red; she was not from Nazareth.

'Hello,' said the woman with a smile.

'David's gone if that's who you are looking for; he left about an hour ago.'

'I guess then there is something wrong with my disguise that says this woman doesn't belong,' said Charlene dropping her smile

'Your toes,' said Mary, 'we don't paint our toes.'

Charlene looked at her feet.

'Right, I had better do something about that then?'

'If you were dressed as a Roman whore I might not have noticed.'

'They paint their toes?'

'They do lots of things we Jewish women don't.'

'I am not Roman.'

'No, you're not. You're from the far-off land where David comes from, where women have more choices in life than they do here.'

Charlene nodded. 'I am also guessing that your men think they are the smart ones, but the women know differently.'

Mary nodded, then gestured for Charlene to come into her home. 'Funny, I was having a similar conversation with my daughter only a moment ago.'

'Is she here?'

'I sent her away when I heard you knock, only the Romans bang on doors.'

'I'm sorry if I frightened you.'

'Yes, you did,' said Mary wiping her hands. 'What do you need to know?'

'How is David? Is he injured?'

'He's a bit bruised, but that's all. David had a fight with the Romans in Nazareth last night. He used his weapon that shoots green light and wind to save my husband, and rescue our friends who were being crucified on the Hill of Kedumim, which is why we helped him and why I am talking to you.'

Charlene nodded her head in thanks.

'Where are the Romans? I didn't see them on the streets.'

'They are hiding behind their walls; they think David used witchcraft.'

'You're not scared, David didn't frighten you?' Charlene realised she was assuming too much of a relationship only moments old. 'Sorry, I haven't even introduced myself, I am Charlene,' she said extending her hand.

Mary took it in her dough- covered one.

'I am Mary, the wife of Joseph. You are welcome as a friend of David.'

'Seriously,' said Charlene, her eyes widening, 'Mary and Joseph of Nazareth?'

'Yes, Joe and I have two sons and a daughter.' Mary chose not to speak of her children who had died, it was not a pain easily shared. 'My daughter is nine years old; her name is Milcah.'

'That's a pretty name.'

'Joe wanted to name her Heli after his mother, I didn't like the thought of that after what happened between us, so we compromised and named our daughter after Joe's favourite aunt.'

'And your sons?'

'My youngest is James, he is not yet one year old. My oldest is 17. He works with his father at the carpentry shop.'

'Your husband is a carpenter, named Joseph?'

'Yes, Joe built all of our furniture and that door behind you,' said Mary proudly.

Charlene couldn't believe what she was hearing.

'Have you ever been to Bethlehem, Mary? I know it's an odd question to ask, but have you?'

Mary nodded. 'Joe's family is from Bethlehem; our oldest son was born there.'

Charlene nearly swore.

'This is going to sound odd, but was your oldest son born in a stable?'

Mary's brow furrowed.

'That is an odd question to ask.'

There was a knock on the door.

'Charlene,' came a whispered call from the street.

'You are not alone?'

'I have two friends with me, one was here yesterday with David.'

'Adrian, David's well-meaning, but clueless cousin.'

'I probably wouldn't have been so blunt, but yes that's a fair description.'

'That is David's description, not mine,' replied Mary. 'I haven't met the man.' Mary went to the door and ushered Will and Adrian inside.

'What's up, Will?' asked Charlene.

'Two Roman soldiers are heading this way; they would have walked right past us if we stayed in the street.'

'Are you sure they didn't see you?' asked Charlene placing a hand on the weapon inside her goat skin bag.

'As much as I can be.'

Charlene addressed Mary, 'Can we hide here until they go past? If it's too dangerous, just say so and we will leave now.'

Mary shook her head. 'Stay here, it's safer and I can tell you what David has planned. The people he is chasing are at the port of Tyre.'

'How far is Tyre?' asked Charlene.

Mary considered the question.

'Four days on foot, two on horseback if you don't rush the horses and they have food and water for the journey.'

'Water won't be a problem,' said Adrian joining in the conversation, 'Uncle Dwight has provided us with a comprehensive survival kit.'

Mary nodded, 'You can make water appear out of dry air like David?'

'Did he show you that?' asked Adrian in surprise.

'He showed me a lot of things,' said Mary. 'David told me you would come for him and that I was to tell you not to follow him because it is too dangerous.'

'That's not going to happen,' said Charlene, 'it's not just his problem anymore. I need to get my life back. Will needs to actually have a life and Adrian, well Adrian probably needs to rethink his family relationships.' Charlene looked to Adrian. 'No offence, Doc.'

'No offence taken, Sergeant Wilson' replied Adrian.

Mary looked into Charlene's eyes. What she saw was determination.

'Then I will tell you what I know.'

'Thank you,' said Charlene, taking her hand out of her bag.

'David is on his way to Tyre to capture the man and the woman who hurt Jenifer Rostig. My sister Hannah, and Polykarpos the Greek school master, are travelling with him.'

'Peter and John talked about a Polykarpos,' said Adrian. 'I gathered he was a somewhat important chap.'

'It was because the Romans took Polykarpos that Peter and his gang put on their idiotic display,' said Mary with disdain. 'They wanted to rescue Polykarpos and whisk him away to safety. Luckily, my oldest was on an errand for his master or he could have been involved. Peter has too much influence on my son with his ideas for changing the world.'

'Ah,' said Adrian shamefaced, 'David and I rather upset their plans.'

'I am glad you did. Joe and I are in your debt for saving our stupid friends' lives, not that they deserved to be saved. I don't know what they were thinking, but I do know what they were thinking with.' Mary held up her hand and wiggled the smallest finger.

Charlene nodded. She understood Mary's sign language perfectly.

'You're welcome,' replied Adrian. 'Sorry, it's unforgivably rude of me, I should introduce myself.'

'This is Mary,' said Charlene, 'Mary, of Nazareth.' Charlene paused to see if anything registered.

'Well, isn't that a lovely coincidence,' said Adrian extending a hand to Mary. 'Will's mother is also a Mary. It's a lovely old-world name with so much more class to it than say, Aaliyah, or Charmayanne. Sometimes I think that parents push random letters of the alphabet together to make a name and think it's acceptable. Surely, they must realise how debilitating a carelessly chosen name can be. A chap's life can be difficult enough without having been forced to answer to Anomaly, or Panda as a name. I feel somewhat blessed that my parents named me simply, Adrian.'

Charlene continued the introduction. 'Mary is the wife of *Joseph*. They live in *Nazareth*.'

'My apologies, Mary. Do you prefer Mrs Joseph or simply Ms Mary? Some people are rather particular about such things.'

'None of this is registering with you, is it?'

'Sorry, Sergeant Wilson, am I missing something?'

Charlene looked to Will who was peering through a gap in the door. 'Will?' Will turned.

'They're about 60 metres away.'

'Okay then, let's not make too much noise and they won't know we are here.' Will closed the door and stepped into the room.

'Mary, this is Will. He is also a relative of David.'

Mary now understood the greeting protocol of these people and extended her hand. 'You don't look like David.'

'You could say that I am a distant relative.'

'Mary is married to Joseph,' said Charlene. 'Joe, as Mary refers to her husband, is a carpenter. He built all their furniture, isn't that correct, Mary?'

Mary was puzzled why Charlene was putting so much detail into her introduction.

Will nodded distractedly, thinking of the threat approaching down the street.

'Joe is a carpenter here in, Nazareth.' Charlene waited for it to sink in, 'Mary has three children, two boys and a girl.' Adrian and Will smiled politely. 'Her first-born son works with his father as a *carpenter* in *Nazareth*.' Charlene was obvious with her emphases. 'Joseph, the carpenter, built all the furniture in their home.'

Will's brow furrowed as he realised that Charlene was trying to convey a particular message, he just wasn't grasping it yet. It was something important, Will could tell that much from the way Charlene was speaking. He was puzzled why Charlene didn't just say it.

'Really?' said Adrian impressed, 'Your husband built all of this? I do like the workmanship. Will, have a look at the detail on the table legs. Can you see the donkey heads carved into the wood? Tell me this isn't the sign of a first-rate artisan.'

Will bent down and studied the carving. 'Yes, that is a very good donkey.'

'Will's father is also an artisan, Mary,' said Adrian, 'and one of the most profoundly wise people of his time.'

Charlene remembered Colin and Mary Thomas spending hours with her parents. Nothing stood out about either, they were just ordinary people, Will was the anomaly. Charlene dropped these thoughts and went back to her introduction.

'Will, Joe's family was originally from the town of *Bethlehem*.'

That was when it clicked into place, right then with that one word. Will's mouth fell open.

'Seriously? Like in three kings and frankincense?'

'Yes, Will,' replied Charlene. 'In fact, Mary and Joseph's oldest son was actually born in...'

Before Charlene could say the words, Will did, '*Bethlehem*!'

'That's nice,' said Adrian, 'having your son in Bethlehem so that family could be close at such important occasions.'

Mary shook her head.

'Joe's parents weren't there; it was just Joe and my mother.' Mary was angry as she spoke. 'It was decided I would marry Joe's brother, Cleopas, a *shadchan* made the match and when I turned 16, I thought we would be betrothed.' Mary shook her head in disgust. 'Cleopas didn't ask me to be his wife, I thought he loved me, he said the words and I said them back, but he didn't mean them.' Mary looked at Charlene. 'Do you remember your first love, how hard it was to say the words because you were afraid that he wouldn't say them back?'

'I remember,' said Charlene quietly.

'Cleopas used the words just to get what he wanted.' Mary looked away; she was afraid Charlene would think less of her. 'Cleopas told me I was fun to be with, he made that point very clear, then he said that I was not suitable to be his wife.' Without thinking, Mary moved to the table and began to clean up the flour and water. 'It was a hard lesson to learn that men can say one thing and mean another.' Mary paused, unsure why she was telling these strangers any of this. 'I married Joe. He is a better man than his brother could ever be, he was there when I needed him, which is more than I can say of most men.'

'Yes, they can be bastards,' said Charlene looking at Adrian and Will and making them flinch.

'We moved to Nazareth after our son was born, saved our shekels and bought this house. If we hadn't, Joe and I probably wouldn't be together.

She has a mouth on her, Joe's mother,' said Mary with an edge to her voice. 'I tried to forgive her, I really tried for Joe's sake, but I can't. I refuse to turn the other cheek. People said she didn't know what she was doing. Goat shit, I say to that, she knew exactly what she was saying.' Mary began to sweep flour into a jar. 'Joe has plans to open his own business with our boys. I have encouraged him to think about the future, you have to have dreams, if you don't then what is the point?'

'Yes, you do,' said Charlene picking up a jar to help clean up.

Mary dipped a cloth in a bowl of water and began to wipe the remnants of flour from the table.

'Heli has never been happy about Joe and I being together. She chooses to believe that I rejected Cleopas rather than the other way around. Maybe he said something to her?' Mary faced Charlene. 'Heli called me a whore when she found out I was pregnant. She did everything she could to split us up and it nearly worked. After I told Joe about the baby, I didn't see him for a week. I was so disappointed I thought about telling him to go to hell. Then Joe looked at me with that silly look on his face and smiled like he was the happiest man in Galilee. Joe told me he loved me and I could tell he meant it; I seriously think Joe can't lie to anybody. He really is a good man, my Joseph. I wouldn't swap him even for a whole herd of milking goats.'

'This Heli woman had no right to judge you, she sounds like an obnoxious cow,' commented Charlene.

'What really made me mad was I found out Heli knew how Cleopas was with girls. I was only 15, still a child.' Mary looked defiantly around the room. 'It's not uncommon, Joe and I had been seeing each other for a while, sometimes things happen you don't plan for. We are happy and our children are well cared for, that's what's important.'

'Yes, it bloody well is, you should tell this Heli woman to get stuffed,' said Charlene. 'If you and your family are happy, what does anybody else's opinion matter?'

'It doesn't,' agreed Mary. 'I don't know what "getting stuffed" means, but that sounds good to me.'

'My mother would wet herself,' whispered Will. 'Here I am, in Mary's actual house, talking with the woman she idolises almost as much as Ita Buttrose.'

'Sorry, am I missing something important?' asked Adrian.

'This is Mary,' said Will keeping his voice down, 'the wife of Joseph.' Seeing no reaction Will tried again. 'Joseph is a *carpenter*, from *Nazareth*.

Their son was born in *Bethlehem*.' Will had to physically stop himself from wiggling his fingers.

'I still don't understand the significance,' puzzled Adrian.

Charlene put a hand on Will's arm.

'Don't, you can explain it to Doc later.'

'Explain what?' asked Mary.

Will was horrified. 'It's nothing.'

'What's nothing? You must tell me.'

'I can't, Mary. My mum would kill me if I offended you.'

'Are you making fun of my family?'

'There is no offence meant, Mary,' said Charlene coming to Will's aid.

'David told me why he is here. He showed me his home, he showed me his Jenifer Rostig. If you know something about my family, then you should tell me.'

'What do we know?' asked Adrian.

'You're not helping, Doc,' said Charlene sharply. 'Go and check how close our friends are.'

Adrian was surprised by the rebuke but moved to peer through a gap in the door.

Charlene turned to Mary, 'I swear on my oath as a police officer that we mean no offence. It's just important that we disrupt your life as little as possible.'

'So, you do know something,' said Mary, 'you have to tell me if my family are in danger.' Mary looked from Will to Adrian, then back to Charlene in desperation. 'I can see it in your faces, you know something bad will happen to my children. Do they all die from the shits? Does Joe die because of Peter and his gang of idiots?'

'Yes, we have secrets,' said Charlene, 'everybody does. The problem is that sometimes telling what you know can do more harm than saying nothing.'

Will felt awful watching Mary's agony.

'If we thought it was safe or sensible to tell you, we would.'

'That's not good enough,' replied Mary raising her voice.

'They are nearly here,' interrupted Adrian. 'I know the taller chap; he's the officer I met yesterday. I'm not sure about the other one, he may have accompanied David out of town.'

Mary put an eye to the gap in the door. 'That's the centurio in charge in Nazareth. His name is Maximus. I don't know the short one with the black eye.'

Charlene reached over Mary's head and gently closed the door.

'Let's take a seat and sit quietly as they go past.'

Charlene sat on the bench seat nestled beside the table made by Joseph. She slipped a hand inside the goat skin bag, curling her fingers around the pistol grip of the weapon. Will held his breath as he sat opposite Charlene; she put a finger to her lips in the universal sign for silence, adding a glare at Adrian who was wriggling on the seat in excitement. The sound of marching feet faded. Charlene took her hand from the bag, opened the door a crack and peered into the street.

'Okay, they're gone.'

'Wasn't that exhilarating,' gushed Adrian. 'I don't know how you do this, Sergeant Wilson. I am truly admiring of your calmness.'

Will breathed out, 'What now?'

'We find some transport and hit the road to Tyre,' replied Charlene, 'With luck we can catch David up.'

'You are the leader?' asked Mary.

'Yes,' said Will taking the opportunity to deflect the conversation, 'Sergeant Wilson is in charge.' He didn't want to lie to Mary; his mum would kick his arse if she found out, and there probably weren't enough Hail Marys to be said in the entire world to be forgiven for that sin.

Mary addressed Charlene, 'David said Jenifer Rostig was his leader, is that true?'

'Yes, I believe she had seniority.'

Mary forced herself to calm down.

'I was wrong about David; I didn't believe Joe when he could see the truth. I guess I am used to seeing the bad in people and can't just assume they are good.' Mary paused in thought. 'Maybe Polykarpos is right when he says only a man who is without sin should be allowed to throw stones at those who have sinned.'

'That is very profound, Mary,' said Adrian, 'I have heard something similar before, do you know where this is from Will?'

Will realised the conversation was heading in a dangerous direction so changed the subject.

'Mary, can you tell us where we can find some horses for transport?'

'You need to see Peter's cousin Simon, he sells horses, though mostly to the Romans.'

'Is this Simon an honest horse dealer?' asked Charlene.

'No, of course not, none of them can be trusted, which is why you must ride the horse, check its age and talk with the previous owner about its temperament before you part with your coin. Do all the standard checks on a horse or donkey you were looking to buy, feel the tendons, inspect its teeth, raise its hooves and feel for soreness.'

Charlene looked at Will.

'Do you know about horses?'

Will shook his head, 'My father is a mechanic, I know about engines if that helps.'

'I am afraid that the inspection of equine livestock has not featured in my education portfolio either,' chimed in Adrian. 'Though I have a reasonable amount of experience of riding of horses in the holographic suites at the costumery. I favour dressage over jumping and racing programs.'

'Great,' said Charlene, 'if we run into Princes Anne, and she needs somebody for her equestrian team, I will know who to go to.'

'Blessed goat crap,' spat Mary shaking her head, 'I promised to help David, you are his family, so I must help you.'

'You don't have to,' said Charlene.

'Yes, I do,' said Mary balling up her hands into fists. 'I will take you to Simon and introduce you, then make sure he doesn't rob you like a blind man. You do have coin?'

'Yes, we have money,' replied Charlene.

'Let me check on my children and I will take you to Simon,' said Mary heading to the door.

'Thank you,' said Charlene.

Adrian held the door open for Mary.

'Thank you, dear lady,' he said as Mary exited. Adrian closed the door and turned to his companions. 'Mary has quite the aura of strength; I wouldn't be surprised if her offspring turned out to be quite successful in life.'

'Seriously Adrian, are you really saying you have no idea who Mary probably is?' asked Will.

'Sorry? I really am missing something important?'

'Don't Will,' said Charlene, 'there is no point speculating. Let's just stay focused on the mission and say as little as possible from now on.'

'What are we not saying?' asked Adrian, 'Did I commit a dreadful faux pas?'

'No Doc, it's just that sometimes it's best to listen and ask questions when we are alone.'

Adrian furrowed his brow.

'Message received, Sergeant Wilson. I will be the model of discretion from now on.'

'It's my fault,' said Will.

'No, it's mine,' said Charlene. 'When Mary told me who she was, I guess I was a bit star struck to be honest.'

'I did the same,' said Will, 'but I should have picked up on it earlier, what with the way Mum is.'

'I thought your mum would have given up the divine thing after what your family went through. I read the files, the local god botherers were pretty rugged once the *W* rumours started.'

'It really was crap,' said Will, 'it nearly broke Mum's heart.'

'Is this something that I need to be aware of?' asked Adrian in confusion.

Mary slipped back into the room.

'Are you ready to go?'

Charlene slung her bag over a shoulder.

'How do we play this Simon?'

Mary looked directly at Charlene.

'A man will have to make the bargain and put silver in Simon's palm.'

'I'll do it,' said Will shouldering his own bag. 'Just give me a thumbs up or a wink and nod if the deal looks good.'

'No, not you,' said Mary. 'Adrian will make the bargain. You have a good and trusting heart. Simon will see you as a somebody whose purse he can lighten very easily.'

'Should a chap be offended?' asked Adrian.

Mary ran a hand along the table made by her husband.

'My Joe is like you in many ways, that is a good thing in a husband and a father, but not when dealing with a man like Simon.' Mary lifted her hand. 'You will pay a fair price, if not, Simon will be suspicious and could go running to the Romans.'

'What do I do then?' asked Will.

'You will be my cousin, Elon, the wagon maker from Hebron; Simon has heard Joe and I talk of Elon.'

'I assume that while Mr Simon is aware of your cousin, he hasn't had the pleasure of meeting him?' asked Adrian.

Mary nodded.

'What's the reason for Elon meeting Simon?' asked Will.

Mary didn't hesitate, 'Elon needs good horses to cart timber for his work. You heard about Simon from me and decided to inspect his merchandise. If the horses Simon sells are good enough for the empire, they should be good enough for you. I would make that point; Simon likes to feel important.'

'What's Doc's angle in this?' asked Charlene.

'Adrian is Elon's half-brother, Aaron. Elon makes wagons, Aaron manages the finances of the family business. Aaron will make the deal and hand over the coins.'

'That doesn't explain me,' said Charlene.

'You are Elon's wife, Eve,' continued Mary. 'While Elon and Aaron are keeping Simon busy, Eve and I can inspect the horses and giving winks and nods when we have picked the right animals.'

'And when the price is right,' said Adrian.

'Yes,' said Mary.

'That sounds like a plan,' said Charlene. 'Not the best plan, but it will do.'

Adrian grinned broadly.

'An adventure awaits my good friends. What could possibly go wrong?'

# CHAPTER THIRTY-FOUR

OCTAVIAN MADE HIS WAY to the private rooms in his villa where he kept the drawings of his wife and children. These simple sketches made less than a year ago were a reminder of why Octavian's existence had meaning and purpose. He recognised Adalburg the instant he had seen her likeness, right down to the glint in her eye that marked the start of laughter. They had laughed a lot, Octavian, and the chieftain's daughter. It had been easy to fall in love with her.

Octavian had wanted to wed Adalburg. It had to be done in secret as it was against the rules for a serving soldier to marry. Octavian swore to Max it was to secure peace with the Germanic tribe. Max agreed it made political sense to bond the chieftain to the empire with blood, but he also knew it was not the only reason his friend needed to take this barbarian woman as his bride.

Berard was their first-born. Adalburg called him her little bear, so he became Berard the bear. A year later, Eadgyo was born, their little princess. Octavian could not imagine ever being without her in his life. He had been content to serve out his remaining years with the legion on the edge of the empire, as long as he had his family at his side.

Then everything changed. Octavian was to be rewarded for bringing the warrior chieftain, Arminius, into the fold of the empire, thus ending years of hostility. He was to be promoted to the rank of *Praefectus Castrorum* with the Sixth Legion based in the lands of the Israelites. Augustus himself had suggested the reward, just as he thought it prudent to move a man capable of such achievement far from his loyal soldiers and any thoughts of greater leadership aspirations.

Octavian was disturbed by the news. As great as this honour was, it would have a devastating impact on Adalburg and the children. He talked with Max of taking his family into the forest and not returning, then as quickly, rejected the idea which might save Adalburg and his children on the fringe of the empire, but bring retribution down on his family in Capua.

Adalburg convinced Octavian that he must finish his service in the legions with the Sixth while she and the children hid from the eyes of Rome. When his duty was complete and he was rewarded with citizenship, they could be reunited. Octavian arranged for a veteran who had served with his father to be paid a regular wage in gold to watch over his family as they hid in the town of Autricum in Gaul. Adalburg was provided with a warm house, on good land where she could grow crops in spring and summer, to provide food through the winter and the children could go to school to be educated as a child of Rome.

Being the Praefectus Castrorum had allowed this arrangement to continue, and now his partnership with Julia would make the plan for his family come true. He just had to serve out the remainder of his time, continue to build his nest egg of gold, then bring them home to Capua.

Octavian sat on his favourite chair and called for his personal servant.

The sound of footfalls heralded the entrance of the 16-year-old Asher.

'Yes, Praefectus?'

'Was there correspondence while I was away?'

'On the desk, Praefectus, there are two letters, one from the Lady Julia,' he hesitated, 'the second has the seal of the Prefectus Animus Rufus, which I thought best to place here for your eyes alone.'

Octavian nodded, then asked, 'Why do I not have wine in my hand?'

Asher considered the question, 'Because I am an incompetent servant who has yet again failed to read my master's mind?'

'Can you read it now Asher?'

The youth nodded.

'Is there anything else you desire while I am finding your wine, Praefectus?'

Octavian raised a single eyebrow.

'You want a horse and an escort for a visit to the Lady Julia?'

Octavian nodded.

'I will see to the arrangements, Praefectus,' said Asher turning to leave.

'Asher.'

'Yes, Praefectus?'

'What does Annius Rufus want?'

Asher turned to face his master.

'I am not that good a mind reader, Praefectus. I will have to wait to find out if I need to know.'

'A good answer, Asher. Just next time take more care when you reseal the scroll.'

'Praefectus?'

'There is a barely visible mark where the seal had been applied, but no longer sits. I expect attention to detail from my personal servant.'

The boy didn't flinch.

'I will endeavour to live up to your standards, Praefectus.'

'I enjoy having you around, Asher. It would make me sad if you weren't here anymore.'

'It would also make me sad, Praefectus,' replied Asher with a bow.

Octavian waved a hand to dismiss the boy, 'Go, before I reconsider how much I enjoy you company.'

'As you wish, Praefectus.'

Julia's correspondence was dated four days previous.

*Octavian.*

*On the day of your return, you will receive a letter from Annius Rufus. It will announce his visit to inspect the port facilities in Tyre on the fourth of this month. Don't waste too much time with Rufus, Tiberius plans to replace him with Valerius Gratus within a few months.*

*Julia.*

Octavian picked up the scroll sealed with a wax impression of the ring of the Prefectus of Judea and Samaria. It had not been tampered with, the stain around the seal was a result of the wax cooling and shrinking. Still, it was good to keep Asher on his toes, he really didn't want to find a replacement.

Octavian read the scroll; it was as Julia described. The date of issue two days after she had written her note.

'Asher?'

The servant hurried into the room with goblet of wine in hand. 'Praefectus?'

'We will have guests staying in two days, plan for 10 for three nights.' Octavian drank from the goblet and thought. 'Plan meals for eleven, the Lady Julia will be joining us, and make arrangements for entertainment after supper.'

'I will see to the arrangements,' replied Asher as he turned to leave.

'Asher.'

'Yes, Praefectus?'

'Does Julia have a spy in our household?'

'Not to my knowledge, Praefectus.'

'Let's keep it that way.'

'Yes, Praefectus,' replied Asher leaving the room. He had thought his method of resealing the parchment was undetectable, now he wasn't so certain. His resistance contact had been very interested in the visit of Annius Rufus. Now he could report that the mystery woman, Julia, would be in the villa on the same night.

Atarah, the head of the household staff, led Octavian to Julia's sitting room.

'Hello Octavian,' said Julia, 'take a seat, you look positively worn out.'

Octavian found his partnership with Julia of immense value; her information was unerringly correct and Julia knew it. What Octavian didn't understand was what Julia truly wanted. Yes, there was wealth generated by the partnership, but there had to be more than that.

'Can I offer you supper?' Julia indicated to the seat opposite for Octavian to take the weight off. 'I showed the girls how to make éclairs today,' she smiled, 'the problem is finding sugar and the prices are ridiculous. I am hoping we can reduce some honey to a candied state and try that.'

'I don't know what you are talking about, Julia?'

'I am talking about baking, Octavian, not a secret woman's plot to take over the world so you can relax. Would you like some wine, though to be frank, the local wine is only suited to sprinkling on fish and chips. The problem with that thought is nobody here has discovered the potato yet; God, I miss deep-fried chips.'

'No wine, thank you,' replied Octavian sitting opposite Julia.

'You got my note?'

'Yes and the correspondence from Annius Rufus. How did you know?' Julia smiled.

'I told you I collect information, it's not magic, I promise.'

Octavian believed Julia to be a spy master with agents in even the highest offices of the empire, which made her dangerous and a very valuable ally.'

'Annius Rufus will only intrude on your privacy for two nights before heading north to start trade negotiations with some minor tribal leader. Something to do with wool, I believe.' Octavian furrowed his brow at the information. Julia noted the look of concern. 'You have nothing to worry about. Annius Rufus has no idea of our arrangement or your interests outside of Galilee.'

Julia looked toward the curtained entrance to the room.

'Sapphira,' she called, 'could you please bring a jug of water with lemon juice if we have any, thank you.'

Octavian noted the shadow of Julia's bodyguard move beneath the curtain. He expected nothing less.

'You have your part of the supply chain moving as efficiently as it can. That's all a public servant like Annius Rufus cares about. He doesn't want to have issues to deal with.'

Octavian nodded in agreement.

'That is also my opinion of Rufus. Is there an opportunity with these trade negotiations?'

Julia shook her head.

'They won't come to anything, but Annius will inform you that Tiberius has commissioned a temple in honour of Augustus to be built in Galilee. Construction will start next year.'

Octavian raised an eyebrow. There were many opportunities associated with such an undertaking. Before Octavian could ask for specifics, Sapphira entered with a jug and two goblets which she placed on a table. As she turned away, Octavian could see the shape of a dagger beneath her robe. Julia was not taking anything for granted.

'Thank you for the coin, by the way,' said Julia as she poured the water. 'Are you pleased with the return on investment?' Octavian nodded. Julia had lived up to her part of the bargain, as had he. 'I didn't come just to talk about Annius Rufus, I have other news.

Have you had a letter from Gaul, how are Berard and Eadgyo getting on at school?'

Octavian stiffened.

'I thought we agreed to treat our relationship purely on a business level.'

'Sorry, my bad. I forgot the Praefectus Castrorum needs to maintain a professional image.'

Octavian relaxed as he took a glass from Julia.

'No, you are right. If we are to trust one another, a certain level of intimacy between us should exist.'

'Wow Octavian, that really is big of you, and don't worry I'm not going to talk about anything we discuss on a business or any other level.'

Octavian placed the goblet on the table.

'As you have asked, I have received a parchment from Adalburg. She and the children are alive and well.'

'That's good, anything else to report?'

Octavian nodded.

'Adalburg had a good harvest of beets and cabbage from her garden. She will pickle the cabbage so it can last through winter.'

'Well then, I guess that is very good news.'

'Yes, it is,' replied Octavian, 'though I hate pickled cabbage. It gives me wind.'

'Okay,' said Julia, 'now the pleasantries are done with, what's really on your mind?'

Octavian placed a lanyard with *Police,* stencilled along its length, on the table. It held the image of a badge and the likeness of David Thomas.

'It happened then, where I said it would?'

'Yes, on the street opposite the carpentry shop. He was not alone, there was a taller man, not a brother, but closely related.'

Julia nodded.

'Adrian, why would he bring Adrian?'

Octavian picked up the police ID.

'This one fought well, was he a soldier?'

'Yes, of sorts.' Julia stood. 'You took care of it as I asked?'

'As we agreed,' replied Octavian, 'he no longer poses a threat, that is as you wished?'

'Yes, that's what I wanted; I just wasn't expecting it to be so simple.'

'Still, as you asked, the first of your demands has been met.'

'Thank you,' said Julia. 'I am grateful and reassured with the outcome.'

'Do you want to know the fate of the other one?'

Julia hesitated, 'Is Adrian in a position to cause problems?'

'No.'

'Then I don't need to hear the details.'

'As you wish.'

Octavian dropped the ID on the table.

'I believe you wish me to find somebody else?'

Julia nodded.

'There is a woman, a girl named Mary, aged somewhere between a newborn and 18 years old, though she could be in her early twenties, but that's unlikely. Nobody knows when she was actually born. There has been lots of guess work, but no solid evidence. Mary is only mentioned a dozen times in the book and there is confusion between Mary the mother, Mary of Bethany and Mary the disciple. She isn't married, neither is she a prostitute as some people claimed.'

Octavian was surprised, this was the first time he had seen Julia unclear on her facts.

'Is it important that this Mary is a virgin?'

'Of course not, it has no bearing on any woman's worth,' snapped Julia.

Octavian could have stated that a virgin, especially a young virgin, was worth more in the slave market than a woman who had lain with a man. He chose to hold his tongue.

'I am sorry,' said Julia composing herself, 'that was unprofessional of me.'

'There is no need to apologise, tell me what you know.'

'Yes, of course,' replied Julia in control again. 'Mary was born in Magdala and comes from a family, wealthy enough to allow her to travel for months on end across Galilee and Judea, without the need to work.'

'Do you want me to find every Mary from a wealthy family in Magdala, aged between birth and 25 years?'

'No, I need you to find one specific Mary.'

'That will not be easy. Magdala is home to 40,000 men, women and children.'

'Yes, I know the demography,' said Julia. 'Around half of the population is male, which reduces the number by 20,000, then if you factor in the women not named Mary and eliminate Marys who are too old, or have married, it will probably bring the number down to say, 20 or 30 girls and women.'

'My men can't go to every house in Magdala looking for your Mary, it would raise not just questions, but suspicions. I will not risk the future of my family just to find a Jewish girl.'

Julia shook her head.

'I am not asking you to do that Octavian. I will never ask you to put Adalburg, or your children in jeopardy.' Julia paused, then started again. 'There must be records you could access. Surely you have a register of people in Judea and Galilee you use to tax the population?'

'The Jewish elders collect taxes on our behalf, if they don't the empire has ways to make sure we collect what is due.'

'What about conducting a census? How else do you plan for future roads, infrastructure, aqueducts? That is why your empire is a success by reaping the rewards of forward planning.'

Octavian nodded. 'That and the legions.'

'Can you organise a census in Magdala?'

'It's not in my power to order a census for no reason.' Octavian sat forward on his seat. 'However, if the Prefectus of Judea was to order such a thing, it would be incumbent on the legion to assist in making it happen. I could place my Immunes at the disposal of the Prefectus to check and consolidate the data.'

Julia smiled, 'See, that wasn't so hard.'

'Wanting a census and making it happen are two different things. Annius Rufus won't do anything unless it is in the interest of the empire. He will need a sound administrative reason for such an undertaking.'

'You have a new emperor, Octavian. I would have thought a career diplomat like Annius Rufus would be feeling a little anxious and eager to make a good impression on the new boss. He could, for example, increase revenue to Rome by conducting a census to establish exactly how many people there are in this corner of the empire to make sure that every person who benefits from being in the empire, pays their fair share.'

Octavian nodded, then surprised Julia with a request.

'I would like to invite you to dine at my villa.'

'Are you asking me out on a date?' Julia saw the look of confusion on Octavian's face and tried again. 'Sorry, you said you want me to come to your villa for a meal?'

'The Prefectus of Judea and Samaria will expect to be entertained while he is visiting. He would also expect a man in my position to have a mistress to act as a hostess.'

Julia feigned shock.

'I don't know whether to be appalled or titillated. What is a chaste woman to think?'

Octavian ignored Julia's sarcasm.

'My servants believe we are engaged in such a relationship; the rumours would have travelled to the ears of the Prefectus. It is better to present you as my mistress than to have questions asked behind our backs.'

'Ok, I can play your vacuous and uninterestingly pleasant lover, if that's what I need to be.'

Octavian shook his head.

'No, Annius Rufus's spies would have reported on you.'

'Then how do you want me to play this?'

'Be the woman the people of Tyre believe you to be. A woman of wealth in a relationship with the Praefectus Castrorum because she sees advantages in such an arrangement.'

Julia nodded.

'It's not exactly a love story like Elizabeth Bennet and Mr Darcy locking eyes across the dance floor at Netherfield Park, still a girl has got to do what she has to survive in the first century. The question is, what are you going to tell Annius Rufus about our relationship?'

Octavian pondered the question.

'If Annius Rufus asks, I can say that you are the only woman in Tyre that is intelligent and attractive enough to be my lover. You are not a prostitute, so you carry no disease. You speak Latin, so we can converse and you have money, so you are not a drain on my purse.'

'You know, if I ever get home, Octavian, I'm going to use that for my on-line dating profile.'

# CHAPTER THIRTY-FIVE

MARY LED THE WAY through the alleys of Nazareth to a track that led to the stables of Simon. She had an obligation to David and the warrior, the happy fool and the sad, serious one, who had come to take him home They would be lambs in front of a hungry lion when they met Simon without her help. Mary couldn't have that on her conscience.

Charlene followed next. The weight of her bag a reminder of the dangers ahead. She would have been more comfortable carrying the weapon in her arms. That wasn't practical, it could draw attention. As a compromise, Charlene held her taser in the sleeve of her dress, she wouldn't hesitate to use it.

Adrian followed Charlene, keeping his head down as Sergeant Wilson had told him to, his eyes locked on her feet four paces to his front. Then he noticed Sergeant Wilson's red toenails. *How wonderful,* he thought and smiled.

Will watched Mary. She reminded him of an angry ewok marching off to battle in her woollen dress and wind-frizzled hair. Of course, she wasn't covered in fur and they were in a stony desert, not a Redwood Forest and he and Adrian weren't anything like Luke or Han. Charlene was a bit like Leia, well not to look at, then Will had a vision of Charlene wearing Leia's gold bikini which made him blush. It was bad enough that Charlene was dragged in to any of this without him fantasising about the impossible.

Then Will thought about Mary again, the woman his mother worshiped almost as much as Ita Buttrose. He was now involved in corrupting Mary, if he had believed in a divine being, he would definitely burn in hell forever. Will locked eyes on Charlene's back. She was taller than Mary, her hips seemed to sway more, then he thought about the gold bikini again and had to look away.

Mary halted on a rise above the domain of Peter's Uncle Simon, which consisted of a double-storey stone house, three times the size of Mary's, four three-sided structures containing fodder, ropes and harness and a large round yard constructed of wooden poles that held a dozen or so horses.

'This is the home of Simon,' said Mary, 'as you can see doing business with the Romans has its advantages.'

'I count 14 horses; we only need three,' said Charlene using Dwight's glasses to zoom in on the horse yard.

'You need the right three,' replied Mary. 'Simon will want to keep the best for his Roman friends.'

'Surely a businessman can be persuaded by the right price?' chipped in Adrian.

'Simon is ... ' Mary hesitated, unsure of the words. 'Simon is driven by his...' Mary again held up a hand and wiggled her little finger.

'He is a dick?' asked Charlene.

'Yes, that is the best way to explain Simon. Which is odd, as his son, Judas, is the kindest, most honest boy you could meet. Judas and my son are as close as brothers.' Mary paused, 'His is another life I owe David.'

'Did you just say Simon has a son named Judas?' asked Will.

'Yes, Simon's son is Judas. Does that matter?'

Will looked at Charlene and mouthed, *holy shit batman* before turning back to Mary. 'Is Cousin Simon's last name Iscariot, by any chance?'

'Yes,' replied Mary in surprise, 'have you heard of him?'

'No, I haven't heard of a Simon Iscariot.'

'I don't understand.'

Charlene mouthed an emphatic, *No*, then faced Mary.

'It's just a coincidence. We know of a person named Judas Iscariot where we come from.'

'What does your Judas Iscariot do in your land?'

Will could have said Judas was a guy in a book who dobbed on his best mate for money and got him killed, then followed up by saying that the story had been turned into a couple of movies and a musical, but he didn't. Because of the look on Charlene's face, he decided to make something up instead.

'He was a singer and played lead guitar in a band.'

Mary frowned, 'I don't understand.'

'No, no you wouldn't,' replied Will realising his mistake. 'What I meant was Judas was a musician, you know, rock n roll.' Will raised his pinkie and index finger skyward making the heavy metal devil horn symbol. Charlene looked horrified and Will dropped his hand.

'Why is this musician, your Judas Iscariot, well known in your land?'

Will didn't know how to answer. What were rock stars famous for? He opened his mouth and it just came out.

'He died young, well, relatively young. I think it was an overdose, you know, don't take the brown acid man.' Will could see the look of confusion on Mary's face. 'He took the brown acid, it killed him.'

'He is famous because he died?'

'Well, no, and yes. He was a great guitar player, song writer and singer.'

'What is a guitar?'

'It's a stringed instrument,' said Charlene, 'you play it with your fingers.'

Will played air guitar to demonstrate. He felt like an idiot.

'Not like a harp?' asked Mary miming playing.

'No, it sits over your shoulder on a strap balanced around hip height.' Will mimed playing again. 'You can't play a rock song without one, or a bass guitar.'

'Is a rock song like the songs in temple?'

'Not really,' replied Will, thinking of the hymns he had been subjected to as a child. Will looked at Charlene. 'How do I explain a rock song?'

'You could always sing one,' she replied holding up one hand and with her pinkie and index fingers raised. 'You started this conversation; I'm just dying to see how it ends.'

'Yes, you must sing me a song about rocks,' said Mary mimicking Charlene with her index and pinkie finger extended. 'Is it like the music David played for me when he showed me his home?'

'David was a classical music fan when we were growing up,' interrupted Adrian. 'Mary may have heard something from AC/DC, or even dare I speculate, one of my all-time favourite classical performers, Barry Manilow. He did write the songs after all.'

'Really?! Barry Manilow?!' replied Will in horror.

'Yes,' said Adrian closing his eyes and singing the opening verse of Copacabana.

'Don't,' pleaded Will. 'No way man. There is no way that Manilow can match anything that Judas Iscariot played.'

'Sing for me,' said Mary.

'I like Manilow,' said Charlene, 'let's see what you've got, Will.'

'No, I can't sing to save myself.'

'I think that you must, William Thomas,' said Mary. 'I insist upon hearing one of your Judas Iscariot songs. David would have sung; I know he would.'

'Yes, David would have sung for Mary,' chimed in Adrian.

'Bloody hell, Adrian, I thought we were on the same side.'

'A valid point, but I support Mary's proposal old chap.'

'Charlene?' Will pleaded.

'Like Mary, I am dying to hear which one of the great musician's hits you pick.'

'Please,' said Mary, sitting on a rock to listen.

'I'm not taking another step until Mary gets her wish,' said Adrian sitting next to Mary.

'You should sing something from the double live album,' said Charlene taking a seat and making the two-finger rock salute. 'Rock on Will.'

'Yes, on with the rocks,' said Mary making the rock n roll hand signal.

'Okay, be it on your own heads. I am just going to sing the first few lines and the chorus, so you get an idea, Mary.'

Mary nodded.

'I want to hear a song that your Judas Iscariot is famous for.'

'Well, this is one of his best, one of the band's best. I just hope I don't screw it up.'

Will closed his eyes, then sang the first two lines of *When the War is Over*. He didn't have a terrible voice, it just wasn't Ian Moss singing, or Barry Manilow for that matter.

Charlene's eyes widened in surprise. 'Chisel! Good choice.' Mary looked quizzically at Charlene. 'Cold Chisel is the name of Judas's band; you could be pleasantly surprised.'

Will sang the next few lines with heart- felt passion, then Charlene joined in and sang harmony on the chorus. Her voice wrapped around the lyrics and caressed the tune. She could really sing.

'Well done you, Will,' applauded Adrian rising to his feet. 'And Sergeant Wilson, I had no idea that you had such talent. Bravo to both of you.'

Charlene smiled at Will. It was the same smile she had used in the hospital waiting room in Adelaide, only now Charlene wasn't the 14-year-old girl who had smiled and winked at him. This Charlene disturbed Will on a whole different level.

Mary clapped as vigorously as Adrian.

'Thank you for singing, it was better than I had hoped for.'

'You're welcome,' replied Will, 'Can we go now?'

'Yes, now I will introduce you to Cousin Simon,' said Mary heading towards the horse yards.

Charlene and Mary moved ahead, Adrian and Will brought up the rear.

'What an odd coincidence,' said Adrian, starting a conversation with Will. 'Why would you name your child Judas, especially if your last name was Iscariot. I would hate to be stuck with that by an unthinking parent. It's even more of a coincidence when you think of where we are, what with Judas being friends with Mary's son, and Mary being married to a carpenter named Joseph.' Adrian shook his head staggered at the thought. 'What do you think the odds are? There can't be many Mary and Josephs living in Nazareth whose son is friends with a chap named Judas.'

Will grabbed Adrian's arm to prevent Mary overhearing the conversation. 'Just stop and think Adrian.'

'I really have missed something important?'

'Yes, you have.'

Adrian frowned in concentration, 'Nazareth is a smallish town when you think about it.'

'Yes, it is.'

'You don't think?'

'Yes Adrian, as does Charlene. We could be wrong, but what are the chances?'

'Does that mean that Mary's oldest son is...?'

'We don't know. He could just be a bloke who wants to get a girlfriend, own a donkey and not die from whatever disease kills people around here.'

'We could ask. I'm sure Mary wouldn't mind.'

'No, you heard what Emil and Dwight said, Mary could get suspicious and do something which could change everything.'

'Surely not, by just asking Mary about her son's name?'

'No Adrian, we can't risk it. We find David, help him then get home. That's it, nothing else.'

'But surely.'

'Haven't you screwed up enough lives Adrian?'

'Sorry?'

'Forget it. Let's just meet this Simon bloke, get what we need and then find your cousin.'

'Yes, of course, Will,' said Adrian apologetically.

'Good,' said Will as he hurried to catch up with Mary and Charlene.


'Simon Iscariot, are you at home? It's Mary, the wife of Joseph, the carpenter.'

A short, grey bearded middle-aged man emerged from the building.

'What do you want, Mary?'

'I brought people who would like to trade with you.'

'If you brought Hannah, this conversation is over.'

'Hannah is not with me.'

'Your sister said something to Cyborea and now she is acting strange. Can you believe my wife told me to have a bath and get my own breakfast?'

'Sorry, I don't know what you are talking about Simon.'

'How old is Hannah?' asked Simon, more as an accusation than a question.

'Hannah is 23.'

'Twenty-three, I don't understand why Peter is interested. She is practically beyond getting a decent marriage at her age.'

'I am not Hannah.'

Simon looked Mary up and down as if appraising a brood mare.

'No, you obey your husband, just as it is written in the scriptures. The husband leads, the wife follows and she should be happy to do so.'

Mary fought the urge to punch Simon in the face.

'Shalom and salutations, my good man,' said Adrian approaching.

Simon looked over Mary's head.

'Who is this?'

'That is my cousin, Aaron. He would like to talk to you about purchasing some horses.'

'I don't sell to strangers, Mary; my inventory is for my regular customers.'

'The Romans you mean.'

'Yes, of course the Romans. They have gold, I don't barter for chickens. If it's a goat, or a donkey your cousin is after, he should try the markets in Magdala.'

'Is there a problem cousin Mary?' interjected Adrian. 'If this merchant is unwilling to trade with the Hebron Wagon Company, then Elon and I can take our business elsewhere. I understand there is an excellent supply of quality equine bloodstock in Tyre.'

Simon looked at Mary. 'The Hebron Wagon Company?'

'Cousin Aaron and Cousin Elon own the wagon manufacturing business in Hebron, you've heard Joe and I talk about them. They have supply and repair contracts with the Romans for all of Judea and Samaria.'

Mary addressed Adrian, 'How many carpenters, blacksmiths, wheelwrights, upholsterers and saddle makers does the Hebron Wagon Company employ Aaron? Is it 30 or 40 tradesmen?'

'Personnel management falls under Elon's portfolio, Mary, but I believe that staffing numbers are approaching 80. That doesn't include our intake of interns during the school holiday period.' Adrian put on his best concerned corporate citizen expression. 'We, at the Hebron Wagon Company, feel that it is important to give back to the community in which we live. As such, we offer work experience to a small number of students from the less privileged families to gain an appreciation of the manufacturing industry from the shop floor perspective. It adds something extra to a curriculum vitae if a young person starting on their career path has real-world work experience to present to a prospective employer. I may have one of our promotional pamphlets on my person, which provides a brief summary of our community engagement program.'

Adrian withdrew a bag stuffed with gold and silver coins from his robes as he made the show of searching for the non-existent brochure.

'Mr Iscariot, I hate to impose, but could you please hold this for me?' Adrian handed over the bag which clinked as it dropped into Simon's hands.

'There is no need to bother, Mr Aaron,' said Simon staring at the wealth in his hands. 'I would be honoured for you and your brother to view my inventory. I regret that stock levels are limited at the moment, but I will have additional inventory on site next week if you don't find exactly what you are after today.'

'That is good to know, Mr Iscariot,' replied Adrian with a smile. 'Today, Elon and I are simply after transport to continue our journey. We had planned an extended visit with cousin Mary ahead of traveling to Tyre, but given the unpleasantness of last night, Elon and I feel it judicious to cut our visit short and progress to our appointment ahead of schedule. Regrettably, the actions last night of that group of miscreants has upset our transportation arrangements, hence the introduction by our dear cousin Mary.'

'I totally understand,' said Simon solemnly feeling the weight of gold in his hands.

'Please think of today as a small step towards possibly establishing a longer-term relationship. The Hebron Wagon Company is in need of an additional supplier of horses, perhaps you may be able to help in this regard, Mr Iscariot?'

'Please call me Simon, Mr Aaron,' replied the horse dealer deferentially.

'I would be pleased to, Simon,' replied Adrian as he took back the bag of coins. 'And you must call me Aaron.'

'Mary, could you please assist Eve?' called Will.

Mary turned to Simon.

'Elon's wife is with child, it's her first pregnancy. She is suffering the morning vomiting.'

'Of course, you must assist your sister-in-law, Mary,' said Simon sympathetically. 'Aaron and I have business to discuss. You would only find it boring.'

'No doubt,' said Mary bluntly. 'I will attend to my cousin while you talk about matters that are way beyond a woman's understanding.'

'Thank you, Mary,' said Adrian flashing his best smile.

Mary talked to herself as she walked away.

'Simon you really are a dick. A small, pink, flaccid dick covered in pimples.'

'Any problems with Simon?' asked Charlene.

'No, he's in love with Aaron's bag of coins. That will keep his attention away from us.'

'Good, which horses do we want?'

Mary moved from animal to animal, lifting hooves, looking at girth marks and legs.

'Don't touch the bay. See how he shows the whites of his eyes as he looks at us. That horse has a bad temperament.'

'Noted,' said Charlene.

'What about the grey one?' asked Will.

'No, she is in foal. Not that far along, but she would not be good to ride at the moment.'

'How can you tell?' asked Will.

Mary touched the mare's neck, then put her hand in the horse's mouth to grip the animal's tongue and look inside her mouth.

'When a mare is pregnant, the flesh either side of her throat swells and turns pink. You can see for yourself.'

'I believe you,' said Will stepping away from the animal, which was obviously not happy about having her tongue pulled out of her mouth.

'Which ones then Mary?' asked Charlene.

'The two bay geldings by the gate and the black mare behind you. They are good tempered, not too old and have been ridden many times.'

'How do you know that?' asked Will.

'You can see marks where they have carried a saddle and they allowed me to approach without any sign of fear. They are experienced mounts. The horse will know what to do, even if you don't.' Mary looked directly at Will. 'You don't know how to ride, do you?'

'No, I don't,' said Will, feeling less than useful.

'Thank you, we are very much in your debt,' said Charlene.

'There are no debts between us. David saved Joe's life and there is nothing else to say.'

Charlene touched Mary's arm. 'I have one last favour to ask.'

'You want to know how much to pay?'

Charlene nodded.

'We don't want to offer too much or too little.'

Mary pointed.

'Thirty Roman Aureus is more than the mare is worth. I would offer 27 then settle at 30. The two geldings are worth less, offer 20 each. When Simon tells you they are worth 25, settle on 23. If you don't haggle, Simon will be suspicious.'

'Understood,' said Charlene. 'It looks like it's your turn, Elon.'

'Ok, I guess I will just walk up and introduce myself.'

'You will need to go too, Charlene,' said Mary. 'First Aaron should introduce his brother, then his brother's wife. Stand behind the men and say nothing, unless Simon talks directly to you.'

'Seriously?'

'Remember what sort of a man Simon Iscariot is,' said Mary wriggling her pinkie finger.

'Got it,' said Charlene putting her arm through Will's. 'Come on husband, let's go and buy some horses from the dodgy used car salesman.'

'This is my brother Elon,' said Adrian as Will, Charlene and Mary approached.

'Pleased to meet you, Mr Iscariot,' said Will extending a hand.

Simon looked confused.

'Sorry,' apologised Will dropping his arm.

'Elon has just completed negotiations with the Roman delegation in Judea. It's a symbolic gesture to demonstrate that you haven't brought a weapon to the discussions,' explained Adrian making up a story to cover Will's attempted handshake.

'Why?'

Adrian's looked blank so Will jumped in to save the moment.

'It goes back to ancient history and the death of Julius Caesar. You know, *Et tu, Brute.*' Will almost made a stabbing gesture but stopped himself.

'Don't you mean recent history, Mr Elon? My father was a child when Gaius Julius Caesar died?'

Simon Iscariot looked to where Charlene was standing to the rear with Mary. Adrian realised he had neglected to offer an introduction.

'Simon, may I introduce the wife of my brother Elon. This is Eve, the daughter of Tracey and the delightfully named Scooter.'

Charlene lifted her head to lock eyes with Simon, then looked away as if embarrassed.

'You are a lucky man, Mr Elon. Your wife is comely and has the hips to bear you many sons.'

'Thank you?' said Will unsure how to reply to this observation.

Simon addressed Charlene, 'Congratulations on your pregnancy, if you eat toasted bread first thing each morning, it will help your stomach.'

Charlene whispered to Mary, 'I'm pregnant?'

'It's your first child, you are still vomiting in the mornings.'

'Why am I pregnant?'

'I needed an excuse to look at the horses. Simon was happy for me to go and help a poor pregnant woman.'

'Do I say anything?'

'Just thank him like you mean it, he likes to feel important.'

Charlene lifted her head.

'I am grateful for your wise words, Mr Iscariot.' Charlene hesitated, then looked to the ground as if afraid to speak. 'I must however obey my husband's wishes, if he tells me to eat toast, then I will, if he forbids it, then I must obey. I hope this does not offend you, Mr Iscariot.'

Simon nodded seriously.

'Your wife is a good woman, Mr Elon; you are going to have a happy marriage.'

'Thank you?' said Will.

'Down to business, you wish to purchase three of my horses?'

'Yes, three of your best,' replied Will

'Might I recommend the grey mare for your wife? She is placid and will not unduly bounce your unborn son on the road.'

'No,' said Will flatly, 'the mare is in foal.'

Simon looked again at the grey.

'I don't believe she is Mr Elon; the mare has no swelling in her belly.'

'Look in her mouth, Mr Simon. It's only early in the pregnancy, but the grey is in foal.'

Simon Iscariot put a hand on the horse's head, then slipped a hand into the animal's mouth to grip her tongue and looked at the mare's throat.

'I apologise; the grey is indeed with foal.'

'No apology is necessary; it would be easy to miss at this early stage.'

'You know your horse flesh, Mr Elon.'

'I had an excellent teacher, Mr Iscariot.'

'In that case, please cast your eye over my inventory and give an honest judgement of what you see.'

Will nodded.

'The bay on the far side of the yard has a bad disposition, I wouldn't sell it to your best customers.'

'Yes, we have had trouble with that one. I agree, not for my best customers.' Will pointed to the black mare.

'I will take her for my wife.' Will pretended to study the remainder of the horses. 'That gelding there where I am pointing, Mr Iscariot.'

'Yes, a fine animal, Mr Elon.'

'And the bay gelding in front of us, Mr Iscariot.'

'Excellent choices,' agreed Simon, 'they are the pick of my current inventory.'

'We will need tack as well,' said Adrian from behind.

'I can supply saddles and bridles from my store,' replied Simon looking at the bag of coins in Adrian's hands. 'Let me call on my sons to prepare the horses. While they are doing so, we can settle on a price.'

'Great job, Doc,' said Charlene. 'Well done Will, though next time at least buy me a drink before you get me pregnant.'

Will blushed.

'Mary, it's time you to get back to your family,' said Charlene. 'I don't know how we could ever repay you for your help.'

'Save David and get him home to his Jenifer Rostig, is all I ask.' Mary shook Charlene's hand then Adrian's and Will's. 'Take the road north until you reach Magdala. Stay there overnight, then travel on to Tyre tomorrow.' Mary turned to go then stopped. 'David promised to keep my sister Hannah safe. Help him do that.'

'I won't let anybody get hurt if I can,' said Will.

'Don't worry, Mary, between the skills of Sergeant Wilson, Will and myself, all will go absolutely swimmingly,' reassured Adrian.

'The moment we find David, I'll send Hannah home, and if I don't, may I marry a Collingwood supporter,' promised Charlene.

'It is a powerful curse?'

'My father would disown me if I did that,' said Will.

'Then I am happy if you swear on such a thing, Sergeant Wilson.'

'Somebody is coming,' said Will.

All heads turned towards the road. Charlene slid her hand into her bag to grip the weapon.

'Watch the sky where the road disappears around the bend,' instructed Will. Two crows were circling slowly, they were joined by a third, then a fourth. 'The birds are following something on the road.'

'Well done, Will,' said Adrian. 'I wouldn't have even thought to notice something like that.'

Mary took one more look at the circling birds and started to move off.

'Mary,' called Adrian, 'please wait, just for a second.'

'I have to get to my children.'

'Just a few seconds, that's all I ask.' Adrian turned to Will and Charlene. 'I can't let this moment just pass; I mean this is Mary, the wife of Joseph, the carpenter from Nazareth.'

'What are you doing, Doc?'

'Please Sergeant Wilson, it's for Will's mother.'

'What?' asked Will.

'Sergeant Wilson, stand next to Mary. Will, the other side please.'

Will stood next to Mary. 'We don't have time for this Adrian.'

Adrian pointed the face of his *Sainter* at the trio.

'Will scrunch in closer to Mary, Charlene, turn in slightly.'

'Are you seriously doing what I think you are, Doc?'

'Now everybody say, Nazareth.'

'I can see two men,' said Will moving in front of Mary, 'go while I distract them.'

'It's the soldiers we saw on the street. Doc, pay for the horses, get them saddled and Will and I will come to you.'

'How much do I pay?'

Charlene pointed, 'The black one is 30, the two brown ones 25 gold coins. Haggle a bit over the price, just don't take too long. If it goes wrong, don't hang around, that's an order, Doc. Find David and finish the job.'

'I understand Sergeant Wilson.'

Charlene picked up her bag and put her hand on the weapon's pistol grip. With luck, she wouldn't need to use it, the problem was Charlene had learnt long ago not to trust in luck.

# CHAPTER THIRTY-SIX

MAXIMUS' SANDALS CRUNCHED ON the sandy track. Dax marched in formation exactly four paces to his rear. Because the Nazareth garrison were behaving like frightened children, they would have to chase the fugitives alone. They needed horses and Simon Iscariot had what they needed.

Maximus watched the circling crows above his head. They had learnt to associate carrion with the sight of a legion uniform. He had seen the same thing in Gaul, where the legion marched, crows followed. Maybe the birds would get lucky today?

'We're not Iscariot's only visitors,' said Maximus as Simon's home came into view. 'I recognise the boys with the horses, they are his sons.'

Dax shaded his eyes against the morning glare.

'A person just disappeared over the hill behind the house.'

Maximus frowned.

'Let's see what the Jew walking towards us has to say. If it's David, don't hesitate, kill him.'

Dax unslung his bow and notched an arrow to its string.

'That's Iscariot near the house. I don't recognise the Jew with him, if he tries to run, bring him down.'

Dax moved wider to ensure a clear field of fire. There was a woman hurrying behind the Jew walking to meet them, she was carrying a bag made from an animal pelt. The thought crossed Maximus's mind that it could hold a dagger, then he thought it was not the way of the Jews. The man would be armed not his woman. If this was the forests, the *Bucinobante*, he would have Dax train his arrow at the woman's heart.

'G'day, hi, hello,' called Will as he slowed his walk. 'It's a beautiful day, but I don't think there is much of a chance of rain, which is a pity as the crops could do with a drink.'

Dax aiming at the stranger's chest. Will waved in a gesture of friendliness.

'Sorry, we just moved into town last week, looking to set up a small business in the main drag. Nothing too big, just selling essentials that you would normally have to travel to the big smoke to get and a few touristy type lines. You know the sort of thing you pick up on holiday then wonder why the hell you wasted your money on it. My mum has a drawer full of commemorative teaspoons she just had to buy.' Will stopped talking expecting a reply, Dax tightened his bow string. 'Anyway, I thought we should introduce ourselves, as my dad says, be a good neighbour and your neighbours will be good to you.'

'Who are you?' demanded Maximus.

'The name's Adam,' said Will, picking the first biblical name that came to mind then immediately wishing he had stuck with Elon. 'This is my wife, Eve.'

Charlene moved to stand a few metres to Will's left in a mirror image of the position Dax had taken.

'Adam and Eve?'

'That's us, Adam, and my wife Eve.' Will tried a smile but just couldn't do it. 'We had an afternoon tea place in Hebron up until last week, didn't we Eve?' Will turned his head to look at Charlene, she was watching the soldier with the bow and arrow. 'We specialised in apple products, had a big orchard out the back of the shop.' There was no reaction. 'Do you know Hebron much?'

'I have been to Hebron,' replied Dax.

'Did you visit our shop? It was next to the wagon factory.'

'No.'

'That's a pity, we had a 20 percent discount for gentlemen such as yourselves. Like Eve is always saying, you guys do a marvellous job, it's only right that we show our appreciation.'

'Why are you here?' demanded Maximus.

The question hung in the air as an accusation, like why did you strangle your wife? Or why is your licence picture different to your face? Will almost faltered, then the words tumbled out.

'The Hebron Wagon Company needed to expand the factory; the brothers that run the business made us an offer we couldn't refuse. Hebron was getting all hustle and bustle; the traffic is a nightmare to be honest. It's all nose-to-tail horse and carts during business hours. Eve and I discussed it and decided to move to Nazareth where our children can have the advantages of living in a small community rather than a big city. Did I mention we only found out today that Eve and I are having our first child?'

'Yes, it was a surprise,' said Charlene, flicking the safety on the weapon in its bag.

'You remind me of somebody who made me feel uncomfortable yesterday,' said Maximus putting a hand on his pugio.

'Sorry to have bothered you,' apologised Will turning to walk away.

'Where do you think you are going?'

'Over there,' said Will, pointing to where Adrian was mounting one of the geldings.

Dax shifted his aim to Adrian.

'Take him out of the saddle,' ordered Maximus drawing his dagger.

Dax breathed in, held his breath and steadied his aim. Charlene shot Dax. The bag absorbed some of the force but not enough to prevent the shockwave from blowing the archer off his feet.

Dax felt as if a horse had kicked him in the chest. The bow snapped in half, the arrow flew backwards, its head gouging a path across the right side of his face severing an earlobe. Then everything went black as Dax's head hit the ground.

Maximus swung his head in time to see Dax's body propelled backwards, attack was how the legion defended itself from an ambush. He rushed towards his enemy.

Will watched the soldier with the bow and arrow blown off his feet, there was no warning, no "halt or I will shoot", like in the movies. Charlene had just fired. Then the big bloke charged. *Bullshit,* Will thought, *no bloody way, mate.*

Will moved to knock Maximus over with a hip and shoulder. The guy pushed a hand connecting full-bore with Will's face. This slowed the big bloke down for maybe half a stride.

'Shit!' yelled Will as he was brushed aside. Charlene fired a second time, some of the blast rebounded and struck Will in the back of his leg. Now he was spinning, the sky was blue, then it was brown, then it was blue and finally it was on his face as he slid head- first into the road.

Will tried to get up but couldn't. The big bloke was on top of him.

'Hold on a second,' said Charlene.

'Sergeant Wilson! That was spectacular, well done you. I can't believe how brave you are, it was, fabulous.'

'Can you get him off me?' asked Will as he struggled to move.

'Roll him towards me,' Will heard Charlene say. 'On the count of three. One.'

Will felt the armour of the centurio roll across his spine.

'Two,' the weight rocked again. 'Three,' said Charlene and Adrian together. The weight flopped with a hard thump and soft thud to Will's side. Hands helped him to his feet.

'Are you okay?' asked Charlene.

'I'm good,' said Will, more embarrassed than hurt.

'Ok,' said Charlene, 'let's get going. From what Dwight said, these guys should be out for the count for a couple of hours.'

Adrian handed Will the reins of his horse.

'Put your left foot in the stirrup, grip the horse's mane here, then swing your right leg up and over the saddle.'

Will looked at Maximus and Dax on the ground.

'Won't they just talk to Simon when they wake up and then go after us and Mary?'

Charlene looked towards the house, Simon and his sons were staring at them.

'I think I had better do a little community liaison work to make sure that isn't going to be a problem. You did pay Simon what we agreed?'

'Yes, I haggled quite successfully, as well,' replied Adrian with a note of pride.

'Then, all I have to do is make it clear it's in their best interest to keep their mouths shut,' said Charlene shouldering the weapon and striding towards Simon and his sons.

'Come on then, Will,' said Adrian mounting his horse and leading the black mare to follow Charlene.

Will couldn't believe how embarrassed he felt. Charlene had saved his arse, probably his life.

'Shit, shit, shit, bloody shit.' He pulled on the reins of his horse, it pulled back. 'Seriously horse, don't you think I have been punished enough without you embarrassing me as well?'

The horse snorted, then moved to follow Will.

'Thank you, I owe you one.'

# CHAPTER THIRTY-SEVEN

POLYKARPOS AND DAVID RODE side by side, Hannah trailed behind, it was in the rules of being female in Galilee and it felt degrading. What made Hannah really angry was that women reinforced this behaviour right from the moment a girl was old enough to understand and yet these rules were often ignored in the family home. Take Mary and Joe as an example. Joe was a great father and probably a wonderful husband, but Mary made most of the decisions that were supposed to be his as the man of the house. Hannah knew there were times when Mary wished Joe would take charge, but she loved her husband and Joe adored Mary. Hannah was happy for her sister; she just didn't want to be her.

Then there was Peter. Hannah had tried to be what he expected of a dutiful Jewish wife, but she just couldn't be what Peter wanted. Their differences were like Peter's body odour, Hannah couldn't ignore it and she definitely couldn't live with it.

Hannah dug in her heels; her horse pushed between David and Polykarpos.

'What are you talking about?'

'Nothing important, Hannah. We're just talking to spend the time,' said David.

'So don't tell me, it's not like you want me to know what is really going on,' said Hannah.

David looked at Hannah, then at Polykarpos.

'I can tell you what I know, it's just not as much as you might think,' replied David.

'You and David should talk, I'll ride ahead, it's not far to Magdala. I can see what's happening at the gate,' said Polykarpos moving off at a trot.

'What would you like to know, Hannah? I won't keep anything a secret that shouldn't be.'

'But you will keep some things secret?'

'Yes, but only to keep you and Polykarpos safe.'

'You promise not to lie?'

'Cross my heart and hope to die.' David made the shape of a cross over his heart.

'Is that a curse?'

'No, it's just means that I promise to tell the truth.'

'I would be happier if it was a curse, where you grew a great boil on your bum if you lie.'

David rode in silence, thinking.

'There is a way in my land to make a sacred oath between two people. We can use it if you are game.'

Hannah believed David was being serious.

'Alright, I can keep a secret, what do I have to do?'

'Hold out your hand.'

'If this is where you cut me and we share each other's blood, you can forget it.'

'No, this is an oath sworn between two people based on trust. I trust you to keep my secrets, and you trust me to tell the truth. Does that sound fair?'

'Alright,' she said holding out her hand, 'but if you cut me, I swear I will beat you.'

David looped his little finger around Hannah's.

'I, David Thomas, pinkie swear to tell the truth, the whole truth, and nothing but the truth, in all of my conversations with Hannah of Nazareth.'

Hannah looked at the fingers locked together.

'What do I do?'

'You have to pinkie swear, then we have to do what we promise for as long as we live.'

'Alright then, I pinkie swear to keep the secrets that you tell me, David of?'

'Warrnambool, Hannah, I live in Warrnambool.'

'You really are from a different land.' Hannah pulled her finger tight. 'I, Hannah of Nazareth, pinkie swear to keep the secrets, no matter how tempting it may be to tell somebody that David of Warn Am Bool tells me.'

'Ok Hannah, what do you want to know?'

'Is it true that women in your land have the same rights as men, being able to choose how they live and who they marry.'

'Yes, in Warrnambool, men and women can do the same work, go to the same schools and are paid the same wage for doing the same job. To put it into a context relevant to Galilee, women can own land, or goats, or carpentry shops. They can choose not to marry at all, or they can marry another woman if that's what their heart desires.'

'Women, can marry women?'

'It's not against the law, or even considered unusual.'

'They would be stoned to death in Galilee.'

'It's just different where I come from Hannah. Nobody is punished for their beliefs or lifestyle as long as it doesn't harm others.'

'Why is Polykarpos helping you?'

'He says it's because I saved his life, and I do need both your help to get to Tyre, but once we get there, I want you both to go home. I don't want you or Polykarpos in danger for one second longer than is necessary.'

'There has to be more to it than that,' said Hannah shaking her head. 'Everything that Polykarpos does is somehow connected to his fight to free the Jewish people. I want that too; I just can't see it happening just because Peter and Polykarpos want it to happen.'

'Things will change. It takes ideas to bring about real change, not weapons and Polykarpos knows that.'

Hannah thought about this, then asked the question she really wanted to know.

'Tell me about Jenifer Rostig.'

'I really don't want to talk about Jen.'

'Would telling me put me in danger?'

'No.'

'Then by your pinkie swear you must tell me about her.'

David nodded, 'What do you want to know?'

'Are you betrothed? Are you secret lovers?'

'No.'

'Is she married to another man and you want her for your own?'

'No.'

'Is she related to you?'

'No.'

'Then why do you care so much about her?'

'It's complicated,' said David.

'That's not an answer and you pinkie swore to tell the truth.'

'Alright, if you really want to know, I do love Jen.'

Hannah's eyes widened.

'Liar! You said that you didn't want her for your wife.'

David shook his head.

'I love Jen like a big sister. She taught me how to separate bullshit from the truth and she would cut her right arm off if she had to save my arse. Jen always had my back, not just on the job, but in the real world where it really counts.'

'That's why you are hunting the people who hurt her?'

'No, that's only a part of it.'

'I don't understand.'

'Jen was stabbed because I was protecting a family secret when I should have been keeping her safe. She wouldn't have left me to fend for myself in that situation, no way.'

'What do you mean you left her?'

'I could try to explain but I don't know if it would make sense.'

'No, that's just you not wanting to tell me the truth, David.'

David reined his horse to a stop. Hannah turned her horse to face David.

'This morning, I wiggled my little finger in front of my nine-year-old niece to explain that men are driven by the thing between their legs more than their brains. Is that why you came to Nazareth, because the thing between your legs is telling you to do something stupid? Would your Jen have done what you are doing?'

Hannah glared at David, then turned her horse again to head in the direction of Magdala.

'We had better catch up with Polykarpos and find a place to stay for the night. That is the sort of decision I would make using my head if I was Jenifer Rostig.' Hannah slowed her horse to allow David to catch up. 'I know I shouldn't be jealous of anybody but when I saw that woman Julia riding a horse, I wished I had one of my own.'

'You have one now,' said David quietly. 'The horse is yours if you want it.'

'I can't take your horse, that's ridiculous. I could feed a family for a year for the price of a horse like this one.'

'I can't take it home with me; you and Polykarpos might as well keep them.'

'Are you serious? You're not expecting something else because you give me a horse, because that's just not going to happen.'

'No, I just want you to have the horse. I will pinkie swear if you need me to.'

Hannah patted her mount.

'Alright, I accept the horse as payment for being your guide, and only for being your guide. I don't want anybody thinking you gave me a horse because of something else I might have done.'

'Then consider the horse as payment for being my guide.'

'Done,' said Hannah with a nod.

There was a pause with only the sound of the horses' hooves breaking the silence.

'Is owning a horse what you expected?'

'Well, it's better than walking,' replied Hannah patting the neck of her ride. 'It's a bit smellier than I had hoped it would be. They really produce a lot of, well, shit.'

'They eat a lot so it only follows that they would produce a lot of waste.'

'You don't understand David, when you spend your life depending on a vegetable garden more shit for fertiliser is better than less shit. Mary will be jealous.'

'Mary wanted Joe to buy her a goat.'

'Yes, goat shit is good. Probably not as good as my horse's shit, but still good.'

They rode on in silence. Hannah was thinking she had been too truthful with David, and David was thinking that Hannah was right about at least some of his motivation.

'Being a horse owner does have a drawback,' said Hannah breaking the silence.

'If you are worried about the cost of keeping him, don't. I will leave you all the coins I have to help with that.'

'He's a her, David.'

'I didn't notice, sorry.'

'It's not the money, I don't care about that. The problem I am having with being a horse owner is that it is hurting my bum no end and the stirrup leathers have worn a hole in the skin on the inside of both of my knees. Maybe this is why the Roman cavalry walk funny?'

'Do they?'

'No, I was just trying to make you smile seeing as I went full obnoxious bitch on you before.'

'It's ok, all you did was speak some truths. The problem is, I already knew most of them.'

'I'm sorry, David, and now you understand why no man, other than stinky Peter, the bad breath fisherman, wants to marry me.'

'Then I would say the men you know are fools.'

Hannah felt herself blush.

'To answer your question, Jen would chase these people with her last breath if she knew what I know. This is not just about what they did, it's about the damage they can still do. This only ends when I bring them in or die trying. It won't change what happened to Jen, but it might stop it from happening to somebody else.'

Hannah was overcome with the strangest feeling when David finished his speech and smiled at her. What was she thinking? Yes, David was different to any man she knew. Firstly, he didn't stink, he was easy to talk to and seemed to find her interesting and was a long way from ugly, if she was to be honest with herself. Hannah knew she was just being silly but that strange feeling in her gut just wouldn't go away.

Polykarpos was galloping towards them, waving to attract their attention and indicating for David to hurry and join him.

'Stay here, Hannah. If this is something bad go home, don't even look back.'

'What? No!'

'That's not a request; we will come back for you if it's safe.'

David sunk his heels into his horse cantering off to join Polykarpos.

'No. Definitely not. Come on girl, let's see what the silly men are all excited about.' The mare bounced forward as Hannah dug her into her sides.

'My poor bloody bum,' said Hannah as her blisters bounced up and down on the saddle.

David caught up with Polykarpos, 'What is it?'

'There's been an accident, I am hoping you can help.'

David pulled on the reins.

'What are you doing Polykarpos? I can't risk the mission.'

'It's a father and his son, the man could die and leave the boy an orphan.'

'What's at stake is bigger than one man's life.'

Polykarpos could see indecision on David's face.

'It's the right thing to do.'

People gathering around an ox-cart further up the road, there was no sign of Romans. David looked back towards Nazareth; Hannah was getting closer.

'This is not good, Polykarpos.'

'It's not good for the boy and his father, David.'

'All right, I might be able to help with my first aid kit, but there will be no miracles, is that clear?'

'Yes, David.'

'I will need you to use your body as a shield so that the crowd doesn't see what I am doing.'

'Yes of course. I will distract their attention as best I can.'

'Okay, let's see what we can do.

Six people were gathered around an ox cart filled with firewood. A man lay on the road struggling to breathe. At his side stood a boy of eight or nine with tears streaming down his face.

'What's happened?' asked Polykarpos as he secured the reins of the horses to the cart.

'He has been stung by a bee,' said a man kneeling beside the casualty to hold his hand. 'His father died the same way when I was the age of his son, Noah.'

David moved past the onlookers with his first aid kit hidden under his shirt.

'Can you move everybody back a bit, mate, I'm going to need a bit of room to work.'

Polykarpos took the hint.

'Good people, my friend is a healer. He may well be able to help this man if you all move back a few steps.'

David squatted next to the wood cutter. The man's face and arms were swelling, indicating an allergic reaction to the bee venom.

'Hello,' said David to the boy, 'my name is David, can you tell me your father's name?'

'His name is Timothy of Magdala,' said the man holding Timothy's hand. 'He is in my employ, just as his father was for my father. If you want to help, take Noah away so he doesn't have to watch his father die.'

'Not today he isn't,' said David, 'not if I can help it.'

'It's too late,' said the man sadly.

Timothy was turning blue, shortly his heart would go into an irregular rhythm and then stop.

'Then I guess there is no time to be subtle about this,' said David removing an epi- pen from the first aid kit and plunging it into the man's thigh. David turned the patient on his side, inserted a finger into his mouth to check for obstructions before rolling Timothy on to his back again.

David sat one hand on Timothy's forehead, forcing it back to open his airway, the other supported the chin and opened his mouth. David placing his mouth to his patient's and breathed two quick breaths into his lungs before checking for a pulse.

'Shit.' David clasped one hand over the other and began chest compressions, counting until he reached 30, then breathed into the man twice more. The colour was a little better, however, Timothy could not breathe on his own, nor would his heart move oxygen around the body unaided.

Hannah flopped on the opposite side of Timothy, 'What can I do to help?'

Timothy's employer looked at Hannah.

'I don't know what David is doing, but Timothy is alive when he should have gone to meet Jehovah.'

'I thought that we weren't doing the name thing?' asked Hannah.

'No time,' said David between breaths.

'What can I do?'

'In the red and white bag there are two round metal discs.' Compresses one, two, three, four, five, six. 'They have what looks like a red shiny stone in the middle.' Breathe, count two, three. Breathe.

'Found them.'

'I need you to put them on Tim. Six, seven, eight.'

Hannah ripped open the bag that held the two discs.

'Where, where do I put them?'

'Eighteen, nineteen, twenty. There's a picture, just follow the directions. Twenty-eight, twenty-nine.'

Hannah found the laminated instruction card with a drawing of a man and a child with the discs sitting on the skin of their body. Hannah held the card up David to see.

'You want me to do this?'

'Yes,' breathe, two, three, 'as quickly as you can. One, two, three, four, five.'

Hannah looked to the man in the expensive clothes.

'Do you have a knife?'

'Yes, I have a blade I use to peel apples.'

Hannah held out a hand. 'Give.'

The man passed Hannah the blade. The knife went through Timothy's tunic making a hand width incision, before Hannah used her hands to widen the hole. She placed a disc onto the man's skin. It stuck.

'Now the second one,' said David.

Hannah hopped across Timothy's torso and repeated the process.

David halted the resuscitation and touched the closest disc to activate it. The discs flashed green as a computer-generated female voice spoke, *'Evaluating heart rhythm.'*

'What? Who?' asked Hannah in surprise.

'It's okay,' said David calmly. 'Just move back, you don't want to be touching Tim if it has to administer a shock.'

*'Standby. Everyone clear. Administering shock. Do not touch patient.'* There was a two second pause, then the female voice continued, *'Delivering shock.'* Four loud rapid beeps were admitted from the discs followed by a pulse of electricity. Timothy's body jumped slightly.

David moved back to the patient's head and resumed his pattern of breaths.

'What's happening?' asked Timothy's employer.

'I'm not sure,' replied Hannah, 'I think that David—'

Timothy's arms rose and fell as if struggling to wake, his eyes opened wide as David released the grip on his chin.

'It's alright, you're going to be fine, Tim.'

David addressed Hannah, 'I am going to put Mr Timothy into the recovery position. What I need you to do is help me roll him on to his side.' David moved Timothy's left arm out straight from his body and his right arm across his chest. 'On three, we'll roll him. Once we have him over, take his right leg and move it so that it is out like his left arm. Bend it at the knee to stop him from rolling on his stomach.'

'Yes, I understand,' replied Hannah moving into position.

'One, two, three, roll,' counted David. Hannah pushed Tim at the hip then moved his leg into position.

'The swelling is going down and his colour looks good,' said David as he moved into Timothy's eyeline. 'Can you tell me your name, mate?'

Timothy looked a little frightened. 'Timothy.'

'I think we are done here,' said David removing the defibrillator discs.

'Noah?'

'He's fine,' said David. 'In fact, I think he should sit with you until you get your breath back properly.'

David moved so the boy could see his father. He had tears in his eyes, but his face was smiling.

'I'm going to mix you up something to drink. It will make you feel a lot better.'

David went to his horse to find a hydration tablet and a lemon flavoured electrolyte tablet. Polykarpos joined him.

'A miracle, David?'

The group watching had grown to eleven people.

'Did they see anything?'

'They are not sure what they saw. They know the man should be dead, but he is not.'

'I think we should just get moving as quickly as we can then.'

'Agreed. I will get the horses ready.'

'You were right, Polykarpos, one man's life is as important as another. Thank you for reminding me.'

The crowd parted in silence as David moved to return to Timothy. A woman touched David's shoulder, he looked at her and the woman shied away.

'Does anybody have something that will hold water?'

'I do,' said a man from the back. A pottery jar was passed to David.

'Thank you, I'll get it back to you shortly.'

'Please, keep it, David.'

'Thank you,' replied David with a frown.

Hannah was holding both Timothy and Noah's hands.

'How are they doing?'

'A lot better,' replied Hannah smiling at the pair.

'Tim, I am going to make you some medicine. You need to drink it slowly over the next hour or so. You can give some to Noah if you want, it won't hurt him, I promise.'

Timothy nodded wide-eyed in understanding. David put the pot on the ground to hide it from the crowd. The hydration tablet was pinched, water appeared and David added a lemon flavoured electrolyte tablet, turning the water yellow. Hannah watched it happen; she just couldn't think how it was possible.

'Are you okay?' David asked.

Hannah nodded in astonishment.

'Can you see if anybody has a cup we can use?'

'Yes, yes I can,' Hannah replied jumping to her feet.

David put a hand on Timothy's shoulder.

'You are going to feel a bit off colour for the rest of the day, I want you to have a decent meal and a good night's sleep.'

David turned to Timothy's employer.

'Is it alright that he has the rest of the day off?'

'I will make sure it happens David.'

'Thank you.'

Hannah returned with a shallow wooden bowl.

'It's perfect, thank you, Hannah.'

David helped Tim to sit up.

'Could you kneel behind Tim to give him some back support?'

'Yes of course I can,' said the employer wriggling into position. 'My name is Andrew; I am a fish merchant from Magdala. Timothy's family have served my family for many generations.'

'Your point being, Andrew?'

'Timothy is more than an employee; he is my friend. I feel blessed that you have brought him back from the dead.'

'Tim wasn't dead. I just helped him breathe until he could do it for himself. Please don't say anything about what you think you saw, Andrew.'

Andrew accepted the request, 'I will do as you ask.'

David held the bowl for Tim, who drank the liquid in great gulps.

'Steady there, Tim,' said David putting a hand on his shoulder, 'save some for Noah.'

'Thank you,' came a croaked reply, 'I owe you my life.'

David looked at Hannah.

'I think it's time we buggered off.'

Hannah blinked a couple of times.

'Yes, we should go.'

The crowd gasped as David and Andrew lifted Timothy to his feet.

David led Hannah by the hand, the crowd parted then closed around them; Hannah felt her dress being held. She turned to find a man gripping the fabric.

'What do you think you are doing?'

'Keep moving,' said David dragging Hannah by the hand.

The woman who had first touched David, fell to her knees.

'Bless me,' she said.

'No, definitely not,' said David to himself

'What did you expect?' said Hannah, 'You just brought a man back from the dead.'

'No, I didn't,' David whispered.

'Yes, you did. I don't believe it, but I saw it. When we get out of here, we are going to have another talk about who you really are, David.'

An old man fell at David's feet.

'Heal my fading eyes, David. Let me see my children's faces one more time before I die.'

'You had better do something before the Romans turn up, or my mother finds out I refused to marry you and believe me, I am hoping the Romans find us first,' said Hannah.

'I heard the voice of an angel' said a voice from the crowd. 'It spoke and David told the angel to bring Timothy the woodcutter back to his son.'

'I saw his soul jump back into his body.'

'Timothy the woodcutter could not breathe. David kissed him as he lay dying and brought life breath back to his body.'

'Get to the horses,' said David, pulling Hannah by the hand, 'we have to go now.'

Polykarpos watched it unfold. It was all he had hoped for.

'Do you believe this, Peter?' he asked the man hiding behind the cart.

'It's true, Polykarpos. David can perform miracles.'

'Yes and so much more. He may not be the leader we planned for, but he can help light the way for others to follow.'

'I don't like Hannah being with him.'

'If we are to free our people, Peter, sacrifices will need to be made.'

'Hannah should be mine; we were betrothed.'

'Hannah doesn't want you, she made that abundantly clear.'

'She isn't thinking clearly. Hannah needs a husband to keep her safe, to love her and bring up a family with.'

Polykarpos watched as a woman dropped to her knees in front of David.

'We have to use this. David can bring the people to our side.'

'How? Not by doing whatever he did. People will think it's witchcraft and stone him to death, or the Romans will crucify him.'

'Exactly Peter, that's how we are going to build our movement.'

'By getting this David killed by the Romans?'

'Yes, by encouraging the Romans to turn David into a martyr.'

Peter watched a blind man drop in front of David.

'So, this is about creating a story like your Greek ancestors with their story of gods and their heroic labours?'

'No, we want the story to be about a simple man of the people doing good, like saving the life of a woodcutter. Our hero needs to be someone that the carpenters, the fishermen and the farmers can relate to.'

'I had better go,' said Peter moving away.

David and Hannah had made it to their horses.

'Please, just go home and enjoy the remainder of the evening,' said David.

Timothy pushed through the crowd and grasped David's hand to kiss it, then reached for Hannah's.

'No, no thank you,' said Hannah pulling her hand away. 'We hardly know each other, and besides I was promised to David as a wife only this morning.'

The women in the crowd oohed and ahhed, then clapped.

'You will make a good wife,' came a call from the crowd.

'May Jehovah bless your wedding bed with many sons and daughters,' called a man who had asked for David's blessing.

'Thank you,' waved Hannah, 'please go home like David said.' Then under her breath so that only David and Polykarpos could hear it, 'Please just bugger off, you all smell very badly.'

The travellers moved slowly past the crowd and continued northwards to Magdala.

'Well, that was interesting,' said Hannah.

'We can't afford to do anything like that again,' said David, 'it's too dangerous for everybody.'

'I am sorry, David,' replied Polykarpos.

'I know you believe we did the right thing, Polykarpos, but there is too much at stake.'

'Yes, I agree, there is a great deal at stake,' nodded the old teacher.

# CHAPTER THIRTY-EIGHT

'ANNIUS RUFUS IS LATE,' said Octavian.

'Is that important?' asked Julia who was sitting on the steps in front of Octavian's residence.

'No,' replied Octavian passing his helmet to an Immune. 'The Prefectus will have been intent on his administrative duties and lost track of time. If it was another official from the Senate, the delay would mean something else.'

'A show of importance by making you wait?'

'That's what men like the Prefectus of Samaria and Judea do to ensure lesser men understand our positions.'

'You're not in favour of this sort of behaviour?' asked Julia.

'It's not how you earn respect.'

'Your men's respect is important to you?'

'I need my men to trust that when I give my word, I will keep it. It starts with simple things, like being on time and making sure your men are fed before you. Making them wait in armour in the sun for no sensible reason, just annoys them. They need a leader who makes sensible decisions if they are going to follow them in battle.'

'So, they don't have to like you, but they do have to believe you have their welfare in mind.'

'Yes, that way I am less likely to have my throat cut while I sleep.'

A rider appeared at the end of street, waving an arm to draw their attention.

'It looks like our wait is over,' said Octavian taking Julia's hand to help her up. 'You know your part?'

'Yes, I am your wealthy, non-threatening, disease-free friend with benefits, and don't worry, I won't embarrass you in front of the boss.'

Octavian nodded to the nearest officer, an order was barked, a bugle call made and the honour guard was erect, still and focused in seconds.

The mounted escort trotted past the steps. A carriage followed, trailed by additional mounted troops, their armour jingling with each rise and fall of hooves on the paved road.

'Fashionably late and with theatrical flair,' said Julia watching the procession come to a halt. 'Do we roll out a red carpet, or is it a bugle call?'

'Neither,' replied Octavian, snapping to attention. 'Just be civil and let me do the talking.'

'As you wish, my love,' replied Julia with a smile.

An Immune placed a wooden step beside the carriage, then sprang to attention as he opened the door. Julia smiled; it was all so familiar. She recalled her father standing in Octavian's position, waiting to receive a general or a minister of the government, her mother in dress uniform subservient behind her father, her brothers springing to attention in time with the RSM barking orders to present arms. She would be in her best dress, hair in a bow, shoes polished and face scrubbed. The dignitary would receive a salute from her parents, handshakes would be offered to her brothers, then she would be expected to curtsey. The general would nod and smile at her. If it was a politician, Julia would be subjected to a few polite words along the lines of how pretty she looked.

It had been humiliating being expected to represent everything her parents, and those who had come before, dedicated their lives to protect. The whole production was a lie, it was really about feeling superior to all the little girls in party dresses and what they represented. If you were born male, you could join the club, if you were a girl, they let you think you were a member. On the surface, the right words were invoked. Policy, procedure, doctrine all carried the same lies. The truth was, only boys mattered which had led Julia here, pretending to be Octavian's mistress, in order to undo all the humiliation which was to come.

Annius Rufus was tall with grey hair, dressed in a white toga with a purple stripe identifying him as a member of the Senate. Julia was curious about the Prefectus of Samaria. If he had been Pontius Pilate, Julia would know much more about the man in front of her. Annius Rufus was a mystery. She liked the thought of the challenge.

Octavian gripped the arm of the senator.

'Welcome to Tyre, Prefectus Rufus.'

'Thank you Praefectus Castrorum for opening your home to me,' replied Annius Rufus. 'I am sorry for the inconvenience to your men, I understand the protocol, but let's be honest Octavian it's not worth the disruption it causes. You don't object to me calling you Octavian? I think there is a time for formalities,' Annius Rufus turned to indicate the legionnaires standing at attention, 'and there is a place for honest, frank and direct dealings. I like to engage with the man, not just the position they hold.'

'As you wish, Prefectus Rufus, please call me Octavian.'

'Thank you, Octavian, and you may call me Annius. If Tiberius presents at your door, we can revert to a more formal stance.'

'Agreed, Prefectus,' replied Octavian, maintaining his military bearing like a mask.

'Shall we go inside? We have much to discuss before the business of the day is done.'

Octavian nodded to the guard commander to dismiss his men, then indicated toward the entrance of his villa.

'This way if you please, Prefectus.'

Annius looked up the steps to the waiting figure of Julia.

'Octavian, you have very much fallen in my estimations.'

'Sir?'

'You have yet to introduce me, I assume this is the Lady Julia?'

Julia radiated a welcoming smile.

'I am flattered to think that you would have heard of me Prefectus Rufus.'

'Please call me Annius, that is if you will allow me to address you as Julia.'

'Of course, Annius,' said Julia as she led him up the steps. 'I will be your hostess during your visit, if there is anything you need, please just ask.'

Annius fell in to step with Julia.

'May I ask why you were not surprised that I knew your name? We have not met before; I am sure of it.'

'No, we haven't met. I would have remembered you Annius, just as I am sure you would not have recalled such an unremarkable woman as myself.'

'I disagree,' replied the Prefectus. 'If nothing else you are taller than women I normally encounter. That alone is a point of difference.'

'I would be disappointed if you could only recall me because of my height, and not because of my smile,' flirted Julia.

'I see lots of smiles Julia, if we had met, I would have remembered your eyes for the intelligence behind them.'

Julia led Annius to Octavian's sitting room.

'You know about me because you have spies watching all the important men and women in the province you govern, and yet, I am still something different to what you expected?'

'Yes, you are an oddity, Julia. You can understand my curiosity.'

Julia indicated for the Prefectus to take a seat. 'Something to eat, some wine?'

'No thank you, I'm afraid it's business before pleasure.'

'Then I will leave you to your business,' replied Julia smiling. 'When you have finished, I will introduce you to the pleasure of an éclair.'

'That sounds Gaullist?'

Julia laughed, 'It's a pastry, Annius, not something which will tarnish your reputation.' With this Julia turned to leave the room, brushing a hand against Octavian's to lightly grip his fingers before locking eyes, until she disappeared through the doorway. The touch surprised Octavian, who turned to watch Julia walking away. It was the exact effect she wanted, creating a moment Annius Rufus could not miss.

Octavian swung back to Annius, looking slightly disturbed by the contact that Annius could not but help witnessing.

'What do you know of this Julia?' asked Annius.

Octavian had been expecting the question.

'As much as I need to know, Prefectus.'

'She has the accent and manner of a nobleman's daughter, but I don't know of her family.'

'Julia is not Roman.'

'Explain?'

'Julia is from a land beyond the empire; I suspect she moved to Tyre to avoid an arranged marriage.'

Annius nodded. It was plausible for a woman of means to defy her father in such matters.

'What does she want, Octavian? Not your gold. My spies tell me she has a sizable fortune.'

'I will be blunt, Prefectus. I provide security and safety; I have no illusions that Julia's needs are more than that. For a woman alone, unprotected, she must always fear that somebody will take what she has.'

'And what do you get from the relationship? I can't believe you would be interested in a woman purely for the pleasure of having a pretty face in your bed?'

'No, it's not because I might find her pleasing to look at Prefectus.'

'Then why take the risk on a woman you know so little about?'

'Because she is not a threat to me, or to Rome.'

'Go on.'

'Julia doesn't need my income; her fortune is larger and she keeps her own household. If I just needed a woman for my bed, I could avail myself of the brothels in Tyre, but many of the women in these houses are just children sold into a life of misery. I refuse to make their lives worse than they are.'

'Yes, that is less than desirable, but the empire needs the commerce of the sea and sailors have needs which the brothels satisfy. It's regrettable, but the needs of Rome outweigh the plight of a few girls whose families have abandoned them.'

Octavian thought it best not to comment further on the plight of these children and continued, 'Julia has no ties to the Empire or for that matter the nobility of Samaria and Judea.'

'Your point being?'

'There is no benefit to Julia on any political level in sharing my bed.'

'That you know of Octavian. You said yourself that you know little about this woman.'

'I intend no insult when I say this, Prefectus, but Julia's interests lie in commerce, not white togas with purple trimmings.'

Annius stiffened, then relaxed. Octavian didn't have the connections to be a threat; his father was a retired soldier not a nobleman with ambitious intent for his son.

'Then there are the practical aspects, Prefectus. Julia is an unattached, attractive, intelligent, and disease-free woman in a city whose brothels are filled with sailors. I may not marry as a soldier of the empire but am expected to have a mistress. Julia is probably the only real choice I have in my position.'

'Are you certain that protection is all Julia is seeking from your relationship?'

Octavian paused before answering, 'Men in positions such as ours underestimate the value of security to a woman such as Julia. Yes, she sleeps in my bed, acts as a hostess for honoured guests and probably pretends to care for me more than she actually does. To Julia, that is probably a small price to pay to feel safe.'

'And you can always take her head, Octavian, if Julia is not what she seems.'

'There is always that option, Prefectus,' agreed Octavian. 'It's a mutually beneficial relationship. Julia refers to it as "friends with benefits".'

This made Annius laugh.

'Maybe you truly are the one getting less from the relationship.'

'Prefectus?'

'Never mind, Octavian. We should move on to the more pressing matters. You would not be aware, but your port is about to become very busy. Very busy indeed.'

Octavian raised an eyebrow in pretend surprise.

'Tiberius has commissioned the building of a temple dedicated to the late Emperor Augustus at Caesarea.'

'A large temple, Prefectus?'

'A very large temple, according to the plans which arrived yesterday. There is no shortage of stone and labour to construct the structure, but timber and the finer materials, to decorate the interior, will need to be imported.'

'We will need to prepare the port for the influx of shipping.'

Annius nodded in agreement.

'Yes, we will, and I admit to having a limited working knowledge of the civilian maritime world and its logistical requirements.'

Octavian walked to the window that overlooked the docks and warehouses of Tyre. 'The port is well sheltered and large enough to hold a significant flotilla, Prefectus.'

'But the docks and warehousing have a limited capacity for the landing and storage of cargo, I read your reports Octavian. Now I would like to hear your proposal to increase the efficiency of the port to accommodate Tiberius' project.'

Octavian launched into his recommendations, 'The docks can be expanded to the west, the lay of the land and the depth of water will allow for this. Warehousing does not have to be adjacent to the waterfront, temporary storage facilities could be constructed at the temple's site using our road network and a fleet of wagons to transport cargo directly from the wharf to the construction site, which would reduce the risk of theft at the port and ensure a rapid turnaround of the transport vessels.'

Annius moved to stand at Octavian's side. The view across the bay with its peninsula of land, forming a protected anchorage, was spectacular.

'Planning the process is only one component of the task before us, I need this project to be a success. Tiberius must be satisfied with my service in his name.'

Octavian understood that Annius needed the expansion of the port facility to happen in order to ensure the emperor's first building project ran smoothly. A safe and profitable position in Rome would be the reward for Annius Rufus. For Octavian, there would be the advantage of having a friend of high status who owed him a debt of gratitude. Failure would not be an acceptable outcome.

'I can find the materials and labour to expand the wharf,' replied Octavian. 'The Iron Legion's engineering cadre can design and supervise the building of the facilities.'

'But that is not the issue, as you would realise Octavian.'

'Gold is the issue, Prefectus,' stated Octavian, 'How is the expansion of Tyre's port to be funded?'

'I had hoped you were as clever as I had been led to believe,' replied Annius with a smile. 'The Senate, while applauding the vision of Tiberius in expanding the worship of Augustus, sees investment in the wheat fields of Gallia and Hispania as a higher priority than a temple in the desert of Samaria and Judea.'

'Tiberius will not fund the temple from his own purse?'

'Tiberius is a more prudent manager of his finances than Augustus.'

'Then the coin will need to be found here.'

'Obviously Octavian, but how? The Senate will not accept a reduction in grain tributes to fund the expansion of Tyre's port. In the eyes of the Senate, a well-fed population in Rome is a happy and safe population. If children in Judea, Galilee or Samaria starve, that would be regrettable, but preferable to the children of Rome going hungry.'

Octavian didn't like the thought of any child going hungry.

'It's not grain we need, Prefectus, it's gold.'

'I agree, a well-fed population is less likely to cause difficulties, which inevitably costs more than if hunger was simply avoided.'

Octavian pretended to consider the problem.

'If we cannot increase the grain tax, then we must look further afield for revenue.'

'How? The town leaders already complain about Rome's taxes.'

'Then we should not increase the burden on these men of importance, instead we should broaden the tax base. If we spread the cost across a very large number of people, the impact on any one family will be minimal, the return potentially quite large.'

'Go on,' said Annius with interest.

'We don't need to impose an additional tax across the entirety of Judea, Galilee and Samaria, we could localise it to a single community. For example, Magdala, which has a large population built around its fishing industry. There, merchants who run the industry, pay the wages of thousands who catch and process fish caught in the Sea of Galilee for export via Tyre across the length of the empire. The entire population of Magdala would benefit by an improvement in the export facilities of this port. The more fish that are able to be exported, the greater the number of people the merchants will need to employ.'

'I see your logic, Octavian. It would be tax to benefit the prosperity of Magdala as a whole.'

'Shall we call it a levy, Prefectus?' suggested Octavian. 'A tax imposed by Rome sounds less appealing than a levy to benefit the people of Magdala.'

Annius nodded gravely.

'Though, I doubt a peasant working on the fish drying racks would see how contributing coin to the building of a wharf in Tyre puts food on their table.'

'If the contribution they make is small enough, I doubt complaints will rise above a muttered grumble, Prefectus.'

'Do you have a plan in mind for how we achieve this Octavian?'

Octavian nodded in assent. Yes, Julia had a plan.

'Firstly, we conduct a census of the entire population of Magdala. This could be completed with the help of the priesthood, the Kohanim and my Immunes. Births and deaths are recorded in a ledger to ensure that all members of the Jewish community can be gathered to the *Beit Knesset*, their temple, for prayer. I also believe this is done so that nobody is missed from contributing to the temple funds.'

'Which is why any list will be incomplete,' reasoned Annius. 'There are Syrians, Egyptians, Greeks, Romans and Gauls working in Magdala.'

'And there will be those who have been expelled from the *Beit Knesset*, such as slaves, thieves, prostitutes, unwed mothers and other undesirables in the eyes of the *Kohanim*.'

'This cadre of outsiders would not be contributing to the taxes gathered by the leaders of the temple.'

'Hence the need of an accurate census, to ensure that all who share in the benefits Rome brings, contribute to the empire's administrative costs, which are small compared to the economic benefits when Rome builds infrastructure such as a wharf or a temple.'

'Yes, there will be an opportunity to provide labour, materials and skills to be paid for with gold and silver, much of which will end up in the hands of the merchants and priests that sit at the head of the community.'

'If that was explained, I am sure the leaders of the city would be cooperative in conducting an accurate census, Prefectus.'

'I have no doubt,' replied Annius barely hiding his sarcasm.

'I believe Prefectus,' continued Octavian, 'that Tiberius would be pleased to know the Prefectus of Samaria and Judea was able to ensure the construction of a temple to the god Augustus without increasing the financial burden on Rome. Such an administrator would be of great benefit closer to Rome, rather than wasting his talents on the outer rim of the empire.'

Annius Rufus laughed, 'Well played Octavian.'

'Have I said something inappropriate, Prefectus?'

'No, Octavian, not at all. In your case it is simply a matter of a good man believing that other men have the same honesty in their hearts as you do. Sadly, the truth is that the higher the position of power, the less likely you will be to encounter true honesty. Stay a soldier, Octavian, stay where you can be rewarded with true loyalty by those you lead.'

Octavian wasn't sure if he was being insulted or praised.

Annius Rufus put a hand on Octavian's shoulder.

'Your idea is sound. We shall conduct a census in Magdala, then move on to Tyre, Hebron, Jerusalem and all the villages that have more than two goats to brag about. I will draft a parchment informing your *Legatus Legionis* that I require the services of yourself and your Immunes to conduct a census of the population of Magdala. If open rebellion breaks out, then you will, of course, return immediately to your military duties as required.'

Octavian bowed in acknowledgment of his orders.

'I serve Rome as required, Prefectus.'

'As do I, Octavian,' replied Annius Rufus dropping his hand. 'Now that business has been sorted, shall we take up the Lady Julia's offer of refreshments? I must admit to being quite intrigued by this éclair she mentioned.'

Julia removed the earpiece connected to the hidden listening device in Octavian's office. Annius Rufus had seen the benefits of her plan, rationalising that what was good for the empire, could also be good for himself. She would get her search for the Mary who lived in Magdala, the child she had come so far and risked so much to find.

Julia looked at Atarah, who was guarding the entrance to the kitchen.

'You can take the cheese and wine in now please, Atarah, then you should head off home and spend some time with the children. We are in for a busy day tomorrow.' Atarah nodded in understanding. 'Give them a hug from me.'

'I will,' replied Atarah with a smile.

Julia picked up a tray of éclairs, dusted with desiccated honey and filled with whipped cream. They contained the last of the chocolate she had brought with her, she would miss this indulgence for now. Tyre was not going to be her home forever. Soon she would find the child, Mary, and with luck, change, not just her destiny, but the lives of all women that were to follow. Asher slipped from behind the curtain which separated the kitchen from larder where he had been hiding. He had watched Julia pull an object from her gown, then place it inside her ear. Asher didn't understand. *Why Julia, would you do this?*

He waited and listened, as Julia sat on a stool while Atarah kept watch at the kitchen door. There was no conversation to guard, no activity at all, Julia just sat there. Then Asher heard a faint sound, like the noise of an insect beneath the bark of a tree. He would have sworn it was coming from Julia! He held his breath to eliminate that as background noise. It was two different sounds: first one, then the other, then both together.

Asher watched Julia adjust the object in her ear. When she did, the sound was louder, it was the unmistakable voice of the Praefectus Castrorum. But it couldn't be. Julia moved her head to one side, as if straining to hear a conversation, nodded as if a question had been answered, then directed Atarah to take food and wine to his master before the call came from the guard outside Octavian's rooms. Julia had known the call would come. She had been listening to the conversation between his master and the Prefect. Asher had to report what he knew quickly; this was too important to wait.

Sapphira moved in her hiding spot to ease the muscles that had been frozen in a squat. She had been searching the larder, when a shaft of light filled the room. Sapphira turned to ask whoever it was, to hold the curtain open. But instead of a member of the kitchen staff entering the room, Sapphira saw the legs of Asher coming through the window that overlooked the garden. Something stopped her calling out. She slumped into the shadow of the storage jars to hide and watch.

Asher moved on the balls of his feet to peer through a gap in the curtain and listen to Julia's conversation. What made Sapphira incredibly angry, was not the spying, but who was doing it. Sapphira had looked forward to her conversations with Asher. He asked about her day while she asked about his family, now she was realising how often Asher had asked questions about Julia. It wasn't the only thing they talked about; Asher had been clever steering her to discuss what she knew about her mistress. Sapphira was more than angry; she was disgusted. This was worse than what Damian had done, at least he had been up front with his manipulation.

Sapphira heard Julia ask Atarah to take cheese and wine to Octavian as Asher moved to leave the way he came. Once Asher was gone, she peeked from behind the larder curtain to make sure that none of Octavian's staff were present to see her leave the kitchen. If Asher could deceive her, then none of Octavian's household could be trusted. Sapphira took a knife from the kitchen, used to cleave the bones of goats and oxen, as she left the room. If the fate that befell Damian for his deceit was also the destiny of Asher, she was prepared to make it happen.

# CHAPTER THIRTY-NINE

'DAVID, HANNAH, WAIT PLEASE,' called a voice.

Polykarpos swivelled in his saddle.

'It's Andrew, the fish merchant.'

'Shalom Polykarpos, I need to talk with your master.'

Hannah turned to look; Andrew waved at her.

'I think he really wants to talk, David.'

'I gathered that,' replied David, keeping his focus on the gate to Magdala. 'The plan was to remain inconspicuous.'

'I don't think ignoring him is going to achieve that, do you?' said Hannah.

David reined in his horse.

'This is why we needed to stick to the plan.'

Hannah slowed her horse.

'I think you should talk to him before we get any closer to the soldiers guarding the gate.'

David risked a look. The fish merchant waved enthusiastically.

'Agreed, but if our friend draws the attention of the Romans, neither of you have seen me before and you walk away and don't look back.'

'I'm not just going to abandon you at the first sign of trouble,' said Hannah with a shake of her head.

'If Hannah is staying, then so must I,' said Polykarpos.

David looked towards the gate; the guards seemed only half interested in the noisy fish merchant, but things could easily change.

'Alright, we'll have a talk with Andrew to stop him drawing attention, then move on. Does anybody have a problem with that?'

'No, I am happy,' said Hannah.

'I am at your service David,' replied Polykarpos.

David waved to Andrew.

'He could be an asset. Andrew must know where we can find lodging for the night and a stable for the horses.'

'What if he wants to tell all his friends about the *miracle*?' asked Hannah. 'If the Romans hear about a man raising the dead, don't you think they will come looking for him?'

'Then we had best make sure that doesn't happen,' replied David.

'What are you suggesting?' asked Polykarpos watching Andrew approach.

'Hopefully, nothing other than talk the man into keeping his mouth shut.'

'*Shalom aleichem*,' called Andrew as he drew his horse up alongside David. 'I just had to stop and talk with you before you entered the city.'

'How can we help you, mate?' asked David.

'It is I that can be of service to you, David, and Hannah your *erusin*, and of course, your servant, Polykarpos. We mustn't forget those who Jehovah has placed in our care.'

'I don't understand.'

'An *erusin* is your betrothed,' whispered Polykarpos in Egyptian.

David looked at Hannah. 'Actually, Hannah and I..'

'David and my father have yet to finalise the details of the *Kiddushin*, it is premature to refer to me as David's *erusin*,' interrupted Hannah.

'The *Kiddushin* is the contract between families that has to be agreed before a marriage can take place,' whispered Polykarpos.

'My apologies to you both. I assumed that, as you were travelling without a family chaperone, your Kiddushin and the date of your wedding was settled.'

'I am Hannah's uncle and her chaperone,' said Polykarpos.

Andrew was flustered.

'I had assumed that you Mr Polykarpos were David's servant. I am embarrassed and must humbly apologise.'

'It's fine,' said David, 'actually, Polykarpos is a teacher with his own school in Nazareth.'

'Then I am not only embarrassed, but ashamed,' replied Andrew. 'I was going to thank you again for saving Timothy, but that is not nearly enough for what you have done.'

'You don't have to say, or do, anything. In fact, I would be very grateful if you didn't tell anybody what you saw today.'

'I don't understand. You deserve to be rewarded for your actions, you didn't just bring a man back from death, you saved a family.'

'Isn't Tim your friend?'

'Yes, Timothy and I were very close as children and I admit that, despite our different positions, I think of him very much as my friend.'

'Would you have looked after his family if Tim had died?'

'Yes of course. Timothy has been like a brother to me my entire life?'

'Then, you are the hero of the story, Andrew,' said David. 'I was just in the right place at the right time for one day. You have been looking out for Tim his entire life. That is of far greater value than what happened today.'

Andrew was stunned.

'I don't know what to say David. Thank you.'

'The line at the gate has thinned,' said Polykarpos, breaking the moment.

'Come and stay at my home as my guests,' said Andrew.

'We couldn't impose on your hospitality,' replied David.

'It would be an insult not to provide you with a bed after what you have done for Timothy and for me. I will not take "no" as an answer.'

Andrew addressed Hannah, 'I can offer you a bath and a soft bed, it would, however, be with my daughters, I am afraid. They can be very talkative and my eldest is rather forthright in her opinions. If she causes you offense, you have my blessing to instruct her to be silent.'

Hannah's eyes widened.

'I would love a bath, Andrew, and I would be honoured to share with your daughters.' Hannah placed a hand on David's arm. 'David needs a bath as well; I don't think he will be too upset if I was to compare his smell to that of a wet goat.'

Andrew wasn't sure if Hannah was insulting her betrothed or being playful.

'I will ensure your horses are fed, watered, and saddled for your departure in the morning. I assume you plan to go on from Magdala tomorrow?'

'Yes, we had only planned to stay tonight.'

'Then it is settled, you will be honoured guests in my humble home.'

'I would be even more honoured if you could extend your offer of a bath to me as well,' said Polykarpos. 'I am afraid I smell worse than David.'

'Yes, of course. I had noticed a slight odour but was reluctant to mention it.'

'I think the most appropriate description would be to suggest that we all stink. I, in particular, am sporting a combination of body odour, goat shit and horse sweat and would prefer not to be attracting flies to your dinner table.'

Andrew smiled, 'I might not be able to match your goat shit, Morah Polykarpos, but I would be willing to wager that my handling of pickled fish has left its own unforgettable odour.'

'Morah?' David asked Hannah.

'It means teacher,' whispered Hannah.

'Then if we agreed that we all stink,' stated Andrew, 'please follow me to my home where we can all bathe before supper.'

Polykarpos risked a look over his shoulder. Peter was amongst the many entering the city before the night curfew. Peter would spread the word of the miracle on the road to Magdala. The few who had witnessed it, would add to the story which would help to build a myth. The myth would build belief and belief would build resistance. From such small things, revolutions grew.

Will slowed his horse. A man was waving and yelling to somebody ahead of himself, near the city gate. The noise was beginning to draw the attention of the guards at the city entrance.

'We should go through the gates right now,' said Will. 'The blokes checking bags or taking tickets, or whatever they are doing, are distracted.'

Charlene stood in the stirrups to get a better look. The guards were focused on the noise. It was the sort of distraction gangs of shoplifters used to sneak past the security with something stuffed up their jumper or down their pants. Charlene got the up-the-jumper idea, but not the down-the-pants approach. A bulge in a person's pants was a dead giveaway that they were secreting a jigsaw or a walkman in a place it was never designed to be operated safely.

'Okay, Doc, you go first, then Will and I'll bring up the rear.'

# CHAPTER FORTY

'I **WOULD LIKE TO** introduce my beloved wife and the mother of our three daughters, Lydia, the daughter of Solomon.'

'Nicely done, Andrew,' said Lydia smiling at her guests, '*Shalom aleichem.*'

'I am very pleased to meet you, Lydia,' said David extending a hand for Lydia to shake. 'I am David, the son of Dwight.'

Lydia smiled, hid her surprise at the gesture and gripped David's hand. 'Never mind that formal nonsense, you are all most welcome.'

'Thank you,' replied David, stepping into the entrance hall.

'My girls have told me a tale of how you saved Timothy. They say you performed a miracle and summoned an angel, is that true David?'

'No, there was no miracle, no angels. We just had the right medicine and good luck.'

'Well, that's both disappointing and a relief at the same time. I really wouldn't know what to serve for supper to a person who could perform miracles. Though, you wouldn't be the first man claiming to be the messenger of Jehovah. You're not another messiah are you, David?'

'No, I am not.'

'Good, I am glad that's settled, though my girls will be devastated. They had their hearts set on you being an angel in disguise.'

'I'm sorry to be a disappointment.'

'Nobody said you were a disappointment, David; I like what I see.'

'I don't understand.'

'Modest as well,' noted Lydia with a chuckle, 'maybe you were sent by Jehovah not to save Timothy, but to brighten the lives of servant girls and their mistresses merely by your presence.'

'I still don't think I understand.'

'That, David, just makes you all the more charming.' Lydia looked at Hannah. 'And you must be Hannah?'

'I am afraid I am not an angel either, just the daughter of Joachim of Nazareth.'

'We are never just the daughter of anybody, Hannah, nor are we just somebody's wife.' Lydia turned to her husband. 'Andrew is my husband; I am his wife. Is either role more important than the other? Don't bother to answer, Hannah, men think one thing, but we know they would fall apart if we weren't there to point them in the right direction. They don't always think with their heads before doing things.'

Hannah wiggled her little finger.

'Exactly,' said Lydia.

'I don't understand,' said Andrew.

'It's just a code we women use to conceptualise where some of your more brilliant ideas come from.' Lydia leaned into Hannah. 'It's important to let them have their little victories, now and then. When it comes to important decisions, we have an equal voice.' Lydia straightened and raised her voice. 'That is the secret to a successful marriage, Hannah. That and the ability to sleep through snoring.'

'I don't snore,' interjected Andrew.

'Yes, Dear.' Lydia leaned in again. 'Little victories, Hannah, let them have them.'

Hannah smiled, 'I think I like you, Lydia.'

'Good, I think I like the look of you too, and my girls, dreadful gossips that they are, swear that you are the newly intended of David.'

'David? Well...'

'We can discuss that over dinner, all the juicy details. In the meantime, can I get you something? A bath? A change of clothes?'

'I will be your friend forever if I can soak in a bath. Today was my first horse ride and bits of me were not prepared for so many hours in a saddle.'

'Of course.' Lydia indicated to a servant, 'Ada could you please arrange a bath and a change of clothes for our guest? My light blue gown should fit Hannah, but before you do, please let the kitchen know we will be having three extras for supper.' Lydia turned to Hannah. 'What does David like to eat, he's not a fish man is he?'

David mouthed, *anything will be fine,* behind Lydia's back.

'No, David is not a *fish man*. Neither am I to be honest, there's something about the smell that puts me off.'

'Lamb it is then. You can't go wrong with a lamb roast and vegetables.'

'Please don't go to too much trouble,' said David.

'It's no trouble at all,' said Andrew happily.

Lydia raised an eyebrow.

'Andrew, I think it's time you showed David, and, sorry, my husband has been negligent in failing to introduce us.'

'I am Polykarpos,' said Polykarpos bowing, 'I am Hannah's uncle.'

'Really, you don't look like her uncle; you look like a Greek school master. I hope you aren't offended, Mr Polykarpos, but you are tall and dark, while your niece is rather short and has red hair.'

'I am *mishpacha*, a distant relative rather than the brother of Joachim or Anne.'

'We are all *mishpacha*, family of some sort, Mr Polykarpos, if we look far enough afield.' Lydia extended a hand to Polykarpos, 'I hope I'm doing this right; this is how you greet people where David comes from?'

'David is from a land called Warn Am Bool,' said Hannah.

'Mysterious, good looking and foreign. Hannah, we are definitely talking over dinner. I don't suppose David is rich as well? Let me guess, today was your first horse ride because David gave you a horse as a betrothal gift?'

Hannah blushed.

'Don't feel embarrassed, it's not a sin to land the right sort of a wealthy husband.'

'David is a good man,' interrupted Andrew. 'I saw the light of goodness in him today.'

'That's lovely, Dear,' said Lydia giving her husband a please shut up smile. 'As I was trying to say, could you please show David and Hannah's Uncle Polykarpos, where they can wash before supper. And lend them some of your clothes Andrew. Jehovah only knows why we have so many when the poor have so little.' Lydia looked at Polykarpos, then at David. 'If that is agreeable with you two gentlemen?'

'You are too kind,' replied Polykarpos.

Lydia had an awful thought. 'I never thought to ask, but is lamb something you would like to eat? You do have sheep in Warn Am Bool?'

'Yes, we have sheep. A roast would be wonderful.'

# CHAPTER FORTY-ONE

WILL AND CHARLENE WAITED on the street in the dark for Adrian to return. Adrian was key to their search. He would recognise David on sight, just as David would recognise him. Charlene and Will had watched a hologram recording taken at a family celebration which portrayed David Thomas as a quiet, polite, and intelligent man who was about as far from his extrovert cousin Adrian's personality as it was possible to imagine.

David had looks that Hollywood casting directors dreamt about; Charlene had raised an eyebrow of approval. Will had nodded, acknowledging yet another man he could not compete with on so many levels.

After securing stabling for the horses, the team began a search amongst the inns of Magdala for David. Adrian would inquire if a man answering David's description, accompanied by a young woman and an older gentleman, were staying the night, using the payment of a silver coin to remove any impediments management might have around customer confidentiality.

After conducting enquiries at nine inns, there was no sign of David and his companions and Charlene was beginning to question if they had bypassed the city and were spending the night in the countryside. If they couldn't find a lead on David soon, they would find a room for the night and travel to Tyre at first light to continue the search there.

Will stiffened.

'There's people coming, at least six walking together in step.' Will could hear the unmistakable jangle of metal. 'It's soldiers.'

Charlene couldn't see anybody in the darkness, but she trusted Will's senses.

'Over here,' she said, moving to the shadow of a building entrance opposite the inn. Will pressed into a corner, Charlene backed into Will, removed the weapon from her bag and raised it to her shoulder. Charlene's buttocks pressed up against Will's body. He didn't know what to do with his hands, which couldn't help but be in contact with the sergeant as six legionnaires marched past their position.

'A street patrol,' said Charlene once the soldiers were out of earshot. 'I don't think they are looking for anybody in particular.' Will didn't dare move until Charlene did. 'Are you alright?'

'Yes, I'm okay.'

'I am glad you're on the ball, Will. I get the feeling the Romans aren't good at playing nice with the locals.' Will stiffened. 'You sure you're okay?'

'There's somebody else.'

Charlene leant backwards to whisper in Will's ear, 'Where?'

'Across the street, hiding behind the corner of the inn,' whispered Will.

Charlene nodded. It could be somebody urinating in the alley, or it could be a mugger waiting in the dark. Charlene handed the weapon to Will, lifted her robe and withdrew the taser from her underwear.

As if on cue, the door to the inn opened, spilling light on to the road.

'Thank you very much,' came Adrian's happy voice. 'I will definitely give you a positive review for customer service and a friendly demeanour when I fill in my trip adviser blog.' Adrian paused, 'I wonder how that works in ancient Magdala?'

A shape moved from the corner of the building.

'Oh, hello!' said Adrian in surprise.

'Where is she?' hissed someone angrily from the darkness.

Charlene was across the street before Will had time to register the threat.

'Wait, Sergeant Wilson!' called Adrian in horror as the police officer struck a blow to the back of the knees, before ramming the arcing taser against the man's neck causing jerking convulsions until the body slumped to the ground.

'Are you alright, Doc?'

'I was just a little startled, Sergeant Wilson; I doubt he can say the same.'

Will moved into position beside Charlene, the weapon raised to his shoulder aimed in the direction the legionnaires had marched.

'They're still going away,' he said quietly. Then the smell hit him. 'God, what is that? Did he shit his pants when you zapped him?'

Charlene straightened, then had to step away from the man on the ground; the smell was overpowering.

'What is that stink?'

'I would like to say that you get used to it,' said Adrian, 'unfortunately, the best you can hope for is that your olfactory nerves give up trying to make sense of it and switch off.'

'What the hell?' said Will getting a second lungful.

'Don't stand in front of him when he is speaking,' advised Adrian, 'His body odour pales into insignificance, once you experience his breath.'

'You know this bloke, Doc?'

'Yes, we were briefly acquainted. This is Peter, the resistance leader from Nazareth. I only called out because I was somewhat startled to bump into him again, and as you can smell, it can be quite confronting when Peter is in close proximity.'

'Why would he be here?' asked Will.

'That's what I was going to ask, until Sergeant Wilson cut our conversation short.'

'Okay,' said Charlene holding a hand over her nose, 'he might be a source of information. He is friends with the Polykarpos guy, right?'

'Yes, I believe they are close,' said Adrian. 'Hence the attempt to rescue Mr Polykarpos which is how this mess started.'

'It started because a criminal stabbed a police officer,' said Charlene bluntly.

'There's a stable behind the inn, let's get him off the street and ask questions there,' said Will being practical.

'Take the lead, Will,' said Charlene. 'Hang on to the weapon, but don't fire unless it's absolutely necessary.'

Will nodded, then moved down the alley, his *W* senses on full alert.

Adrian squatted behind Peter, put both arms under his armpits then bending at the knees, pushed up, pulling Peter into an upright position. Adrian gripped Peter's right arm at the wrist with his left hand, held it high, then bent forward placing his right arm between Peter's legs while pulling his left arm down and across his body. The limp form slid across Adrian's shoulders as he stood upright.

'Just tell me where you would like me to put him down.'

Charlene was impressed.

'Follow Will, Doc, let's see if we can find a manger.'

'A manger? Oh, well done, Sergeant Wilson, well done indeed.'

Peter raised his head, it felt like he had been kicked by a donkey.

'How do you feel old chap? I am sorry for the misunderstanding. Sergeant Wilson takes her role very seriously.'

Peter's head dropped back to the stable floor. 'The clueless cousin.'

'I think that is a little unfair,' replied Adrian feeling somewhat offended.

'Where is she? I mean where are they?'

'Who?' asked a female voice.

Peter raised his body to see a woman holding something that reminded him of David's weapon.

'You're the same as David. You used what you call technology to do this to me.'

'Where is David?'

'Answer my question first, where are they?'

Charlene flicked the taser's safety to off, then placed it in the waist band of her underwear.

'If you are asking about David Thomas, Polykarpos the school teacher and Mary's sister, Hannah, we think they're in Magdala and so do you or you wouldn't be searching for them.'

Peter shook his head, 'I wasn't looking for David. He can look after himself. Polykarpos said he could perform miracles; I didn't believe it until I saw it myself.'

'What did you see?' asked Charlene.

'He brought a dead man back to life.'

'How is that possible?' Adrian asked. 'We are talking properly living and breathing back to life. David didn't create one of the undead by accident?' Adrian looked directly at Peter. 'The person David brought back to life didn't try and bite anybody did they?'

'No, he hugged his son, there was no biting.'

'Well, that's a relief. Well done, cousin David.'

'Ignore it, Doc. If David used medical technology, for your time it would have looked like scary magic. For all you know he just revived somebody who'd fainted.' Charlene turned her attention back to Peter. 'Where did you see David last?'

'They were not afraid. We don't fear Jehovah like the Romans fear their gods,' said Peter defiantly. 'They believed David to be a messenger of Jehovah put on earth to show the way.'

'Great,' said Will, 'it's the Life of Brian Monty Python script.'

Charlene glared at Will.

'Let's not get distracted, we stick to the plan.'

'Okay, let's just say you're right and we do everything we can not to screw up history, good on us. The problem is that while we're playing by the rules, cousin David is busily giving the sports almanac to Biff. If we get home, I don't want to find out that my Mum's had a boob job and is married to some wanker millionaire who's the president of Collingwood,' said Will.

'Who's Biff?' asked Adrian, 'and what's a boob job?'

'We can't do anything about what's already happened,' said Charlene. 'We just have to stick to the plan. Are you good with that, Will?'

'I guess I just have to be.'

'Doc?'

'Yes, we stick to the plan, Sergeant Wilson; you are in charge.'

'Good, then what we need to know is where Peter saw David last.'

'At the southern gate,' said Peter angrily. 'I wanted to follow them through the gate, but I had to keep moving and lost them in the city.'

'Why did you leave them behind?' asked Charlene.

'Because the fish merchant named Andrew was talking to them, he was there when David brought the woodcutter, who had been stung by a bee, back from the dead.'

'What happened?' asked Adrian.

'Polykarpos found the woodcutter and his son on the road. He asked David to save the man.'

'David had to help; he didn't have a choice,' said Adrian.

'No, he could have left it alone and not drawn attention to himself,' said Charlene bluntly.

'You couldn't just let a man die in front of his son, Sergeant Wilson?'

'We're trying to save everybody, Doc. That's the mission, that's what we focus on.'

Adrian was shocked.

'Saving one chap's life is going to change everything.'

'Yes, it could,' said Will. 'Think about when Marty McFly was knocked over by his grandfather's car at Lorraine's house, instead of his father.'

Adrian was confused.

'Lorraine? Does she have some sort of a relationship with this Biff?'

'No, not since Marty repaired the timeline,' replied Will.

'Am I missing something?'

'Yes, but it doesn't matter because Charlene is right.'

'I don't think that is particularly fair for the woodcutter?'

'Maybe he was supposed to die,' said Charlene.

'No, he was supposed to be saved by David,' replied Adrian indignantly. 'I refuse to think otherwise, Sergeant Wilson and if that is wrong, then everything we are doing is wrong.'

'The fish merchant was calling for them to stop,' said Peter interrupting the argument. 'The Romans couldn't help noticing the noise he was making.'

'Bugger it, they were the distraction at the gate,' said Will, feeling guilty for missing David.

'Don't beat yourself up, we'll find them in the morning,' said Charlene.

'Good,' said Peter. 'Find David and let Hannah go home, where she and Polykarpos can be safe.'

'I don't know how that is going to keep them safe,' said Adrian. 'I seem to recall that some Italian gentlemen were rather annoyed with you and Mr Polykarpos.'

'Bullies don't just give up, not unless they find somebody else to focus on,' said Will.

Peter said nothing. 'That's why you don't care about David, shit, you probably don't really care about Polykarpos either.'

'Polykarpos is my friend, I would give my life for him.'

'But you would rather that David gave his instead,' said Will.

'Sacrifices have to be made; David can help unite the people in our struggle.'

Will looked at Charlene, 'Does this sound familiar?' He snapped his attention back to Peter. 'Whose idea was it to help this woodcutter bloke? I bet it wasn't David's, he knows the risks. What did Dwight call it?'

'The Grandfather Paradox,' said Adrian quietly.

'Whose idea was it, Pete? Was it your idea? No? How about Hannah's?'

'You leave Hannah out of this.'

'No, not Hannah,' said Will thinking. 'It was Polykarpos, he's the boss. What was the plan, to turn David's good deed into a publicity stunt for the cause?'

Peter moved in anger but stopped when Charlene pulled the taser from under her robes.

'Why didn't you just wait for them inside the gate? If you had, you wouldn't need to be sneaking around after dark trying to find them,' asked Will.

'What was so important that made you abandon your friends?' asked Charlene.

'I was following orders.'

Charlene nodded, something smelled and it wasn't just Peter. Charlene handed her taser to Adrian.

'If Peter gets funny ideas, use this.'

Adrian took the weapon.

'I think we can be civilised enough for it not to come to that.'

'What are you thinking?' Charlene asked Will as they moved out of earshot.

'I'm thinking Mum would be really disappointed. You do know who Pete is?'

'We're just guessing and it's not relevant to the mission,' said Charlene.

'He's friends with Mary and her husband, I bet he is mates with their son as well.'

'Your point being?'

'Think about it. Judas is in Pete's gang and they all went to school with this Polykarpos bloke. I bet if we asked smelly Pete, he has a mate named Matthew, and another named James and John, and what was the guy who didn't believe any of it, Thommo?'

'So, what if Peter is who we think he may be, it's still not relevant.'

Will shook his head, 'Yes, it is relevant.'

'Where are you going with this, Will?'

'They made my Mum's life hell, Charlene. Pete and his mates caused a shit storm of misery across the entire planet. People died, or will die, in God knows how many wars because of what they started. I know it was supposed to be all about doing good and making rules to live by, like don't kill anybody. Yep, Pete and his mates get the medal for that one. The problem is, it turned in to, don't kill anybody who believes exactly what we believe. Everybody else can either join the team or suffer the consequences. Look at Ireland. What a bloody awful cluster that is and for what?'

'I understand Will, but it has nothing to do with our mission.'

'You know, they missed a commandment. The eleventh should have been, *don't be an arsehole to anybody*. Maybe I should suggest it to Pete. Do you reckon he's open to constructive criticism on Moses's work?'

'Are you done?'

'It's bullshit!' said Will angrily.

'Are you good? Because if you're not, say so now and Doc and I can go on without you.'

'Yes, I'm good. Let's just find David, fix up his stuff up and get home.'

'Okay, now that you have that out of your system, what do you think Peter was up to?'

Will forced himself to calm down before he answered.

'My guess is that Pete was busy spreading the word to come and meet the miracle man. He and this Polykarpos have seen what David's weapon can do. Just imagine the propaganda value if he is backed into a corner and has to use his weapon to protect Polykarpos and Mary's sister from the Romans.'

'You really think that's it?'

'Why else would he be so reluctant to tell us.'

'If we don't find David before he is surrounded by a curious crowd—'

'Then David, along with Mary's sister and the teacher, will be in deep shit,' said Will finishing Charlene's sentence. 'Pete did say sacrifices have to be made.'

'Thanks Will, that helps.'

'Peter, we should explain who we are and why we are here,' said Charlene.

'I'm not deaf, your name is Charlene, you are the leader. Adrian is, well he must have some use or he wouldn't be here. And that one, Will, is your bodyguard.'

Charlene couldn't help but smile. Thankfully, she had her back to Will, so he didn't feel embarrassed.

'I am a police officer.' Charlene handed Peter her ID. 'We are here to help David. If we fail, it could have devastating consequences for you and everybody you know and love.'

Peter didn't care about David, he cared about Hannah and right now Polykarpos's plan to use David for the cause didn't seem worth what he might lose.

'The people we are after are working with the Romans. The woman named Julia showed them where David and Adrian could be found, which is where they took you and your friends and were going to kill you. That was until David risked his life to save you.' Charlene could see guilt in Peter's eyes. Now was the time to press the advantage. 'If the Romans try to take David tomorrow, he will either run, or fight as a last resort. The people we are chasing will want David, and anybody he has been in contact with, dead.' Charlene could see Peter wavering. 'I would hate to be the person to tell Mary her sister was killed with David.'

'I was only following orders.'

'I can't tell you how many times that excuse has been used to justify absolutely horrible disgusting and evil things, Peter. The ends never justify the means. You have a choice, either help us or stand by and watch Hannah die.'

'The only thing necessary for the triumph of evil, is for good men to do nothing,' said Will. Then before Adrian could ask, he continued, 'That's John F Kennedy, not my dad.'

'What were you doing in Magdala?' Charlene asked.

Peter stared at Charlene, then at Will and Adrian.

'I was doing what I must for my people.'

'I know this one,' interrupted Adrian. 'The road to hell is paved with good intentions, I believe Charlotte Brontë, Byron and Ozzy Osbourne have used that quote.' Charlene gave Adrian the look. 'Ah, I think I will just be quiet and listen, Sergeant Wilson.'

Charlene turned to Peter.

'What specifically were you told to do?'

Peter sighed, 'I was to spread the word, to talk about the miracle. The story was already circulating in the town, gossip is faster than the wind.'

'What else?'

'Polykarpos said to tell people that David would be at the northern gate one hour after sunrise tomorrow. He said to suggest if one miracle could happen, why not more.'

'It's Brian,' said Will.

'Did Polykarpos tell you which street he would take to get to the gate?'

'No, that's why I was visiting inns after curfew to find them.'

'Could they be staying with the fish merchant?'

'Possibly, but there is no point searching for his home with the Romans patrolling the streets.'

'I guess we are staying here tonight,' said Will.

'I will help you,' said Peter abruptly, 'I know Magdala. I will lead you to the gate.'

'Thank you,' said Charlene, 'we could use a guide and a friend.'

'I am not doing this to be your friend, I am doing this to keep Hannah and Polykarpos safe. Polykarpos is wrong about David. This land belongs to the Jews it should be us that sets it free.'

Charlene nodded in understanding.

'Then as soon as we find David take Hannah and Polykarpos home and forget you ever met us.'

'We need a plan,' said Will, 'we can't just wander the streets hoping to find them before the Romans do.' Will activated the data storage device. 'Show map of ancient Magdala.'

'It's a maze,' said Charlene studying the hologram, 'the only open space is near the gate.'

'Well, we know where the crowd will be.'

Charlene pointed at the map.

'We have to find them before they enter this space. If the Romans even half know their job, they would have heard about the *miracle* and the planned rally and have troops in position to pick David up the moment he pokes his head out of one of these streets.'

'We need a distraction,' said Will finding what he was looking for on the map. 'Something else for the Romans to focus on.'

'What are you thinking?'

'I am thinking something, biblical,' said Will as he upended Adrian's sack and found what he was looking for. 'The crowd has come to witness a miracle; I say let's give them one.'

# CHAPTER FORTY-TWO

HANNAH CLIMBED OUT OF the tub to find that her clothes were missing. A polite knock on the bathroom door made her jump.

'Are you ready to be dressed?'

'Where are my clothes?'

Two women entered, one holding bath towels, the other a blue dress and clean undergarments.

'Don't worry,' said the older woman, 'your clothes are being washed. You'll get them back before you leave.'

'Relax,' said the younger woman, who was around Hannah's age, 'this is something you can tell your daughters about one day.'

'My name is Ruth,' said the older woman, 'this is my daughter Kelilah. Don't worry, we have seen it all before, though I can't recall any of the mistress's guests telling us to bugger off before when we helped them undress for a bath.'

'I'm sorry,' apologised Hannah feeling ashamed.

'You don't need to apologise,' said Kelilah. 'Compared to what comes out of Mistress Mary's mouth, you were singing with the voice of a lark.'

'Mary?'

'You may meet her at supper tonight,' said Ruth with a wry smile. 'Though Mistress Lydia might keep her in her room, seeing as she wouldn't want to offend you.'

'How could I be offended?'

Ruth and Kelilah laughed.

'Mistress Mary is rather open to sharing her thoughts,' explained Kelilah, 'I don't find her offensive myself, but some find her opinions difficult to hear.'

Ruth handed Hannah a towel, 'Use these to dry yourself.'

Hannah felt the towel. it was a finer cloth than anything she had for clothing.

'I couldn't, it will ruin them.'

'It's just a towel,' said Ruth, 'Lydia has a cupboard full of them.'

Kelilah watched Hannah wrap herself in one towel and use the second to dry her hair. 'We should do something with your hair.'

'What's wrong with my hair?'

'Nothing, dear,' said Ruth looking at the frizz of red running in all directions. 'It just needs a bit of a brush.'

Hannah entered, wearing the gown picked out by her hostess, her hair upright in the Roman style, held in place with jewel tipped pins. It was a strange sensation wearing a wealthy woman's clothes.

Polykarpos smiled, Andrew clapped in appreciation. David stared as if he had never seen Hannah before. They locked eyes, David smiled, then looked away as if embarrassed. Lydia took Hannah by the arm and directed her to a seat at her side.

'You look stunning, Hannah. I have a feeling that your David wishes it was closer to your wedding day than it is,' said Lydia for all in the room to hear, which made Hannah blush.

'Now that we are seated, it is my honour to welcome you at our table,' said Andrew.

Polykarpos stood to give the reply.

'On behalf of Hannah, the daughter of Joachim, David, the son of Dwight, and myself, a humble teacher, I thank you for your gift of hospitality.'

Andrew cleared his throat to reply, Lydia cut him short.

'Shall we eat before the lamb goes cold?'

'Yes, of course, let's eat.'

Platters of meat and vegetables were placed on the table, wine was poured and bread and cheese placed for all to share.

Andrew addressed the table, 'I would be honoured if you would give the blessing David.'

'I am afraid I wouldn't have the right words,' David replied truthfully. 'Polykarpos, as the elder from Hannah's family, should have the honour.'

Andrew furrowed his brow.

'If that is your wish, David?'

'Somebody just say something,' interjected Lydia, 'Hannah and I will faint from hunger if you men don't hurry up.' Lydia put a hand on Hannah's. 'This is why women should be in charge, we at least know when to make speeches and when to eat.'

Polykarpos bowed his head.

'Bless us, Jehovah. Bless our food and our drink. Since you redeemed us so dearly, and delivered us from evil, as you gave us a share in this food, so may you give us a share in eternal life.'

'Now let's eat,' said Lydia, plunging a fork into the lamb, 'I would hate to think this animal died for nothing.'

There was silence, only broken by the sounds of eating and drinking for several minutes. It was late and David, Polykarpos and Hannah were very hungry.

'Tell me, David, what sees you travelling through Magdala?' asked Andrew.

'I have business in Tyre,' replied David sipping his wine.

'Might I enquire as to the type of business? I have many contacts at the port, I would be happy to write you a letter of introduction.'

'That is very kind, but I am not an importer or an exporter of goods.'

'That is unfortunate,' replied Andrew in disappointment. 'Is your family in business?'

'Yes, my father and his brothers are in business together.'

'What sort of business is your father, Dwight, I do have that right don't I?'

'Yes.'

'What business is *Dwight* and your uncles engaged in, David? Is it a profitable business?'

'Husband,' interrupted Lydia, 'I think it might be rude to question our guests about their business affairs.' Lydia looked to David. 'I am sorry. Andrew means no offence, but I swear if he had not been born a man, he would have made the perfect *yenta*.'

'There is no offence taken. My family is in the clothing business, and it is profitable.'

'But you are not in the family business?'

'No, it wasn't for me.'

'Then we are back to my original question,' said Andrew with a laugh. 'What is it that you do?

'If David doesn't want to tell you how he makes his living, then that is his business, not ours Andrew,' interrupted Lydia. 'We should just be thankful that David, Hannah and Polykarpos came into our lives when they did. I can't imagine how sad we would all be if Timothy had gone to *shamayim* today.'

'Yes, yes of course,' said Andrew embarrassed at his actions. 'I must apologise for my rudeness; I am, as Lydia said, no better than a *yenta*.'

'It's not a secret,' said David, deciding to end his host's embarrassment. 'I am a police officer, a detective.' David looked to Polykarpos for help with the translation.

'David is a *shoṭerim*,' said Polykarpos. 'He is an enforcer of the law.'

Andrew's eyes widened.

'You are on a mission to apprehend a law breaker?'

'It is a delicate matter; I can't reveal any of the details.'

'I understand,' said Andrew. 'Say no more, I might be a *yenta* for trivial matters, but I can keep a secret if asked.'

'Thank you,' said David raising his wine glass in thanks.

'Enough of this conversation,' said Lydia, 'it is getting tedious and boring. It's my turn to ask the questions I am dying to know.' Lydia turned to Hannah. 'How did you and the mysterious, and obviously too handsome David first meet? Was it love at first sight, or did you make him chase you until you caught him?'

Hannah choked on her wine. David sat bolt upright as if hit with the blast from his stunner and Polykarpos grinned from ear to ear.

'I too, would like to hear the story,' said Polykarpos leaning across the table. 'I was surprised when Mary told me of your engagement. It seemed so sudden. David is of course an excellent choice; may Jehovah bless you with many children.'

'Praise Jehovah that is so,' said Andrew. 'Children are the greatest blessing that marriage can bring, may you have many sons.'

'And daughters,' added Polykarpos. 'It is also a blessing to have daughters. Where would sons find their wives if it was not for daughters?'

'Yes, you must have girls as well,' added Andrew, 'they are also a blessing.'

'Thank you for your kind wishes,' said Hannah, doing her best to hide her annoyance.

'What surprised me the most about your engagement was that I thought you were opposed to marriage.'

'I have never been opposed to the principle of marriage, Uncle; I just don't believe a wife should be subservient to her husband. Why should a woman give up her right to make decisions the moment she marries? Does marrying somehow lower a woman's intelligence?' Hannah glared at the three men in the room. 'If you told a man that the moment he married he would be condemned to a life of washing, cooking, cleaning, and raising children, along with obeying every petty demand of his wife until the day he died, would he marry?'

Hannah glared at Polykarpos.

'Well, Uncle, would you?'

'Marriage is the outlet for men and women to express their urges,' said Andrew.

Hannah turned to Lydia, 'Did you marry Andrew because of your urges?'

'Jehovah, no,' laughed Lydia. 'Don't get me wrong, I like expressing my urges with my husband, but that is not why I married him.' Lydia lowered her voice. 'The secret is to marry a man who doesn't treat you like a servant and uses his head, not his...' Lydia wiggled her little finger, 'to think with. It also doesn't hurt if he makes you laugh, but you already know that, Hannah.'

'What was that you said, Lydia?' asked Andrew.

'I was just telling Hannah that I married you because you are a good man.' Then almost as an afterthought, 'and of course, because I loved you.'

'And that's why I married you too, my wife.' Andrew raising his glass in salute. 'I really would be lost without Lydia.'

'But love is not enough. There has to be equality, women deserve to have rights.'

All heads swivelled towards the voice. Standing in the doorway was a teenage girl with an angry look on her face.

'I can't believe you continue to spout the propaganda pushed by old men to keep women living as little better than slaves, Father.'

'Mary!' barked Lydia. 'You forget your place, we have guests.'

'Shouldn't they hear the truth?' asked Mary defiantly.

'Enough,' said Andrew, rising angrily to his feet. 'What have our guests done to deserve your wrath, Daughter? Why should you force your opinions on people you have never met?'

Mary dropped her eyes.

'I apologise for my behaviour Father, but I cannot apologise for the truth.'

'Enough, Mary,' growled Lydia, 'that is enough.'

Mary looked at her mother and conceded.

'I'm sorry, I meant no offence to our guests.'

'I was not offended,' said Hannah.

'Youth should have a voice,' said Polykarpos, 'they are the elders of the future. If Mary was a boy I would offer her a place at my academy.'

'But I am not a boy,' said Mary, 'I am forbidden from attending a school.'

'That is the wish of Jehovah as written in the holy scrolls' said Andrew.

'Why can't we change it? And why should we have so much and the poor so little?'

'Because life is not fair,' said Lydia. 'Like it or not, that is the truth. We do what we can to protect the less fortunate, it's just not simple and it's not easy.'

'It's not enough,' said Mary. 'The children of Galilee may never forgive their parents if they are unwilling to make a better world for them to inherit.'

Andrew thrust his chair back.

'Say goodnight, Mary. I think you have entertained us enough for one evening.'

Lydia put a hand on her daughter's arm.

'We will discuss this in the morning.'

Mary dropped her stare, then nodded a good night to all at the table.

'Mary, what do we say to guests when they are about to leave the safety of our home?' asked Andrew. 'Do we just send them on their way?'

'No, Father,' replied Mary realising her father was offering an opportunity to redeem herself.

'Would you like to say the words?'

Mary bowed to Polykarpos, then to David and finally to Hannah.

'May you have a safe journey tomorrow. May Jehovah save you from every enemy and ambush, from robbers and wild beasts on the trip. And from all kinds of punishments that rage and come to the world.'

'Thank you for your blessing,' replied Polykarpos.

Hannah touched Mary's hand.

'I understand, you are not alone, Mary Magdalene.'

Mary took one last look, then left through the door she had entered.

'I must apologise,' said Andrew, 'there is no excuse for such behaviour.'

'We were not offended,' said David. 'Mary was only being honest with what she believes.'

'How old is Mary?' Hannah asked.

'Mary is 14,' replied Lydia. 'Our daughter is privileged but doesn't understand the responsibilities that come with our position. There are families who depend on our success to keep them fed. Mary has never gone hungry; nor has she spent her childhood in hard labour. If she had, maybe she would understand how hard it is to change what is.'

'Mary wasn't always so forthright,' explained Andrew. 'I blame that boy, the apprentice. What was his name, the son of the carpenter from Nazareth?'

'What Andrew is referring to is an infatuation that Mary had with the son of the carpenter who built our dining table. We had it built in Nazareth at a carpentry shop owned by a man called Isaac. Do you know it, Hannah?'

'Yes, I know Isaac's shop.'

'Do you know his head craftsman?' What was his name Andrew? Jabin, Jesse, John?'

'Joseph.'

'Do you know him?' asked Lydia.

'Nazareth is a small town,' said Polykarpos, 'it's a *yenta's* paradise, there are no secrets.'

'That must be difficult at times,' said Lydia.

'Yes, it can be,' said Hannah with a sigh.

'I understand,' said Lydia touching Hannah's arm. 'Anyway, Joseph brought his son with him to install this table along with the chairs in three separate journeys. It's very clever the way it fits together like a puzzle.'

'Yeshua,' said Andrew, 'that was the boy's name.'

'Mary was quite taken with Joseph's son,' continued Lydia. 'He broke a wine glass showing Mary a magic trick. His father offered to pay for a replacement.'

'I wouldn't hear of it,' said Andrew, 'a carpenter earns little enough. Joseph offered a set of carved wooden cups as a replacement, which I accepted as a gesture of good will.' Andrew pointed to six wooden cups on a table against the wall, 'I would far rather have those cups than the most expensive glass goblet from Rome.'

Lydia addressed her husband.

'We should give Hannah and David a pair for their wedding. They are as much *mishpacha* for saving Timothy as any family member.'

'Yes, Lydia,' said Andrew, rising from his seat. 'Lydia and I would be honoured if you would accept a gift with which to drink your wedding toast.' Andrew handed two cups to Polykarpos. 'I place these in your keeping until that day. May they never run dry with the love of a husband and wife for as long as Jehovah blesses their union.'

Polykarpos accepted with a smile.

'I will keep these safe until that joyous day.'

'No,' said Hannah horrified, 'we can't accept such a generous gift.'

'Nonsense,' replied Lydia, 'I would feel insulted if you could not accept such a small gift for the life that you have given us.'

Hannah looked at David. 'It's not right, David.'

David didn't want to cause an insult. 'We are honoured to accept your generous gift.'

'Good, that's settled then,' said Lydia closing the matter. 'Now, what was I saying?'

'You were talking about our daughter Mary and the son of Joseph the carpenter from Nazareth' said Andrew, retaking his seat.

# CHAPTER FORTY-THREE

## MAGDALA, NOVEMBER 3<sup>RD</sup> 15 CE, DAWN

PETER GUIDED THE TEAM through the streets of Magdala the moment the curfew lifted. Once the team was at its destination, he was to retrieve the horses and wait at a rallying point. Charlene's role was to coordinate the operation from a position where she could create a distraction to allow the team to withdraw if need be. Will would position himself to provide a warning of either a build-up of hostile forces or the sighting of David. If Charlene was forced to create a diversion, Will's job was to retrieve Adrian and then make contact with David.

Adrian's mission was to make the *miracle* happen, disrupting the Roman operation and providing time for both David's and Charlene's teams to melt away in the confusion.

The closer the four approached their destination, the more people they encountered heading towards the city's northern exit.

'It's just ahead,' said Peter, stopping at the last curve of the narrow alley before the open space in front of the gate. 'If you keep walking you will see the gate in front of you.'

'What's that noise?' Adrian asked.

Will's *W* senses were going off at what he knew had to be around the bend.

'Lots of people, something like down the main street on Christmas Pageant morning in the Mount.'

'Are you sure?'

Will nodded, 'It's a pity you didn't bring your Santa costume.'

Charlene turned to Peter, 'it's time you headed off to pick up our rides.'

Peter nodded, turned, and began pushing through the foot traffic.

'Be quick,' he called over his shoulder. 'Even if the Romans were not aware before, they will come and investigate why so many people are gathering at the gate.'

'Are we clear on our tasks?' asked Charlene.

'Yes,' said Will grim-faced.

'Affirmative, Sergeant Wilson,' replied Adrian smiling.

'Ok then, let's go make a miracle.'

Adrian made his way towards the well that sat near the centre of the public space. If things went to plan, he would use the well to perform the miracle which should trigger a response from the crowd and the Romans. Charlene believed the Romans would have undercover operatives in the crowd, as well as troops at strategic locations, ready to surround and remove David the moment he was identified. That's how she would have planned an operation to snatch up a body off a street amongst a potentially hostile population. She would have used a highly trained team with set rules of engagement designed not to injure members of the public. The problem was, the Romans were only trained in the art of war which meant the use of lethal force was their first option.

Adrian was bombarded with calls from stall holders who had set up with their wares in a semi-circle, some 15 metres from the well. Adrian smiled at the offers of the finest bread, the sturdiest sandals and the freshest fish in all Magdala. As he navigated the tide of bodies, Sergeant Wilson, then Will, confirmed they had eyes on his movements in his earpiece. They were depending on him and he wouldn't let them down. Then an opportunity presented itself. It was better than using the well and it would be spectacular. Adrian liked that thought.

'I have an idea, a slight variation from the plan.'

'We spoke about this, Doc.'

'There are too many people at the well, Sergeant Wilson. This will be less risky and we can activate the miracle precisely when we want.'

Charlene was silent, thinking.

'Please trust my judgement, Sergeant Wilson, I know about theatrical performance.'

'Is Doc in the clear, Will?'

'There are soldiers hiding in the buildings leading into the square and four of the men, sitting in front of the gate with the families waiting for David, don't belong. They stick out like footy players in an under-11 ballet class, but other than that, I don't see an immediate threat.'

'What have you in mind, Doc?'

Adrian briefly explained. It was simple, Charlene liked simple and the timing could be controlled more effectively.

'Okay, just don't be too theatrical, Doc.'

'*Shalom Aleichem*,' called a stall holder catching Adrian's eye.

'*Shalom Aleichem*,' replied Adrian, slowing his walk as if half interested in the goods on display.

'Are you in need of earthenware, friend? The finest storage jars in all of Galilee can be yours for just a few shekels. I am having a sale in honour of the miracle of Magdala. You should buy what your heart desires, it is a lucky day.'

'A miracle?' asked Adrian, feigning ignorance.

'Friend, have you not heard of the miracle of Magdala?'

'I am afraid I missed the local news.'

'Praise be to Jehovah; a woodcutter was brought back to life yesterday on the road from Nazareth, not more than 2,000 cubits from where we stand. My wife knows another man's wife, whose cousin saw it happen with her own eyes. A traveller named David breathed life into the woodcutter's dead body. The voice of an angel was heard to speak and the woodcutter was raised to live again.'

'That does sound like a miracle,' said Adrian looking to the heavens.

'Which is why all of my wares have been reduced in price by 15 percent, friend. For one day only, all of my customers are *mishpacha* and if a second miracle happens today, as foretold, I will take another two percent off in celebration. Of course, as these are special prices, there will be no return on goods bought on sale.'

Adrian studied the display.

'I'm not sure that you have what I need. I need a container absolutely certain not to leak.'

'Friend, this is the workmanship of my cousin, Immanuel. He is a potter without peer in Magdala.'

'I am not from Magdala,' said Adrian pleasantly. 'If your cousin was the finest potter in Hebron, I would not need to ask about the quality.' Adrian smiled at the stall holder. 'I mean no disrespect to your cousin.'

'If you were from Magdala, you would not question the quality of any good made by Immanuel,' replied the stall holder picking up a cooking pot. 'Look at the lines of this pottery. Are not the handles well placed to allow your wife to lift this vessel from a cooking fire without burning her hands? This pot will not crack, even if it is left too long on the flames. It is a cooking pot that any wife would be happy to have in her home.'

'I don't have a wife.'

'You don't have a wife?'

Adrian could see the look of disbelief on the stall holder's face.

'Why don't you have a wife, Doc? It's what's expected?' whispered Charlene's voice in the earpiece.

'My wife died,' said Adrian loudly.

'How did your wife die, Doc? Keep it simple.'

'She was killed.'

'Killed?'

'Yes, she died tragically. It's not a story I feel comfortable talking about.' Adrian could see curiosity in the stall holder's eyes. 'All right, the truth is she was trampled by a herd of goats.'

'Goats! Why didn't she just die from an infection, or in childbirth?' whispered Charlene.

'Yes, in hindsight that would have been more logical, Sergeant Wilson,' whispered Adrian.

'It has been known to happen,' said the stall holder bowing his head. 'May your wife find peace, resting in *Sheol*.'

'Thank you,' said Adrian also bowing his head.

'You have no wife, but you have children to care for?'

'Yes, a dozen children.' Adrian could see a look of admiration on the stall holder's face. 'My wife was generous in her affections, hence, so many sons, and indeed daughters. That's why I am interested in these,' said Adrian touching a large storage jar.

'An excellent choice, friend and by chance, I am having a special on these jars today. Buy five and get a sixth half price.'

'Will it hold milk? We have lots of milk to store, because we have a lot of the goats.' Adrian paused. 'It's tragic and a blessing at the same time.'

'Smooth, Doc,' whispered Charlene, 'now close the deal.'

'These storage jars will keep your milk sweet and cool even on the hottest of days.'

Adrian examined the jar.

'How much milk will this hold?'

The stall holder was surprised by the question.

'They hold enough, but not too much to carry, that is important to wives.'

'I have a lot of goats. I might need five jars, or perhaps six. It's a long journey from Hebron if I need one more.'

'If you buy six, friend, I will give you a seventh as a gift.'

'I would really rather know,' said Adrian, placing the equivalent of a month's earnings in gold in the stall holder's hand, 'this is to show that I am not wasting your time.' Adrian looked at the well. 'If you filled the jar with water, we will know how much milk it will hold. Does that sound reasonable?'

'I have a milking bucket in my inventory we could use.'

'Wonderful,' grinned Adrian, 'perhaps the second miracle will happen today after all?'

'Perhaps it already has,' said the stall holder feeling the coins in his hand.

'Is Doc in the clear, Will?' asked Charlene.

'Yes, the Romans seem happy to wait and watch.'

'The hour after curfew is nearly up. Is there any sign of David?'

Will touched the glasses and zoomed out the magnification.

'No. Wait. The third alley to your right, there is an old bloke, a woman with red hair, and a man whose face I can't see approaching on horseback.'

'That will be them,' said Charlene. 'Do it now, Doc. Will, head to intercept them, don't run but get a wriggle on. Doc, as soon as it starts, you go as well.'

'Okay,' said Will pushing through the crowd.

'Affirmative, Sergeant Wilson,' replied Adrian, watching the stall holder head to the well with a bucket in his hand.

Adrian carried a storage jar to a point mid-way between the stalls and the well where foot traffic was at its greatest. It was exactly where the miracle needed to happen. Adrian removed a jar of hydration tablets from his robes and tipped the contents into the empty vessel, followed by the contents of a jar of raspberry-flavoured electrolyte supplement tablets.

'Spectacular,' Adrian said to himself.

The stall holder returned with a bucket of water.

'Shall I pour it in?'

'Please do, I bet we are in for a surprise on how much one jar can hold.'

The stall holder concentrated on not spilling the bucket's contents as he poured, then looked up to see if his customer approved. Adrian was gone. The stall holder felt his feet grow wet; he looked down hoping his cousin had not sold him another load of jars that leaked.

What he saw made him leap back in fright. The jar was overflowing with blood. It boiled, splashed, and gurgled from the vessel. A woman screamed, men began to yell, people pushed, ran, and stumbled away from the flood. Red liquid covered the stall holder from head to toe, soaking his beard and dripping from his nose to his lips where he tasted, not blood, but the sweetest of wines! He cupped his hands and caught the liquid as it rained down.

'It's wine,' he yelled, 'the water has turned to wine!' The stall holder drank, the electrolyte did what it was designed to do, he felt well, more alert than he could ever remember. 'It's a miracle!' The stall holder looked to the men and women falling to their knees around the miracle fountain of wine. 'I will reduce my prices by another two percent,' he yelled to the heavens. 'Thank you, Jehovah, for choosing me.'

A dark shadow fell across his face. The stall holder turned to see the blunt pommel of a gladius just before it impacted and everything went black.

Polykarpos insisted on waiting a half hour after curfew for the morning rush at the gate to slow and the guards to settle into their routine. David thought it reasonable, people with nothing to hide could afford to take their time.

Andrew apologised for not breaking the fast with his guests. He had business to attend to and wanted to see how Timothy was recovering.

Lydia had no such obligations. She fussed around her guests making sure they were fed and provisioned for their journey. Mary brought Hannah her clothes, along with an apology for her behaviour at supper. Hannah felt Mary was a kindred spirit in a world where few women could safely speak for themselves. David glimpsed them in conversation. As he watched, Hannah raised a hand and wiggled her pinkie finger. Both girls laughed, then abruptly stopped when they noticed David. David averted his eyes and moved on which increased the laughter.

Lydia handed a basket of food to Hannah for the trip, then presented the blue gown as a gift.

'For your wedding, Hannah. Let it start with love. If you find it slipping, wear the gown and let it do its magic.'

Hannah had no choice but to accept. She didn't want to offend Lydia or break their cover story. Much to her shame, she liked how the dress made her feel, especially when David had first seen her in it.

Polykarpos led the way, David brought up the rear. The streets were narrow and the increasing flow of people heading in the same direction, forced them to ride single file. David was concerned at the number of family groups; he had expected the foot traffic to be mostly men going to work. There were children, the elderly, the sick and disabled, this wasn't the normal traffic of a city going about its daily routine.

'What's up ahead?' David called to Hannah, 'What's at the end of this street?'

Hannah turned in her saddle.

'Just the square in front of the gate.'

David looked behind. There were more people joining the procession.

'Why are there so many people heading towards the gate? Is this normal?'

Hannah blinked at the question, then turned to look ahead.

'No. I wouldn't ever see so many babies being carried by mothers in Nazareth this early and the men should already be at their work.'

'Somethings wrong. Tell Polykarpos to stop.'

'Uncle,' Hannah called. Polykarpos didn't look back. 'Uncle,' she called louder. 'Polykarpos!' Hannah yelled for a third time.

Hannah thought she saw Polykarpos nudge the flanks of his horse as it moved further away. She dug in her heels and bounced forward, sending a stab of pain to the blisters on her backside.

'Didn't you hear me?' demanded Hannah as she finally managed to weave her way through the clogged street to catch Polykarpos.

'Were you calling?'

'You must have heard me yelling.'

'I am old, Hannah; my hearing has faded with age.'

'David wants you to stop.'

'We are almost at the gate,' replied Polykarpos urging his horse forward.

'I said, stop!' barked Hannah grabbing the reins of Polykarpos's horse.

David's horse pushed up against the rump of Hannah's.

'Let's just turn around and go.'

'We are almost at the gate,' said Polykarpos pointing to the end of the street. 'The road to Tyre is outside the northern gate.'

'See the last house on the left, watch the door,' said David turning his horse.

'What am I looking at?' asked Hannah.

David withdrew the stunner from the bag on his saddle.

'There is nothing we can do, just turn around and head towards the southern gate.'

Light flashed off the metal of a legionnaire's helmet. As Hannah watched, a second, then a third helmet emerged through the doorway.

There was a great roar of voices: women and children screaming, men yelling. As Hannah watched, legionnaires rushed from the doorway, shields up, swords drawn to seal the exit from the square. Hannah turned her horse; David had probably saved her life, just as he had saved Joe and Polykarpos in Nazareth. She felt sick. Who was this man she was following?

Polykarpos had no idea why the Romans acted early. There were so many people who could have borne witness if David was forced to defend himself. The Jewish people had to believe they could push the empire out of Galilee. David could have provided the spark for that belief in Magdala. Now it was gone because David was more cautious than Polykarpos hoped. There would be other opportunities, Tyre could be the place where the spark turned into a fire. Still, the word was filtering out to the young, they were the future of the rebellion. Yeshua, the son of Joseph the carpenter had already passed the idea to Mary, the daughter of Andrew the fish merchant. There was always hope that his Mary of Magdala, Mary Magdalene, might play some part in what was to come.

Being a head taller than most of the crowd, Adrian could at least see where he was going as he pushed through the panicked crowd.

'How are you travelling, Doc?'

'I am making progress, Sergeant Wilson, though it is somewhat difficult.'

'Keep pushing, you have about 20 metres to go.'

'What's going on?' asked Will planting his feet to brace against a change in the crowd's flow.

'The Romans have opened the gate,' replied Charlene. 'Their checking all the men before pushing them out one at a time.'

Charlene increased the magnification on her glasses. The store holder was standing at the gate with a Roman non-commissioned officer at his side. If the store holder shook his head, the next man in line would be allowed through the gap. If he shrugged, the man would be placed under guard. The unlucky few were tall, clean shaven and in their twenties or thirties. They were searching for Adrian.

'Doc, I need you to come to my position as quick as possible.'

'Where are you?' asked Adrian, then jumped as a hand grasped his shoulder.

'I have got him,' said Will.

'Can you get to my position?' asked Charlene as she watched the crowd exit through the gate.

'Yes, we can,' replied Will grimly. 'Hang on to my belt Adrian and follow me.'

Charlene watched Will and Adrian emerge from the mass of people. They looked uninjured, but obviously fatigued. She scanned the area. Families with babies in arms, or toddlers at their feet, were waiting outside the moving crowd for the pressure to reduce. The sick, lame, blind and deformed who had come for a healing miracle were nowhere to be seen. The Romans had ejected them through the gate first. Bodies of those injured or killed in the panicked crush, lay on the cobblestones, surrounded by relatives or friends who refused to abandon them. What had she said to Peter about the end justifying the means? Was keeping their world the same really worth the cost? It was crap, absolute bullshit, but what else could she do?

'Wait there,' instructed Charlene, 'I'll come to you.'

Will scanned his surroundings. Legionnaires were guarding all the exits; they couldn't escape via the streets that led from the market square. The buildings abutting the space were flat roofed. If they could climb on top of one of these structures, they could move over the roofs to get away; the problem was how to get up there without being spotted. The Romans at the gate had their hands full sorting the men, the soldiers guarding the street exits were concentrating on the crowd at the gate with an occasional glance at the family groups either waiting their turn or grieving over the dead and injured.

'We need to move,' said Will. 'Standing here, we stick out from everybody else.'

Charlene nodded.

'Head towards that body, it doesn't look like anyone has claimed it.'

They made their way to an elderly man who had been trampled in the rush.

'Is he dead?' asked Adrian.

'Don't worry, Doc, he can't hurt you,' said Charlene sitting beside the corpse.

Will sat opposite Charlene.

'The poor bugger.'

'I hope this adventure of yours is everything you wanted it to be, Doc.'

'I am so sorry, Sergeant Wilson,' said Adrian lowering himself to the ground.

'We all are,' said Will sadly as he gently rolled the man onto his back. 'Sorry mate.'

'Time to focus, guys,' said Charlene. 'Any ideas how we get out of here?'

'We could jump forward in time, Sergeant Wilson, then reappear after dark.'

'That's a last resort, Doc. It might push the Romans over the edge and they could come in swinging. It's too big a risk.'

'Adrian can't get out the gate and I am not leaving him to fend for himself,' said Will.

'Agreed,' said Charlene. 'Doc comes with us, or we don't go.'

'Thank you,' said Adrian with relief in his voice.

'If we can't go through them and can't go around them, then let's go over them,' said Will.

Adrian placed the body across Will's shoulders, who carried the man towards the shortest building on the edge of the square. The legionnaires at street entrances watched Will's progress, until he laid the man down in front of the structure. Charlene sat next to the body, arranged his limbs in a respectful pose, before she clasped her hands as if in prayer.

Adrian carried an injured older woman to join the deceased man in the building's shade where Charlene made her comfortable and gave her water. Back and forth, Will, then Adrian, gathered the dead and injured; the mourning families joined in the procession, carrying their loved ones to the communal point of grief. The legionnaires began to lose interest, the activity at the gate was more entertaining.

Will gave the command on his fifth trip. The few soldiers who had a line of sight with the pile of bodies were looking away.

'Do it now.'

Charlene and Adrian moved to the building's wall. Adrian clasped his hands together to form a step, Charlene placed her foot in Adrian's hands. Will saw the attention of one soldier drift towards the bodies. He had hoped it wouldn't come to this. On Will's shoulder was the deceased body of a young woman, he could smell urine on her clothes and sweat from her body. Will stumbled, the weight came off his shoulder and slid toward the ground. He tripped on the woman's robes, tumbling into the paving stones. His hand impacted into the still warm flesh, he felt like vomiting. He heard laughter which was cut short by a barked command. Will looked up. Charlene was gone, Adrian was hurrying to help him to his feet. They had done it, but at what cost?

Adrian had launched Charlene upwards with just enough elevation to grasp the roof edge then haul herself up and over.

'Are we good?'

'No reaction down here,' replied Will.

'Okay. Once I am in position, I will give you the call.'

'Affirmative, Sergeant Wilson,' came a subdued reply from Adrian.

'Keep your heads up, focus on the job.'

'Yes, Sergeant,' replied Adrian, 'let's get it done.'

Charlene leopard-crawled to the end of the roof, keeping her head and backside as low as possible, just as her father had taught her. When she was well out of sight, Charlene lowered her body over the end of the roof and dropped into an alley and walked away as if she was meant to be there.

'Who's that?' said a voice in her ear.

'Peter?'

'Yes, this is Peter of Magdala.'

'Are you at the rally point?'

'No, I heard the screaming, I had to move closer.'

'Your blood's worth bottling, mate. Bring the horses to the last street on the land side of the city.'

'Yes, I can do that.' There was a pause. 'If you had not told me about this technology you call radio, I would have believed I was hearing the voice of an angel.'

'I bet you say that to all the girls, Peter. I'll see you soon, mate.'


'I'm in position,' said Charlene.

'We're ready,' replied Will.

'I am sorry,' said Adrian, looking into the dead eyes of a youth on the ground.

'So am I,' said Will, 'and I know what you meant; this is not your fault.'

'This is the responsibility of the Thomas family. My family, Will, you are not responsible for the sins of your great, great, great-grandchildren.'

'Thanks for the vote of confidence, Adrian, though wouldn't it be a kick in the bum if you are descended from Brian and Loni?'

'I am so sorry, Will.'

'You're just trying to do the right thing; let's leave it at that.'

Charlene voice filled their earpieces again.

'When I signal, Will, you go right, Doc, hard left.'

'Okay,' replied Will.

Adrian and Will walked towards three legionnaires guarding the entrance of the northern most alley leading to the market square. The legionnaire in the centre of the formation was scarred and leathered from years of service; the two either side were young and nervous. Will gripped his taser behind his leg.

'Have you got your taser?'

'Yes, it's in my underpants,' replied Adrian.

'Wouldn't it be better in your hand?'

'Yes, it probably would,' said Adrian searching for his weapon.

'Stop where you are,' commanded the veteran. 'Turn around and go to the gate.'

Will looked over the man's head, Charlene held five fingers aloft, then four, then three.

'I am the man you are looking for,' said Will.

'Take them,' said the veteran.

Will moved to his right to break up the soldiers' formation.

Adrian raised his taser, squeezed the trigger and watched electricity arc at the end of his arm. The young soldier before him hesitated, then moved with his gladius aimed at Adrian's stomach.

'What in the name of Apollo?!' exclaimed the veteran, followed by a series of shuddering vocal sounds as Charlene placed her taser against the soldier's neck and pulled the trigger.

'Golly,' squealed Adrian as he dodged the sword. 'Perhaps we can come to some understanding that is a little less aggressive?'

Will hip-and-shouldered Adrian's attacker into a wall, knocking the wind out of the soldier and sending Will staggering sideways. The legionnaire swung his attention from Adrian to Will. Gasping for breath, he thrust his gladius at Will's face. Will stepped to the side of the blade as it lost momentum, pushed his taser against skin and pulled the trigger. The soldier dropped, convulsing from the electrical charge as it arced across nerve receptors.

Adrian swayed to dodge a sword thrust from the remaining soldier still standing. The sword would have gone into Will's back if Adrian hadn't jumped in front of the attacker.

'It's me you want,' Adrian yelled as the blade caught his robe and ripped a ragged hole.

Charlene drove her foot into the knee of the soldier breaking cartilage and tearing tendons. The legionnaire dropped as his leg collapsed. His neck and face were impacted by the flat of Charlene's hand as she straight-armed thrust it upwards into the exposed chin. His head snapped backwards and the lights went out.

'Peter has the horses somewhere down this alley. Don't walk, Doc, run as quick as you can.'

Will took a last look across the square. There were only 20 or 30 people still at the gate. He turned and ran as if every person he had ever encountered as the *W* was chasing him with evil intent.

# CHAPTER FORTY-FOUR

DAMIAN SHUDDERED, REMEMBERING THE knife slicing into his flesh. Julia didn't remove all his manhood; she left his penis as a torment to remind him he was no longer the man he believed himself to be. Julia had been clinical, as if he was no more than a sheep that needed castration. He would not accept this fate; Julia would pay a price. He would make her suffer and then he would find a way to go home.

Doctors might not be able to give back his balls, but they could replace his testosterone. After all, it was the hormone he needed, not the organs that produced it. Anger boiled, it was that bitch Sapphira's doing, her and Atarah, they would pay as well.

Light flooded the cellar. The door normally opened twice a day, once after dawn, once on dusk. The bucket which served as a toilet was emptied at dawn.

'Hello, my love.'

Damian stared in hatred at the woman who had literally cut off his balls.

'You could do with a shave. Don't get me wrong, it doesn't look bad on you, the whole "I don't give a damn" image.'

'What do you want, Julia?'

'I have news. Guess what it is.'

'You've changed your mind and are going to set me free?' Damian said sarcastically.

'No.'

'You're sending me home. That's all I want, Julia.'

'If I did that, you could reoffend, and you must never be given the opportunity to fall prey to your urges again.'

'You cut my balls off, beat and imprisoned me, tricked me into helping you. Don't you think I have been punished enough?'

Julia placed a bowl of food on the floor.

'If Atarah and Sapphira had decided your punishment, it wouldn't have just been your testicles you lost.'

Damian picked up the bowl and began to eat.

'Do I live out my days tied up like an unwanted dog in this dungeon? If that's what you have in mind, I will kill myself.'

'No, you are going on a sea journey. A change is, after all, as good as a holiday.'

'Where?'

'Italy is a possibility. Morocco and Gibraltar are also nice this time of year.'

'Have I been sold as a galley slave?'

'The Romans don't use slaves to row their ships, Damian. Imagine having a crew of slaves rowing into battle, what would be the incentive to play the game?'

'Am I to be a slave in a household like ours?'

'You were never the master of this house, my love. That's where you came unstuck, if you remember.'

'Am I going to the games?' asked Damian in horror.

'Now you have ruined the surprise.'

'No Julia, sooner or later Octavian, or a man like him, will take this away from you. You need me to be the voice of a man for you. It's the only way you will survive.'

'I have heard your argument before, which is why I know I can't trust you. You are... well, you are exactly who you are, and don't compare yourself to Octavian. His ethics are far more admirable than yours will ever be, which is sad when you think about it.' Julia looked Damian up and down. 'A sea voyage and some exercise will do you good. I hate to say it, but you have been getting a little flabby of late.' Julia headed to the steps. 'You leave at dawn; Atarah will bring an early breakfast.'

'Wait, you can't just walk away.'

Julia hesitated, 'You have a question or a farewell message for your friends? Sorry, that's cruel, you don't have any friends, do you?'

'Why?'

'Because they offered good money. Octavian says I will double my investment.'

'No, why did you bring me here? I thought that this was just a brief visit to see Jesus and Mary, then we were going to time jump to set ourselves up for the good life. Or was that just another lie? I don't deserve to die just because you hate men.'

'I don't hate men; I hate the way men treat women. And you are getting what you deserve.'

Damian rattled his chain.

'Nobody deserves this. I thought your faith was all about forgiveness and turning the other cheek.'

'Who said I was a believer? What has any religion done for the world, other than bring conflict and oppression? No Damian, I am here to change what Christianity has done to women, not to bathe in its misogynistic beginnings.'

'I don't understand.'

'No, how could you?' said Julia moving up the steps.

'Explain it to me, I at least deserve that.'

Julia hesitated, 'Alright, if you really want to know. I read about the *Cabinet* in Cynthia Horrigan's journals. Everybody who read them thought it was a fantasy, the plot of a novel or the writings of a lunatic. I didn't think so. She wrote about things that only a person who had lived in our time could know.'

'I only met Cynthia twice. She had a certain strength, courage you would call it.'

'Cynthia wasn't as kind in her description of you, my love.'

'I admit it was partially my fault.'

'I think it was wholly your fault. Still, water under the bridge, just desserts etc.'

'You did this because of Cynthia?'

'No, she just showed me how to make it happen. Cynthia was, is and will, be an inspiration. That's a time travel joke, Damian.'

'I got it, very clever Julia.'

'Good, you will need a sense of humour where you are going.'

'You haven't said why.'

'To change the world obviously. To change how women are treated from now until the end of time.'

'That's not possible in this time, especially not by a woman. Men make the rules, that's why you need me.'

'Just accept it, Damian. I am not going to set you free.'

Damian shook his head.

'Octavian won't be able to help you, even if you could convince him to.'

'You're right, Octavian isn't the right person, but he is helping by making it possible to find the person I have come here to meet.'

'Who are you looking for Julia? The Apostles? The Virgin Mary? That's if they are real.'

'They are real people, but God didn't impregnate Mary while she wasn't looking and there were no angels or kings bringing gifts to a stable on the night Mary's son was born.' Julia sat on the steps. 'Mary is shorter than I imagined, with red hair. Who would have guessed she was a ginger? Joseph is a nice man, but out of his depth with Mary.'

'You weren't looking for them?'

'I will admit, I was curious; Mary could have been the one, but when I saw her with her children, it was obvious they were her world and I couldn't disrupt that.'

'So, not Mary?'

'Well, not that particular Mary. It's the other Mary I am here to influence, to make her the hero of the story, rather than a foot note to a man betrayed by his best friend and killed for annoying the powers that be. When you think about it, he didn't really achieve anything other than being bad at playing politics. It was those who followed, used his story to build the brand, then sell it to the world, who benefited.'

'You're talking about Mary Magdalene, the girlfriend?'

'Don't forget prostitute and sinful woman, none of which is true. Those stories were created by Pope Gregory the first, because he wanted to put women in their place and how better than by slut-shaming their idol.'

'All of this was done just to meet a girl? I still don't understand.'

'You never will, my love. You and Gregory would be right at home sharing a beer and bragging about your conquests while watching football. Mary is the one woman in the story, other than Mary, the mother, whose name most people know. Mary is mentioned twelve times in the book, that's more than anybody else other than our friendly neighbourhood martyr. With the right mentoring, the story could be about her, Mary could be the one on the cross. Imagine how that would change the way women are viewed right from the beginning.'

Damian was shocked, Julia was insane.

'You will get stoned to death for just suggesting a woman could be the leader.'

'Stoned, crucified, or fed to the lions, it doesn't matter how she becomes a martyr, it's about the spin you put on the story. That's how the Christian religion got off the ground, propaganda and a social welfare program for the poor. That's why there were so many early converts, people were fed and given medical care by the Christians. The other religions didn't think about the welfare of their followers, it was all about appeasing the gods. They lost out because of something as simple as providing bread to the hungry.' Julia smiled, 'I know how it is supposed to happen, who, when, and where. I have gold, political influence at the local level, and the best technology our century has to offer. I can make Mary Magdalene a god, a rockstar, or a martyr. I can make her the focus of the story and that's what I plan to do.'

# CHAPTER FORTY-FIVE

PREPARATIONS FOR A FEAST in honour of the Prefectus of Samaria and Judea had been underway since dawn. Julia had her staff preparing a meal for 33 guests of Annius Rufus and 120 retainers, assistants, secretaries, and bodyguards who were being catered for in the stables behind Octavian's villa.

Annius and Octavian had spent the day with the management of Tyre's port and the Nasi of Tyre's Sanhedrin, discussing the proposed expansion of the port. Julia greeted Annius on his return then placed a hand on Octavian's shoulder, followed by her lips on his cheek. Octavian realised that Julia was just continuing the deception.

'Did you have a productive day?' Julia asked.

'Yes, it was a useful day,' replied Octavian as he handed his sword to Asher.

'Not as productive a day as you, Julia,' said Annius noting the preparations for the feast.

'I was just hoping not to disappoint, Annius.'

'I don't think you know how to Julia; I will think far less of Octavian if he does not make you his wife when his service with the Sixth ends. I meant that as a kindly wish, not as a command Octavian.'

'I would indeed be a fool if I did not take the woman I love as my wife when my military service ends,' replied Octavian.

'Do those words comfort you, Julia?' asked Annius.

'I would be disappointed if Octavian did anything else,' she replied with a smile.

'If you will excuse me, I think I will wash and change robes,' said Annius taking his leave.

Julia leaned into Octavian, 'How was it really?'

'The Sanhedrin agreed to provide labour for expansion of the docks, in exchange Annius proposed that a percentage of the increase in revenue in the form of a levy, be funnelled back into Tyre's economy.'

'Let me guess,' said Julia, taking a goblet of wine from Asher then handing it to Octavian, 'Annius suggested the Sanhedrin should administer the levy fund.'

'Annius made it sound as if the Sanhedrin were relieving the community of a burden, he thanked them for their service.'

'Are you happy with the Sanhedrin skimming the profits at the expense of those they are supposed to represent?'

'I don't get to be happy or sad about anything that is in the best interest of Rome. It's the cost of getting your census and finding the girl in Magdala.'

'The end justifying the means Octavian?'

'Do you want to find the girl or not? The morals of how you do this are your issue, Julia, not mine.'

'Yes, I have to find Mary, there is no other option. There is too much at stake to fail.'

'Then, as the census in Magdala has already been ordered by Annius, you have answered your own question. The means has justified the end.'

The travellers arrived in Tyre mid-afternoon. Hannah approached a group of women collecting water from a communal well; they were happy to gossip with the young woman from Nazareth. While Hannah gathered intelligence, David and Polykarpos sought out stabling for the animals. They would be an encumbrance if this turned into a drawn out surveillance operation. They returned to the well just as Hannah was bidding a farewell to her new friends.

'What did you find out?' David asked.

'Julia lives in that villa on the hill,' Hannah pointed to the house. 'She has established a homeless shelter for destitute and abused women in Tyre, where she provides food and safety for all those who ask for help. The Praefectus Castrorum is providing guards for the shelter to keep unwanted men away. The women told me that Julia only has women in her household. I got the impression they are as much Julia's bodyguards as servants.'

'Did they say anything about Damian Treffer?'

Hannah nodded.

'I didn't understand exactly what they were saying, but I think the man Damian is at the villa. They were all odd when I asked about him.'

'What exactly did they tell you?'

'They said the Lady Julia came to Tyre with a man called Damian, and that Julia doesn't have men in her household anymore. Then they said the price of a man's betrayal is on display in her cellar.'

'What did they mean by that?' asked Polykarpos.

'They said Damian was a man you could not leave alone with your mother or daughter, but he wasn't that man anymore.'

'Is Treffer dead?' asked David.

'No, I don't think so. They said Julia and the Praefectus Castrorum are lovers, so Julia no longer needs a man in her household to protect her. I asked if Octavian had taken Damian's head. They laughed and said it wasn't his head and it wasn't Octavian. They talked as if Julia is an angel sent to protect the women of Tyre.'

'Julia stabbed Jen in the back with a knife, then she smashed the handle into her head and followed up by kicking her while she was bleeding on the floor. Does that sound like the actions of an angel?'

'No,' said Hannah quietly.

'Maybe this Julia is the jackal, and Damian the lamb?' suggested Polykarpos.

'You might be right,' said David. 'Octavian has power and resources at his disposal. Julia may have side-lined Treffer for a better offer. If Julia is the brains behind this caper, it's probably what she did to Treffer to gain access to the *Cabinet*.'

David turned his attention back to Hannah.

'What else did the women tell you, there was a lot of laughing going on.'

Hannah could have taken offense at the insinuation that she had behaved like a yenta but chose to ignore it.

'Well, David, my new girlfriends told me about a big party in town tonight, which I think it might be of interest.'

Charlene's team arrived an hour after David's.

'This is nice,' said Adrian looking towards the Mediterranean. 'You know, I have been to Tyre before,' he said, looking for landmarks he could recognise.

'Has it changed much?' asked Will.

'There is definitely less traffic and jet skis on the water than I recall. There are also more donkeys.'

'Where do the wealthy people live?' asked Charlene. 'I can't imagine our fugitives have come here to live in the slums.'

Peter pointed to higher ground, south of the causeway, that joined the island port to the mainland.

'The villas of the wealthy are on that hill. The Roman Governor of Tyre lives there,' said Peter pointing to a large structure north of their position.

'Ok, let's start making inquiries to see if any of the locals have heard of a Damian Treffer or a Julia Howard. You never know, we might get lucky.'

'I may be able to help,' said Peter reluctantly.

'How?' asked Charlene.

Peter hesitated, 'Some graduates from the academy of Polykarpos find work with the Romans.'

'I thought you and this Polykarpos bloke were dead against the Romans?' asked Will.

'That is true.'

'But some of your mates are happy to work for them?' queried Will affronted by the idea. 'Isn't that a bit like working as a contractor for the Nazis to build a holiday resort at Auschwitz in 1940?'

'Peter won't get the reference,' said Charlene, placing a hand on Will's arm. 'You have a contact who could help us?'

Peter hesitated, 'If the Romans knew we have a man inside their organisation...'

'Are we talking about a spy?' asked Adrian loudly.

Charlene fixed Adrian with a glare.

'Sorry, mum's the word, Sergeant Wilson,' replied Adrian, realising his mistake. 'I will take my pony to the water trough and leave you to continue your discussion of,' Adrian mouthed the word, *espionage*, 'amongst yourselves.'

'My horse needs a drink too,' said Will following Adrian.

Charlene turned to Peter.

'The people David is hunting, can do more harm to your people than the Romans ever will.'

Peter sighed in resignation.

'His name is Asher; he is 16 years old and works for the Praefectus Castrorum as his personal servant.'

'Will he help us?'

'Yes, if I ask,' said Peter sadly. 'I will put Asher's life in peril because of what you tell me of the woman who now shares Octavian's bed.'

Annius and Octavian waited at the top of the steps to welcome the important guests to the feast. The less privileged were directed to the stables where the centurio, who commanded the city guard, would act as host.

Julia provided Octavian with a reassuring smile, then shook her body as if warming up for a morning run. Octavian turned to face the first of the arriving dignitaries.

'I hate these occasions,' said Annius. 'I should have followed my brother and joined the legions.'

'That would have been Rome's loss, Prefectus,' replied Octavian, smiling at the approaching Philip, the Tetrarch of Iturea and Trachonitis, and half-brother of Herod Antipas, the Tetrarch of Galilee and Peranea.

'I suspect it would have been less hazardous. In my profession, it is difficult to tell your enemies from your friends. Take Philip, educated in Rome with powerful friends, a favourable family line and no future other than to attend events such as ours on behalf of his brother. You may think Philip is here on behalf of his people. That, of course is not the real reason. He is here for politics and politics alone.'

'I would have thought that was obvious, Prefectus.'

'That, Octavian, is why you should remain a soldier and I a politician. Philip is here because he wants to ingratiate himself with Tiberius' representatives in Galilee. He would like us to view him as a viable alternative to his half-brother.'

'Is Philip a threat to Rome?'

'All men within reach of power should be considered dangerous Octavian.' Philip was now only a step away. '*Shalom* Philip, son of Herod.'

'*Ave*, Annius Rufus, Prefectus of Samaria and Judea,' replied Philip with a bow.

'You are most welcome, my friend.'

'And I am humbled by the invitation, Annius,' replied Philip with a smile. 'I take it that you are our host, the Praefectus Castrorum?'

'You are most welcome in my home,' replied Octavian bowing.

'Please go through to the banquet, Philip,' said Annius. 'We will have ample opportunity to talk shortly.'

'Of course, Annius,' replied Philip. 'I promise not to bore you with my views of how I wish the world was, provided you introduce me to your friend.'

Octavian swung to where Philip's eyes were focused.

'May I introduce the Lady Julia.'

Philip bowed at the waist.

'The rumours of your beauty were not exaggerated, Lady Julia. It is an affront to the relationship between Rome and my people that you were not first in line to greet the guests.'

Julia curtseyed.

'My place is to stand behind the men of importance, to serve them and Rome as best I can.'

'The right words, at the right time. I see why Octavian seeks your friendship.'

'You are too kind, your Highness.'

'Will you be sitting to my left, Julia?'

'If you wish, with the agreement of Annius.'

'I would be happy for you to entertain Philip, though it would be more prudent to ask Octavian's permission, rather than mine.'

Phillip turned to Octavian.

'Do I have permission to share the companionship and conversation of your lady over dinner, Praefectus Castrorum?'

'Julia does not need my permission on any matter that is not within the realm of my obligations as a soldier of Rome,' replied Octavian.

Philip smiled, 'If this is the level of diplomacy that you display with your lover's feelings, Jehovah help my brother in his negotiations with you.'

'I meant no offence, your Highness.'

'None taken on my behalf, I was thinking of the Lady Julia's feelings.'

'Octavian and I understand each other perfectly,' replied Julia. 'There was no offence in my dear Octavian's words. That's how successful partnerships work, through honesty and directness. I wouldn't want it any other way.'

Philip nodded at Julia's words.

'I think Rome would be better served if you took your place at the front of the line, Lady Julia, rather than hiding your diplomatic skills in the background.'

'I am but a woman,' replied Julia putting her arm through Philip's to lead him to the dining room, 'our time at the front of the line has yet to come.'

David used his glasses to observe the women hustling to and from Julia's villa.

'I think you will fit in better in the blue dress that Lydia gave you,' said David. 'I know I shouldn't be asking you to wear it, you can say "no" if you don't want to.'

'It's just a dress, besides I think I look good in it.'

'Yes, you do, Hannah,' said David quietly.

Hannah felt herself blush.

'Turn your back. Even a real *erusin* shouldn't see his bride-to-be in her underwear before the wedding night.'

Now it was David's turn to blush. There was a rustle of cloth as Hannah dressed in the blue gown.

'How do I look?'

'Like Aphrodite,' said Polykarpos.

'Seriously, how do I look?' Hannah asked looking at David.

'Good, you will fit right in.'

'Ignore David, you look beautiful Hannah,' said Polykarpos.

'We're on,' said David abruptly.

Hannah nodded, then walked off to join the 20 or so women dressed in colourful gowns, assembling in front of the villa.

'Be careful,' said David in Hannah's earpiece. 'Remember, have a quick look at the building layout then get out.'

'Don't worry, nobody will even notice I am anything other than another servant girl.'

'I didn't mean it like that.'

'I better stop talking,' replied Hannah.

'My name is Atarah; I am the head of Julia's household staff. Thank you for arriving on time, and for wearing the dresses supplied for tonight, which Julia wishes you to keep as a gift, along with a gold aureus for your labours.'

This brought about surprise and joy from the assembled women. Atarah raised a hand for silence.

'I will explain the rules for tonight, they are simple. It is your task to carry food and drink from the kitchen of the Lady Julia's home to the tables at the Praefectus Castrorum's stables, where you will serve the food and drink, remove plates and uneaten meals, with the permission of the guests, and withdraw. You are not to engage with the guests other than with what is required to serve at the tables. Any offence against your dignity will be dealt with severely. The Praefectus Castrorum's soldiers have been directed to intervene the moment any man even thinks of touching you or talking to you in an inappropriate manner. Is that clearly understood?'

'Yes, Atarah,' replied one of the women.

'Is that clearly understood?'

'Yes, Atarah,' replied all the women.

'Good, now follow me inside.'

David removed his earpiece, then indicated for Polykarpos to do the same.

'If this goes wrong, if Hannah is discovered, your job is to retrieve the horses, then get Hannah away from Tyre, is that clear?'

Polykarpos nodded in understanding.

'You will not be coming with us?'

'It depends on what happens. If you or Hannah's safety is compromised, that changes the mission focus. If you are safe, I can finish what I started because it will only be my head on the chopping block.'

'I will see Hannah home to her family, that is my sacred vow.'

David gripped Polykarpos by the hand.

'Thank you Polykarpos, I am in your debt.'

'We are *mishpacha*, David, there is no greater bond.'

David released Polykarpos's hand.

'I think your niece might want us covering her backside again.'

David replaced his earpiece. Atarah was speaking to Hannah.

'I don't know you, did Sapphira ask you to help?'

'Yes, Sapphira did,' replied Hannah cautiously.

'Are you new to Tyre?'

'Yes I am.'

'What's your name?'

'I am Hannah, the daughter of Joachim and Anne from Nazareth. My uncle has brought me to Tyre to find a husband before I turn into an old crone who no man will want. I would rather that happens than to be forced to marry a man I couldn't respect.'

Atarah nodded in understanding.

'I am a widow; my husband was a good man; we had a happy marriage.'

'If I was to be honest, Atarah, I can't see myself sharing a life with any man, not that I haven't been asked. There is a fisherman who has been particularly attentive, but so have the flies that follow his every move, and there is no way I am sharing a bed with somebody that smells like a four-day old herring left in the sun.'

Atarah smiled, 'Nor should any woman, Hannah. Your father doesn't understand?'

'Joachim of Nazareth is not amused,' replied Hannah with a smile. 'Which is why dear father asked my uncle to find me a match in Tyre.'

'How is your uncle progressing in his task?'

'I am not currently encumbered with an *erusin* so I thought that while I am waiting, I might as well earn a few extra shekels for my purse. I would like to keep my financial independence for as long as I can.'

'I only wish more girls were as sensible,' replied Atarah. 'Good luck with your uncle and thank you for helping tonight.'

There was a pause in the conversation as Atarah could be heard giving instructions to the other women before returning to Hannah.

'Please come with me, Hannah.'

David could hear Hannah was walking, the sound of voices reduced in the background.

'Could you take this barrel of beer to the stables? If it's too heavy one of the other women can help you.'

'No, it's not too heavy.'

'Thank you, Hannah, I am glad of your help.'

'I am glad of the opportunity.'

David could hear liquid moving as Hannah picked up the barrel.

'If it doesn't work out with your uncle, the Lady Julia is always looking for intelligent women to join her staff.'

'I will keep that in mind.'

'If you want to talk about a position, come and see me, but now I had best make sure the rolls arrive while they are still warm.'

David could hear the sound of receding footsteps.

'Atarah has gone David.'

'Where are you?'

'In the larder behind the kitchen.'

David heard a thump as Hannah had put the barrel down.

'Can you see where the bedrooms are located?'

'There is a passage behind the kitchen, I can see where it goes.'

'Is it safe?'

'I don't think there is anybody in the back of the villa.'

'Take the barrel with you. If somebody comes, wave it around and say you got lost.'

'If that doesn't work, I will say *goat shit*. That can be the signal to come and get me.'

'All right, goat shit means you need help.'

David pulled a note pad and pencil from his bag to sketch a basic outline of the villa. 'Tell me what you see Hannah, explain the room layout.'

'The kitchen is to the right of the entrance hall. It's 10 paces long and five paces wide. The longest side runs towards the rear of the villa.'

David added to his drawing, 'How many doors?'

'One from the entrance hall, one leading to the larder and the passage behind the kitchen.'

'How big is the larder?'

'It's three paces wide and the length of the kitchen.'

'Does it have an exit out of the villa?'

'No, it only has a door to the kitchen, and a door to the passage.'

'Okay, hold your breath and listen. If you hear anybody in the passage, leave.'

Hannah held her breath, all she could hear was the beating of her heart.

'I am going into the passage.'

'Tell me what you see.'

'There are four doors on the left of the passage and one on the right at the far end.' Hannah hefted the barrel, striding the passage as if she belonged.

'The first door leads into a big room; my parent's house would fit inside it. How wealthy are these people?'

'It's not their wealth. They stole the coins to pay for all of this when they stabbed Jen.'

'I'm sorry,' said Hannah, 'I don't think I really understood until now.'

'Describe the room.'

Hannah stepped into the room and slid behind the door to hide.

'There are two seats in the middle of the room facing each other with a table between. There is another table with one chair at the back of the room with a cupboard filled with scrolls behind it. The room is eight or ten or paces deep and there is a door leading to the entrance hall. I can see women coming out of the kitchen.'

'Is there another door?'

'There is one behind the table with the one chair.'

David wrote, *reception room / office* on his plan. Hannah could hear voices coming from the larder.

'Thank Jehovah, this is the last time we have to feed him.'

'I hate going down those steps,' said a second female voice. 'It makes me feel like throwing up when he puts on that voice and that smile, like he is Jehovah's gift to all women.'

'You won't have to look at him after tomorrow, Anna,' replied the first voice.

'I never understood why Julia just didn't finish it when he did that to Sapphira.'

'I wouldn't have just taken his balls, I would have taken everything and let the bastard bleed to death,' replied Anna.

'Let's just get this over with. We still have the lamb to take to Octavian's villa.'

Hannah peered through a gap between the door and the wall. Two women walked past the door; one was carrying a plate of food.

'Hurry up, Ruth,' called the woman with the plate turning to look back towards the larder.

'Don't be impatient, Anna,' called a third female voice. 'If I hurry, the water will spill and somebody will have to mop it up.'

A shadow passed the doorway, Hannah risked a look.

'Why are we giving him water to wash?' asked Susanna. 'I thought, *the great master of the household,* was sold to the games.'

'Julia is still punishing him,' replied Anna. 'Tiberius has banned the gladiatorial games; he thinks the slaves of the empire are more use building roads and aqueducts.'

'Did Julia know?' asked Ruth.

'Yes, she knew. He thinks he is off to Rome to be lion food,' laughed Susanna.

'If he still had balls, they would have shrunk to the size of raisins,' said Ruth.

The women laughed.

'What has he been sold for then?' asked Ruth.

'To work in a stone quarry. Can you imagine him getting his hands dirty?' said Anna.

'Not having his hair brushed,' said Susanna miming brushing her hair.

'Smelling of sweat instead of lavender,' said Anna raising an arm to smell her armpit.

'I hope the bastard dies a broken cripple after the way he threatened Atarah's children,' said Ruth.

Hannah watched the women disappeared into the cellar.

'Did you hear any of that David?'

'Only a few words.'

'I think I have found your Damian Treffer.' David was silent, processing the information. 'The women are coming back.' Hannah hid behind the door.

'I just want him gone,' said Anna with revulsion in her tone.

'You have to give him points for trying,' said Susanna. 'Did you see him giving Ruth the look? Even without his balls he thinks he can have his way with any woman he sees.'

The three women laughed as they exited towards the villa's kitchen. Hannah held her breath and listened. There were no voices, no footsteps.

'I am going to look in the room.'

'Ok, listen at the door. If it's quiet, take a quick look then leave. I want you out of that building in the next few minutes.'

Hannah listened at the door, then lifted the latch. The door moved on well-oiled hinges. She listened again, then pushed the door all the way open. Light from the passage spilled down stone steps. There was a shape in the dark which Hannah couldn't make out.

'Hannah,' said David firmly but calmly in Hannah's ear, 'there are two soldiers approaching the building in a hurry, I want you out now.'

'I'm going.'

Noise, lots of noise from the direction of the larder. There were voices, men and Atarah talking quickly. Hannah peered around the door; Atarah was running to keep up with two legionnaires marching towards the cellar.

'*Goat shit, goat shit, goat shit David,*' whispered Hannah as she closed the cellar door behind herself.

'Polykarpos, go,' said David tightening his grip on his weapon. 'Hannah, where are you?'

'I'm in the cellar,' whispered Hannah, 'the Romans are in the passage.'

'Hide and I will come and get you.'

'Oh, I am definitely going to hide,' said Hannah, moving down the stairs. 'If you don't, you can forget about being my pretend *erusin* ever again.'

'*Hello,*' said a voice in English from the darkness.

Hannah jumped in fright. 'Who's there?'

'*You're new. Welcome.* Shalom. *I don't get many unexpected visitors.*'

Hannah only understood the single word of Hebrew, but the voice sounded friendly.

'That's Damian Treffer,' said David in her ear, 'get out of the room, Hannah.'

'It is him?'

'Yes, that's Treffer.'

'He can't reach me; he's chained to the floor. That's what the women meant about the price of treachery being on display in Julia's cellar.'

'Don't let him touch you.'

'*So, you have heard of me?*' said the voice. '*I am afraid you have me at a disadvantage. Let me introduce myself, I am* Damian, *who might you be?*'

Octavian slid away from the banquet table; Julia turned to see an Immune whispering in Octavian's ear.

'Is there something wrong?'

'Max is here.'

'I thought he was in Nazareth?'

'He was, but now he is here asking to speak with me urgently.' Octavian stood, 'your Highness, Prefectus, I have a small matter requiring my attention.'

'Is it something that I need to be informed of?' asked Annius.

'No, it is a routine matter, but some things are best dealt with immediately.'

'I understand Octavian, go and attend to your duties with my blessing.'

Maximus reported on the events in Nazareth following the capture of the rebels and their leader Polykarpos. The description of the escape of Adrian caused Octavian to furrow his brow in disbelief. Dax then spoke with brevity of the escape of Polykarpos, and a man called David. He reported the death of his fellow guard, then his pursuit to capture the men responsible.

Maximus continued covering what occurred on the Hill of Kedumim, then finding Dax injured and unconscious. When Maximus reported the reaction of his soldiers in Nazareth the following morning, Octavian was surprised, then shocked when Maximus moved on to the encounter at the stables of Simon Iscariot. The description of how he and Dax were attacked by a woman with the power of the wind was brief. Dax lifted the dressing on his face to show his scar. Then Maximus talked of waking hours later and Iscariot blurting out a story claiming his family had been the victims of witchcraft and theft. He swore the two men and the woman had fled north on horses stolen without payment. The description of Aaron of Hebron was remarkably similar to the Jew, Adrian.

Finally, Maximus talked of how he and Dax travelled to Magdala to find the legion post in disorder. The centurio in charge reported two miracles and the chaos that followed. The descriptions of the men involved matched David and the cousin Adrian.

Octavian thanked his friend, then directed Maximus and Dax to go to the stables to be fed. He promised to talk with them again shortly, then sent his Immunes to summon Julia and the centurio in charge of the garrison of Tyre. Octavian directed the centurio to send two of his best men to Julia's villa to secure the slave, Damian of Treffer. Nobody was to be allowed access to the slave without the direct authorisation of Octavian, Centurio Maximus or the Lady Julia. The centurio acknowledged his instructions and left to carry them out.

Octavian wondered if the advantages of having a friend with benefits were about to disappear. The safety of Adalburg and his children could be at risk. It would not give him pleasure to take Julia's head, but he may have no choice.

Charlene marvelled at the technology of Dwight's glasses as she used them to observe the comings and goings at Octavian's villa from a nearby rooftop. Peter was lying next to Charlene, also wearing glasses supplied by Dwight.

'That is the Prefect of Samaria and Judea,' he said, pointing out Annius Rufus. 'I saw him in Magdala once.'

'Who's the soldier next to him?'

'That is Octavian,' replied Peter bitterly.

'I assume the woman in the red is Julia?'

Peter nodded. 'That is the woman David showed us with his picture painted with light.'

Charlene zoomed in the focus. Julia's arms were bare, which probably meant her *Sainter* was secured under lock and key in her home.

'That is Philip, the brother of Herod Antipas,' said Peter in surprise. 'He is the Tetrarch of Iturea and Trachonitis.'

'Is Herod the king who killed all the children?'

Peter was surprised by the question.

'No, he has never slaughtered children. Herod is the Tetrarch Galilee and Perea, which is like a Roman governor. The Romans made him the Tetrarch as compensation for taking his throne. When Herod the Great, the father of Herod Antipas and Philip, died, Augustus divided his kingdom amongst his sons and daughter to weaken their power.'

'Divide and conquer. I had heard it was a Roman invention.'

Charlene resumed her observation; Julia was arm in arm with Philip. It looked like her influence went beyond just being the girlfriend of the local sheriff.

'Will, Doc, did you set eyes on Julia?'

'From here, we could see part of a red dress, but not her face,' replied Will.

'It was definitely Julia?' asked Adrian.

'Yes, Peter confirmed it. let's consider her out of bounds for the moment. If I was David, I would make the same assessment and set up surveillance at her residence. If Cinderella has a big night at this royal event thing and decides not to have a sleep-over with her boyfriend she will head home later tonight. That's where I would be looking to put the cuffs on her. That's where David will be.' Charlene turned to Peter. 'You're up, Pete. Stay outside if you can, we may lose communications inside the building.'

'I will do my best,' replied Peter sliding backwards across the roof.

'Doc, Will, make your way to my position. If we have to move, I don't want us spread out like Brown's cows.'

'Affirmative, Sergeant Wilson, though I have never met Mr Brown's cattle.'

'We're coming,' said Will moving Adrian along.

'Peter,' said Charlene, 'be polite. People are more cooperative if you treat them nice.'

'I will smile, even if it is a Roman who comes to the door.'

'Don't overplay it, just be your happy self.'

Peter approached the villa. The soldier standing guard straightened.

'I am here to see Asher on an urgent matter.'

'What business do you have with the boy?'

'His uncle, a schoolteacher from Nazareth is gravely ill. Asher, as the oldest male relative, must pray the *Kaddish* on the day his uncle dies.'

'Nice act at being happy,' whispered Charlene.

The guard considered the request, 'What's your name?'

'I am Peter of Magdala.'

Peter stood waiting as the guard went to find Asher.

'Come with me,' said the soldier holding the servant's door open.

'Thank you,' said Peter stepping through the entrance. Once the door closed at his back, Peter depressed the on/off button on the earpiece. What he had to discuss with Asher should be for their ears only.

Asher hid his surprise when Peter entered his room.

'*Shalom,* Peter, you have news of my uncle?'

'Sadly, yes,' Peter replied dropping his head. 'Your uncle Polykarpos is on his death bed.'

The guard closed the door to give Asher privacy.

Asher put a finger to his lips, then pressed an ear against the door to check the guard was not listening.

'I thought Polykarpos was dead. Octavian told Julia that Polykarpos and somebody called David had been taken care of.'

'They escaped; I believe they are here in Tyre.'

'If the Romans capture Polykarpos they will torture him for the names of all of us in the resistance. He was better off dead once the Romans knew who he was. Now he is a liability.'

'Agreed, but Polykarpos is alive, and in Tyre with David.'

'Who is this David? I hadn't heard of him until Julia and Octavian made plans to have him killed.'

'I don't know how to explain it, but Polykarpos believes David is important to the resistance. He has knowledge and access to weapons that could help us in our fight. Polykarpos wants to use David to rally people to the cause.'

'Why does Julia want this David dead?'

'It's a blood feud. Julia stabbed a woman who is important to David. He is here to take her and the man, Damian of Treffer, home to face punishment for this crime.'

Asher shook his head at the absurdity.

'Octavian will kill any man who tries to harm her.'

'If you had seen the weapons, the tools that David and the others from the land of Warn Am Bool have, you would not think that way. I saw David raise a man from the dead with my own eyes. He has a weapon that uses the power of the wind to smite his enemies.' Peter removed his earpiece and showed it to Asher. 'This lets me hear the words of others from a thousand paces as if they were whispered in my ear.' Peter turned the radio on and placed it alongside Asher's ear. 'Sergeant Wilson?'

'I can hear you, Peter, we lost communications for a while.'

'Can you speak with Asher, Sergeant Wilson? Explain to him what you need?'

There was silence for a moment.

'Okay, give him the earpiece.' Peter placed the device in Asher's ear. 'Hello Asher, this may seem strange, but it's not magic, it's just a tool.'

'I have seen this before. The Lady Julia used something the same to listen to Octavian and Annius Rufus. I thought it was witchcraft.'

'It's not. There is no magic involved.'

Asher fell silent, then asked the obvious question, 'Why do you hunt Julia?'

'Straight to the point, I like that. To put it simply, Julia is evil. She has travelled to your land to gain influence and power, which is why she has become friends with Octavian. She doesn't care who she kills to get what she wants and can do more harm to your people than the Romans ever could.'

'What do you want me to do?'

'We need to know where Julia lives, the layout of her home and what the security is in place.' Asher handed the earpiece to Peter. 'Julia is a threat to the resistance; she ordered Octavian to capture Polykarpos.'

'And she would have killed all the members of the resistance in Nazareth if David hadn't saved our lives,' said Peter.

'I will take you to the villa of the Lady Julia, I know where Damian is and how to get to him,' said Asher.

'Did you hear that, Sergeant Wilson?'

'Yes, I did, well done mate. We'll make contact when I see you back on the street.'

Peter turned off the earpiece.

'She can't hear what I am about to say. Polykarpos tricked David into performing a miracle at Magdala; he knew about the woodcutter's father dying from a bee sting. Polykarpos caught a bee in the wildflowers and slipped it into Timothy's robes while he was pretending to ask directions.'

'Why are you telling me this?'

'Because Polykarpos wants a bloodbath. He wants David to fight the

Romans with his technology and if he dies, he becomes a miracle-performing martyr for our people to rally behind.'

'I thought Polykarpos was planning that for Joseph's son?'

'Yes, but David is here now and the boy won't be ready for years.'

'Polykarpos has lost his way,' said Asher shaking his head. 'We can't beat the Romans in a war, we have to be smarter than that if we want their empire to collapse.'

'I agree. We need to kill their gods and replace them with one of our own making, then we can control what they believe and how they behave.'

Asher nodded. If Polykarpos was no longer the right man to lead, then Peter was the next logical choice.

'What do we do?'

'We help these people from Warn Am Bool, then carry out our plan without the threat of the Julia hanging over our heads.'

Sapphira heard all of this from her hiding spot. Asher's betrayal was complete. She waited for Asher and the man Peter to pass, then followed them.

*'I am* Damian, *who might you be?'*

'He's looking at me strangely, David. He thinks I am talking to him.'

'If it stops him from calling for help, talk to him.'

Damian looked up the steps.

*'If you expect me to pretend that you don't exist while you hide in my prison you should at least tell me your name.'*

'Tell him your name, Hannah.'

'I am Hannah' said Hannah, pointing at herself.

*'Nice to meet you,* Hannah.'

'Smile and pretend you are a shy girl who is afraid to talk.'

Hannah looked directly into Damian eyes, then looked away as if embarrassed.

*'Perhaps we can get to know each other, I have nothing much else planned for today.'*

'Come and get me, he makes my skin crawl,' said Hannah in a timid voice while looking at Damian.'

*'If only we could understand each other, though, sometimes words just get in the way.'*

The door opened. Light ran down the steps, illuminating Damian. A soldier clanked down the stairs to inspect him.

'*You're a little early, I have this room booked until tomorrow morning.*'

The legionnaire gripped the chain attached to Damian's leg and pulled it to ensure it was secure.

'*Don't worry, I won't be stealing the towels when I leave, I will want my room deposit back.*'

'The eunuch isn't going anywhere,' the soldier said to his companion at the top of the steps before using his gladius to push Damian's clothing aside. 'She did a good job of cutting his balls off. Most men his age would have died.'

'*So, the rumours about you Romans are true,*' said Damian. '*Sorry, but I still like women, even with my minor setback.*'

'Come back up, we can keep watch from up here until we are relieved. Julia's women might even bring us some of that food they are carting about.'

'Not if Atarah has anything to do with it. It's no wonder her husband died; I would lean on my sword if I had to put up with her every day.'

The soldier ascended the steps, the door slammed shut and the room plunged into darkness.

'Stay out of his reach, I will come to you,' instructed David.

'I wouldn't let that thing touch me if my choice was crucifixion or marriage to him.'

'*It would be easier to talk if we could see each other, there's a lamp on a table behind you.*'

'There is a lamp behind you,' interpreted David. 'See if you can work out how Treffer is secured.'

Hannah found the lamp, a flint and a small steel blade, by feeling in the dark. She held the flint against the wick of the lamp, then struck it repeatedly with the knife until the sparks ignited the oil.

'*I am beginning to believe you might be able to understand me,*' said Damian in surprise. '*You are prettier than I first thought. Red hair doesn't normally do anything for me, but it suits you.*'

'What can you see?' asked David.

'There's no windows, just the one door. His chain is bolted to the floor. It looks very solid.'

'How is it secured to him?'

Hannah raised the lamp.

'There are two iron half circles around his ankle, secured with a lock on one side and an iron rivet on the other. The chain is hooked through the hasp of the lock.'

*'Who are you talking to Hannah? You are not one of Atarah's girls, maybe I should ask our Italian friends to come back?'* Damian pointed to the cellar door. *'I don't think you want the Romans to find you, in which case, you should at least pay rent if you want to share my room.'* Damian stepped out of his robes to stand naked in front of Hannah, picked up the sponge, dipped it in the bucket of water and indicated for Hannah to take it and wash his body.

'He wants me to wash him, with a sponge,' said Hannah in disgust. 'He is standing here naked and bits of him look very excited to see me.'

'Don't go near him, it's a trick.'

'I know it's a trick, the problem is, he is going to call the Romans.'

'Show him your earpiece.'

Hannah removed the device and held it in the light. Damian dropped the sponge then stepped towards Hannah with his hand extended.

*'Where did a nice girl like you, get something like that?'* Hannah replaced the radio earpiece covering it with her hair. *'Who's with you, Hannah?'*

'Say my name, my whole name, Hannah.'

'David Thomas, *of* Warn Am Bool,' said Hannah defiantly.

*'Really? Ask David if he gave my regards to his mother, like I asked?'*

'Don't answer that.'

'Answer what? I don't understand what he's saying.'

*'I will take that as a "no",'* said Damian putting his clothes back on. *'Julia said you would come. She also said Octavian would deal with you. Obviously, that didn't work out as planned.'*

'Toss him the earpiece, don't let him touch you.'

Hannah tossed the earpiece underarm to Damian.

*'Thank you,* Hannah. *I was enjoying our little chat.'*

'Shut up and listen,' said David. 'If you want to live and get home for medical treatment you need to cooperate.'

'And, if I don't?'

'I have no problem in rescuing Hannah and leaving you behind in the shit. It's Julia I came for; she used the knife, you're just a bonus if I feel like taking you with me.'

'Point taken.'

'Where are the recall devices?'

'Well, I obviously don't have them.'

'Are they in this building?'

'Maybe.'

'I need better than a maybe.'

'Then I have some leverage, after all. Perhaps we could negotiate where you take me. I am thinking the south of France in the 1960s. I could see myself making quite a good life amongst the wealthy widows and bored English housewives on the Riviera.'

'No.'

'I don't think you have come all this way, at great risk to the Thomas family reputation, to fail because you won't negotiate with me. I know Julia's secrets; the question is what is it worth to you?'

'Give the earpiece to Hannah.'

'Why?'

'Because in about a minute, the guards outside your door will be unconscious and very upset when they wake up and who do you think they are going to take their anger out on?'

'Are you sure that you are Dwight's son and not Gerald's?'

'Give the earpiece to Hannah or you can say goodbye to ever getting home.'

'Julia will have them with her,' said Damian quickly. 'She had a body belt made to hold hers. She took mine the night her bitches locked me in this room.'

David was quiet, thinking. 'Where is the key to your chain?'

'On a leather thong around Atarah's neck. Good luck getting it from her.'

'All right, I'm inclined to take you home, provided you follow my orders to the letter.'

'I understand, Officer Thomas.'

'I need you and Hannah to stay where you are until I come for you. Is that understood?'

'Yes.'

'You can hand the earpiece to Hannah now.' Damian put his hand to the earpiece. 'And Damian.'

'Yes, Officer Thomas.'

'If you touch Hannah, I will cut the rest of your pride and joy off and let you bleed to death, is that understood?'

Octavian had just finished briefing his men when he saw Julia approaching.

'Is something wrong?'

'David is believed to be in Tyre.'

'How is that possible? You told me that issue had been taken care of.'

'It had, then something went wrong.'

'What went wrong?'

'David escaped from the prison transport on the road from Nazareth to Tyre.'

Julia looked angrily at her business partner.

'We had an agreement, I provided you with information and working capital for our business arrangement, in exchange you undertook to take care of David.'

'It will be taken care of,' replied Octavian changing his tone to one of annoyance. 'Two of my best men are guarding Damian and I have issued orders to seal the town gates and increase patrols on the walls. Nobody is getting in or out of Tyre unless I say so. Then tomorrow when Annius Rufus has departed, my men will conduct a house-to-house search. This David will be found and I will present you with his head.'

'I wanted this taken care of two days ago.'

'I understand that, Julia. I also know you didn't tell me how dangerous this David is. Max reported he was responsible for a riot in Magdala and the desertion of the garrison in Nazareth.'

Julia breathed out in frustration, 'I should have insisted you kill him on sight. I admit it was an error, not one I will repeat.'

'We agreed to be honest with each other, Julia. If you knew this man David was a threat to the empire, you should have told me.'

'David is only a threat to me, not a danger to Rome. I'm sorry, Octavian; I should have warned you what to expect.'

'And I should have doubled the guard on the transport. We will kill this David and everybody associated with him tomorrow and end it.'

'It won't be that simple. If you confront him head on with a show of force and he uses his weapon, it won't only be your soldiers in Nazareth running scared of what looks like witchcraft.'

'What do you suggest then?'

'Don't seal the city, don't do anything outside of the normal. David would have already figured out that I am too well protected, but I am not the only person he is looking for.'

'You want to use your slave as bait?'

'Yes, and if I can borrow Max and one or two of your men, I can sort this problem out myself while you return to your duties. Annius will be wondering where you are.'

Will was tail on to Charlene, watching their backs.

'Wait. Something's happening.'

Charlene crawled back to Will's position. 'What is it?'

'Two soldiers in a hurry.'

'Why only two? If David had made a move, I would use overwhelming force?'

'Here comes Pete, there's somebody with him.'

'That's our guide, let's get down to the street.' Charlene shuffled backwards. 'Hang on to your tasers from now on. It's about to get interesting.'

Sapphira waited until Asher and Peter crossed the street before moving to follow them. Once Asher was inside Julia's home, he would have nowhere to hide.

Julia watched Maximus approach. He reminded her of any number of family photos in the display cabinet at her parent's home, the archetype career soldier. Accompanying Max was a short legionnaire whose nose had been recently broken, eyes blackened and face scarred. Despite the injuries, the man's eyes were bright and focused.

'Ave, Maximus,' said Julia, placing a kiss of familiarity on his cheek.

'Ave, Lady Julia,' replied Maximus, feeling uncomfortable with the affectionate greeting of a woman pretending to be Octavian's lover. 'This is Dax.'

'Hello Dax, you look like you have been in the wars.'

'I am a veteran of many campaigns,' Dax replied in a deadpan manner.

'I am pleased to hear you say that,' replied Julia continuing to smile. She then addressed Maximus, 'I know about Adalburg and the children, I am helping Octavian to keep them safe and in exchange, Octavian has asked you to help me.'

Maximus locked his gaze on Julia.

'If this is for Adalburg, then my sword is yours to direct.'

'Thank you, Maximus, thank you, Dax,' replied Julia, not wanting to laugh at the absurdity of having such a mismatched pair called Max and Dax at her service.

David was waiting for Polykarpos to return before making his next move. He knew where Damian, Julia and the recall devices were located, he just needed to bring them all together.

'Polykarpos?'

Silence.

'Hannah?'

'Yes, I can hear you.'

'Just stay where you are, if anything happens, yell.'

'Don't worry, they will hear me screaming in Nazareth, and David, I called goat shit, and I meant it.'

Charlene watched Peter and Asher's approach.

'Keep walking Peter, we'll follow when we're happy nobody is on your tail.'

Peter slowed, then resumed his normal stride. Will spotted Sapphira first.

'They're being followed.'

Charlene pressed back into the shadows.

'Are you sure?'

'Yes, it's a teenage girl dressed like the women carrying food to the party.'

'This is getting exciting,' whispered Adrian. 'It's like the spy scenarios customers play out at the costumery, only not in Fedora hats and trench coats obviously.'

Charlene made a change of plan.

'Follow the girl, Will. We'll keep an eye on Peter from the next street over, that way she shouldn't see us and we won't look like a gang of muggers stalking Peter.'

'No worries.'

'And Will, if there is any risk of us being compromised by the girl, don't hesitate to take her out of the picture with your taser,' instructed Charlene.

'Ok, but I won't hurt her if I don't have to.'

Will's *W* senses made him pause before following Sapphira, then he heard the footsteps of Maximus and Dax on the cobblestone street.

'Remember the two blokes from the gun fight at the OK Corral?'

'Yes.' Charlene was obviously not happy about the question.

'Well, they're on the street out the front of Octavian's place.'

'Where are Holliday and Earp up to?'

'Who?' queried Adrian.

'I'll explain later, Doc. Will, are they following Peter?'

'No, they're heading towards the sea.'

'Okay, let them move off to a safe distance, then follow the girl.'

'Wait,' said Will. He could hear female voices laughing. A woman in a red dress came into view, surrounded by six, no seven, other women in brightly coloured garments.

Julia was prettier than Will imagined a violent criminal should be. He found this hard to reconcile with what his head told him about this woman, laughing with her friends, then he looked at her wrists.

'Another eight women following Peter,' reported Will, 'one is wearing a red dress.'

'Do you think it's Julia,' asked Charlene.

'It's her. She's wearing two *Sainters*.'

'Safety first,' replied Charlene dryly. 'She knows cousin David is here. So much for the element of surprise.'

Charlene and Adrian shadowed Peter until he and Asher arrived across the street from Julia's villa. She could see their heat signatures in the dark and a third heat signature of a body hiding in shadow, observing the entrance of a Julia's villa.

'Peter, can you and your mate disappear? I need you to walk away and take your female fan out of the picture. Go back to the horses, find a spot to hide and wait. Do you understand?'

There was a cough in the earpieces. Charlene watched as two heat signatures moved away. Moments later, the figure of a girl emerged on the street. She moved to follow Peter, then stopped as the sound of massed female voices could be heard approaching. The girl turned and ran towards the noise.

'Not quite how I thought it would go, but it will do,' Charlene said to herself

'Do you have any orders for me, Sergeant Wilson?' asked Adrian in a whisper.

Charlene handing the night vision glasses to Adrian, then pointed towards a building 30 metres away.

'Yes, you can introduce me to your cousin.'

'It's Asher,' Sapphira blurted out. 'He lied to me; he tricked me. I heard him plotting against you with a man named Peter. I followed them and now they are getting away,' said Sapphira with tears in her eyes as she pointed in the direction where Peter and Asher had fled.

'Don't look,' commanded Julia, 'don't anyone turn your head to look. Go to the kitchen, collect the cakes and take them to the feast.'

'I was trying to protect you, Julia.'

'It's alright, Sapphira, you've done nothing wrong.' Julia placed a reassuring hand on the girl's cheek. 'Come inside and tell me what you overheard, and don't worry about Asher, I won't let any man hurt one of my girls ever again.'

Adrian approached the building where David was concealed and began to urinate on the street.

'David, its Adrian.'

'I know, just be careful where you are pointing that.'

'Sorry, I am trying to look inconspicuous.'

'Why are you here?' whispered David.

'To rescue you, of course. Uncle Dwight provided the last of his *Sainters* so you could come home.' Adrian pointed to his wrist. 'We are calling these *Sainters* if you were wondering what I was referring to.'

'Dad is involved?! Shit Adrian, when you got home you should have stayed there, it's too dangerous.'

'Was it too dangerous when you tricked me into helping you?' whispered Adrian.

'I'm sorry, I didn't think I had a choice. I never intended putting you in danger.'

'I know about Jenifer Rostig, I can imagine how I would feel, if I were you,' Adrian paused, 'I was going to give you a telling off, but I can't, not now. As our great ancestor Colin Thomas said, *you will do anything for your family, because they are your family and so you must.*'

'Who's Colin Thomas?'

'Will's father.'

'Who's Will?'

'I'll explain later. Right now, you need to come with me. Julia will be here in a minute and Sergeant Wilson wants to discuss tactics.'

Sapphira collected a box from beside Julia's bed. Inside resided the knife that once belonged to Cynthia Horrigan and a second much-prized family heirloom.

'Is this what you wanted?'

'Thank you,' said Julia removing both objects from the box. The knife went into the sash at her waist. The second object was checked with swift hand movements and mechanical clicks, then slipped into the sash behind her back.

'Ask Atarah to come and see me, please.' Julia said, giving Sapphira a smile.

'Yes, Lady Julia,' replied the teenager hurrying away into the depths of the villa.

'You can come out now.' Maximus emerged from a cloak room on the side of the entrance hall, his gladius in his right hand, his pugio in his left. 'Where's your friend?'

Dax emerged from the door that led to Julia's sitting room. He held a bow with an arrow notched in its string.

'Are you going to be able to use that in my home?'

'An arrow through the neck is as effective at five paces as it is at 50,' answered Maximus.

'Good,' said Julia with a nod. 'Then if you two gentlemen are happy, I will get into position and wait.'

Maximus, then Dax, stepped back into the shadows to wait.

'This is my cousin David,' said Adrian, 'David, this is our team leader, Sergeant Wilson.'

'I prefer Charlene, and it's Brevet Sergeant from SAPOL in 1987, not the Salvos,' added Charlene extending a hand. David took Charlene's hand.

'I know I should ask questions, but I am not going to. I am pleased to meet you, Charlene.'

'This is Will,' said Charlene. 'Will's not a cop, but he's brilliant at covert surveillance and spotting trouble before it happens. I can't think of a better man to have backing us up.'

Will extended his hand.

'Nice to finally meet you, I have been waiting for this moment since I was 14.'

'Fourteen?'

'Yep, ever since the day Adrian turned my family's life upside down.'

David looked at Adrian.

'Will is our great, great, great grandfather, or uncle, we're not really sure.'

'Of course, he is,' replied David. 'Who else would Dad and Emil send but another relative?'

'You're not going to get all bent out of shape are you, Dave?' asked Charlene. 'Will and I might not be from the Flash Gordon Police Academy of the future, but Will can handle any sort of shit that comes his way and I'm a bloody good cop with advanced weapons and tactical training, and we saved your arse in Magdala. If I were you, I would be handing out flowers and chocolates, not looking like you just found out your best mate is bonking your girlfriend.'

'I'm sorry, I just don't want to get anybody killed. It's bad enough that I dragged Adrian and Emil into this mess, and now all of you as well.'

'I could have stayed at home,' said Will. 'but I chose to come and make a difference, Dave. I am doing this to keep my family safe, the same as you are. If it goes wrong, if I stuff this up, it's on me, not you.'

David nodded in understanding.

'I am here because a crim stuck a knife into a copper doing her job,' stated Charlene. 'That can't go unpunished, no matter how far they run or where they hide. Is that fair enough?'

'Yes, it is,' said David extending his hand to Charlene and Will again.

'Good, now that everybody has finished being knobs, you can brief us on the plan.'

'Yes, I can hear you,' replied Hannah.

*'Tell David to hurry up, I doubt* Julia *is sitting around waiting for him to make the first move.'*

'Shut up, I am trying to hear what David is saying.'

*'I don't know what you said, but that sounded bitchy to me.'*

'We're coming to get you. There will be lots of noise but just stay where you are,' said David.

'Don't worry, I'm not going anywhere. And just in case you forget David, I called goat shit.'

David changed to the earpiece in his right earpiece and spoke again, 'Will, are you in position?'

'Yes.'

'Adrian?'

'That would be an affirmative,' replied Adrian from his position behind the villa.

'I'll try Polykarpos again, he should have been back by now.'

'And I'll try Peter just to make sure he's safe,' said Charlene.

'Peter?' asked David.

'Yep, a big bloke, smells like a tuna sandwich on a 40-degree day. He has a thing, which borders on stalking, for Mary's sister and is connected to a teenager named Asher who works for Julia's boyfriend Octavian. The plan was to use Asher to provide intel on Julia's security arrangements. Peter and the kid picked up a tail from Octavian's place, so I diverted him away, which is a good thing, grandfather paradoxically speaking,' said Charlene.

'I don't follow?'

'You do know who Peter probably is?'

'A fisherman who fancies himself as a sort of local resistance leader.'

'You and Adrian really are cousins, aren't you!'

'Am I missing something?'

'No, it's probably crap. We can talk about it over a beer when we get home.'

Polykarpos approached the sentry at the stables of the Praefectus Castrorum.

'I need to speak with the guard commander.'

'Go away, Grandfather, come back tomorrow.'

'It cannot wait.'

'I say it can, old man. Come back tomorrow.'

'There is going to be a rebel attack in Tyre tonight.'

The sentry looked Polykarpos up and down.

'Are you telling the truth, Grandfather? If you are telling tales walk away while I am still feeling good about you.'

'It's happening tonight, the commander of the guard must be told.'

The sentry sighed, 'All right, I will ask the centurio to talk with you. If you are lying, it could cost your head, you do understand that?'

'Yes, I understand and so must the centurio, there is not much time.'

David walked up the steps of Julia's villa. Charlene followed; the butt of her weapon tucked firmly into her shoulder. David stepped to the right of the entrance, Charlene to the left. David counted to three, then moved through the door sticking to the right, Charlene followed on the left. Their weapons travelled an arc from left to right, then right to left covering standing, squatting, and ceiling heights. The room was empty.

David moved to the door of the kitchen on the right of the hall. Charlene went left, David right. Charlene placed her back against the wall and aimed her weapon at the door from the entrance hall to Julia's office cum reception room. Her job was to cover David's back. David knelt beside the door, held his breath and listened. There was the sound of movement on the far side of the door. A person was lying in wait, probably hard up against the wall beside the doorframe.

'I can hear you behind the door,' said David calmly. 'We are here for Julia Howard and Damian Treffer, to take them home to be tried for the crimes they have committed.' David paused, 'I will give you until I count to three to put your weapons on the floor and move away from the door. If you don't do as I say, you may be harmed.'

'Take the door off the hinges on my count,' said David shifting focus to the entrance of Julia's reception room, which was the logical place for a second assailant to be hiding.

Charlene aimed at the centre of the wooden door and waited.

'One, two, three.'

Charlene fired. The door to the kitchen blew inwards dragging the hinge side of the door frame with it.

Something red moved across the doorway to Julia's study. David fired his stunner into the opening, more by instinct than conscious thought. The pressure wave from the weapon burst across the open space as Dax launched an arrow at David's heart. The rush of air deflected the projectile. The metal tip rose then fell as the air current slowed its momentum. The steel pierced cloth and flesh before striking bone, skipping along the curve of David's seventh rib until it impacted the wall separating the entrance hall from the kitchen. David instinctively moved away from the object that struck him. Cloth ripped and the shaft of the arrow splintered as his body weight pulled against the anchor that pinned his robe to the wall.

Charlene's reaction came less than a second later. Three rapid blasts from her weapon hammered through the opening where the attack had been launched. Dust, parchment, cloth and splintered wood filled the air. The sound of breaking overwhelmed the noise of rushing air with each trigger pull.

'What's happening?' called Will over the radio.

'Sergeant Wilson? David?' whispered Adrian in shock.

'We're okay,' replied David. 'Just keep your eyes open.'

'All clear front,' replied Will in a calmer tone than he felt.

'All clear rear. Over,' said Adrian breathlessly.

'Are you okay?' asked Charlene.

David pulled the remains of the arrow from the gash in his robes.

'Let's keep moving.'

Charlene nodded, 'I'll take the lead.'

David moved to the left side of the door frame as Charlene finger counted to three, then moved through the opening.

A hand grasped the barrel of her weapon. It was ripped upwards then away from Charlene to bounce across the wooden bench in the centre of the kitchen. Charlene moved with the momentum of the weapon, using her thigh muscles to increase the distance beyond the reach of her assailant, just as her father had taught when practicing room to room clearance techniques. While many parents spent time teaching their children how to ride a bicycle or kick a ball, Scooter Wilson had instructed his children in the art of survival in a potentially hostile world.

Charlene swivelled at the hips as she collided against the bench. The first knife thrust went between arm and hip; she twisted her body to avoid the blade. Maximus had chosen to stab with his gladius; the pugio would follow at the throat. Both blades missed as Charlene slid sideways out of his reach.

'Don't fire, that thing will turn everything in this kitchen into shrapnel.'

David lowered his stunner. Charlene moved to face Maximus.

'Are we just going to dance with each other, or shall we move on to the climax now? I just hope you don't disappoint like all the other men I have dated in my life.'

'I promise to finish this quickly and as painlessly as I can,' replied Maximus.

'Are you sure we haven't dated?' retorted Charlene, 'I seem to recall hearing that line a lot in the past.'

Maximus shifted his grip on the pugio moving from a backhand to a forehand grip. Charlene eyed the blade; it was what she would have used. The big flat sword would be ok to lunge with but swinging it would expose the soldier's body to counterattack. Charlene looked for a weapon. There was a carving knife and a meat cleaver within reach.

'You can't kill him,' called David.

'Let me guess, the Grandfather Paradox? I guess it's your lucky day after all, mate,' said Charlene smiling at Maximus. 'I can't kill you, but you can use your little prick on me as much as you want. It sounds like every boof-headed bloke who ever drank too much on a Saturday night's dream, doesn't it?'

'Let's end this, I have a feast to get back to.'

'I hate a man in a hurry,' replied Charlene, picking up a wicker basket.

Maximus thrust the gladius at Charlene's abdomen. Charlene swivelled the cane basket by the handle impaling it on the blade, covering the cutting edge in a flexible condom of woven wood. Maximus dropped the sword and lunged with his pugio, rapidly flicking the dagger at Charlene's face. The blade tip sliced millimetres short of flesh as she jerked her head backwards. Maximus thrust forward again. His aim was to inflict cuts that would sting with burning pain to shock and frighten his enemy. They would back away, hands would be used to fend off the weapon, more cuts would come, more blood loss, more pain. Panic would set in, then would come the killing strike.

Charlene knew what Maximus was doing. It was straight out of the knife fighting manual. The counter was to move quickly, parry the knife, then strike the exposed points of vulnerability. It was good against an inexperienced opponent, but the soldier in front of her was far from inexperienced. His foot work was good, his balance and eye focused, he knew how to kill.

There was a crash. David couldn't risk firing his stunner, so he hurled a vase half filled with water and a bouquet of flowers. The thump against Maximus's helmet had surprised him more than anything, the cold water spilling down his helmet and inside his armour, making him flinch. This was the opening Charlene was looking for.

*Right hand forward in contact with the inside of the wrist; left hand strikes the outside of the knife hand; the wrist bends inward; the arm movement is held; fingers open; the knife flies away from the broken grip.*

Charlene's foot collided at speed between spread thighs, followed by her forehead crashing into the bridge of Max's nose. Maximus staggered, then dropped to one knee. Charlene shook her head to clear the pain. Maximus tried to rise. Charlene punched the centurio in the side of his neck, impacting the carotid artery, disrupting blood supply to the brain and causing him to slump to the floor unconscious.

'Like I said, quick, and disappointing.'

David crossed the kitchen; stunner up aimed at the entry to the pantry. 'Are you okay?'

'I've had worse dates,' replied Charlene, wiping Maximus's blood from her face. 'How about you?'

'My ribs are hurting like hell.'

Charlene widened the tear in David's robes, his chest was covered in bruising. Charlene's eyes widened in recognition of the amount of pain David must have been in even before they had entered the villa.

'There's not much bleeding.' David flinched as Charlene prodded the injury. 'Nothing's broken; you'll just have to suck it up.'

'And you wonder why you have trouble dating.'

'We have company,' interrupted Will. 'Eight soldiers and a civilian in a hurry.'

'Doc?'

'Yes Sergeant Wilson?'

'You know what to do if we call goat shit.'

'I do, but I don't like the idea.'

'You don't have to like it, Doc, you just have to do it, understood?'

'Affirmative.'

'Will?'

'I'm with Adrian.'

'Is it understood?'

'Yes.'

'Just keep us in the loop, both of you,' said David.

'If the cavalry gets inside the building, call it, then push the go home button. No ifs, buts or maybes. Is that clear?' said Charlene.

'Affirmative, Sergeant Wilson.'

'Okay, Charlene. I know how to disappear, that's what the *W* is good at.'

Will watched the formation approach. The civilian leading the march was near enough to running. This wasn't Will's only issue; the neighbours were now gathering on the street in front of the villa.

'The rebels are inside that building,' said Polykarpos pointing.

A boom rattled roof tiles; the crowd gasped.

'If this is a trap!' threatened the Decanus in charge.

'It's not, I hate the rebels. We poor struggle enough without these zealots stinging the legion like a tiny wasp, then running away leaving us to face your anger?'

'You're happy to betray your fellow Jews?' asked the Decanus in disgust.

'I am not a Jew, I am Greek. Why should I suffer because of the acts of these fools?'

'Stand over there and don't move, but I swear if you have lied...'

'You will take my head,' interrupted Polykarpos, 'I would expect nothing else.'

Will watched the Decanus brief his men from his roof top observation point. It was like watching the half- time huddle at the footy. The civilian stood nearby listening. He could have been 40 or 70, the one standout feature on his thin face was a row of blackened teeth.

The soldiers broke the huddle. Any moment now, they would go through the villa's door. Will searched the roof for something to create a distraction, his eye fell on a row of pots sown with vegetables.

'Julius Cesar wore his sister's undies!' Will yelled as he hurled a projectile. The pot spun through the air spewing loose soil until it crashed to the street.

The military men turned as one to stare at the mess.

'How come the legion has only one word for attack and ten for retreat?' yelled Will as he launched a second projectile, which impacted against the raised shield of the Decanus.

'You two, deal with that idiot,' was the instruction.

'Roma FC is a poor man's Arsenal!' came the taunt, followed by a third pot that collided with a sickening crash into the helmet of a legionnaire.

'Change of plan. We cut off his head, then deal with whatever is going on in the villa.'

The first two legionnaires on the roof approached with shields locked defensively. Will waited, hands behind his back as if standing at ease on a parade ground. The soldiers separated to allow the Decanus to pass.

'You're a dead man,' said the Decanus drawing his gladius.

'I don't think so mate,' replied Will. 'Go Saints.'

There was a flash of green light, the air pulsed. Will disappeared. The Decanus rushed to where Will had been standing, the remainder of his men bolted up the steps on to the roof. The Decanus paced from one side of the roof to the other, looking down to street level.

'Find him, he can't have gone far.'

A gentle breeze wafted across the roof picking up particles of spilt soil which impacted the Decanus' eyes and nose. He sneezed.

There was a flash of green, followed by a roar of wind. The men on the roof top were hurled from their feet. Two tumbled from the roof, crashing with a metallic thump on the cobbled street below. One somersaulted down the steps, sliding to a halt in a shower of sparks as armour scraped against stone. The remaining five tumbled about the roof until the wind died as suddenly as it had arrived.

Will landed, feet spread and balanced, his finger poised over his *Sainter* as he rematerialised. The soldiers rose to their feet, one ran towards the steps.

'Stay where you are,' bellowed the Decanus. The soldier hesitated, then stopped wild- eyed, staring at Will.

'Go Saints,' said Will taking a step in the soldier's direction. The man leapt from the roof flailing his arms as he plummeted to the street with a sickening thud, followed by a scream of pain. Will glanced over the roof to see the soldier lying on his side with one leg bent at an unnatural angle.

'I am going to kill you,' spat the Decanus drawing his pugio.

'No, you won't,' replied Will activating his *Sainter*.

The roof top glowed green, the air pulsed and Will disappeared again.

'Get off the roof!' screamed the Decanus. Scattered vegetables, spilt soil and broken pottery moved in a sudden breeze. The Decanus looked to where Will had disappeared. 'Bugger.'

Men tumbled from the roof as the rush of wind exploded. The Decanus slid backwards on his stomach, shards of pottery impaled his skin as his momentum slowed, then stopped as quickly as it started. He hung precariously, legs in space, his right arm tucked under the weight of his armour, his left arm, fingers extended like a claw, clinging to the surface of the roof.

'Have you had enough?' asked Will.

'Who are you?'

'I'm somebody you can't bully or frighten. Believe me, you're an amateur compared to Viki and Glenis in high school.' The Decanus stared back in angry confusion. 'The smartest thing you could do is pack up your bongos, go home, run a hot bath and get an early night. We can call it a nil- all draw if anybody asks.' The Decanus began to slide again. Will grabbed his hand to hold him in place. 'Let's be sensible. I promise not to push you off the roof, if you promise to pack up the band and go home. And no sneaking back once you get out of sight. I won't be happy if you break your word.'

The Decanus stared in hatred.

'What's your name mate? It can't hurt to tell me.'

'I am Decanus Lucius of the Sixth Legion Ferrata.'

'See, that didn't hurt. I am Will Thomas, of the Saint Kilda Football Club. The Saints play real footy, not soccer.' The Decanus continued to fume in anger. 'What I propose is that I stand over there, while you and your mates bugger off home. If you come back, well then, we can just keep going the way we started. Does that sound fair?'

'I will kill you.'

'No Lucius, you won't. If you try something silly, I will call upon the power of Plugger Lockett and smite you with lightning.' Will lifted his hand pulling the trigger on his taser, electricity arced across the electrodes. 'Don't be the bloke who won't take the hint to bugger off home when the party is over. It's a sure way not to get invited again.'

The Decanus edged his way back onto the roof, then dismounted the steps to the street below. Will watched as Lucius and his men limped away.

'All clear out front,' Will reported.

'Understood,' replied Charlene. This was followed by a rattling of the villa's tiles.

It was bloody obvious that Lucius and his mates would be back, Will needed to be somewhere else, the logical place being inside Julia's villa. Will scrambled down the steps, the residents on the street stared at him in awe.

'Are you an angel?' asked an elderly woman.

'Are you here to spread the word of Jehovah?' came a call from the crowd.

'No,' replied Will, 'I don't own a suit or a bicycle.'

'Are you here to lead a revolt against the Romans?'

'No, I'm not here to do that,' replied Will pushing through the gathering.

'What do you want us to do, Will Thomas, of the Saint Kilda Football Club?'

This stopped Will in his tracks.

'You heard that?'

'You ordered the Decanus to pack up his bongos and go home,' said Meschach, the cloth merchant. 'I don't know what a bongo is, but the legion ran in fear.'

'Right. What I want you all to do is go home and stay inside until lunch time tomorrow. Lucius is fairly pissed off, so he and his friends will be back, and if they ask what happened, use the Sergeant Schultz defence. I know nothing. I saw nothing. I heard nothing. Are we clear on that?'

'Your herald told us the people of Galilee must rise up against the empire and cast them out.'

'He said David Thomas was sent to show us the way,' called a voice from the crowd. 'Are you not David?'

'Sorry, you have the wrong bloke,' replied Will. 'Who told you this anyway?'

'Your herald, the Greek with black teeth. He said he led the Romans here so that we might witness their weakness in the face of your power.'

'Where is he?'

'Gone,' replied Meschach.'

'And you believed some bloke who you don't know, who just turned up and told you to pick a fight with the Romans because he was an agent for the David Thomas miracle show?'

'He said he was sent by Jehovah.'

'You people are in a lot of trouble when the Avon lady finds out where you live.'

'You want us to deny our own eyes and ears? Did you not defeat the might of the legion with the avenging light of an angel?'

'There was only eight of them and one looked to be carrying a hamstring injury.'

'Kneel, we should kneel and pray before Will Thomas, the instrument of Jehovah,' said the old woman.

'No, don't do that.' Will lifted the woman to her feet. 'No man, or woman, is better or more important than any of you. Don't ever go thinking that.'

'What is it you want of us, Will Thomas?' asked the woman.

'I want you go home and forget what you think you saw.'

'I don't understand,' said Meschach. 'Why should we fear the Romans with you here?'

Will realised he had to do something to protect these people.

'Sorry, what's your name, mate?'

'I am Meschach, the cloth merchant.'

'Okay, Meschach. If the Romans fear me, isn't it logical that you might want to as well? I told you, I wasn't an angel, I told you I wasn't a man of Jehovah. What does that leave? What is the opposite of an angel sent by Jehovah?'

Meschach's face dropped in horror.

'The evil one? Satan? Lucifer himself?'

'Okay, I see what you're thinking. He also goes by Rodney Elliot if you're making a list.' Will lifted the taser for all to see and pulled the trigger. Electricity arced, sparked, and buzzed blue. 'Go, home, now. All of you.'

Meschach turned, ashen- faced to push through the crowd.

'Run, don't look in his eye, run to your homes and hide.'

The crowd dispersed leaving Will feeling awful.

'Mum would be disgusted with me.'


Atarah and Sapphira met Julia at the entrance to the cellar.

'Is it happening?' asked the housekeeper.

'Yes, David Thomas didn't take the smart option when he had the chance.'

'Should I call the women to come?'

'No, we are going to deal with Mr Thomas and his friends by ourselves.'

The villa shook, once, then three times in rapid succession.

'Our guest has arrived,' said Julia, placing a hand on Atarah's and Sapphira's arms. 'You have nothing to fear, just do as we practiced.'

Julia addressed the Immunes standing guard, 'You are dismissed.'

Crashing and banging could be heard from the direction of the kitchen. The Immunes gripped the hilts of their swords.

'Go and play if you want,' said Julia. 'You have my permission to kill anybody who you think doesn't belong.'

Atarah lit the wick on a lamp, Sapphira tightened her grip on the carving knife from Octavian's villa and the women descended into the cellar.


Hannah snuffed out the lamp, then slid the knife used to light the lamp into the sleeve of her gown. It wasn't much of a weapon, but it was better than being unarmed.

'*We have visitors*' said Julia in English as she walked down the cellar steps.
'*That will be* David Thomas,' replied Damian.
'*How could you know that?*'
'*A little bird told me. I am looking forward to a change of scenery, clean sheets, medical attention for my horrific injury inflicted by a deranged woman.*'
Julia handed the keys to Sapphira, 'Unlock him.'
'*I am happy to wait.*'
Julia drew Cynthia Horrigan's knife.
'*I have no qualms in finishing the job I started Damian, if you won't cooperate.*'
Atarah raised her lamp spreading illumination to the corners of the room.
'Hello?' said Julia, seeing Hannah hiding.
'Hannah? What are you doing here?' asked Atarah in surprise.
'You know this woman?'
Atarah turned to Sapphira, 'You didn't ask her to help with the feast?'
Sapphira shook her head.
'I'm sorry Julia, she said Sapphira had invited her.'
Julia took the lamp.
'We have met before, just the once in Nazareth.' Julia turned to Damian, '*Your little bird?*'
'*I thought you must have sent her to brighten my day.*'
Julia turned from Damian in disgust.
'There was something about our meeting.' Julia clicked her fingers. 'You gave me directions to the carpentry shop, your brother-in-law, Joseph, sorry Joe works there. Which makes you, Mary's sister,' Julia smiled. 'David chose his little bird very well, but sadly you have been lied to, Hannah. Women like Atarah, Sapphira and me are not your enemy. We have to work together to liberate women from misogynistic oppression. It can start for you tonight, if you choose to join us.'
'I am here because I want to be, not because David tricked me. There are good men in the world like David, just as there are evil women,' replied Hannah defiantly.
'Then you have made your choice.'
Atarah and Sapphira moved to take hold of Hannah. She pushed Sapphira away, Atarah punched Hannah in the face then pushed an arm high behind her back.
'Little birds that whisper secrets have to hear them first.' Julia removed Hannah's earpiece and crushed it under her heel.
'We won't be needing Damian after all,' said Julia indicating for Atarah

403

to release Hannah. 'Go and move into your positions as we practiced and keep hold of the key, please Sapphira, just in case we have to change plans.'

Sapphira placing the key to Damian's lock around her neck as she hurried away.

Atarah paused on the steps.

'Are you sure you want to do this? You could have Octavian deal with them.'

'We could, but sometimes women just have to do it for themselves.'

Charlene secured Maximus with zip ties to the kitchen bench. The last thing they needed was him coming for them again.

'This is broken,' said David holding up the weapon made by his father.

Charlene picked up Max's dagger and drew her the taser.

'Then I guess I go old school.'

David looked around the frame of the pantry door, then held up two fingers to indicate the two soldiers approaching.

'All clear out front,' said Will in Charlene's ear.

'Understood.'

David fired into the pantry, jars of flour, seeds and spices were flung from their shelves and shattered. The result was a fog of white that billowed along the corridor turning it into a tunnel of near zero visibility. Coughing could be heard from the approaching soldiers.

'Use the infra-red,' instructed David.

Charlene touched her glasses, 'I've got this, cover my backside.'

David faced into the kitchen; the pain of his ribs stabbed and burnt, none of which mattered, he had a partner to protect.

The sound of electricity arcing was followed by a series of crashes and bangs, then silence.

'Clear,' called Charlene.

David lowered the stunner, then stepped into the passageway.

'Are you okay?'

'I will be in a minute,' coughed Charlene.

'Hello, Officer Thomas. We haven't formally met, but I know of you from a mutual acquaintance.'

David switched his glasses to infra-red. At the end of the passage were two figures. Cynthia Horrigan's blade stood out black and cold against the warmer white of Hannah's throat.

'I can see you both clearly, my night vision glasses are military grade. Please ask your friend to remain still. I can see her blade, just as I can see your sidearm. It would be tempting to just blast away; the problem is, Officer Thomas, or do you prefer David?'

'David is fine, if I can call you Julia?'

'Of course, and might I ask who your friend is?'

'Brevet Sergeant Wilson,' replied Charlene.

'I apologise for the incident at the costumery, it was regrettable.'

'It wasn't me you stabbed.'

'Then why are you here, Sergeant?'

'Because you stabbed a cop.'

'Dedication to duty, I can respect that.'

'She's stalling,' said Charlene, 'just shoot her.'

'I wouldn't do that; Cynthia's knife is pressing against Hannah's carotid artery.'

'This is goat shit, David,' said Hannah angrily.

'If that was meant for you, David, I would feel a little hurt.'

'You won't be able to hold us in this position for ever,' said Charlene.

'I don't have to, do I? How long do you think it will be before Octavian sends reinforcements? You can push the buttons on Dwight's invention and jump away, at which point Hannah will find out how sharp my favourite toy is. Or?'

'Or we can lay down our weapons,' said David.

'What's to stop you killing her then coming after us?' asked Charlene.

'I give you my word, one woman to another.'

'Bullshit! Just shoot the bitch before she disappears.'

'Julia is not going anywhere,' said David.

'How perceptive. Yes, I have commitments which tie me to my present locality for the moment.'

'Put down the knife,' said David aiming his weapon at Julia.

'This is goat shit,' repeated Hannah. 'Why do I have to die because you are thinking with your thing, like every man I have ever known?' Hannah raised her hand and wiggled her little finger so David could see the knife protruding from the sleeve of her dress. 'It would be just like you, stabbing me in the leg if you don't do what Julia wants.'

Hannah slipped the blade into the palm of her hand as she dropped her arm. David lowered his weapon.

'I'll put my stunner on the floor, if you take the knife away from Hannah's throat.'

'You first,' said Julia.

'Put down the knife, Charlene,' instructed David.

'No. This goes against everything I know and what my gut is telling me.'

'There won't be a hostage if Julia uses the knife. We have her history of violence to consider.'

Charlene dropped Max's pugio.

'And the taser,' said Julia.

Charlene bent to place the taser next to the pugio. David leant forward to place his weapon on the floor, then stopped. There was a blade was at his throat.

David looked to his left. Charlene was on the floor, her right arm twisted behind her back, an invisible blow struck the side of her head, bringing a trickle blood from a cut above her eye. Flour dust from the floor settled on the invisible object pinning her. David could see the shape of a leg, an arm and part of a torso.

'The stealth suits,' David said to himself.

'Relieve Officer Thomas of his weapon, Sapphira, then put Hannah in the cellar with Damian. When this is over Hannah you can go home to Nazareth.'

An invisible hand took the stunner from David's fingers. Atarah removed the hood from her stealth suit, climbed off Charlene's back and kicked the taser toward Julia. David watched as Sapphira removed the hood from her suit, handed his stunner to Julia, then pushed Hannah towards the cellar.

Charlene rose to her knees and looked directly at Atarah.

'I don't normally punch women, but I am going to make an exception for you.'

Atarah flicked the blade of Max's pugio to indicate for Charlene to get to her feet.

'Now what?' David asked.

'Now I have a decision to make. Sergeant Wilson is easy to place, many men would be happy to have you as a slave in their household.'

'No man will ever own me.'

'If that is your final word on the matter, so be it.'

The door from Julia's reception room opened. Adrian stepped into the passage. He saw David, then Charlene and smiled. He saw Atarah and frowned, then turned and laid eyes on Julia.

'Julie Diesel! What are you doing here?'

'Adrian, still as clueless as ever.'

Adrian frowned.

'Your name isn't Julie Diesel, is it?'

'No.'

'I see. That's why you joined my genealogy society, to get to the *Cabinet* through me.'

'Believe it or not, I was even willing to sleep with you to get what I needed. Thankfully I discovered Damian before I had to endure that particular horror.'

'I don't like you, either. I found your presentations at the society boring to be truthful.'

'Go and join your cousin please.'

Adrian moved to stand between David and Charlene.

'Now what?' queried David.

Julia reached behind her back to withdraw the heirloom which had belonged to the United Sates Marine Sergeant who emigrated to Melbourne at the end of World War Two. Charlene and David raised their arms. Adrian looked confused.

'What is it?'

'That is a 45 calibre M1911A1 semi-automatic pistol, Doc. It was the standard side arm of the US military, until it was replaced by the Berretta M9 in 1985. I prefer the Browning 9mm High Power, it has a thirteen round magazine to start with and the 45 calibre is just wank factor.'

'We are full of surprises, Sergeant,' said Julia aiming the pistol two- handed at David's chest, 'I am sorry, Officer Thomas.'

Will burst through the door of Julia's bedroom, hurling his buzzing taser at Julia's head. The pistol discharged as Will collided with Julia knocking her off her feet.

Charlene smacked the pugio from Atarah's hand and followed through with a straight left. Atarah blocked the blow with her forearm and kicked Charlene in the stomach. Charlene smiled, then stepped in to deliver a rapid fire right then left to Atarah's jaw, before finishing the job with an elbow to the side of her head. Charlene rolled Atarah on her front, clasped both wrists together and zip- tied them.

'I told you I was going to make an exception for you.'

Will was lying on top of the swearing and kicking Julia, his hands wrapped around her wrists to prevent her from pushing buttons on her *Sainters*. David grabbed Charlene's taser from the floor to go to Will's aid. Sapphira, then Hannah, screamed.

Adrian took the taser from David.

'Go save Hannah.'

David ran to the cellar door.

Adrian smiled at Julia.

'I swear, if you touch me Adrian Thomas...'

'I have no intention of touching you, the thought positively makes me nauseous.'

Julia kicked and pushed against Will.

'Just hurry up Adrian, she's digging her nails in,' said Will.

'We can't have that,' said Adrian, 'it's against the rules of civilised behaviour.'

Adrian placed the taser against Julia's side and pulled the trigger.

'I hope that was as good for you as it was for me, Ms Diesel.'

Will slid off Julia, then pushed himself into a sitting position against the wall. He looked at the blood oozing out of his robes. If this was how he died, he could live with it.

Charlene dropped in front of Will.

'What the bloody hell were you thinking?'

'I got shot.'

'I can see that.' Charlene used Cynthia's blade to cut away at the bloody robes. 'Will, it's time you called me Charlie, that's what my friends call me, my best friends.'

'Alright, Charlie.'

'Doc, go and find the first aid kit and be quick about it.'

'Yes of course, Sergeant Wilson.'

Charlene widened the hole. The bullet had cut a furrow just above the pelvis, the wound was a gash, not a penetration. Will had been very lucky.

Charlene pressed Will's hand against the wound.

'Apply pressure until I tell you to stop.'

'I got it,' said Will. 'Hadn't you better arrest Julia?'

'Yes, I can do that.'

Charlene rolled Julia on her stomach, removed the *Sainters* and zip-tied her hands and ankles. Adrian returned with the first aid kit.

'I hate to be a worry wort, but we have company.'

'How many?'

'Let's just assume it's too many, Sergeant Wilson.'

Charlene pressed a wound dressing into place. Adrian attached an antibiotic then a pain-relieving patch to Will's arm.

'Thanks mate,' said Will grasping Adrian's hand.

'I don't think you'll need stitches, but we had better have a doctor look at it,' said Charlene. I'm afraid you won't be wearing a bikini with the scar it will leave.'

'No problem, I was never much of a swimmer,' said Will.

Charlene patted Will on the shoulder.

'That was very brave. Stupid, incredibly stupid, just to be really clear, but wonderfully brave.'

'Yes, well done you, Will,' said Adrian.

'It's goat shit time,' said Charlene. 'Doc you're going home.'

Charlene pushed the button on the *Sainter* on Adrian's wrist, the air pulsed, folded in on itself and Adrian was gone.

'Julia next,' said Will.

Charlene attached her *Sainter* to Julia's ankle and pushed the return button.

Will handed Charlene Julia's *Sainters*.

'I've set these for just after we left.'

'Thank you,' said Charlene strapping a *Sainter* to her wrist. 'Now you.'

'Not until I know you are coming with me.'

'Of course I am, I'm your knocked-up pretend wife, after all.' Charlene leant across as if to kiss Will. Will's eyes widened in surprise, Charlene placed a finger on Will's wrist, 'Go Saints.' The air pulsed and Will and was gone.

Charlene picked up the M1911A1 and ran to the cellar.

# CHAPTER FORTY-SIX

WILL WAS ALONE IN the dark with the wreck of his car and a police vehicle parked behind it. He waited for Charlie; an hour went by, then two. Finally, the realisation hit that standing next to an abandoned police car in the middle of the night was not sensible, so he drove home.

In less than two minutes, Will parked in his driveway, applied the handbrake, turned off the car's remaining lights, shut down the engine and made his way inside. The keys went on their hook in the kitchen, his bloody robes in the rubbish bin and his body into the shower. The waterproof wound dressing stayed in place, the patches on Will's arm looked like band aids, they would be easy to explain. The wound on his side had best just stay hidden. He would put mercurochrome on it in the morning then raid his first aid kit for a fresh dressing and plaster strips to hold it in place, Will had no intention of showing it to a doctor.

He eventually lay on his bed, just for a moment, just to rest his eyes, then nothing.

# CHAPTER FORTY-SEVEN

DWIGHT STOOD AT THE computer interface as if his presence alone could prevent malfunctions. Emil wanted to pace but knew it wouldn't bring any of them back faster. The *Cabinet* shook, boomed and Adrian materialised.

Emil opened the *Cabinet's* door.

'Are you alright?'

'Yes, apart from an incredible thirst and the desperate need for a shower.'

'Where is my son?' demanded Dwight.

'Don't worry, David won't be far behind me, Uncle Dwight, and apart from the arrow wound, bruising and minor lacerations, he is a picture of health.'

'Where did he get hit by an arrow?'

'The kitchen, I think, though I am not a 100 percent certain, what with the weapons fire and the hand-to-hand combat, it was all a bit confusing.'

'Where was he wounded on his body, Adrian?' asked Emil trying to remain calm.

Adrian pointed to his ribcage.

'I believe the arrow struck here and made a bit of a gash here as it bounced off a rib.' Adrian could see the looks of concern on his uncles' faces.

'Sergeant Wilson patched David up and he was straight back into the fight. He will have a scar, but as Sergeant Wilson said, he will live.'

'Why did you leave him behind?' demanded Dwight.

'Because Sergeant Wilson called goat shit. Will had just been shot with a 45 calibre semi-automatic pistol, though she said that was a bit of *wank factor*. Apparently, the Browning Hi Power is a preferable weapon with its 13-round magazine.'

'Is William Thomas dead?' asked Emil.

'No, Will is going to survive, though he will also have quite a scar.'

'Tell me what happened to David?' asked Dwight with growing alarm.

'Well, just before I left, David was in pursuit of Sapphira who was escorting Hannah at knife point to where Damian was imprisoned. Julia had earlier inflicted a rather appalling injury on Mr Treffer for, I am led to believe, was inappropriate and unwanted sexual advances against Julia's household staff.'

'Who is Hannah?' asked Emil.

'I haven't actually met Hannah, though I know her sister, Mary. She was very helpful when we arrived in Nazareth. Mary introduced us to Simon Iscariot the horse dealer. He has a son named Judas.'

'Judas Iscariot?' asked Emil in surprise.

'That's right, Judas is the best friend of Mary's son, who works as an apprentice carpenter with his father Joseph.'

'What?' asked Dwight, struggling to comprehend what Adrian was explaining. 'You were helped by the wife of a carpenter, named Mary, in Nazareth, who introduced you to the father of Judas Iscariot?'

'That's right,' smiled Adrian. 'It's been an interesting adventure.'

The *Cabinet* boomed; Julia materialised.

'Untie me,' snapped Julia, 'or I will expose all of you for what you did to Cynthia Horrigan and bring the Thomas family to its knees forever.'

Adrian smiled as he dragged Julia clear of the machine.

'May I introduce Julia Howard, or as we were first introduced, Julie Diesel. Julia is a deceitful, scheming, violent criminal, who, given half a chance, would kill every one of us without a single qualm. Julia, these are my Uncles Emil and Dwight.'

# CHAPTER FORTY-EIGHT

HANNAH TOOK THE STEPS two at a time to distance herself from Sapphira and the knife pressed against her back.

'*What is going on?*' demanded Damian.

Sapphira barely glanced at Damian. 'I will let you out when it's safe.'

'You can't leave me alone with him.'

'He can't harm you as long as you stay out of his reach,' said Sapphira.

Hannah slapped the flat of the blade she had been hiding across Sapphira's knuckles, the butcher's knife clattered to the floor. Sapphira looked down at her hand then backed away in fright. Damian lunged, grabbing Sapphira from behind. She had been out of reach until Hannah had forced her to move.

Sapphira screamed as Damian wrapped his arms around her waist and throat. Hannah lunged to wrestle the teenager from Damian's grip. Sapphira bit down on Hannah's hand, thinking it was Damian. Hannah screamed, pulling away a bleeding digit.

Damian tightened his grip around Sapphira's throat while he thrust a hand inside her stealth suit, searching for the key to his shackles. Sapphira thrashed against the invasion of her body, Damian tightened his grip.

Hannah could see Sapphira's eyes bulge as Damian cut the air supply to her lungs.

'*Where is the key?*' Damian growled as his hand moved back and forth across Sapphira's chest.

Sapphira was dying in front of Hannah's eyes. Hannah raised the blade, then plunged it into the hollow between the collar bone and Damian's neck.

'*What have you done?*' screamed Damian in surprise, pulling the blade from his body. Blood gushed from the wound; he fell to his knees then collapsed to the floor as his heart pumped away his life.

David made it to the door in time to see Hannah plunge the blade home and Damian collapse into a pool of his own blood. Sapphira crawled away, crying hysterically. Hannah moved to comfort her.

'Adrian, Will and Julia have gone,' said Charlene as she appeared behind David. 'You don't need to bring him, there's no point.'

David moved down the steps.

'We have company,' said Charlene. 'It's time to go.'

'You go, I'll just be a minute.'

'No, we leave together.'

David knelt beside Hannah and Sapphira, 'Is she alright?'

'No, not after what he did to her,' said Hannah.

'We have to go, Hannah. It's not safe to stay here.'

'Don't worry about me, I'll stay with Sapphira.'

A gun shot rang out.

'I won't be able to hold them off for long, if I can't actually shoot anybody, David,' said Charlene

'Go,' said Hannah, 'they won't harm us.'

Charlene fired twice putting holes in a shield.

'Let's go Dave.'

'Do you have a spare *Sainter*?'

Charlene threw a bracelet to David who attached it to Sapphira then placed the device meant for Damian on Hannah's wrist.'

'What's this?'

'Do you trust me, Hannah?'

'Do I have to?'

'No. Where we are going you can choose to trust or not trust anybody; it will be entirely your decision how you live your life. If you don't like it, I promise to bring you back home.'

'Warn Am Bool?'

'Yes, Warrnambool, Hannah.'

'Alright, David Thomas, take us home.'

'Goat shit,' David called.

Charlene pushed the button, and she was gone.

David pushed the button on Sapphira's *Sainter*, then the one on Hannah's. The cellar filled with swirling green light.

Octavian arrived at the door with Maximus at his back.

David stood.

'Julia has been arrested and will not be back.'

Green light swirled, the air folded in upon itself and David disappeared.

Polykarpos watched from the crowd on the street, the death of Hannah and David was a small price to pay for what was at stake. If the story of David's battle didn't gain traction, there was always the long-term plan of moulding Joe and Mary's son into an instrument to use. All would not be lost.

Dax stood on the steps of the villa searching for faces in the crowd. It was the blackened smile that betrayed Polykarpos. Dax fitted the string to the nock of his arrow, aimed for the centre mass of his target, held his breath then let his fingers slide from the string.

# CHAPTER FORTY-NINE

IT WAS THE SOUND of banging that woke Will. Once he realised it was his family at the door of his house, he pulled on a pair of jeans and a top to cover his wound before letting them in.

Mary kissed Will's cheek then headed to put the kettle on while Will led his visitors to the lounge room.

'You look a bit stiff,' said Colin taking a seat.

'It's just a bit of bruising.'

'I'll take your car to the panel beaters tomorrow, and don't worry about anything mechanical, I will deal with that.'

'We're going to pay for the repairs,' said Loni. 'Brian and I are ashamed of what happened. Aren't we Brian?'

Brian hung his head.

'I'm sorry, Will, I don't know what I was thinking,'

'Nobody died, that's the main thing,' said Will holding his hand out to his brother.

'No,' said Colin. 'Brian, I want you to learn from this mess. From now on, every one of us has each other's backs, no matter what.'

'Because you will do anything for your family, because they are your family and so you must,' said Will.

'How did you know I was going to say that?'

'Tea's up,' interrupted Mary, carrying cups on a tray. 'I'm going to give you my mother's tea set, William, it will be just the thing when you are married and have visitors.'

Will smiled at his mother.

'I don't think that's likely, Mum. No woman in her right mind wants to go out with the *W*, much less marry me. And even if I did manage to get a girlfriend, I doubt Ita Buttrose will be dropping around for tea.'

'Of course you will find a girlfriend, William, or I will have something to say about it.'

'You know she will,' said Colin. 'Get a girlfriend, Will, that's an order.'

'Yes Dad, I'll get right on to it tomorrow, just to keep Mum happy.'

Mary ordered everybody to sit.

'Lonica, do you have a friend that might like to meet Will?'

Loni almost dropped her cup as tea went up her nose.

'I don't know, I would have to ask?'

'Of course, Loni will ask,' said Brian, 'someone must owe you a favour or two.'

'You don't have to Loni; I wouldn't ask you to do that,' said Will.

'I will pray to the Virgin Mary to find you a girlfriend, William, a nice girl, just like Mary herself.'

'What, a short, red-headed arse-kicker who takes crap from nobody?'

'William Thomas, how can you say such things?!'

'No reason,' said Will. 'It's just how I imagined she would be if we ever met.'

Brian laughed, Loni looked daggers and he stopped.

'Did you see a police car near the Army Depot on your way here?' asked Will.

'I didn't notice one,' said Loni. 'Why?'

'There was one parked there last night.'

'They do move them around,' said Brian.

'Talking of police cars, there is one pulling up in the driveway,' said Mary, moving the curtains aside. 'I hope this isn't about last night again, Colin.'

'It might be, I'll go and see. Will, if I get arrested, drive the Monaro home for your mother.'

'Don't joke about things like that,' said Mary crossing herself.

'They're probably here to see Will,' said Brian.

'There's only one policewoman,' said Mary. 'It's not a they; it's a her.'

'She is a police officer,' corrected Will. 'We don't have police men, or women anymore.'

Brian peered through the blinds.

'I wouldn't mind being arrested by that police officer.'

Loni slapped her fiancé on the arm.

'Aren't you in enough trouble?'

'There is no harm in looking.'

'Wanna bet?' said Loni.

'Look who it is, Mary. Charlene Wilson, all grown up, and a police officer as well,' said Colin as he led her into the room.

'Well, I never. Move over Brian. Loni, can you bring another cup from the kitchen? I am sure there is another one in the pot.'

'No please, don't make any fuss, I can't stay long. I have reports to write up after taking those three gentlemen off the streets last night, and don't worry, there are no repercussions for any of you. I would have defended myself just as you did in that situation.'

'Thank you, Officer Wilson,' said Mary, 'that is something to be thankful for.'

'Charlie, please call me Charlie, that's what my friends call me.'

'If you haven't come about last night, Charlie, is this a social call?' asked Loni.

'Sort of, I was on my way to see somebody, my boyfriend actually. I saw your cars, so I thought...'

'You thought that you would drop in and just say "hello"?' said Will. 'On the way to visit your boyfriend?'

'Is your boyfriend somebody we know, Charlie?' asked Mary.

'Yes, I am sure you know him. He's not much to look at in the morning if he hasn't had a good night's sleep, but he has the biggest bravest heart of any man I have ever met.'

'Well, that counts Will out,' joked Brian.

'Why would you say that?' asked Charlene.

Brian couldn't answer.

Charlene smiled at Loni, 'I hope you have a fabulous wedding.'

'Thank you?' replied Loni, confused by what Charlene meant.

Charlene smiled, 'Will, can I see you outside for a minute?'

'Sure.'

'Fabulous to see you all again. Mum and Dad said to say "hello". Don't get up, I will make a point of catching up properly when I'm not on duty.'

Mary pushed the curtain aside to watch Will and Charlene standing in the driveway.

'You know, the first time I met Charlie I told Will never to have anything to do with her. Now I wish I hadn't said anything.'

'Are you alright?' asked Will. 'I waited, but you didn't appear.'

'I went back to the bat cave to help Dave with Julia. He brought back the knife which linked Julia's DNA to the stabbing. I don't think there will be any problems when it goes to trial.'

'Did she try to use the *Cabinet* as a get- out- of- jail card?'

'Yes, she did, but it was like claiming you talked to Jesus.'

'Nobody took her seriously,' nodded Will.

'Talking of Mary. Doc gave me something for you, he made a couple of copies, he thought she might like one.' Charlene handed Will two framed photographs. 'I think they're great, but I don't know if your mum will understand.'

'She'll love it,' said Will looking at the image of Charlie, Mary and himself smiling like a family holiday snap.

'Are they watching?'

'Who?'

'Your family, Will, who else?'

'Of course. Mum is probably nearly exploding because she can't hear what is going on. I think Loni is also keeping an eye on you.'

'Well, she picked the wrong brother.'

'What?'

'Just shut up and kiss me,' said Charlie wrapping her arms around Will and pulling him close.

'Yes, of course, Sergeant Wilson.'

Mary closed the curtain. 'Thank you, Ita, thank you Mother Mary. I knew I could count on you.'

# CHAPTER FIFTY

## WARRNAMBOOL BASE HOSPITAL, JULY 28TH 2117 CE

'DON'T JUST STAND THERE, Dave, come in,' said Jen from her bed.

'How are you?' asked David looking for a place to put the flowers he was holding.

'You do know I would have preferred a beer to more flowers.'

'I will see what I can do next visit,' said David quietly.

'Stop that crap, this was not your fault. I should have waited for backup before charging in and besides, you saved my arse when it counted. I would have died if you hadn't found me.'

'I owe you a shirt.'

'Yes, you do, and while you're at it, you can cough up for a skirt to match, and a pair of shoes.'

'Done,' said David with a smile. 'How are you really?'

'Sore, and I have to be careful with what I drink until they grow me back a replacement kidney, but other than that, I'm good. I heard about the arrest of Howard; well done Dave. I might have made a decent copper out of you after all.'

David nodded his thanks, then bit the bullet.

'There is something I need to talk to you about. Something I wanted you to hear from me before anybody else said anything. It's nothing bad, but something I wanted you to know as my partner.'

'All right, what have you done? Got yourself a dog, or, heaven bloody help me, a cat? You know I can't stand cats.'

'No, nothing like that.'

'What, then? You haven't actually managed to find a girlfriend, have you? What would that do to my reputation at the station if they find out I am not actually jumping you after hours?'

'Sorry,' said David dropping his eyes.

'Shit Dave, you mean I'm right?'

'Would you like to meet her?'

'Bloody hell, I get stabbed at work just once and the whole world turns upside down.'

'You don't have to if you don't want to.'

'Bullshit, if you don't bring her in, I'm getting out of bed to track her down.'

'Hannah is from Israel; she doesn't speak much English yet.'

'I lost a kidney, not my universal translator. Bring her in Dave, I would love to meet her.'

'I have Hannah's teenage cousin, Sapphira, here as well,' said David. 'Sapphira is staying with Hannah and me for a while. We are going to be looking for a school for her to attend while she is staying with us on a sort of gap year. Do you mind if she meets you as well?'

'Wait, did you say that your girlfriend is actually living with you?'

'Yes, Hannah is living at my home. I know it might seem odd that you haven't heard of her, but Hannah and I met a very long time ago and we have been through a lot together. Hannah moving in just seemed to feel right for both of us.'

'Stop the world, you have a live-in girlfriend who you have never mentioned before?'

'It's a long story, maybe for another day.'

'Bring them in Dave, I want to meet your girlfriend and her cousin, Sapphira. That is a pretty name. This has quite made my day.'

'Hannah, Sapphira, please come and meet my best friend in the world, Jen Rostig.'

Hannah entered, followed by Sapphira carrying a tray of éclairs she had baked for Jen.

'I am so pleased to meet you,' said Hannah, taking David by the hand while smiling broadly, 'I have heard so much about you from David, my *erusin*.'

# EPILOGUE

CYNTHIA STOOD IN THE falling snow outside the tiny wooden church that had become a hospital for the wounded and dying. Her husband was dead, her mother dying and all she could think of was saving her son.

The boy held up the bracelet.

'We should sell this for food.'

'No Michael, it has far more value than a silver dollar or two.'

'Major Howard said he would take us back east where I could go to school, and we could pretend this never happened.'

'If we give in to men like Major Howard, who will remember your father? Who would remember Spotted Quail, your grandmother and Yellow Flower, your aunt?'

'So, what do we do?'

'We call for help, Michael, and we survive until it comes. For now, we must be whatever Silas Howard needs us to be.'

'I would rather die.'

'No, you have to survive and remember, if you die it will be as if they never existed.'

The boy wanted to weep but held the tears back. Cynthia took the journal from under her cloak, ripped the last page from the book, then placed it inside the bracelet.

'Emil will come for us, Michael. He promised he would.'

Cynthia laid the bracelet in the snow, touched the largest button on its face, then watched as the green light flared and the plea for help disappeared.'

'Now what do we do?'

'Now, we find Major Howard and ask for his help.'

New Found Books Australia Pty Ltd

**www.newfoundbooks.au**